# THE WIFE OF RILEY

Mercy Watts Mysteries Book Six

A.W. HARTOIN

www.awhartoin.com

This book is a work of fiction. Names, characters, places and incidents either are products of the author's imagination or are used fictitiously. Any resemblance to actual events or locales or persons, living or dead, is entirely coincidental.

# ALSO BY A.W. HARTOIN

**Historical Thriller**

The Paris Package (Stella Bled Book One)

Strangers in Venice (Stella Bled Book Two)

One Child in Berlin (Stella Bled Book Three)

Dark Victory (Stella Bled Book Four)

A Quiet Little Place on Rue de Lille (Stella Bled Book Five)

**Young Adult fantasy**

Flare-up (Away From Whipplethorn Short)

A Fairy's Guide To Disaster (Away From Whipplethorn Book One)

Fierce Creatures (Away From Whipplethorn Book Two)

A Monster's Paradise (Away From Whipplethorn Book Three)

A Wicked Chill (Away From Whipplethorn Book Four)

To the Eternal (Away From Whipplethorn Book Five)

**Mercy Watts Mysteries**

Novels

A Good Man Gone (Mercy Watts Mysteries Book One)

Diver Down (A Mercy Watts Mystery Book Two)

Double Black Diamond (Mercy Watts Mysteries BookThree)

Drop Dead Red (Mercy Watts Mysteries Book Four)

In the Worst Way (Mercy Watts Mysteries Book Five)

The Wife of Riley (Mercy Watts Mysteries Book Six)

My Bad Grandad (Mercy Watts Mysteries Book Seven)

Brain Trust (Mercy Watts Mysteries Book Eight)

Down and Dirty (Mercy Watts Mysteries Book Nine)

Small Time Crime (Mercy Watts Mysteries Book Ten)

Bottle Blonde (Mercy Watts Mysteries Book Eleven)

Mean Evergreen (Mercy Watts Mysteries Book Twelve)

Silver Bells at Hotel Hell (Mercy Watts Mysteries Book Thirteen)

Short stories

Coke with a Twist

Touch and Go

Nowhere Fast

Dry Spell

A Sin and a Shame

**Paranormal**

It Started with a Whisper

*For my Grandpa Ace, who gifted me with the love of travel. I miss his adventurous spirit every day.*

# CHAPTER ONE

I stared at the wide double doors along with everyone else in the clinic. Unlike everyone else, I didn't know what I was waiting for. From the expression on the practice receptionist's face, we were waiting for doom.

The Columbia Clinic was usually a friendly place but not that afternoon. I was seven weeks into an eight-week temp job as a nurse for the clinic's nurse practitioner, Shawna Davis, a tireless woman with four kids and a husband with so much energy she had to walk him every night or he'd take apart the microwave. Even Shawna's shoulders sagged when she saw the schedule. I'd taken a look but could garner no clues about what was coming. One of the other nurses suddenly discovered that her toddler had a fever and left after she saw the schedule. Nobody would tell me anything and I'm usually good at getting information out of people.

The Columbia Clinic was a normal general practice in a small picturesque town just over the Illinois border and I was lucky to get the gig. I needed a steady paycheck after having to take a couple weeks off for a broken ankle and the clinic was a prime place to work by everyone's account. I was filling in for the regular nurse, Kellie Greenwald, who was out on maternity leave. Kelly's newborn had a raging case of colic, but I'd heard several people say they wished they were her for the day.

That wasn't a good sign. Colic could drive parents to the brink of insanity—just ask my mother. It also wasn't a good sign when the entire place flinched whenever the doors rattled. Neither was the huge sigh of relief when a harried mother managed to open the doors with a double baby stroller while holding a screaming four-year-old on her hip.

Karen, one of the other nurses, ran over, calling out, "I've got her." Karen helped Mrs. Bellringer with a big smile on her face as the twins in the stroller started screeching and tugging at their ears. I went to help and Karen panicked, holding up her palm. "No, no. I've got it. You stay right there."

"Why do I feel like I'm being set up?" I asked Steve, the receptionist.

He gave me a blank look. "I don't know what you mean."

"Yeah, right."

"Don't let this affect your decision."

"It won't. Believe me," I said.

The whole office had been trying to talk me into going back to school to get my masters and become a nurse practitioner. The main argument was that I could give up dangerous detective work and not have things happen like broken ankles and the occasional murder attempt. They made it sound like I had a choice. I did not. I was Tommy Watts' daughter, and there weren't a lot of choices left up to me. He was a famous retired police detective who had opened his own shop, and I, as his only child, was expected to support the family business for free. The office thought I was making money chasing down lunatics, but it was costing me in more ways than one. Crimes showed up unannounced and demanding attention whether I wanted to give it or not.

"Mercy," said Steve. "You really should consider it. You'd be great. The patients love you."

"Let's just see how this goes."

More patients showed up, eliciting the same flinch and sighs of relief, until there was only one left. Stanley Cadell. Stanley was the one, but I had no idea why. He was a sixty-seven-year-old diabetes patient in a wheelchair, but the man could clear a room. There was a thump on the doors, and all the sudden, I was alone behind the desk with Steve, who immediately picked up the phone, saying, "He's here." There was a pause. "Mercy." Another pause. "Right away."

Steve looked up at me. "Can you get the door?"

"Sure," I said, not moving.

"What are you waiting for?"

"For you to read me the warning label."

"It's better if you don't know."

"Nothing good comes after that sentence."

Steve shook his head. "I know."

I got the door and found a thin man with the pallor of the recently deceased waiting outside. His comb-over had flipped up and was waving at me in the breeze.

"Mr. Cadell?" I asked.

He brightened up and ran his eyes up and down my scrubs a couple of times, not in a creepy way more like he was sizing up the competition. "So...you're the one they've been talking about."

"Are you Mr. Cadell?"

"I don't want one of those others," he said, shifting in his seat to peer through the open door behind me.

"Others?" I asked.

"I want the girl, the pretty one with the big eyes."

"Shawna?"

"That's the one. I don't want one of those useless doctors, and I'm not going over to Dr. Sidaway. You can't make me. She has a mole. A big one with hairs."

*Definitely the dreaded Stanley Cadell.*

"Okay. I don't think that'll be a problem, Mr. Cadell. You have an appointment here. Let me help you in," I said.

"I'm not a cripple. I get around fine on my own."

I glanced out into the mostly empty patient parking lot. There was no one waiting and no car with a handicap tag. "How did you get here?"

"Taxicab. Uber won't take me anymore, the commie bastards," said

Mr. Cadell, laying the stink eye on me like I too might be a commie bastard.

"Alright then." I opened the door wider for him to wheel through. "Come on in."

"Aren't you going to help me? I'm missing a foot here or didn't your fancy medical training teach you to detect that?"

"I thought...oh, never mind." I wheeled Mr. Cadell in and Steve braced himself on the desk and plastered a patently false smile on his face.

"Good afternoon, Mr. Cadell," said Steve.

Mr. Cadell grumbled as I wheeled him past the desk and muttered something about faggots under his breath. Steve gave me his chart and whispered, "Check the chair."

I nodded, but I had no clue what he was talking about. The chair seemed fine to me. It rolled well and had serviceable brakes. I took him into Room Three and took his vitals. They weren't great, matching how he looked and probably felt. Mr. Cadell had one of his feet amputated since it started to rot as a complication of his diabetes and he was released from rehab the day before. I thought they'd jumped the gun on that. He had pretty much every complication you could get, from diabetes from coronary artery disease to impaired kidney function. The man was a mess and he knew it. He glared at me, questioning my technique for taking his blood pressure and lecturing me on why the new-fangled thermometers weren't accurate. I never wanted to escape a patient so much and that's saying something, considering I have a tendency to get vomited on.

"Can you dance?" he asked when I'd finished.

I jerked upright from looking at his stump. "What?"

"You look like Marilyn Monroe. I guess you got the surgery. Did you take the dance lessons?"

"I didn't get surgery, Mr. Cadell. This is what I look like."

"You look like a slut. What did your mother say about this?"

I swallowed and took a breath. It seemed pointless to say that my mother and I both were spitting images of Marilyn Monroe through no fault of our own. Mr. Cadell wasn't interested. "She didn't say anything. I'll see what's keeping Shawna." I had a pretty good idea what was keeping our big-eyed nurse practitioner—a sense of self-preservation.

"Well, can you dance?" he insisted.

"I never thought of Marilyn as a dancer," I said, heading for the door.

"Can you sing?"

"Not if I can help it." I left the room and found Shawna standing in the hall, twisting her white coat in her hands.

"Is he ready for me?"

"It's more a question of are you ready for him," I said.

She sighed. "Let's do it. Come on, Mercy."

"What? He's all yours. I'm done, unless you have a procedure."

*Please don't have a procedure. Please don't have a procedure.*

"I need a witness and it's your turn," said Shawna.

"A witness?"

"In case things go bad."

"How bad can they go? He's a 130-pound amputee in a wheelchair."

"He bites. There's pending litigation."

"With us?"

"Not so far. He likes me."

"God help you."

"He hasn't so far. Mr. Cadell is still my patient."

Shawna went in and I reluctantly followed. The checkup went pretty well until Shawna got to Mr. Cadell's stump. It wasn't healing as it should. Shawna had me clean and bandage the wound as she started talking about sending him to a dietitian. I got the feeling this wasn't the first time they'd had this talk.

"I don't need some woman telling me how to eat," said Mr. Cadell.

"What have you been eating?" asked Shawna.

"Food."

"Be more specific. Did you bring your food diary?"

Mr. Cadell started plucking at his American flag lap blanket. "I don't need to do that. I know what I eat."

"Fantastic," she said. "What did you eat for breakfast?"

"Oatmeal," he said with a triumphant look.

"What was in the oatmeal?"

My alarm bells went off. This was when things were going to go wrong. I finished the bandaging and backed away slowly.

"A little sugar. You have to have sugar in oatmeal," said Mr. Cadell.

"Did you test your blood before you ate?"

"I forgot."

Shawna rubbed her forehead. "Mr. Cadell, diet is a major factor in your disease progression."

"I'm not fat," he said with a certain amount of pride. In my opinion, he could've used some fat.

"We've discussed this," said Shawna. "In your case, weight isn't a factor. Diet is."

Mr. Cadell rummaged around under his blanket and I was afraid he'd come out with something I very much didn't want to see. In a weird way, he did. Mr. Cadell pulled out a Twinkie.

"Mr. Cadell!" exclaimed Shawna.

He ripped open the Twinkie and stuffed half of it in his mouth. Shawna smacked the rest out of his hand. "You can't eat that."

"I can eat what I want!" he yelled, pulling out another Twinkie.

*I should've checked the wheelchair.*

Shawna lunged for the Twinkie and I lunged for Shawna. I managed to hold her back from throttling the old loon.

"Do you want to lose another foot?" she yelled.

"It's your job to make sure I don't!" he yelled before ripping open another Twinkie.

"You make my job impossible! You must control your diet!"

"I am controlling it!"

She snatched the Twinkie away. "This is the opposite of control!"

"I want some Xanax!"

"Not unless you get therapy," said Shawna, panting with my arms around her middle.

"I'm depressed!"

"Then get some therapy!"

"No!"

That's when it broke loose. Twinkies were everywhere. Dingdongs and HoHos, too. Mr. Cadell had a whole Quick Mart under his blanket. It was a real sugar storm.

# CHAPTER TWO

I trudged up the stairs to my apartment covered in gooey white filling, knowing without a doubt that I wasn't cut out to be a nurse practitioner. Heck. I wasn't sure I was cut out to be a nurse. That had gotten totally out of hand and the worst part was that Mr. Cadell was coming back next week. I wished I could have an infant with a fever on that day. Kellie was so lucky. On the upside, Mr. Cadell was happy. I tipped the cab driver an extra twenty to take the coot off our hands, and Mr. Cadell said he couldn't wait to see me next Wednesday. Apparently, we were the highlight of his week. He called me "Cutie" before I slammed the door. What the heck? Murderers made more sense and they never shoved yellow sponge cake up my nose. Not going to be furthering my education for more of that. I'd take the criminal lunatics over the hometown loons any day.

I made it to the last step when a bout of cursing burst out of the hall ahead of me. I'd like to say it couldn't be, but there was no mistaking that voice. I turned the corner to find Uncle Morty kneeling in front of my door with lock picks in hand and a black backpack at his side. Uncle Morty wasn't my blood uncle. He was my father's best friend and the ever-present grump in my life.

He kept fiddling with the lock until there was a faint clink. He tried the knob and cursed again when it failed to open.

"What're you doing?" I asked.

Uncle Morty started and then glared up at me, much like Mr. Cadell, but I knew he didn't have any Twinkies. He was a baked goods snob like me.

"Trying to get in your apartment. What's it look like?"

"May I ask why?" I asked, but I didn't really care. I was sticky, tired, and, in a week, I had to come up with another job that paid as well as the Columbia Clinic.

Uncle Morty lurched to his feet and put his picks away in their little leather carrying case. "I got a situation."

"Is that situation called Melvin, by chance?"

His upper lip twitched. "Open the door."

I crossed my arms and leaned on the wall. "What's your plan?"

"I'm gonna stay with you until he goes back to Jersey."

My mouth fell open. Uncle Morty couldn't stay with me. What a nightmare. A smelly, grumpy, onion pizza-loving nightmare.

I snapped my mouth shut so hard it hurt my teeth and then said, "You can't stay with me. You're supposed to be bonding with Melvin."

"Screw it. I hate that guy," he growled.

"That guy is your only brother."

"Not my fault. I didn't pick him. Let me in. I'm holing up here until he leaves next Saturday."

*That's over a week. Noooo!*

"You have to spend time with Melvin. Minnie said so."

Minnie was my best hope. She was Morty's elderly and very beloved mother. She lived with Melvin, at least officially. I think Melvin lived with her. There is a difference. Once a year, Minnie went on a Wild Widows cruise with her friends and Melvin was required to visit his brother, Morty, so they could, in Minnie's words, reconnect. Personally, I thought it was so Melvin wouldn't burn the house down.

"I'll have dinner with the bastard. Once."

"How long has he been here?" I asked.

"Two days. It's been freaking hell."

I put on a cheerful expression. "Two days? That's hardly enough to say hello. You have to go back to your place."

"I've had enough of that sanctimonious bastard."

*Oh no! Not the sanctimonious.*

"I'm sure he didn't mean it. Give him a chance to apologize."

"He compared my work to Sheldon Hawke," said Uncle Morty in a low, hateful tone.

Sheldon Hawke? Why'd it have to be him? Uncle Morty considered him to be a hack writer. I thought he was pretty decent, but my opinion didn't count.

"Then he said that I don't have any discipline. I just make things up."

"Um..." I didn't know how to combat that. Uncle Morty was a fantasy writer. He did make things up, hence the fantasy label. That would've been fine if Melvin wasn't a historical fiction writer, known for his exquisite attention to detail and historical accuracy. The fight about who was the better, more valid writer was long-running and tedious.

Then it came to me. "You're very disciplined. Super disciplined. Go home and tell Melvin I said so."

"I don't have to research, he said. I can do anything I want, he said." Uncle Morty ground his fist into his hand.

"Tell him I said—"

"He don't care what you think. You're a kid."

I was too tired to inform him that I was hardly a kid, so I elbowed him aside and put my key in the door. It was only a week. I could stand anything for a week. "Minnie's going to be mad."

"I'll explain it to my mother," he said.

"Good luck with that." I sighed and opened the door wide enough to see a figure standing in the middle of my tiny living room. It was a trim man with dark, wavy hair, wearing pastel golfing clothes. Oz Urbani, nephew of mafia queen, Calpurnia Fibonacci. He was the last man Uncle Morty should see in my living room. My parents would kill me if they knew about our association. I slammed the door, my heart pounding.

"What're you doing?" Morty grabbed the doorknob.

"Mom and Dad."

"What about your parents?"

I peeled his thick fingers off the knob. "You should stay with Mom and Dad. They have six bedrooms. They'll never notice you're there."

That wasn't true. Nobody could miss Morty. He was unmissable.

"Your place was closer," he said.

*Think Mercy. Think.*

"That's no way to choose your living arrangements for the next week. I don't have any food."

"I'll order pizza."

*Oh my god. Not the pizza.*

"I'm not quiet. Aren't you editing the new book? I'll bother you."

"Screw that. I'm here."

I smiled and hoped it looked genuine, not incredibly panicked. "Okay. If you insist. Hey, I can play you the new Taylor Swift album. You're going to love it. It's so happy."

"I hate happy." He frowned and unzipped his jacket, revealing large pit stains. I had to get rid of him for so many reasons.

"But Taylor will make you happy, I swear. Have you been looking at YouTube lately? I have the cutest collection of cat videos to show—"

"I'm outta here." He picked up his backpack and stomped down the stairs. Thank God.

I leaned on the door to slow my breathing and to work myself up to facing whatever Oz wanted. It couldn't be good. I owed Calpurnia Fibonacci my life. The Costilla gang had put a price on my head a few months ago just because I happened to shoot Richard Costilla in the face when he tried to knife me. Calpurnia took care of it without being asked and now I owed her a favor. It was time to ante up. I'd been dreading this eventuality since the day Oz told me Calpurnia spared my life.

The knob turned in my hand, and Oz said through the opening, "Are you coming in?"

"I guess I have to."

"You do live here."

"Now seems like a good time to move," I said.

"Don't be like that. We've always been friends."

I pushed open the door and walked in past Oz. We had always been friends, but it was a peculiar kind of friendship. I saved his sister in Honduras. Calpurnia helped out my godmothers in a family squabble to repay me and so forth. I was starting to get the feeling that once you got involved with Calpurnia, you were stuck. At least Oz was nice and his handsome face didn't hurt either. He sat on my sofa and my cat, Skanky, leapt on his lap and began purring like a buzz saw. Some watchcat he was. If a homicidal manic broke in, he'd give my would-be murderer love.

"What's your cat's name?" asked Oz, giving my worthless feline a serious scratch.

"Skanky."

He gave my cat the once-over. "What's wrong with him?"

"Nothing now." I dropped my purse on a chair and pulled the ponytail holder out of my hair.

"I have to ask," he said. "What happened to you?"

"Twinkie fight."

He eyed my scrubs. "Weren't you at work?"

"Yep. All in a nurse's day's work. Lay it on me, Oz. What does she want?"

"What makes you think I'm here for my aunt? Maybe I wanted to hang out with you," he said with a winning grin. Oz was smooth. I'd give him that. He looked perfect, sitting there in his bright pink golf shirt that showed off his deep tan, courtesy of the June sunshine. Oz was a golf pro and not supposed to be part of the Fibonacci family business, but I had my doubts as to his involvement.

"Yeah. We always hang out," I said.

"We could. I like you."

"My parents would freak. How did you get in here?"

"I'm better at picking locks than Morty," he said.

"What if he'd gotten in?" I asked.

He shrugged. "It didn't happen. Why worry about it?"

"Fine. Somebody could've been here," I said.

"Like who? That cop you're dating?" Oz smiled wickedly at me.

"Well, yeah."

My parents would freak if they knew my connection to the

Fibonaccis, but it was nothing to how Chuck would react. He wasn't a retired cop like my father. He was a St. Louis police detective and having a girlfriend with organized crime connections would be bad for his career and could possibly call into question his cases. If I was involved with Calpurnia, who was to say he wasn't?

"Not likely," he said.

"Why not?"

"He's not spending the night."

"Creepy," I said. "How do you know that?'

"Aunt Calpurnia likes to keep track of the friends of her friends."

"Fantastic. So what does she want?"

"I don't know, but she made it clear that I'm not to let you slip away. She wants to see you today at her house."

I shook off the dread and said, "Fine. Let's go."

"Not like that. This is Calpurnia Fibonacci. You can't go in scrubs, and you've got stuff." Oz stood up and plucked a brown spongey glob out of my hair. "What is this?"

"There were Dingdongs, too."

"Your life fascinates me."

"I'm glad it fascinates somebody, 'cause it irritates me," I said.

Oz spun me around and pushed me toward my bathroom. "Shower and I'll take you over."

"Do I have to be blindfolded?" I asked before heading into the bathroom.

"What in the world for?" he asked with frown.

"Maybe I'm not supposed to know where she lives."

He snorted and rolled his eyes.

"I don't know. I was just asking."

"Everyone knows where Calpurnia lives, from the FBI to the lowliest beat cop in our fair city."

I sucked in a breath. "What if her house is under surveillance? I'll be seen going in."

"It's not. I checked."

"How do you know?"

He raised an eyebrow. "You think my aunt doesn't know when she's being watched?"

"Never mind."

I took a boiling hot shower to get the sugar off and mulled over what to wear until Oz yelled for me to hurry it up.

"I'm coming. What should I wear?" I yelled back.

"Something sexy and conservative," he said through the door.

"Those things don't go together."

"Yes, they do. Hurry up. Calpurnia doesn't like to be kept waiting."

I had no idea what to wear, but the choice seemed important. After another ten minutes of pondering and Oz squawking through the door, I choose a1930's dress that I bought at the vintage shop on McPherson Avenue. It was oxblood red with a full skirt and a snug waist. It covered everything, but Chuck called it sexy. When I emerged from the bedroom, Oz whistled. "Perfect."

My dress was the only thing that was perfect about that day.

# CHAPTER THREE

Oz drove through an open gate onto Calpurnia's property. No wonder Oz rolled his eyes at me. Fibonacci was written in cursive wrought iron in an arch over the entrance. I guess Calpurnia didn't believe in either subtlety or hiding. I had to respect the lack of pretense.

We drove down a winding driveway, past a small golf course and a driving range with well-manicured trees and flowers in free-form beds.

"Does your aunt golf?" I asked to break the silence.

"No. She put those in for me," Oz said.

"You must be her favorite."

"One of them."

"Please. You're the favorite," I said.

He grinned at me. "Could be."

I wondered if that was why he was allowed to stay out of the family business. Being a favorite has its privileges, not that I would know. I was an only child, but Chuck was my father's favorite. His mother married my uncle, who adopted Chuck before Delilah dumped him. Chuck was the son I refused to be. He was a cop, very impressed with Dad, and was the only detective on the force with a rep that rivaled my father's. I was the disobedient daughter who became a nurse and thought she ought to be paid to surveil cheating husbands and gym rats claiming disability. Chuck would've done it for free and thanked Dad for the opportunity. What a suck-up. Constantly making me look bad. It was a good thing he was so hot and charming and unexpectedly sweet or I would've had nothing to say to him.

Oz pulled up in front of an ultra-modern house, all straight lines and glass. It reminded me of Frank Lloyd Wright's Falling Water but less blocky. We got out and walked up the slate stairs to the door that was unlocked. I don't know what I was expecting exactly. I hadn't given Calpurnia's home any thought whatsoever, but I wouldn't have expected this house if I had. A woman named Calpurnia Fibonacci, who headed a mafia family, should've had a traditional home, old world with lots of wood and creaking, not some modern masterpiece. There weren't even any knuckle-cracking goombahs playing cards in the foyer while protecting the house. There was no one there at all.

"How do you like the house?" asked Oz.

"It's gorgeous." And it was. The blond hardwood floors gleamed like glass and all the furniture was Danish Modern in design. It was totally different from my style—early garage sale—but I liked the clean, crisp feel of it.

Oz pressed an intercom button next to the door. "Aunt Cal? It's Oz."

"Kitchen, baby," said a throaty voice that could almost have belonged to a man. Calpurnia Fibonacci. I was so nervous; I think I peed a little.

Oz put his hand on the small of my back and guided me through the house. The clean lines continued throughout. We passed through a living room with a fireplace that covered the entire wide wall. Displayed there were dozens of family photos, a happy family, a normal, average family. I had a hard time reconciling what little I knew of the Fibonaccis with those faces. How could bad look so good?

Calpurnia read *Architectural Digest*, *La Cucina Italiana*, and *Harper's*. Was she a murderer? A drug trafficker or worse, a human trafficker? I hoped Calpurnia would give me a clue. From the look of her house, if she did, it would only confuse me.

We turned into a short hall and the smell of garlic and searing meat reached us along with the sound of Linda Ronstadt singing "You're No Good." Oz breathed in deeply. "Dinner."

Dinner smelled awesome, but I wasn't staying if I could possibly help it. We walked into a large bright kitchen done in a cappuccino brown and cream. Sun streamed in through a glass wall, highlighting the big center island, topped by a huge slab of blue and silver swirled granite. Calpurnia stood behind the island, opposite us with her back turned. Oz walked me to the island and then stopped, waiting patiently while she stared down into a pale blue Le Creuset Dutch oven, the big one.

Calpurnia might've had a deep voice, but she was no man. She wore a snug black lace dress with cap sleeves. There was a hot pink apron tied around her neck and narrow waist. The dress hugged her curves down to her shapely calves. Her thick, dark brown hair wound around the back of her head in a silky halo and her feet were bare. This was Calpurnia Fibonacci, the woman who saved my life. The woman many men feared and, if I went by the expression on Oz's face, loved and respected. I felt a rush of gratitude to be on her good side. Whatever she asked of me, I would do it as long as it wasn't too illegal. For the first time, I wasn't sorry to owe such a woman. I had my life and it was proper to be grateful. I'd rather owe her than a man anyway.

"Do you like pizzaiola, Miss Watts?" asked Calpurnia in her throaty voice laced with a subtle Italian accent.

"I don't think I've ever had it," I said. "Smells great."

Calpurnia turned, revealing a chiseled jawline and a hooked nose. She smiled at me over her shoulder with a mouth a bit too wide for her face and well-coated in ruby red lipstick. "I knew I'd like you."

"Really? Why?" I asked.

"You aren't afraid."

"I was nervous."

She raised an elegant eyebrow, thickened with a brow pencil. "No more?"

"No," I said.

"Good. Now open that can of tomato paste for me." She pointed to a small can on the counter beside her. I glanced at Oz and he shrugged.

I found an opener in a drawer and opened the can, setting it closer to her.

"Oz, baby, come here," said Calpurnia.

Oz went over dutifully. She kissed his tanned cheek and then rubbed away the ruby smudge with her thumb. "Go out and skim the pool for me. We've been invaded by grasshoppers."

"Yes, ma'am." Oz nodded to me and left through a set of French doors in the glass wall.

Calpurnia got out a chipped platter and took four ribeye steaks out of the pot. They were seared to a rich reddish brown and made me involuntarily lick my lips.

"What do you think is on those?" she asked.

I channeled my inner Aaron. Aaron was my so-called investigating partner and a master cook. "Powdered garlic, salt, and pepper."

"Very good." She took the tomato paste and scooped it into the smoking pan, instantly caramelizing the paste. She worked it around the pot with a wooden spoon and added oregano and red pepper flakes. When the paste was a rusty orange, she lowered the heat and added a whole box of chicken stock.

"Any idea why you're here?" asked Calpurnia.

"Not even a little bit."

"I want you to do something for me."

"Okay," I said.

"That's all you have to say?"

"Pretty much."

She smiled at me. Her teeth were as white and even as her nephew's. "That's what I like to hear." She went on to add salt and pepper to the pot, taste the mixture, and then add more. When she was satisfied, she put the steaks back in, poking them down with a wickedly sharp meat fork. I put the lid on for her and she put the pot in the oven, closing the door with her foot.

"Chianti?" Calpurnia asked.

"Yes, please."

She uncorked a bottle, grabbed a couple glasses, and tucked a plain manila folder under her arm. We followed Oz's path out the French doors to a stone patio made up of several levels. Winding stairs led down to the ice blue pool where, Oz was skimming the water with a long-handled net. We sat at a table covered with an ornate mosaic of a Roman villa.

I poured the Chianti, a Barberino Val d'Elsa vintage. Calpurnia swirled the lux red liquid in her crystal glass and breathed in the scent, closing her light brown eyes, before taking a sip. I followed suit because I didn't know what else to do. She wasn't in a hurry to get to the point and I definitely wasn't in charge.

Oz yelled up, yanking us out of our silence. "Aunt Calpurnia, I'm going to check the water. It smells off."

His aunt raised her glass and nodded before switching her warm, yet piercing gaze on me.

"Can I ask you a question?" I asked.

"You may."

"I thought the Fibonaccis had been in St. Louis for generations. Why do you have an Italian accent?"

She laughed, a surprisingly musical sound for her deep voice. "My mother was a great beauty with an even greater temper. When I was two, she decided my father had been unfaithful to her and took us to her family in Rome. He wasn't able to bring us back to St. Louis until Cosmo and I were sixteen."

"You didn't see your father for fourteen years?"

"Oh no. He was a constant presence in our lives. My sister, Giada, Oz's mother, was born in Rome. Papa couldn't resist my mother. Few could."

"Some women are like that," I said.

Her eyes roved over my face. "It is an advantage. No?"

A smile broke out on my face despite my trying to suppress it. "It is."

We laughed and sipped our fabulous wine under the constant glances of Oz, who checked the pool chemicals and rearranged the deck chairs.

"Miss Watts, does the name Angela Riley mean anything to you?"

I thought it over and said, "Sorry, no."

Calpurnia opened the folder and gave me an eight by ten glossy photo of a family of five. The husband was a balding blond man in his thirties. The wife, also mid-thirties, was a pretty brunette with green eyes and a mass of curls. The children were also brunettes with shy smiles. The little girl was about six and the boys were older, maybe nine and ten.

"Angela's the mother?" I asked.

"Yes."

"And?"

Oz's aunt sipped her wine and gazed at me over the crystal rim. "And I want you to find her for me."

"Is she lost?" I asked.

"She's supposed to be dead."

"Supposed to be?"

"That's what we were led to believe six years ago."

"This is a pretty cold case," I said.

"It was. One week ago, Angela's sister saw her in Paris."

I leaned forward and poured her some more wine. This was going to be interesting.

When Calpurnia finished her story, she excused herself to go check on her pizzaiola. I sat back and watched the shadows extend across the lawn to where Oz was playing fetch with a pair of black Labradors. I ran over the facts in my mind while trying to figure out how in the world I was going to find Angela Riley without anyone knowing I was looking for her—in Paris, of all places. I loved Paris, the city of lights, of love, of art and passion. But why there? Why couldn't Angela Riley show up in someplace convenient like Jeff City or Hannibal? Of course, she wouldn't do that. That would be too easy and finding Phillip Riley's wife wasn't going to be easy.

Phillip Riley was the long-time accountant of the Fibonacci family as his father was before him and his grandfather before that. Six years ago, he'd been a happily married man and father of three. His wife, Angela, was pretty and, in Calpurnia's estimation, unremarkable. She was a stay-at-home mother, belonged to two book clubs, volunteered at her kids' schools, and coached soccer until October six years ago.

Angela took a weekend trip to Chicago with her sister, Gina. They went to museums, saw a Broadway show, and went to bars. That's where Angela got into trouble. It turns out that Phillip Riley wasn't so happily married. While getting drunk on Long Island iced teas with Gina, Angela met a man. After about ten minutes, she was making out with him in a corner. The description was vague—five foot ten, brown hair, square jaw. Angela called him Tom. No last name.

The bar was hopping that night. Some sports team had won something and the party was raging. Around one in the morning Angela said she was going to dance with Tom. She left Gina at the table and was never seen again. The cops couldn't even figure out what exit she left by or if she actually left with Tom. She stepped away from the table and vanished. There was no body and no trace other than her stiletto. One shoe had been found in the alley behind the bar. She never came back to the hotel and she left her purse with Gina. The cops concluded that she left with Tom. He forced her into a car and he killed her, although they had no concrete proof of that. Of course, what woman would run off in the middle of the night with one shoe and no money?

Phillip hired a private investigator, Harvey Spoon. According to Calpurnia, he tried to hire my dad, but Dad turned him down flat. Instead, he hired Spoon, a man I'd heard of and Dad respected. Spoon found nothing. Angela hadn't used her social security number or accessed any accounts. Lots of leads turned up, thanks to the reward Phillip and the Fibonaccis offered, but none of the leads panned out.

After two years of fruitless searching, Phillip gave up, accepted that Angela was most likely dead, and began the long wait until he could have her officially declared so.

But that wasn't the end of it. Two weeks before Oz showed up in my apartment, Gina, Angela's sister, was in Paris having lunch with her third husband on Rue Cler when she saw Angela. Or she thought she saw Angela walk by with a man. Gina was sitting in Tribeca, saw the woman but was unable to get out of the restaurant in time to catch her. Calpurnia clearly didn't believe that. She thought that if she saw her long-dead sister, she'd find a way. She hadn't been to Tribeca. I had. Tribeca's tables were tightly wedged together and the place was usually packed at lunchtime. It takes time and agility to get out and Gina didn't have time. She did manage to run down the street and take some pictures with her phone as the woman got in a cab.

I compared the phone shots with the family pictures. Angela had curly hair in the family pictures, but the woman in the phone shot had straight hair with a reddish tinge. Gina only got a couple of profile shots and the profile worked, but it wasn't distinctive. The woman's build was similar, five foot five, small breasted with wide hips. But I realized that the phone shot could be a photo of Angela Riley or one of a million other women.

The French doors opened and Calpurnia came back out. This time, she was accompanied by a man. He was her age with the same silky brown hair and wide mouth. He smiled when he saw me and lots of laugh lines crinkled around his eyes. He had to be Calpurnia's twin, Cosmo. He was supposed to be the head of the family, but, for whatever reason, a woman had taken the mantle from him.

"Miss Watts," he said with a deeper accent than his sister. "How nice to finally meet you."

I stood up and shook his offered hand. It was warm and surprisingly callused. "It's a pleasure to meet you, too."

We sat down and Cosmo took a drink of Calpurnia's wine before saying, "Do you know who I am?"

"I assume you're Cosmo Fibonacci, Calpurnia's twin," I said.

"Correct. I hear you're handling the Riley matter for us."

"I guess so."

He frowned a tiny bit and then quickly covered the disapproval. "You're not enthusiastic about the favor my sister has asked of you?"

"It's not that. I'll do it. I just...I don't know how I'm going to prove this one way or the other."

Cosmos laughed the same musical laugh as his sister. "I don't know either, but I'm sure you'll do your best."

"I will. I always do. But I have some questions."

"Go ahead," said Calpurnia, taking her glass from Cosmo.

"How come Phillip isn't here? He's the husband."

Calpurnia and Cosmo exchanged a look.

"Very perceptive," said Calpurnia. "Phillip doesn't believe Gina."

"You don't seem convinced either, but here I am."

"Gina came to me after trying to get Phillip involved. She asked me a favor. I'm granting it."

"Phillip doesn't want Angela back?" I asked.

She swirled her wine. "Angela will be declared dead in nine months. He has another woman and he will marry her when that happens. Phillip made his peace with this years ago."

Cosmo shook his head. "He made his peace with what the cops say happened. Angela got murdered by the man that she was fooling around with. That was bad enough."

I drained my glass and Cosmo poured me the rest of the bottle. "I see. If Angela is alive, she left him and abandoned her three children."

"Exactly," said Cosmo. "He's done with her, one way or another."

"Do you think she would've abandoned her children?" I asked.

They both shook their heads and Calpurnia said, "Not for a minute. She was a devoted mother."

"You should know that Gina is bi-polar," said Cosmo. "She's been medicated for years for that and for depression since Angela's disappearance."

"That doesn't mean she's wrong," I said.

"No," said Calpurnia. "But it's a factor."

"It is. How thoroughly did the cops and Harvey go through Angela's finances?"

"With a fine-toothed comb," said Cosmo. "If she's alive, she took nothing with her. Not a cent."

"There were no rumors of an affair, someone who might've financed an escape?"

"No," said Calpurnia. "She and Gina were extremely close. She would've known."

I rolled my glass between my palms. "You know she's most likely dead."

"I understand that. When can you leave?"

"I have a week left in my current job. After that. I'm thinking next Friday or Saturday, if I can figure out how to swing this last-minute trip."

Cosmo took a fat envelope and a cellphone out of his breast pocket. "This should help." He slid them across the table. The envelope was filled with hundreds. Several thousand dollars were in there, money I could definitely use, but couldn't accept.

"I can't take that," I said.

"I thought you'd say that," said Calpurnia.

Cosmo shrugged and tucked the envelope back in his pocket.

*Goodbye, sweet cash.*

Calpurnia pushed the cellphone closer to me. "You need this and don't say no. It's non-negotiable."

"Untraceable?" I asked.

"Yes. It's loaded with my private number and Cosmo's. I expect frequent updates."

I took the cellphone, finished my wine, and looked at the pictures again. A nondescript woman wearing a flowered sundress in Paris. Great. That's not hard at all. On the other hand, the man she was with, he wasn't so bland. Tall, silver-haired with a large, hawkish nose. He wore white linen cropped trousers, a silky grey polo shirt with a light navy sweater over it and a pair of pointy loafers with no socks. He couldn't be an American. No way.

"Miss Watts?" asked Calpurnia. "You look like a girl with a plan."

"I'm not going to look for Angela in Paris," I said.

"No?"

I held up the cab picture. "I'm going to look for him."

# CHAPTER FOUR

I didn't even make it through my front door before I smelled it. Stank onion pizza. It was in my apartment. I banged my head on the door, eliciting a yell.

Uncle Morty whipped open the door. "What're you doing?"

"I was coming home. Now I'm rethinking my position."

"What's your problem?"

"Why aren't you at Mom and Dad's?" I asked.

Morty grimaced. "Your cousins are there, planning that gawd awful wedding. Bridget asked my damn opinion on the groom's cake. What the hell do I care?"

I walked in and saw not one but two pizzas on my coffee table, along with two beer bottles, cheesy puffs, pork rinds, and his laptop. Uncle Morty had settled in. I'd have to use a cattle prod to get the man out.

"So how'd you get in? You couldn't pick the lock earlier," I said, opening the window and waving the stink out.

"Chuck let me in."

"He's here?" I headed for the bedroom.

"Nah. He was dropping something off for you. I could've picked that wimpy lock of yours given enough time," he said.

"Yeah, right," I said. "Wait. Did you say he dropped something off?"

"Some contraption. Claims it makes coffee."

I groaned. Not another so-called present. Chuck and I hadn't been dating that long, but he'd proved to be what my mother called generous. I called it bothersome at best. Who needed an ice cream maker and a gelato maker? Not me. I, also, didn't need an espresso maker, a Keurig, and a Mr. Coffee.

"What're you making that face for?" asked Uncle Morty. "The sap loves you. He brings you stuff."

The stuff Chuck brought me reminded me of Mom's evil Siamese bringing her dead mice. She appreciated the gesture, but then she had to do something with the tiny corpses.

"I don't have the space," I said. "My apartment isn't that big."

*Especially with you in it.*

Uncle Morty dropped onto the sofa, making it creak. "You should be grateful."

"He brought me a tap and die set."

"What're you going to do with that?"

"I don't even know what tap and dies are for. I put it with my shoes. Where'd he go?" I asked.

"Ferguson. Another riot is shaping up."

I gave him a look. "You mean protest."

"Whatever," he said.

"But it's pouring."

"Won't last long then," he said with a snort. He didn't have much respect for protesters who couldn't face a summer shower. Of course, I couldn't imagine Uncle Morty caring about anything enough to carry a sign in the rain or even fog. He wasn't a fan of moisture or causes, for that matter.

I marched into the kitchen, hoping Chuck didn't bring me another Keurig. He didn't. Sitting next to my new pasta maker was a Rocket espresso machine. Contraption was right. Compared to the other espresso machine, a normal looking De'Longhi, the Rocket looked like it was imagined by a steam punk author, all chrome with knobs, nozzles, and gauges.

Uncle Morty heaved himself off the sofa and came over to take a look. "Does it make coffee?"

"Yeah, but I don't know how."

"Figure it out before morning. I could use a good espresso to start work."

"So you're staying?"

He scowled at me and returned to the sofa. I attempted to find a place for the Rocket, but it stayed on the counter with all the other stuff. I was going to make dinner, but I couldn't find a spot to do it in.

"I give up," I told Morty, grabbing my purse. "I'm going to Kronos."

Uncle Morty raised a bushy eyebrow at me. "You gonna call Chuck?"

"You said he was working."

"That damn riot is probably over."

I stopped with my hand on the doorknob. "I can call him. Since when are you so interested in us?"

"I ain't interested." He didn't look at me but focused on his disgusting pizza. "What's going on with you two?"

"Nothing."

"That's right. Nothing."

"Huh?"

He pointed toward the bedroom. "Where's Chuck's stuff? My wizard had stuff here."

My last boyfriend was formerly Uncle Morty's wizard in his Dungeons and Dragons crew. He hadn't quite gotten over our breakup. I'd rather not think about Pete and the terrible way I handled the end of our relationship. Must change focus.

"Did you search my apartment? Seriously?" I asked.

"I was looking for some mouthwash."

*Really? Good.*

"I've got to go." I opened the door.

"Where's Chuck's stuff?"

I shrugged. "His place, I assume." I left with a sinking feeling in my stomach. I didn't think anyone else would notice, certainly not Uncle Morty. There was no stuff and I wanted there to be stuff. Chuck avoided the topic and he'd never even spent the night. If I was being honest, he'd barely touched me since the day we decided we were together. Chuck had been everything I wanted in a boyfriend—if I ignored all the appliances—except that he was somehow distant. I'd sunk so low as to try and seduce him with fancy lingerie. The minute I attempted to model it for him, he suddenly had an emergency at work and practically ran out the door. I'd never encountered such a thing before. I didn't have to seduce men. They had to seduce me and since they were usually bad at it, I wasn't nearly as wild as people assumed.

I would've thought he was old-fashioned or just plain odd, but practically every friend I had had dated Chuck. No one ever said he was a prude or distant. He was popular even after the inevitable breakup. He remained friends with his exes. Chuck's hot body and sexual prowess was the stuff of legend. I'd only gotten to experience it once. With the way things were headed, it was going to stay that way.

Kronos was Aaron's restaurant, a Star Trek-themed magnet for cops and firefighters. It was packed as usual. I squeezed in the door and found that Chuck wasn't in Ferguson. He was there, singing. He stood in the center of the restaurant with the rest of Cop-A-Pella, the police a cappella group, singing G.R.L.'s "Ugly Heart." They switched the gender, but I still didn't see that coming.

I made it to the bar and accepted a metaphysical malt from Rodney, the other Kronos owner. The malt was chocolate and sent an icy chill down my throat as I watched Chuck belting out his solo in his damp uniform. I hardly ever got to see him in blues, but it was good to be identifiable in Ferguson.

Chuck winked at me and I couldn't stop smiling. Maybe he was just old-fashioned when it came to me. It was kind of sweet. I was special. I could handle that.

As soon as I thought I was special, I discovered someone who didn't agree at all. Pete sat at a booth with some other doctors. His handsome, intelligent face twisted as Chuck sang about a woman stamped with a beauty mark. The smile fell off my face and he saw me. The other docs followed his gaze, saw me, and started eating like burgers were a new invention. Pete stood up and went for the door. Without thinking about it, I tried to head him off.

I snagged his lab coat as he went through the door. "You don't have to leave."

"Yes, I do." Pete went out. I started to follow, but someone grabbed my arm.

"Don't," said Aaron, turning me around and pushing me toward the bar.

"I want to apologize," I said.

"Don't." He gave me a menu and went into the kitchen.

I sighed and opened the menu, not that I needed to. I'd memorized it long ago, except for Aaron's off-the-wall daily specials, which I never ordered. That Friday was mini crab soufflés with a lemon thyme drizzle. That's a hard pass.

The song ended in thunderous applause and I was quickly surrounded by breathless cops. Chuck put a big hand on my back, not my butt as the old Chuck would've. I gave him a huge grin and went for a kiss, which he avoided by kissing my cheek. What the hell? I couldn't shake the feeling that something wasn't right and it wasn't me. It was Chuck. The other guys didn't seem to notice, thankfully.

"What did you think?" asked Nazir, another detective.

"You were excellent," I said. "That's a new one, isn't it?"

Sidney Wick, a detective that I always seemed to annoy, took a strawberry margarita from Rodney and said, "We're doing it for the benefit."

"Benefit?"

Chuck rubbed my back. "You remember, Cops for Kids. It's for the Children's Hospital."

"Oh, right."

"Chuck says you're considering singing for it," said Nazir.

I snorted. "I am not."

"You should," said Wick. "You'd bring down the house. Gotta go. The wife needs her medicine."

Nazir elbowed me. "Come on, Mercy. You can sing. Think of the children."

"I'd rather do a bikini car wash."

"That could be arranged."

"You're evil."

Nazir laughed and Chuck asked, "Did you see my present?"

Dr. Grace, the head pathologist at St. James, wedged himself in beside me. "What present? Was it a ring with a diamond, per chance?"

"It was not," I said. "He got me a Rocket espresso machine."

Dr. Grace whistled. "I bet that cost a pretty penny."

Both Chuck and Nazir reddened and looked away.

"Or maybe not," said Dr. Grace. "Gotta go."

The good doctor disappeared back into the crowd without ordering a drink.

"What was that about?" I asked. "How much did that thing cost?"

Chuck avoided looking at me and ordered a beer.

"Hello." I tapped him on his hard bicep.

"Don't worry about it, Mercy," he said. "It was a gift."

I got out my phone and googled it. "Are you crazy? 2700 dollars. You're taking it back."

"I didn't pay that." Still no eye contact. Nazir was looking at the ceiling.

"Ebay?"

"Kind of like that," said Chuck.

*I should've known. Police auction.*

"Tell me it wasn't found at the scene of some gruesome murder," I said.

Nazir and every other cops made like they'd been called to a crime scene or maybe like Kronos was about to become one.

"No problem, baby," said Chuck, blue eyes without a hint of deceit.

I narrowed my eyes at him. "Why's it no problem?"

Nazir patted him on the back. "Good luck. I'm going to go...somewhere not here."

"Run away, you coward," I said before turning back to Chuck. "It was, wasn't it?"

"Might've been."

"Which murder?"

"That Calabash murder-suicide."

I groaned. "Didn't that happen in the kitchen?"

"It ended there."

"Tell me there wasn't blood on it."

"I cleaned it," he said.

"Ew. I want that thing out of my apartment," I said with a shudder.

Chuck nuzzled my cheek. "I'm going to make you great lattes with that."

"No, you're not."

"Really. The foam is perfect for latte art."

"No foam."

"You'll change your mind when you taste it."

"Can you hear me?" I asked. "Can my voice penetrate your skull?"

"I hear you, but I know you'll change your mind when you taste the espresso."

"I'll toss that thing out the window."

He held me by the shoulders. "It cost 2,700 dollars new."

"You mean pre-blood spatter."

Chuck grinned with pride. "Yeah. I got it cheap. The family didn't want it."

"You mean nobody else wanted a bloody espresso machine? I'm shocked."

"It was a great deal."

"Fantastic. Where'd the ice cream maker come from? A school shooting?"

"Drug raid. No biggie."

"Can't you just go to Sears like other people?"

"I'm not like other people and neither are you."

I slid off the stool. "I'm going to see Aaron, you cheap maniac."

Chuck leaned in and I thought he would kiss me for real. Instead, I got a peck on the forehead. "You love me."

"You're alright." I wormed my way around the bar and into the kitchen where Aaron had donned a pink hairnet over his permanent case of bedhead.

"You hungry?" he asked.

"Starving."

"I got a cra—"

"No crab. Worf burger and fries, please," I said. Aaron looked so sad, I added, "If you've got a poutine..."

That's all I had to say. The little nut job was at the grill, making a super calorie bomb. That could take a while and I had stuff to do.

"Hey, Aaron," I said. "Can I use your computer?"

He shrugged and I took that as a yes. Kronos' so-called office was in the back corner of the large kitchen surrounded by cans of tomatoes, bins of potatoes and onions, and linens, since they never used linens. I sat down at the little desk and searched flights to Paris. Pricey, especially last minute. I was lucky that my godmothers were Millicent and Myrtle Bled, known as The Girls. Thanks to my godmothers' love of travel, I had a million frequent flyer miles. I could use the corporate advantage, too. Airlines always catered to the Bleds. Millicent and Myrtle Bled were the matriarchs of the Bled Brewing empire. I was seen as an honorary Bled and I'd have to use that if I wanted last-minute tickets during the summer. I might be able to stay at one of the company apartments if they weren't booked. They normally would be, considering it was Paris, and the company apartments were a perk for family and brewery employees over a certain tenure, but there had been a recent death in the Bled Brewery family.

Lester, The Girls' long time chauffeur, had been murdered during a break-in at the Bled mansion. The entire company went into mourning and The Girls said people were afraid to go to the company properties because it had gotten out that Lester's killers hadn't found what they were looking for and were expected to try again. I wasn't worried about that. The Klinefeld Group was behind the break-in. They were a shadowy not-for-profit group that claimed to only be interested in the preservation of art, but they were interested in a lot more than that. They'd sued The Girls over The Bled Collection, trying to get a hold of art that Stella Bled Lawrence had smuggled out of Europe during WWII and hadn't been reclaimed because the owners had fallen victim to the Holocaust or hadn't been located yet. But The Klinefeld Group wanted something else, something they had thought was concealed within the collection. They did get the inventory during the break-in and had dropped the suit when they didn't find what they were looking for on the list.

I logged into the company site and found three properties in Paris would be vacant. Perfect. I took the Rue Montorgueil apartment. It was too big for me, but nobody else wanted it and I loved the quaint pedestrians-only shopping street. I'd have to call the airlines to wheedle my way onto a flight, but that could wait until tomorrow.

The office door swung open and I closed the browser. Aaron put a to-go bag on the desk and left without a word. Normal for him. I picked up the bag and went back into the kitchen as my phone started vibrating in my pocket—my phone, not Calpurnia's. I took a look and groaned. Melvin. When did he get my number? It was an SOS from Uncle Morty's brother so I supposed it wouldn't do to ignore it.

"Hi, Melvin. What's up?" I asked.

"Morty won't let me in," he said in a voice that was indistinguishable from Morty's.

I bit my lip and winced. "In where?"

"Your apartment. Whaddya think?"

"Why are you there?"

"Supposed to be with Morty. Mom said." There was a loud pounding on what I assumed was my door. "Let me in, you best-selling hack!"

My neighbors weren't going to be happy. They liked a quiet building and put up with my occasional stalkers and news crews when I got involved in a criminal investigation like the Bled break-in because I, myself, was quiet and made them cinnamon rolls at Christmas, but inflicting two Van Der Hoof brothers on them was going too far.

"I'll be there in a minute." I hung up and rubbed my forehead. "The sooner I get out of here, the better."

"Where are you going?"

My head jerked up and there was Chuck, standing in the door, holding a spice-encrusted fry.

"Um..."

He frowned. "Did something happen? Did The Klinefeld Group contact you?"

"No."

He relaxed and my purse chirped. I froze. Oh my god.

"What was that?"

"What?"

"That noise," said Chuck. "You look weird. What's wrong? Something happened, didn't it?"

All I could think of was Calpurnia Fibonacci's phone in my purse. Why the hell did I leave that in there? And it wouldn't stop chirping.

"I...um..."

Aaron walked over and stood in front of my purse, pressing it between the wall and his chubbiness. The chirping was barely audible. Thank god.

Chuck moved in closer. I recognized that look. He was in detective mode, ready to suss out the truth at any cost.

"We're going to Paris," said Aaron.

*Oh crap! Did he say Paris? How the—*

"Paris?" asked Chuck. "Are you going without me?"

Oh my god. This cannot be happening.

"Well, no," I said. "I was going to..." I don't know what I was going to do.

"I thought we weren't doing Paris until we had a plan," said Chuck.

Chuck and I had planned to go to Paris to follow-up a lead we got on The Klinefeld Group. Unfortunately our lead, Paul Richter, the brother of a cop from Berlin who investigated a crime in 1963 that possibly involved The Klinefeld Group, had died not long after we found out about him. The cop, Werner Richter, was killed in a hit and run in 1965. There was no rush without something else to go on.

"Cooking school," said Aaron.

"Cooking school?" asked Chuck.

We were both looking at Aaron, who was looking past us at a spot on the wall. Where was this going?

"I guess we were going to go to cooking school," I said after a minute.

"You guess?"

"The plan wasn't set in stone."

"So there's a plan and you didn't tell me?"

"Er..."

My purse stopped chirping and Aaron returned to the grill. "She's helping me."

Chuck tossed the fry in the trash, a sure sign of anger. "At cooking school? You gotta be kidding."

"Um...I know Paris and it wouldn't hurt to talk to the Richter family while I was there."

Chuck straightened up to his considerable height and his face went hard. "Got to go to work. I'll see you later." He stalked out of the kitchen after punching the swinging door open.

"What was that about? Cooking school?" I asked Aaron.

"You need to go to Paris?"

"Yes."

"So we'll go."

I rubbed my head again. "What about the cooking school?"

"I'll find one."

"I guess there's always a cooking class in Paris, but, Aaron, you don't have to come."

"I'm coming. You need me."

That was probably true. Aaron was surprisingly useful, although I could never quite figure out how it worked out that way.

"Okay," I said. "We leave in a week."

He handed me a piece of crusty melted cheese off the grill. So good, but I didn't deserve it. Chuck was upset and I didn't know how to unupset him. He was acting weird before and I couldn't even figure that out.

Nazir came in through the swinging door. "I need to talk to you."

He had never taken that tone with me before. We were friends, but from the expression on his face that might not last the night.

"Okay," I said more guilty-sounding than I wanted it to come out.

"You're going to Paris?"

"It was just decided."

"And you're not taking Chuck." Nazir's voice was so hard, I was a little bit scared and I don't scare easily.

"I didn't get a chance to ask him. He marched out."

*That sounded good. Please let that have sounded good.*

"So Chuck's going?" he asked.

"If he can get the time off," I said.

*Please don't let him get the time off. Please, God. I beg you.*

"I'll make sure he gets it," said Nazir, his whole body relaxing.

*Crap on a cracker!*

"Um...why's it so important to you?" I asked.

"Chuck needs to get away. Can't you see that?"

"He is acting kind of odd."

Nazir headed for the door and I grabbed his arm. "Why does he need to get away?"

He peeled my fingers off his arm. "I doubt he'll ever tell you." Nazir walked out the door, leaving it swinging violently in his wake.

So I was taking Aaron and Chuck to Paris while I worked on a case for Calpurnia Fibonacci. Was there any way I could pull this off without getting caught working for the mafia? It would take a miracle and I'd heard miracles were in short supply.

# CHAPTER FIVE

I spent half that night trying to convince Chuck that I wasn't investigating The Klinefeld Group without him. He took the whole detective thing very personally and I didn't get it. He could investigate them without me. I couldn't care less, but Chuck definitely did care. He thought I would get killed without him by my side. I had to bite back many retorts, pointing out that I seemed to do fine without him. I hadn't been killed once.

All of this talking was done on the phone. I couldn't lure Chuck over to my apartment with promises of back rubs or anything else, but that might not have been due to his recent oddness. Uncle Morty and his brother had taken up residence in my living room. I was in the bedroom with the door closed, but I could still hear them arguing about the merits of *Star Trek*, the original series, versus *The Next Generation*. How they could care so passionately was a mystery to me. They, also, cared about pizza. Were anchovies better than onions? Should the sauce go under the cheese or on top? This mattered. A lot. My living room was covered in stank pizzas for their taste testing. The smell seeped under my door and gave me nightmares where Mr. Cadell from the Colombia Clinic kept throwing fish and onions at me.

I finally got to sleep around two a.m., but the snoring woke me at six. I tried to go back to sleep. It was Saturday, for crying out loud, but the pizza and snoring made that impossible. So I got up and went through the Angela Riley file. It was slim. Calpurnia was right. Angela was unremarkable if you ignored the disappearing thing. I studied Angela's face, every inch of it, until I thought I would recognize her instantly. It wouldn't be as hard as I originally thought. Angela had very round green eyes with thick lashes that didn't need the help of mascara. The eyes were fairly distinctive, but it was the lips that would cinch it. Her upper lip wasn't symmetrical. Her lip line on the right was slightly higher, not very noticeable, but quite unique. Sometimes, she made the sides match with lipstick, but mostly she didn't. If I found the woman in Gina's pictures and got close, I would know for certain if it was Angela.

My Fibonacci phone had remained silent for the rest of the night after I returned Calpurnia's texts. She told me that both Gina and Angela's husband, Phillip, would be expecting me in the morning for interviews. I'd texted that I'd be there and turned the phone to vibrate.

I put my phones in my purse, dressed, and snuck past the snoring Van Der Hoof brothers. They were asleep, side by side, on the sofa. Skanky was draped over Uncle Morty's rumbling belly. He opened an eye when I tiptoed past, but otherwise didn't move. I locked the apartment and heaved a sigh of relief.

"Ahem." A throat-clearing sound that boded nothing but ill for me.

*Oh no.*

"Ahem."

I girded my loins and turned around. "Hi, Mrs. Papadakis."

"Mercy," she said before making a tsking sound.

"Yes, Mrs. Papadakis?"

"You keep me up last night. I need my beauty sleep." Mrs. Papadakis didn't look like she'd been kept up. She looked a lot better than me. At seven in the morning, her black hair had been curled and sprayed into its usual bouffant. She was in full makeup, complete with burgundy lipstick, and wore a silky print wrap dress and slingback heels. I'd never seen her not look exactly like this. Okay. Maybe the dress print varied, but not by much.

"You look great," I said.

She frowned, creasing the heavy foundation on her forehead. "Women must make the effort or the men...you know." She looked at my wrinkled jeans and faded t-shirt and did not approve.

"Right. Uh huh." I could not imagine Mr. Papadakis doing 'you know'. He wouldn't survive long if he did.

"This new boyfriend of yours. He is too much. He must leave and you take that nice doctor back. He was very quiet." She squinted at me. "What did he do to make you leave him, a doctor?"

"Nothing. It was me, not him."

"Then get him back. With your face, it will not be difficult."

"I have a new boyfriend, Chuck. He's a policeman, a detective." I smiled widely to show her that was a good thing. Law and order. Upstanding citizen.

"No, no. That's no good. He get shot. A doctor is better and he didn't make the smells." She waved her hand in front of her face.

"Chuck doesn't smell. I mean, he smells good."

"Then what is that odor?"

I looked back at the door. "Oh that. That's not Chuck. That's Uncle Morty and his brother. They do smell. Not them personally, but the pizza they eat."

"Get rid of them. They yell and smell."

I bit my lip. "I'd love to, but I can't. They're kind of like family."

"Family?" Mrs. Papadakis believed in family in a huge way. When hers came over, they made Uncle Morty and Melvin seem silent in comparison. "What do they do?"

"Morty and Melvin? They're writers."

"Good earners?"

"I guess so. They sell a lot of books."

"How old?" she asked with a glint in her eyes.

"Mid-fifties." This was getting a little scary. "Why? What do you have in mind?"

"They married?" She put her hands on her bony hips.

"No."

*And there's a good reason for that.*

"I take care of it," said Mrs. Papadakis and she spun around, dialing her cellphone. "Nicky, you come over today. I want you to meet someone."

Oh my god. She was bringing over the cousins, Nikki, Nia, and Maria. They weren't married and there was a good reason for that, too. If three extra chatty Greek women didn't scare Morty and Melvin away, they'd be married before Bridget.

I ran down the stairs and made a mental note not to come home for a long time.

Gina was expecting me, but I made her nervous. She sat at her kitchen table with a lit cigarette dangling from her lips and another one in the ashtray on the kitchen table.

"What did Calpurnia tell you?" she asked, her foot tapping incessantly.

"That you saw Angela in Paris."

"Not that. About me. What did she say about me?"

*Oh crap. How do I answer that?*

"Not much," I said. "It's not really relevant."

She flicked a column of ash into the tray and took a deep puff. "I'm not crazy."

"She didn't say you were."

"Really?"

"Really. Now is there anything about Paris that you didn't tell Calpurnia?" I asked.

Gina relaxed and leaned back, the rigidity going out of her spine. "No. It happened exactly the way I told her."

"Did your husband see the woman you think is Angela?"

"Not so much. It happened so quickly. We were eating lunch and there she was. Then she was gone. Calpurnia doesn't believe me, but I tried to catch her. Really, I did." Angela clutched at her robe, tightening it around her neck. She did that every time she said Calpurnia's name.

"I believe you. Tribeca is popular. It's hard to get in or out at lunch."

Gina smiled. Her lips were the same as her sister's, not quite symmetrical. Other than that, they looked nothing alike. Gina was a strawberry blonde with pale green eyes and freckles over her little upturned nose. "So you understand."

"I do," I said.

"It was her." Gina teared up. "I knew it was her. Nobody understands, but I felt it."

"Instincts are powerful and often right."

"You think so?"

"Absolutely." I was starting to get a feeling of my own. Gina saw her sister and it wasn't wishful thinking, not after six years. When people go missing, their loved ones are constantly doing double takes. I knew that from personal experience. But Gina went to Calpurnia, a woman she feared, six years later. She was sure. Calpurnia and Cosmo thought the bi-polar diagnosis was a factor, but, if it was, it wouldn't have taken so long to kick in.

Gina snubbed out her cigarette in the ashtray and picked up her coffee cup, squeezing it but not taking a drink. Her eyes never left me. She wanted to be sure about me, too.

"Whatever you tell me is just between us," I said. "The Fibonaccis don't have to know. Calpurnia asked this favor of me, but, as far as I'm concerned, I work for you."

"There is something else," said Gina.

"Something you didn't tell Calpurnia?"

"Only my husband knows. He doesn't think I'm crazy so it's safe."

"What is it?"

"I followed her. I didn't mean to do it and I know it was impulsive and I'm not supposed to do things like that, but I had to. Ricky didn't care. He understood," she said all in one breath.

A huge grin spread across my face. Somebody up there likes me. "That's the best news I've heard all day. Heck, all month. Where did she go?"

"Please don't tell Phillip." Her little nose wrinkled with dislike. "He'll tell my parents and they'll think I'm off my meds. I'm not. I'm taking them. I am."

I took her hand and squeezed it. "I won't tell anyone. I swear to you on my mother's head. I won't tell a soul."

"Okay," she whispered. "They're always watching me, waiting for me to screw up."

I imagined there'd been quite a few screw ups in the past, but this wasn't a screw up by any means. "Where did she go, Gina?"

She pulled her cellphone out of her robe pocket, typed something in, and gave it to me. "I don't exactly know. It was my first time to Paris, but I bet you can figure it out from the cross streets."

I didn't need to look at the cross streets. I knew exactly where that cab went. "Place des Vosges."

Gina scooted over and peered at the screen. "Is that what it's called? I loved it. So beautiful."

Place des Vosges was a square in the Marais district, an area known for old world elegance, shopping, and falafel. Searching the Marais for Angela would be my pleasure.

"It's a gorgeous area. So did she go to an apartment or a shop?" I asked.

Gina's face fell. "I lost them." She pointed at a set of three stone arches. "They got out of the cab and went through there. I followed, but I couldn't find them. There was a restaurant and lots of people picnicking."

"Not ideal, but I can definitely work with that." I had her send all her pictures to the Fibonacci phone.

"Do you think you can find Angela?" asked Gina.

"I'll do my best and, between you and me, I'm not half bad at this stuff."

Her eyes filled with fresh tears. "Thank you. I've lived with this for so long. I thought that if only I had followed her to the dance floor..."

"Whatever happened, it's not your fault." I didn't point out the obvious. If Angela wasn't kidnapped and murdered, she left and stayed away of her own volition. She put her family through hell. I wasn't a fan, but Gina loved Angela and wanted her back. I'd try to give her what she wanted but knowing what really happened would have a new, painful price.

"That's what I tell myself, but I was there. I should've done something."

"You couldn't have known. Tell me how Angela's relationship with Phillip was," I said.

She lifted one shoulder and twisted her mouth. "It was okay."

"You don't like him?"

"Phillip is...I don't know...kind of cold. He handles everything like it's a business deal. If Angela wanted to do something and it wasn't logical, she couldn't do it. He likes facts, not feelings."

"Is that why he didn't believe you?" I asked.

Gina rolled her eyes. "He's not going to believe *you* unless *you* come back with DNA, fingerprints, and an affidavit."

"No pressure," I said. "Is that why Angela got a little wild that night?"

"I don't know. It wasn't like her at all. Angela was very conservative. I wouldn't have believed it if I hadn't seen it."

"You didn't think she'd have an affair then?"

"I didn't before that night. She was always the good one. My parents practically worshipped her. I was the hot mess."

She went on to describe growing up with Angela. Gina was the wild one, always in trouble, sex early and often, drugs and alcohol. Angela was the honor student, cheerleader, the designated driver, the one who Gina counted on to get her out of her many scrapes. Nothing Gina said fit what happened that night in Chicago. I totally would've bought it if it'd been Gina who disappeared, but it wasn't. Sure, Angela'd been a typical girl, falling wildly in and out of love. Sometimes she acted like a fool. But those were boys she dated. Angela never did anything impetuous. She insisted, even in high school, that dates were formal affairs, dinner and a movie, etc. She never hooked up. When she was a married woman, she was as Calpurnia described her, devoted to her children. Something wasn't right. This was not a woman to make out with a complete stranger and leave her sister, her unstable sister, alone in another city. Nor was she the type to abandon the children she adored. No. Something definitely wasn't right.

Phillip met me at the door, wearing a navy suit and tie at ten o'clock on a Saturday morning. The six years showed in his face, haggard and worn with care. He shook my hand and led me to the formal living room. The centerpiece was a baby grand piano covered in family photos. Angela was among them, smiling at her graduation, on her wedding day, and holding newborns. Phillip might be trying to move on, but he hadn't forgotten her.

I sat on the sofa and he took a tufted wingback chair. A woman with short blonde hair popped her head in and asked, "Can I get you anything? Iced teas? Lemonade?"

"No, thank you," said Phillip so stiff I was surprised he didn't creak.

I smiled and shook my head no and then turned back to Phillip. "I get the feeling you're not thrilled about this."

"Calpurnia is doing Gina a favor and you're repaying one. I understand the situation."

"You wish she'd left it alone?" I asked.

"It's pointless to wish." Phillip sat ramrod straight and watched me, but they weren't cold eyes. They were filled with sorrow and self-restraint. He wasn't what I expected from Gina's description. He was reserved, but he cared deeply. It radiated off him and he could barely stand to go through this again, to talk about what happened when it was so close to being over.

"I'm sorry," I said.

His grey eyes widened slightly. "Are you? Why? This is what you do."

"I'm a nurse, not a private investigator. I don't enjoy digging into your sorrow."

"I appreciate that, but can we get this over with?" he said.

I asked him the standard questions. Phillip's statement jived with what I'd been told. Angela wasn't the type to do what she did. The marriage was solid and so forth.

"Miss Watts, I don't know what else to say. I don't know anything. The police never found anything," he said.

I put my elbows on my knees and clasped my hands under my chin, pondering if I should ask what I really wanted to ask.

"Miss Watts?"

"Do you believe Angela's dead?" It came out quickly and surprised him, but it didn't surprise me.

Phillip jumped at the bluntness but answered without hesitation. "Yes. She has to be."

"Why does she have to be?"

He stood up and went to the window, staring out at the long green lawn. "Because nothing else makes sense."

"What happened that night doesn't make sense," I said.

He didn't look at me again. "I know, but Angela isn't in Paris. It's not something she would do."

"What do you mean?"

Phillip sighed, still not looking at me. "She wouldn't travel abroad. Angela wasn't an adventurous person. She didn't have a passport. Nobody in her family did."

"Gina has one," I said. "She went to Paris."

"Because of her new husband. That's the only reason." Phillip turned away. He was done.

I excused myself and left, feeling his sadness weighing on me as I went out the door to my truck. The blond woman came out the front door and waved at me. I stopped and she closed the door quietly and came over to me.

"Hi. I'm Dara, Phil's girlfriend," she said.

Interesting. She was the first to call him that. He was Phillip to everyone else, including himself.

"I'm Mercy Watts." I shook her hand.

"Can I talk to you for a second?"

"Of course. Do you have something to tell me about Angela?" I asked.

Dara shook her head. "No. I never met her. I only wanted you to know he's not what he seems."

"Phillip?"

"He comes off as cold and uncaring, but he's really sweet and loving on the inside."

"How did you two meet?"

"I was Madison's third grade teacher. We met three years after it happened. I adore those kids. I can't have any of my own and they've made my life complete." She blushed. "That sounds silly, I know."

"It doesn't sound silly at all. It's lovely that they have you," I said. "Is there anything else?"

She bit her lip. "I wanted to ask you if you think it could be true that Angela's alive?"

"It's possible, but I wouldn't bet the farm on it."

Dara laughed nervously. "Phil doesn't believe Gina because of her illness."

"What do you think?"

"I think it would kill him if she's alive."

I leaned back against the truck. "Why?"

"He trusted her completely. He can barely deal with the fact that she went off with that guy and got herself killed. If she ran off..."

"He trusted her completely? I got the impression from Gina that they weren't that close."

"Well, they weren't, not like us." Dara put her hand on her heart. "I said we had to go to therapy or it was over. He wouldn't talk or share anything, but now he does. It took a long time though."

"If they weren't that close, why did he trust her?" I asked. "Wives can cheat like husbands do."

"Don't tell anyone I said this, but Phil says that Angela never had an ounce of imagination. None at all. He didn't think it would occur to her to do something wrong. That's why he was so comfortable being married to her."

I frowned. *Comfortable?*

"Everybody wants to be comfortable with their spouse," I said.

"Yes, but I can only say this because of who you are."

"Who I am?"

"You work for them, too," said Dara and her voice turned to a whisper. "The Fibonaccis. It's important to be discreet and Angela was certainly that. Don't get me wrong. Phil's on the right side of the family." Her voice lowered until I could barely hear her. "The legal side."

"I understand." I offered my hand again and Dara shook it. "Thanks for your help."

"I didn't want you to think that he didn't care."

"I understand and I could tell that he cared."

She thanked me and watched as I drove down the long drive with her forehead in a frown. Now I didn't want to find Angela in Paris. Dara didn't deserve that. But then there were Gina and Angela's parents. I slammed my hands on the steering wheel. "That's just great. Somebody's got to lose."

Why did I have the feeling that it was going to be me?

# CHAPTER SIX

An hour later, I sat at Café Déjeuner, waiting for Spidermonkey to show up. Spidermonkey was my go-to cyber sleuth. He was as good as Uncle Morty but smelled a lot better. I read the *Wall Street Journal* that they kept on hand for him and sipped an iced mocha. I wanted to scour the internet for information on Angela's disappearance, but I didn't dare. Uncle Morty'd been known to get into my phone and root around under the guise of thwarting the occasional stalker, but it was really under my mother's orders. After the Costillas put a hit out on me, she worried more than usual. She was afraid someone would figure out how to track me and that they'd try again. I wasn't worried because I had Calpurnia Fibonacci on my side, but Mom didn't know that.

Spidermonkey used his considerable skills to make our calls and texts look like I was talking to my friend, Ellen. Morty didn't want to know what we went on about so it was a great cover.

Unfortunately, Uncle Morty wouldn't avoid my internet searches like he did girl talk. If Morty saw that I was looking into Angela, he'd put it together. He was the only one who seemed to doubt that my all-powerful father was the one to get the Costillas off me. I had to be very careful that absolutely nothing connected me to Calpurnia.

The bell on the door jingled and Spidermonkey walked in. He was striking with his silver hair and lime green polo. He ordered a black coffee in a lilting South Carolina accent and made Sally, the barista, smile.

She gave him his coffee and flicked a glance at me and rolled her eyes as he went through the pantomime of not knowing me but sitting together because there wasn't room anywhere else. He wasn't fooling Sally. She'd seen us together enough and probably thought we were having an affair. I had to admit it did look that way.

"Is this seat taken?" he asked.

I snorted. "Well, I was waiting for someone, but go ahead handsome stranger sit down."

"Mercy," he whispered. "We don't know each other."

"Yeah, we're stealthy."

"Morty could happen by and see you sitting here with me. If he questioned the staff—"

"Let me stop you right there. Sally thinks we're having an affair and Uncle Morty never comes down to Laclede's Landing. He thinks it's full of hipsters and idiots."

Spidermonkey glanced at a table with four guys, all sporting man buns. "It is."

"Plus, Melvin's in town."

"Oh, it's that time of year. Is he hiding at your parents'?" he asked.

"My apartment, actually."

Spidermonkey made a face. "No wonder you wanted to meet today."

I stirred my mocha with a straw. "That, and I have a situation."

"A situation that you need my expertise for?"

"If you'll take the job."

"Why wouldn't I?"

"Wait until you hear what it is."

I told Spidermonkey that Calpurnia had called in her marker and exactly what I was expected to do. He sat back, listening in his calm way.

"What do you think?' I asked.

"How far are you?"

I gave him my leads: Place des Vosges and the man that the possible Angela had been with as well as a rundown of my interviews.

"Are you going to interview friends or her parents?" he asked.

"I don't see the point. So will you help me on this?" I didn't have a backup plan if he said no, but I couldn't do it without help.

He smiled and waved to Sally, indicating that he needed more coffee. "Of course, I will."

I got dizzy with relief. "Really?"

Sally poured Spidermonkey's coffee and raised an eyebrow at me. "Anything?"

Hunger hit me hard. I'd gone out without eating. Calpurnia's mission did nothing for the appetite, but the smell of all the pastries woke up my taste buds. "What's good?"

She grinned. "Everything, but I'd have the lemon poppyseed cruller."

"Make it two," I said.

Sally headed for the pastry display and Spidermonkey said, "I hope you plan on eating both of those."

"I'm back to normal." I'd lost a lot of weight after I'd killed Richard Costilla. Guilt is a dangerous thing, but I'd evened out my karma by saving a life at Cairngorms Castle and was back on donuts and happiness.

"Does that mean that you're modeling for DBD again?" asked Spidermonkey.

"Not quite. Mickey says I'm still on the skinny side, but I'm curving up."

I was the band, Double Black Diamond's cover girl, but the Costilla incident had lost me my Marilyn curves and my extra income for the time being.

"Well, keep eating. I don't see The Klinefeld Group investigation getting any cheaper. When do you leave for Paris?" he asked.

"I'm hoping for next Friday or Saturday."

"Tickets would be a problem, but the Bleds name will help you out with that."

Sally brought my crullers and I convinced Spidermonkey that he needed to eat one—you know, to keep up his strength. "So you don't mind working for Calpurnia?"

"I'm working for you, which I never mind."

"You know what I mean," I said.

"I do, and I don't care. I assume that Chuck doesn't know."

"He can never know."

We munched our crullers in silence. The problem of keeping Chuck out of this was huge, but he was going and it couldn't be helped. Maybe I should stop by the cathedral and say a prayer or two hundred. I wasn't sure if God would be all that open to helping the Fibonaccis, but maybe I could spin it.

"What do you know about them?" I asked.

"Them or her?" he asked.

"Is there a difference?"

"There is and there isn't. Calpurnia is unusual as are the Fibonaccis. Did you know that no Fibonacci nor any of their people have ever been convicted or even indicted?"

"I heard something about that."

"They're lucky. Everything works out perfectly for the Fibonaccis."

"What are they into?" I asked.

"Everything, except women and kids."

More relief. I got a little light-headed, but it could've been the cruller. "Really?"

"They don't deal in sex of any kind. Calpurnia's orders. Her father wasn't so picky, but Calpurnia dropped that end of the business when she took power. There were a lot of doubts about her leadership when she did that, but the Fibonacci influence has spread exponentially under her."

"So Cosmo's kind of a figurehead?" I asked.

"No one really knows what goes on inside the organization, but I'd guess Cosmo is his sister's right hand man," said Spidermonkey, looking at his watch. "Loretta's going to wonder where I am."

"Where are you supposed to be? I asked.

"Buying milk and eggs."

"Oh my god. You've been here for over forty-five minutes. She'll be suspicious."

Spidermonkey laughed and took out his phone. "Not up to this point. I proved I'm incompetent with shopping long ago. I've got another fifteen minutes before she starts calling. Give me your list."

I asked for all the info he could get on Angela's life and everything the cops had on her disappearance, including any suspicions that the Fibonaccis or Phillip had anything to do with it, just in case. Next, there was The Klinefeld Group. Spidermonkey was splitting the cost of researching them with me. He had a keen interest in tracking down Nazis who escaped justice and thought the Klinefeld Group was up to their eyeballs.

I asked for Paul Richter's will if there was one, addresses of surviving family, that kind of thing.

"Paul Richter isn't going to keep you very busy," said Spidermonkey.

"I'm supposed to be doing a cooking class with Aaron so Chuck will run down the Richters while I find Angela."

Spidermonkey made a few more notes on his phone and then gave me a piercing look. "This plan is less than ideal."

I licked my sugary fingers. "Tell me about it."

"You're going to need more help than either I or Aaron can give you."

"I'm open to suggestions," I said and finished my lukewarm mocha.

He asked for my Fibonacci phone and put a number into it. "That's Novak, my contact in Paris. I don't speak French and you're going to need someone who does."

I looked at the number and got a little queasy. I trusted Spidermonkey completely but adding someone else to the mix seemed ill-advised.

"Novak is top-notch and he's a whiz with secure systems."

"Is there really any such thing as a secure system?"

Spidermonkey pushed his cup back and stood up. "No, thank god, or I'd be out of business."

"Novak? Is he Parisian?"

"No. He's a Serb that emigrated to escape the Bosnian war. He understands France the way only an immigrant can. If Angela is living there, he's your best bet on getting information. Call him as soon as you have something. I'll tell him to expect you."

"How much does he cost?" I winced, ready for the pain.

"Nothing. He owes me a favor or two."

"You don't have to use up your favors on me. This is my problem."

Spidermonkey gave me an unexpected hug. "You're doing the legwork on The Klinefeld Group in Paris. It's the least I can do."

He left and I ordered another iced mocha so maybe Sally wouldn't think he and I were a thing. She kept an eye on me while I worked on the airline tickets for Paris on my regular phone. The flights I wanted were sold out except for first class and even I didn't have that many frequent flyer points. I'd have to call the brewery travel office and see what they could do.

Jordan was on call twenty-four seven. I still hated to bother him on a Saturday. He'd be at one of his kids' many sports—baseball, as it turned out—but he was surprisingly thrilled to hear from me. I'd met the pitching legend, Oliver Jakes when I was at Cairngorms Castle and he was now dating my cousin, Sorcha, aka Weepy as the family called her. I'd almost broken them up while at the castle and during my efforts to fix it, I'd introduced Oliver to Jordan. Oliver had done a mini-camp for Jordan's peewees and Jordan thought I was some kind of miracle worker.

I'd forgotten all about the mini-camp, but Jordan hadn't. He was happy to help. The Bled name was enough to pull any amount of strings and he'd get back to me with confirmation. I ordered four more crullers as a peace offering in case Mrs. Papadakis hadn't been able to run off Uncle Morty and Melvin and drove home expecting at best a terrible stench and, at worst, raging writers.

I got the stench. My apartment was trashed, covered in nasty pizza boxes, used napkins, and to go boxes from Kronos. Skanky lay in the middle of the room, bloated and mewing pitifully.

"For crying out loud. What did you eat?" I asked the cat that was known to eat tin foil.

He burped. I'd never seen a cat burp before. It was really weird to watch.

"I'm calling the vet. It's your own fault if she stomach pumps you."

I did call the vet and she was unimpressed. Considering what Skanky had eaten before and lived, she wasn't worried. I was supposed to watch him and call her if anything exciting happened. By exciting, she meant call her if he died. She wanted to perform a necropsy and see what his stomach was made of. It's time to get a new vet when they start hoping your pet will die so they can dissect them.

"Now we need a new vet," I told Skanky. "Thanks a lot."

Burp.

I peeled an anchovy off his head and then started cleaning around him. It took me an hour to get to the kitchen, where I found a note that made my blood run cold.

You will pay for this.

It was written in Uncle Morty's jagged block lettering. I guess Mrs. Papadakis had sicced her cousins on Morty and Melvin. Uncle Morty could really make my life hell, but considering the mess he left, he'd already done his worst.

I went on to clean the rest of my apartment and, by the time I was done, Chuck had called to say he had a new murder to deal with and we wouldn't be going to whatever comic book hero movie he'd picked out that week. I tried to sound disappointed and did too good of a job. He promised we'd go before Paris. Damn.

So because of some grisly murder in Dogtown, I got to have a girls' night with Claire, Dad's assistant and my old high school rival. Claire was always up for a night of guilty pleasures. It gave her a break from her endless search for her next husband. We made carbonara and watched a marathon of *Scandal* while eating entire pints of ice cream. Skanky didn't die or throw up. Life was good.

# CHAPTER SEVEN

Chuck woke me up the next morning by dumping a load of books on my bed.

"What the?" I asked, rubbing my eyes.

"I got them," he said.

I stared at the pile. "Did you buy every travel book on the market?"

"Only the ones on Paris. How about you take half and I take half?"

"Take them to Paris?"

"No. Read and take notes on where to go and what to do." Chuck was so excited, he was pacing and making huge hand gestures like he was suddenly Sicilian.

"But I've been to Paris. I can get us around," I said with a yawn.

Chuck snorted. "You get lost in the Central West End."

"Not lately." I crossed my arms and managed to look indignant.

"We have to have a plan or we won't be able to cover all the major sites."

"Have you been talking to my mother?"

"I might've. A little."

Groan.

"Never tell Carolina Watts you're going on a trip. She'll plan it for you and then be pissed if you don't stick to the plan."

"Your mom's a good planner."

"If you say so," I said.

He held up a finger. "Wait right there. I almost forgot."

"Forgot what?"

"Wait a minute." Chuck left and returned with a big box. He dropped it on the foot of my bed. It was so heavy; I caught a little air.

"What is that?" I asked.

"Exactly the one you wanted." He opened the box and lifted out a deluxe toaster oven.

I stared. What the what?

"It isn't the one?" he asked with concern all over his handsome face. "I got it at that cooking store Aaron likes. No blood."

"Um...it's great. The best. Who told you I wanted a toaster oven?" I asked.

"Morty."

*Bastard.*

"Did my beloved Uncle tell you anything else?"

"He mentioned a tanning bed." He looked around my smallish bedroom. "But I'm not sure where we'd put it."

*I am going to kill that old man.*

"I changed my mind on the tanning bed. My pale skin can't handle it. Thanks for the toaster thing, though."

I slid out from under the covers and what little sleepiness I had left was instantly gone. Like an idiot, I'd left the Fibonacci phone on my side table next to my regular phone. I jumped up and stood in front of the table. "I'm starving. Are you hungry? Let's eat."

Chuck produced a bag from The Bagel Factory. "I brought you breakfast in bed."

*Crap!*

"Um...what about coffee? I could use some coffee."

He waggled his eyebrows. "I'll make you a latte so good it'll make you want to go to the gym with me this morning."

"No latte is that good."

"They are when they're made with a Rocket." He ran his fingers through his slightly thinning hair, making every muscle on his taut torso flex under his tight tee. If only I could distract him with sex like every other man in the universe.

"How about regular coffee made with a machine that has never been bloody?"

Chuck started over with an arm outstretched. He took my hand and tried to pull me toward the door. He was going to see it. Chuck didn't miss much. It was his job to ask uncomfortable questions and get the truth. My connection to the Fibonaccis was a truth he absolutely could not have, for both our sakes.

"Did you wash it?" I blurted out.

"What?" he asked.

"The Rocket."

"I told you I did."

I spun him around and pushed him through my bedroom and out the door. "Okay. Extra foam."

Chuck kept trying to turn around. "Don't you want me to teach you how to use it?"

"No, I'm good."

He turned around and grabbed me by the shoulders. He was so tall; the extra phone would be in full view. "Are you trying to get rid of me?"

*Say something good.*

"Yes."

*Dammit.*

"What is going on? Suddenly, you don't mind the Rocket and you want me out of your bedroom." He flushed hard and his blue eyes went all glittery. "Is someone in your bedroom?"

I rolled my eyes. "Puhlease. You woke me up. Did you see anyone?"

"No," he said slowly. "What is it then?"

"If you must know, I'm a girl and I have stuff."

He pulled back. "Oh. Why didn't you say so?"

"I was trying to be discreet, but I can tell you about it in detail. You see, there's this little cramp that starts—"

Chuck threw up his hands. "I'm out."

I closed the door behind him and rested my forehead on it for a second. That was close. Then there was a little clattery noise behind me. I whipped around and the Fibonacci phone vibrated itself off my table and landed with a thump on the carpet. It was Calpurnia offering to send a guy named Fats Licata with me to Paris for protection. I told her I was bringing Chuck and Aaron with me. She wasn't happy, but what could I say? It was happening.

Then I stowed the phone in a giant box of pads I bought at Costco and put it behind my ugliest shoes in the closet. If Chuck looked there, there were more things wrong with him than I suspected.

The door opened behind me. "What are you doing?" asked Chuck.

I crawled backward out of the closet and held up a pair of red ballet flats. "Looking for these. Paris shoes."

He frowned and gave me a latte with an apple drawn in foam. It tasted great—better than great, like the best latte ever. "You're taking other shoes, right?"

"What's wrong with these?" I asked, licking the foam off my upper lip.

"They're kind of"—he made a squashy motion with his hand—"flat."

I raised an eyebrow. "They're flats."

"But we're going to Paris. Aren't the women stylish there?" he asked.

I pulled a battered suitcase out of the closet and plopped it on the bed. "Have you ever tried to walk on cobblestone streets in heels?"

"Not lately."

"I'd like to not break another ankle, thank you very much." I put the flats in the suitcase and picked up Rick Steves' Paris guide. "Did you leave any books for the other people?"

"There was a book on Lithuania." He sat on my bed and opened the bagel bag. "Let's stay in bed all day today."

I hopped on the bed and kissed his neck. He smelled great, like bagels with a hint of sweat and expensive cologne. "That's the best idea I've ever heard."

Chuck pulled two highlighters out of his pocket and gave me a green one. "Great. We can get all the planning done today."

*Dammit!*

# CHAPTER EIGHT

We arrived in Paris on Saturday morning. In a fit of cheapness, I insisted on taking the train and then the metro into the city from Charles de Gaulle. So stupid. Both were packed and I wasn't wearing a hat and sunglasses. I should've known. There were advertisements using Marilyn Monroe to sell snacks and perfume plastered on the tiled walls. I looked and felt like I'd been mugged, but people still wanted pictures of me. Mickey Stix wasn't going to be happy. The legendary drummer was always ready for his close-up and thought I should be, too. I did represent the band after all. But makeup was just so much work and in a tiny plane bathroom...forget it. I'd rather look bad.

We made it to the metro's line four after about sixty-eight flashes in my face and it was even more crowded. My laziness wasn't working out for me. As usual, I managed to be wedged in next to tall men who insisted on holding the pole above my head. They didn't smell, but armpit isn't my favorite spot on a man, especially men I didn't know.

The train screeched to a stop and the doors ratcheted open. I hoped a bunch of people would get off. Instead, a bunch got on. Everyone squished up a little more to make room and my suitcase dug into my shins as I pressed it against the pole. We should've taken a cab, but Chuck was so excited to take the metro that I gave in.

People shifted around, trying to prep themselves for the next stop, and I scooted to the left, getting a whiff of hot dog. Chuck and Aaron were on the pole behind me. I glanced back and smiled at Chuck. He swiveled his head around, taking in everything the way everyone does on their first trip to Paris.

He saw me smiling and leaned over to ask, "What's our stop?"

"Etienne Marcel," answered Aaron.

I turned the other way to look at my partner, who was staring at his pole, completely disinterested in anything around him. "How did you know—"

Just then the metro announcer said, "Etienne Marcel. Etienne Marcel."

"This is it," I told Chuck.

"Great." He used his long arm to help me squeeze out the door and onto the platform.

Etienne Marcel was just as I remembered with its white subway tile, harsh lighting, and surprisingly clean floor. I pushed the new rolling bag Chuck bought me so I wouldn't be lugging around Great Uncle Ned's battered old luggage and pointed to the right. Aaron grabbed my arm and turned me left.

"Do you know where you're going?" asked Chuck.

"I know where I'm going. Actually getting there is the challenge," I said.

Aaron didn't say anything but took off at a good clip.

"Should we follow him?" asked Chuck.

"He somehow knew his way around Cairngorms Castle so I'd say yes."

We dashed through Etienne Marcel and followed Aaron out the exit gates, that were conveniently open for our suitcases, past the ticket booth to trot up the concrete stairs into the morning air filled with exhaust and moisture from a recent rain. Two guys tried to give us flyers and another man offered oranges off a little stand between us and the super busy street. I took a deep breath and sucked in the Paris energy. People were going every which way. Horns were honking. A family of tourists were huddled together looking at a guidebook. A woman walked by pushing a little cart filled with round loaves of bread and adjusted the pack on her back that was filled with at least twelve baguettes. Paris. My first love.

The light changed and Aaron trotted into the street without checking to see if we were following. We chased him down a couple streets—those little legs could move fast—until we caught up in front of a children's clothing shop called NotSoBig on Rue Tiquetonne.

"Aaron," I called out as the street swam in front of my eyes. Damn jet lag. If only I could sleep on planes.

Chuck steadied me. "Hold it. Aaron. Stop. Now!"

By some miracle, Aaron stopped and turned around. "Huh?"

"Mercy's tired. Give us a break, man."

"I'm fine," I said. "Let's get to the apartment."

Aaron waited that time and we walked a couple small blocks to Rue Marie Stuart where the Bled apartment was. I found the red door for our building and let us into the dim mailbox room and then through the glass door to the narrow timbered stairs. Chuck and Aaron stopped at the foot of the stairs and looked up. Neither of them would fit very well. I was smaller than both of them and I barely fit.

"Is there an elevator?" asked Chuck.

I pushed the button on the wall next to me and the minuscule elevator opened.

"You've got to be kidding."

I laughed. "When this place was built people didn't come in your size."

"I'll take the stairs."

"Suit yourself. Fourth floor. Green door." I got on the elevator. I would've waited for Aaron, but he wouldn't fit.

The elevator rose to the fourth floor in the glacial manner that I remembered from the last time I stayed there when I was sixteen and ever so impatient with the whole world. I got off to find Chuck looking triumphant in the stairwell.

"I beat you," he crowed.

"Impressive."

"You make it sound like you're not impressed."

I gave him a peck on his stubbly jaw. "I'm totally impressed with everything you do."

"Alright then. Just so we have that straight," he said, satisfied.

Aaron came puffing up the stairs behind Chuck and hurled his orange suitcase on the floor. I think he might've stomped on it if he'd had the energy.

Chuck picked up Aaron's suitcase and I let us in, wondering exactly what Chuck was going to think.

"It's smaller than I imagined," he said.

"Everything is in Paris," I said. "We should take the big bedroom."

I went into the little living room/kitchen combo and opened the shades. Not much sun came in. Most of the sun was blocked by the apartments across the narrow street, but the light cheered up the place. I opened the windows and the lovely scent of someone's lunch wafted in.

Aaron came over and took a sniff. "Lamb. Slow roasted in salt."

"You would know that. Do you want to check out the kitchen?" I asked, but he was already heading for the small space. It was a serviceable little galley arrangement with everything we could need, including a fabulous espresso maker, which Aaron automatically flipped on.

I pushed my suitcase toward the bedrooms and then stopped when I saw Chuck's face. He looked like he was in pain or panicked. I couldn't decide which.

"What?' I asked.

"I thought you said there are three bedrooms," he said.

"There are, but the third is teensy, more like a big closet."

"That's okay," he said brightly. "I'll take the teensy one."

He went down the hall, found the teensy bedroom, went in and closed the door. I looked over at Aaron who, to my surprise, was looking at me. "Do you know what's going on?"

"No."

"That's weird, right? Shouldn't we be sharing a room? Like a couple. We are still a couple."

"Huh?"

"Aaron!"

"Huh?"

"You'd tell me if he was, you know, over me, wouldn't you?" I asked and got a blank look for my trouble. "Look who I'm asking. This jet lag is worse than I thought."

"Rodney says Chuck loves you." Aaron said love like he wasn't quite sure what the fuss was about. He probably didn't.

"Rodney says, huh?"

"Yes."

"Alright. I guess that's something. I'm taking the big room, unless you object."

Nothing happened, so I took the big room. Thirty minutes later, I'd unpacked, making sure to put Dad's gift of pepper spray in my purse, just in case, and taken a super quick shower. Hot water was a scarce commodity, even in a Bled apartment. I put on a swishy sundress and heard something when I stepped into the hall. It was what I suspected would happen. Aaron hadn't unpacked. He hadn't even made it to his room. The little weirdo was crashed out on the sofa, curled up in a tight little ball like a kitten.

"Aaron!" I nudged him, getting no reaction. "You can't sleep. We have to get in the right time zone."

Snore.

"Aaron!"

"I'm awake." His eyes weren't open.

"Where's Chuck? He'll wake you up." I went down the hall, pounded on Chuck's door, and received no answer. I put my ear to the door and, sure enough, there was snoring. I knocked and went in. The room, and especially the bed, was smaller than I remembered. Chuck was stretched out with his feet hanging off the end. It was ridiculous.

I sat on the edge of the twin bed and poked him. "Wake up. You can't sleep until tonight."

"I'm not sleeping," he said.

"What was that snoring then?"

"A figment of your imagination."

"Get up. Let's go out. See stuff."

"You've already seen it." He rolled over, showing me his back.

"You haven't. Isn't that why we're here? To see Paris?"

"We're here to follow a lead on The Klinefeld Group," he muttered.

I traced the muscles in his back with my finger. "That's not the only reason. It's the most romantic city in the world."

"Uh huh."

"I bet I know what will wake you up." I unzipped my dress and was he awake fast. Awake and on his feet.

"I'm ready," he said, avoiding my eyes. "Where should we go first?"

I crossed my arms. "That's it. What is up with you?"

"I don't know what you mean," he said, backing up to the door.

"Don't give me that. You've been trying to get me naked for years. Now I unzip and you run the other way. Are you dumping me in slow motion?"

He took my shoulders and gave them a squeeze before he zipped me up. "No way. I'm never, ever going to dump you. If anything, you'll dump me."

"Do you want me to dump you?" I asked, my stomach doing a half-gainer and landing in my throat.

"No. Of course not. I'm respecting you. Don't you want me to respect you?"

*That seems like a trick question.*

"I guess."

He patted my shoulder and pulled me out the door. "We're taking it slow like they did in the old days."

"But you never say sleazy things to me anymore. Where's the sleaze?" I asked.

"You want me to be sleazy?"

"I think so."

"I'll work on that. Where are we going? The Eiffel Tower? The Louvre?" he asked, avoiding looking at me like crazy.

In ten minutes, he had Aaron up and was pouring espresso down his throat. While they were distracted with finding directions, I texted Calpurnia that I was in Paris and on the case. Well, sort of. First stop, Notre Dame. A few prayers were in order.

Actually, Notre Dame was our second stop. First was Boulangerie Eric Kayser on the end of Rue Montorgueil, the pedestrian-friendly street packed with shops offering pretty much anything you could want or need. It took us thirty minutes to make it to the bakery because Aaron had to look in every cheese shop and inspect the produce stands. I practically had to drag him along, only to get there and find it had a long line as usual. I wasn't that hungry. I just wanted the comfort that a good boulangerie can bring.

We waited and got chocolate croissants before heading to Notre Dame. It was a thirty-minute walk and Chuck held my hand, keeping up a distracting chatter. I think he was afraid I'd ask more questions, but I wasn't going to. I didn't know what to do. There was definitely something going on, but I had bigger things to worry about like the Fibonacci phone in my purse and how in the world I was going to confirm the mystery woman's identity in twelve days. When I decided on the length of our stay, it sounded like more than enough time, but now that I was walking the streets of Paris, looking at the apartments, the millions of people and it seemed impossible. What was I thinking when I said I could do it?

"We're not in the metro," said Chuck. "Can't you take off that hat?"

I wrinkled my nose at him. "I love this hat." I didn't exactly love it. I needed it for more reasons than one. Firstly, I didn't want cameras pointed at me. Second, my hair wasn't the fan of Paris that I was. It always went crazy curly and not in a good way. The Girls said it was the Seine. My hair didn't like the moist air. I lived within miles of the Mississippi, but, apparently, that was different. Whenever I ventured out of Paris, my hair calmed down. The closer to the river the worse the hair.

When I was little, Millicent would put my hair into pigtails that ended up looking like frizzy puffballs. As I got older, we tried a myriad of shampoos and conditioners. No luck. Hats were my only hope.

"It's so floppy, I can't see your face," said Chuck.

"That's the point." I wasn't about to mention the hair. Let him discover the horror naturally.

"Let's test the theory. Maybe nobody will notice you," he said.

"Pass."

Chuck pestered me until he spotted a looming tower. "There it is." He dragged me forward and we practically ran into the square, packed with people, of course.

The cathedral stood in front of us, blocky and impressive. The French called Notre Dame the Temple of Reason for a period after the revolution and I could see why. The perfectly symmetrical towers, the rose window in the center, and three arched doors with their many intricate carvings gave a sense of calm, of reason in a chaotic world. No wonder the revolution that destroyed so much had left Notre Dame standing.

"Oh no. We'll never get in." Chuck's broad shoulders slumped.

There was a line. There pretty much always was. But it went fast. I steered him to the end and we joined the international queue that included five different nationalities just in our little section. Guys came around hawking souvenirs. Chuck wanted to buy me everything. I had to convince him that I didn't need a mini Eiffel tower or a Mona Lisa postcard.

The couple in front of us were trailing a couple of carry-on bags. When they reached security, they were stopped and an argument in French ensued.

"They can't bring luggage in?" asked Chuck.

"No, but people always try to do it."

"Can you understand what they're saying?"

"A bit."

The security guards escorted the enraged couple out of line and then waved us forward. Since we had no bags, except my purse, we got to go right into the dim interior. I pulled off my sunglasses but left my hat in place. Chuck tried to snatch it off my head, but I smacked his hand.

I stalked ahead of him through the crowd. The center nave was blocked off because there was a mass going on. It was easy to forget that Notre Dame was a working icon, the neighborhood church for plenty of Parisians. The sight of so many heads bowed in prayer humbled me as it always did.

"It's massive," whispered Chuck, taking my hand.

I squeezed his warm hand. "It is."

"Is mass always in French?"

"No," I said. "There's an international mass on Sundays."

Aaron put his hand on my back and urged me forward.

The reading ended and the next started. We walked down the right side toward the pulpit, past thick stone columns, looking up at the beams of light jetting down through the air tinged with smoky incense.

We passed behind the choir stalls, a solid wooden wall with carved reliefs. I think Chuck took a picture of every single figure, so it took fifteen minutes to get to the end. We peeked around the edge to watch the priest with his arms extended as he spoke about forgiveness. His green robes were embroidered with gold but managed to seem simple in the grandeur of Notre Dame. One of the other priests gave him a lit thurible with smoke billowing out. The grand organ played as he walked in a semi-circle, swinging it. The scent of the incense filled the air and I missed The Girls. I'd never been to Notre Dame without them before. It felt strange and a bit empty without my godmothers and their prim Chanel suits handing me coins to put in the prayer boxes.

Mass ended and I dug in my purse. I'd come prepared to do what was expected of me. I gave Chuck two euros and he stared at them. "What's this for?"

"A prayer. Pick a saint. Any saint."

"What should I pray for?"

I raised an eyebrow. "Is this your first time?"

"Well, I never paid to pray before," he said.

"It's a donation, you nut."

He got thoughtful. "Maybe I should pray that one of my mother's marriages will stick."

"It can't hurt."

Aaron held out his hand. I gave him some euros and he trotted off into the crowd.

"What do you think he's going to pray for?" asked Chuck.

"Divine food inspiration," I said, hefting my heavy coin purse.

Chuck stared at the large amount of coins. "How many prayers are you doing?"

"I'll cover all the bases. It's tradition."

"The bases?"

"Myrtle asked me to remember Stella, her parents, her friend, Marie, and some others." I turned around and went to Saint Denis, dropped my coin, and lit a candle for my parents. Chuck followed suit and we worked our way through Notre Dame, praying for souls and continued health. At least, that's what I was praying for. I don't know what Chuck was doing.

On the other side of the nave, I stopped at Mary's altar. I dropped my last coin and asked Mary for wisdom.

*Mary, please help me find the truth and to know what to do with it when I do.*

Chuck put his arm around my shoulders. "You look so serious."

I leaned on him and breathed in his scent of cologne and wintergreen gum, mixed with the incense. It went together well.

"Not serious. Hopeful," I said.

Aaron appeared at my side and announced that he was done. We headed outside, squinting in the sunlight and marveling at the line that was now twice as long. I felt renewed and ready to go look for Angela. Unfortunately, Chuck was clamped onto my hand. This was a tourist day, like it or not.

"Where to now?" asked Chuck. "I'm too tired to remember the plan."

"What else do you want to see?" I asked.

"Everything."

"Oh, is that all?" I asked with a laugh.

"That's it." He kissed me lightly on the lips. Progress. Maybe we should take another turn around the cathedral.

"We could go over to Sainte-Chapelle and the Conciergerie," I said. "They're on the island, but they're probably crowded by now and the line doesn't go fast."

"What do you suggest?" he asked.

"I need to go to the Deportation Memorial."

"Where's that?"

I pointed past the cathedral. "Not far."

"Aaron, you good with that?" asked Chuck.

Aaron shrugged, so we walked into the gardens beside the cathedral. A school group of little girls in black and white uniforms giggled and ran around their teachers, kicking up the gravel and breaking into song. Couples were strolling and taking pictures. Parents were trying to soothe screaming toddlers and wailing infants. This all seemed out of sync with the looming grey stone of the cathedral, but it helped to remind me that this wasn't only a monument. Notre Dame was part of everyday life.

I took some pictures of Chuck and Aaron standing at the back of the cathedral with the flying buttresses behind them and sent the pics to Mom. She, like Calpurnia, required frequent updates and proof that I was alive.

Aaron led us straight to the memorial, an austere site at the end of the Ile de Cité. There was a low concrete wall with the years of the Holocaust written in jagged black writing on it. It memorialized the 200,000 Parisians who were deported to their deaths in concentration camps.

Chuck glanced around. The area was empty except for the two guards at the entrance, nothing like the cathedral that was now standing room only. "Where is everybody?"

"People don't really know it's here or realize what it is, I guess. Remembering the Holocaust on your vacation is kind of a downer," I said.

"But you want to go?"

"*Want* is putting it a little strongly. It's what we do. Remember, I mean."

"Are you remembering someone in particular?"

"Absolutely. Big Steve's parents were survivors. His mom was deported from Paris."

Chuck's face registered his shock. Few people knew about Big Steve Warnock's family. He didn't want to make a thing of it. We knew because he was a family friend and my mom worked for him as a paralegal for years.

"I had no idea," said Chuck. "Aaron, did you know?"

"Yeah." Aaron didn't elaborate. He never did. I knew more about Big Steve's parents' Holocaust experience than I did about Aaron, the man I called my partner.

"Besides the Warnocks, is there anyone else?" asked Chuck.

"Stella knew quite a few people that were deported. Some of them were members of the resistance cells she was involved with and some were innocents, friends that she couldn't save. Most of them never knew who she really was or that she was an American."

"How'd she manage that?" he asked.

"She learned seven languages during the war and could do accents really well. Stella spent a lot of time in Paris and she helped quite a few people escape. I always wonder if what The Klinefeld Group is looking for came from here," I said.

"Too bad none of them are alive to ask," he said.

"Margot de Genlis and Marie Galloway Laurence Morris Huntley Huntley Smith are still alive. They both knew all about Stella."

"Whoa. That is a name."

"Marie's a character."

"You've met her?"

"I've met both of them several times, but I don't know what they'd be willing to say. Stella's activities are still classified so, to some extent, their hands are tied."

"How can these women still be alive?"

I glared at him. "Because they didn't die. They're tough women."

Chuck grimaced. "I'm not sure why, but I'm sorry. How old are they? A hundred plus?"

"Hardly. They both joined the resistance in their teens. I think Margot is ninety-three and Marie is probably older, but I'm not sure."

"Do they live in Paris?"

"Margot lives in Tuscany with her daughter. Marie has a house in St. Louis, but she could be anywhere. She's quite the traveler. The family might know, if I can figure out a way to ask them."

"What family? The Bleds?"

"Of course. Marie was married to one of Nicky's brothers. She's family," I said.

"Nicky Lawrence? Stella's husband?"

"The one and only."

"We've got to talk to those ladies. They could know what The Klinefeld Group is after, not to mention the connection between your family and the Bleds. Maybe they know about the meeting here between your great great-grandparents and Stella and Nicky."

"Marie doesn't like to talk about the war. Her scars are deep. She was in Ravensbrück."

Chuck's face, that had been gleeful with the thought of new leads, grew solemn. "How long did the Nazis have her?"

"Fourteen months. She was barely alive when the Soviets liberated the camp. I don't want to ask her if we can avoid it."

"What about Margot?"

"She avoided capture, mostly because Marie wouldn't give up any information. Her memory isn't great, but she remembers her part in the resistance with great pride. Margot will talk to us, but she won't betray any oaths she made."

"But it was so long ago. How can it matter now?" he asked.

I glanced at the memorial. The guards were watching us, wary and alert. The memorial was considered a target for terrorists and they didn't like us standing there. "Time depends on who you ask. I'd better go in. The guards aren't happy."

"We're going, too," said Chuck.

"You don't have to. It's my thing."

"And now it's our thing."

*Our. I like the sound of that.*

We walked over and the guard asked if we spoke French. I did a little and he was happy not to have to get another guard to translate. He ran the metal detector over us and checked my purse before going over the rules. No pictures down in the memorial. It was a quiet place for reflection and remembrance. I told Chuck and Aaron what he said and we were allowed in.

We went down the long concrete stairs to a courtyard with an iron-barred gate and a jagged black sculpture. The sculpture always reminded me of the sign over the gate at Auschwitz. Maybe that was the intent. On the other side of the courtyard was the entrance to the memorial itself. I stepped through the open door into a room with an eternal flame in the center. There was an opening in the wall with bars over it. It was the entrance to a long tunnel. Myrtle and Millicent said it symbolized the journey into darkness from which few returned. The walls were inscribed with names, thousands of names.

I did as I'd been taught, clasped my hands in front of my heart, and remembered each of the names my godmothers had me memorize. It was very important to The Girls that I do this, stand in that spot and remember those men, women, and, especially, the children. Then I remembered Big Steve's parents. He never asked me to, but I thought he'd like it if I did.

"Okay," I said.

Chuck looked down the hall. His eyes roved over the names. "I forgot that the Nazis occupied the city."

"Paris makes it easy to forget, but the past is everywhere you look," I said.

"I think we're going to find something here," he said, still staring into the distant black end of the hall.

"About The Klinefeld Group?"

"I don't know. Something."

# CHAPTER NINE

We stayed up late on our first night in Paris. Dinner at a tiny bistro that Aaron picked because they had great duck confit. He was not pleased when I ordered steak frite instead. He warned that it wasn't going to be great and it wasn't. What can I say? I wanted steak and fries. Chuck did obey our resident food expert and he said the duck confit was fantastic. We all had crème brûlée and, I don't care what anyone says; it's different in Paris —creamier and the sugar melts ever so slowly on your tongue.

I collapsed on my bed at midnight—alone, might I add—and slept until ten the next morning. That was a lot later than I was planning, but I forgot to set the alarm on my phone.

The apartment was quiet, so I crossed my fingers that Chuck and Aaron were still asleep and I could sneak out. I almost talked myself out of taking a shower in the name of saving time, but I couldn't do it. I took a quick shower and put on a pair of jeans and the red ballet flats Chuck kept trying to take out of my suitcase. The man did not like flats, but he didn't have to like them. I wasn't putting them on him. I got a black sweater, my floppy hat that he'd tried to throw into the Seine, and my big sunglasses. I didn't want to be noticed, especially not when I was searching for Angela.

My door creaked open and I winced. So darn loud. I tiptoed past the other bedroom doors and through the kitchen/living room. I unlocked the door when a voice said, "Hey."

*Dammit!*

Aaron trotted across the living room while slipping on a faded 80's-style jean jacket. "I'm ready."

"Shush," I whispered. "I'm going out for croissants."

"No."

"I'm not asking permission," I said.

"You're not getting croissants."

*Double dammit.*

"Okay. I'm getting macaroons. Happy?"

"No."

"Aaron, please, go back to bed."

"I'm ready. I wrote Chuck a note," he said.

"Saying what?"

"That we went to the school to check in for our class." He opened the door, ushered me through, and locked it behind us. He started for the stairs, but I grabbed his arm.

"Aaron, you'll go to the cooking school and I'll do whatever. Understand?"

"No."

"No, you don't understand. Or no you won't do it?"

"I'm going with you. We're partners." Aaron went down the stairs with me on his heels. He was like a tubby steamroller. I couldn't stop him.

"Aaron, we're partners when my dad sends us to do things, not all the time."

"All the time."

We went outside and took a right to Rue Montorgueil. The shopping street was busy, even for a Sunday, with shoppers and the smells were fantastic. Roasting chicken, bread, and hints of ripe cheese danced in the breeze.

"Oh for god's sake. You can't go," I said.

"I'm going. You'll get lost."

That was probably true, but there were metro stops every other block, so I could always find my way back. “I’ll be fine. Where are you going?”

“Here.” Aaron marched into the corner café and sat at a table facing the street.

“I’m in a hurry,” I said. “See ya later.”

“Sit and tell me why you have two phones,” said Aaron.

It was the first order the little weirdo had ever given me and I sat out of sheer surprise. “I was hoping you forgot about that.”

“I didn’t.”

The waitress came over and I ordered café crème and chocolate croissants for both of us. They came out immediately and I sipped the hot heavenly mixture before saying, “You know I have a connection to the Fibonaccis from our time in Honduras.”

Aaron nodded, ripped off a piece of croissant, and eyed the flakiness before stuffing it in his gullet.

I watched Paris walk by, my eyes never straying from the tourists in heavy backpacks, businessmen with their baguettes, and mothers wrangling unruly children while I told him how much I owed Calpurnia Fibonacci and why we were in Paris. I told him Chuck didn’t know and that he couldn’t for his career and our relationship, whatever that was.

“Okay.”

“That’s it?” I asked. “You understand that you’re basically working for the mafia?”

He shrugged. “Okay.”

“We’re going to have to find a cooking school and at least make this sound plausible.”

“Done.”

“You found a school?”

“Yep.”

“Is it the Cordon Bleu?” I asked.

“No.”

That was all the info I was getting. I’d just have to trust Aaron to make the story believable. I wasn’t exactly comfortable with that, but what could I do?

“Let’s go, partner.”

We got off the metro at the Bastille stop with all its revolution artwork and passed the spot where the prison that incited the rage of the people once stood. We walked around the traffic circle into the broad boulevard where the market was bustling. Aaron made a beeline for it, saying he needed stuff. The market definitely had stuff, everything from clothing to fresh fish. I dragged Aaron away down the street, crossing over to an avenue with lovely apartments towering over us with wrought iron balconies dripping with red blossoms. That area I knew. The Marais. My godmothers loved it. My earliest memories of Paris were of the Marais, listening to the street musicians and Millicent feeding me bites of chocolate babka to keep me happy in museums.

I got turned around a couple times, but we found Place des Vosges without much trouble. The buildings around the seventeenth-century square were impressive with their red brick walls and blue slate roofs. We walked under the same vaulted arches that Gina's mystery woman had disappeared through.

Aaron stopped and made a little sound of contentment at the sight of the park in the center. The border was edged with trees shaped into squares. Beyond them were gravel paths through green lawns leading to a cluster of trees with a fountain in the center. It was a peaceful, elegant place and felt a world away from the city it was in.

I hooked my arm through Aaron's. "I know. It's wonderful, isn't it? The Girls wanted to buy an apartment here, but the one they wanted never came up for sale. Let's try the restaurants first."

Café Victor Hugo had just opened, so the staff wasn't too busy. They took a look at my pictures but didn't recognize either the woman or the man with her.

Aaron and I worked our way through every café on the arched promenade. Normally, I would've loved spending time there, imagining all the other people through the centuries that had walked where I was walking, but we had a mission and it was a big, fat fail.

When we made it back to Café Victor Hugo, I asked for a table with a view and we had some more coffee while I stared at Gina's pictures. I was right. The man did stand out. He wasn't like anyone we'd seen that day, but no one knew him. Maybe they were only passing through. Tourists. If that was true, we were screwed. I'd have to track down the cab and see if they used a credit card. What a pain. I didn't have a clear shot of the license plate.

I showed Aaron the picture. "If you saw this guy, who do you think he'd be?"

I expected the little weirdo to shrug, but he surprised me by saying, "Artist."

"He could be an artist. A well-off one, that's for certain. No Paris garret for him." I looked up at the elegant apartments overlooking the square. "But surely if he lived here, someone would've remembered him."

"Dealer?" asked Aaron.

Our waiter came over, smiling at me shyly. "Mademoiselle, may I have a picture with you?"

I was surprised until I realized that I'd taken off my enormous floppy hat and sunglasses. I had no makeup on, but he didn't care. He thought I was Nina Symoan, the wife of Mickey Stix. I corrected him, but he was so disappointed that I showed him the latest publicity shots I'd done for the band. He blushed and asked for pictures. Nina had retired and I'd taken her place as cover girl. I figured this was part of the deal. Mickey would be happy. He thought I should be more of a publicity hound. I got enough publicity just walking around. I didn't care to get any more, but I stood up, fluffed my hair, and applied some Harlot Scarlet to my lips for effect. We took a bunch of pictures and when I was smiled out, he said, "You are looking for that gentleman, Mademoiselle Watts?"

A thrill went through me. "Yes. Do you recognize him?"

"No."

*Dammit.*

The waiter frowned. "You think he is the artist?"

"I was guessing that he might be."

"If he is the artist, he might have his work in the gallery."

I took his hand and he blushed until he was nearly purple. "What gallery?"

"Art Symbol would be my choice." He gave me directions and I kissed him on the cheek, leaving a perfect lip print. I stuffed my hat on my head and put my glasses back on while Aaron paid. We dashed out of the café to the road, Place des Vosges. There were half a dozen galleries on the street. We'd have to work our way through them.

The first three were a bust and I was starting to get discouraged. The fourth gallery, Art Symbol, wasn't going to be much different, except maybe less pleasant. We walked through the door into an ice cold gallery filled with modern pieces that Myrtle and Millicent would quietly say weren't their cup of tea, which is to say they were big, raw canvases with pink stripes in the center. One had a paintbrush fixed to it. There were some interesting panels with human figures coming out of them, but I doubted The Girls would've considered anything there worthy of the Bled Collection.

A girl came out of the back at the tinkle of the doorbell and it was instantly clear that she didn't think that we were worthy of her shop. She looked like it was Halloween and she was going as Mia from *Pulp Fiction*, complete with the Cleopatra haircut, heavy eyeliner, and the starched white shirt. I hoped she didn't fancy herself an artist. She wasn't terribly original.

She asked in French with a German accent if she could assist us. I assumed she didn't want to assist us, since her lip was raised in a sneer. We did not smell bad, I swear. I tried to show her the photos, using my French, which isn't that bad, but she acted like she couldn't understand me and we should simply go away. I wasn't getting anywhere with her and, if we didn't leave, I might just kick her in the shin.

"Let's go," I said to Aaron, who'd remained silent throughout all my interviews.

"Non," he said.

"Huh?"

Aaron went on to speak perfect French in a raised tone that got the girl's attention with a quickness. He was speaking so fast, I couldn't follow what he was saying, but I heard the name, Bled, several times. Then Aaron waved her away like she was an annoying bug and she hustled through a back door. Three seconds later, a man in a fabulous suit and a purple tie came out. There was a hint of pink on his high cheekbones and when the girl attempted to follow him back into the shop, he hissed at her. He actually hissed. It was awesome.

He introduced himself as Monsieur Neel and spoke with Aaron in respectful but not obsequious tones. Then he turned to me. "Welcome, Mademoiselle Watts. We are happy to assist any member of the Bled family. I apologize for my assistant. She is young and not yet well-trained. I will see to her."

I could tell by the glint in his blue eyes that she wasn't going to like how he saw to her. "Thank you, Monsieur Neel. We are looking for this man. He was in the neighborhood about three weeks ago. Do you recognize him?"

"Oui. Of course. That is Monsieur Huppert. He is of the Musée d'Orsay in acquisitions. He was here looking at one of our new artists."

I went a little faint. Monsieur Huppert. Yes! "Thank you so much. Do you perhaps recognize the woman who he is with in this photo?"

Monsieur Neel looked again. "I believe she was with him that day, but I do not recall her name. I apologize."

"There's no need to apologize. You've been extremely kind and helpful," I said. "Do you have a card that I might have?"

He gave me a card out of a slim silver case he kept in his breast pocket. "Thank you for visiting us, Mademoiselle Watts."

"Thank you. I will pass your name on to my godmothers."

He puffed up and said, "Will you? The name of Bled is well-known in the art world."

"I will. I'll tell them that you were very helpful and they will remember."

Monsieur Neel thanked me again and opened the door for us. I stepped outside, feeling lighter than I had since the moment I saw Oz Urbani standing in my living room.

Aaron led the way into the Bastille station with me tugging on his jean jacket. "Since when do you speak French?"

"1985."

"How'd you learn the accent so well?"

"People," he said.

"French people?"

Aaron ignored that and I had to admit it was a pretty stupid question. He didn't answer any of my other stupid questions either, so I called Spidermonkey on the Fibonacci phone, intending to leave a message since it was five in the morning at home. Spidermonkey shocked me by answering, completely awake and working. The night before, he was at a cocktail party with his wife's friends, all podiatrists. I said I'd call back if he needed to sleep, but he wouldn't hear of it. Apparently, the uberization of podiatry biomechanics and practice expansion wasn't quite as fascinating as Loretta thought it was. Usually, Spidermonkey didn't mind. He considered it the price of being married to a doctor who had no interest in retiring, but if he saw a chance to escape, he took it. He ended up snoozing in his host's den for most of the evening with a glass of scotch.

"You're a bad guest," I said, stifling a laugh.

Spidermonkey snorted. "Nobody noticed. Did you get the man's name?"

"Monsieur Huppert. He's in acquisitions at the Orsay," I said. "Do you want me to call Novak?"

"No, that's easy enough. We'll use Novak for the tough stuff."

My purse started to ring as we walked up the stairs to the platform. It was probably Chuck. I gave my regular phone to Aaron and said, "Tell him I'm busy."

Aaron answered with, "Mercy's peeing."

"For the love of god, Aaron." I punched him in the shoulder, jogged up the rest of the stairs, and went back to Spidermonkey.

"What was that about?" asked Spidermonkey.

"Nothing," I said. "Same stuff, different day. How long to do a background on this guy?"

"How much do you want?"

"Not the whole kit and caboodle. Monsieur Huppert isn't the target. If you can get his frequent contacts from email and his phone that will work. I assume he called this woman."

"Certainly. I'll have it for you later tonight. Hopefully, he doesn't have many female friends."

"I didn't show you his picture, did I?"

"No hope, huh?"

"None," I said. "I'm guessing he's Monsieur Popular with the ladies."

"Well, we can't win 'em all."

I said goodbye, looked at the metro map on the platform, and groaned. The little weirdo came up and gave me my phone back. I grabbed his arm and tried to take him back to the stairs. "We're on the wrong platform."

"No."

"I can read a map," I said.

*Sort of.*

"We're going the wrong direction."

"Right direction for our school," said Aaron.

I stopped tugging on his arm. "There's a cooking school for real? I mean, one that we're actually going to?"

He stared off to the left.

"Okay. So where are we going?"

"Atelier Guy Marin."

"Never heard of him. Who is he?"

"Chef."

"I assumed that. What did you tell Chuck? Isn't he waiting for us?"

"He's going for a run and we have to check in at Marin's."

The train rolled in and we got on, headed to the eighth arrondissement, home to the Champs-Élysées. This cooking school was going to be pricey. Doing a favor for Calpurnia was going to cost me what little I'd managed to save up from working at the Columbia Clinic, including the bonus Shawna gave me for getting Twinkie stuffed up my nose.

Aaron knew exactly where he was going and we arrived at a large open door that gave me hope. Maybe it was a little workshop, a startup that was using low prices to lure in cooks. Then we walked in. Atelier Guy Marin wasn't a startup and Marin wasn't a nobody. It was a mansion that confirmed my fears of exorbitant cost. It was surprisingly modern with big plate glass windows at the back overlooking a pretty courtyard.

"How much is this going to cost me?" I hissed in Aaron's ear.

A man wearing a black apron and sporting a shaved head and a neck tattoo of what appeared to be a cornucopia of vegetables came out of the back. "Chef!"

"Chef!" exclaimed Aaron. He almost seemed excited or, at least, what passed for excitement in Aaron. The two embraced and began speaking in French about some restaurant, Guy Marin, and beef, unless my French was worse than I thought.

The chef turned to me, holding out his hands. "Mademoiselle Mercy, I've heard so much about you."

I took his hands and he clasped mine in his big, warm ones. "Really? I mean, thank you."

"I am Mathieu Torres. I will be assisting Aaron with his class," said Mathieu.

"Wait. You'll be assisting him?" I glanced at Aaron, who was staring at the wall. "Somebody's confused and I don't see how it can be me. I know him."

Mathieu reached behind the island and pulled out a chef's coat, shaking it out. "Then you know what an honor it is to work with a chef of his esteem."

"Esteem? Aaron? I know he's good, but..."

Aaron slipped on the chef's coat and buttoned it. I'd like to say he looked like a chef, but, to me, he looked like he'd stolen his dad's chef coat and was playing a game of pretend. He rooted around the drawers, not finding what he wanted, until I took off his glasses and gave them a good clean. Then he pulled out a duck press and various tools that I think I saw in the torture museum in Rothenburg.

"I'll teach duck," said Aaron. "Mercy will take the pâté à choux course."

"No, I'm good. I can do pâté à choux. Millicent taught me," I said quickly.

"Advanced pâté à choux," said Aaron.

*Dammit.*

"Can't I take chopping for dummies?"

Mathieu laughed. "Aaron assures me that you are an accomplished baker."

I was, sort of. The Girls loved baking and they insisted I learn. They thought cookery and baking was part of a well-rounded education. That's how I ended up taking French, instead of Spanish, and the reason I could ride side saddle and English, but not Western. My godmothers weren't always the most practical of women.

Aaron said he needed to get the feel of the kitchen, whatever that meant, and started pulling out ingredients without asking permission. Mathieu looked like he expected it.

"So how do you know Aaron?" I asked.

"I trained under him at Guy Savoy."

"Are you serious?"

"You didn't know?"

I glanced at Aaron, who was doing something with asparagus and scallops. "No. He doesn't talk much."

Mathieu nodded. "He teaches by example and gives his students great confidence. I learned a great deal under his tutelage."

"So Aaron lived here, in Paris?"

"Yes. For five years, I believe."

"That explains the French," I said.

"Excuse me?"

"Nothing." My regular phone rang and I excused myself to answer it.

Chuck breathed hard into the phone. "Where are you?"

"At the cooking school. Are you having an asthma attack?"

"I'm running. I thought I'd go to where you are."

"It's too far. We're in the eighth."

"That's where I am, I think. Champs-Élysées?"

"They'll never let you in. You're all sweaty," I said.

"You don't want me to come?" He sounded hurt through the heavy breathing, and it was a good opportunity to prove that I *was* going to a cooking school.

"Just don't come in. Text me when you get here," I said.

I sent him the address and hung up.

"All is well?" asked Mathieu.

"Yes. My boyfriend wants to come by."

"Of course."

"He's out running."

"Perhaps not."

I smiled and watched Aaron work. I'd never really watched him cook before. I just ate the results. In the kitchen, he was focused and fast-fingered, prepping three plates of asparagus three ways. By the time Chuck showed up, we'd already eaten his appetizer and it was excellent. Somehow, he'd pickled asparagus in ten minutes. He also roasted it and did some weird thing with pancetta. Mathieu was very happy, telling me he'd see me tomorrow afternoon for my advanced class.

When I got downstairs, Chuck was jogging at the door. His tank was sticking to him like he'd been in a wet t-shirt contest. It would've been sexy, but I could smell him at five feet.

"How far did you run?" I asked.

"He checked his phone. "I'm at ten miles."

"That's a lot for a vacation."

"I'm shaking off the jet lag. How's the school look?"

I wrinkled my nose. "Terrible. Aaron put me in an advanced pastry class."

"You'll have fun."

"If you say so." I sounded super reluctant so he wouldn't get suspicious.

"I'll meet you at home. When will you be back? I need lunch," said Chuck.

"Maybe an hour."

Chuck kissed my cheek and ran off, dodging traffic and getting plenty of second looks from the ladies strolling down the street. Aaron came out and said we were done. I took his arm and we headed off down the street after Chuck.

"So you worked at Guy Savoy?" I asked.

"Yeah."

"Any other secrets I should know?"

"Huh?"

"Never mind. What do you want to do after lunch?"

Predictably, Aaron wanted to go to E. Dehillerin, the cooking store, and some store that only sold antique linens for some reason. I agreed, because there was nothing I could do on the Angela issue until Spider-monkey got back to me and I wanted to see what Chuck would say about spending an hour in Paris looking at whisks. And an hour was conservative. The Girls once bought twenty whisks at E. Dehillerin and they were all different. It took so long I fell asleep on a stool in flatware.

When we got back to the apartment, Chuck was showered and smelling great. "That took forever."

"We stopped for supplies." I held up a bottle of wine and a bag of sandwiches. Aaron unpacked a basket of tiny strawberries and several varieties of cheese.

"I'm starving," said Chuck.

We ate at the sofa table, spreading Brie de Meaux on the baguette we bought and having the sandwiches with butter, speck, and Comté cheese. Chuck swirled his wine and took a sip. "Don't take this the wrong way, but I still like beer better."

"I thought as much, but we're in France. Hello."

He laughed and grabbed my laptop off the side table. A thrill of fear went through me before I remembered that I'd been careful not to use it to look up anything on Angela or the Fibonaccis. I fixed a smile on my face and took a bite of brie.

Chuck gave me a suspicious look before saying, "I hope you don't mind that I used your laptop."

"Of course not."

He opened it and showed me the screen. It was a street view from Google Maps of a typical Parisian apartment building with a fromagerie on the first floor. "That's where Paul Richter's daughter lives. She and her husband moved into her mother's apartment. We can interview her tomorrow," he said. "I think she'll be home or at the shop. Her husband runs it now."

"I doubt she kept her uncle's stuff."

"You don't want to try?"

I stretched and stared up at the blackened beams decorating the ceiling. "I totally want to try. But sometimes, it feels like the past is getting further and further away and we'll never know what The Klinefeld Group wants or what it has to do with my parents."

He put his arm around me and drew me to him. I thought he would kiss me, but, of course, he didn't. "I know, but I have a feeling that we're close to something."

"Really?"

"Yeah. Ever since we got here, I don't know...something about this city. I was running and I saw bullet holes from the war. You're right. The past isn't that far away and it all started here. Your family, the Bleds, The Klinefeld Group. It's all here."

"That's Paris. It makes you feel things you didn't know you could."

He shook his head and kissed my forehead. "I wish I could feel less."

I looked up into his eyes and he looked away.

Then Aaron stood up. "I'm ready."

"For what?" asked Chuck.

"Shopping."

"You want to go shopping?" He looked over Aaron's Spiderman tee and jean shorts.

I elbowed Chuck. "Are you nuts? Not that kind of shopping. We're going to the cooking store."

"Do we have to?"

Aaron was bouncing up and down on the balls of his feet.

"What do you think?" I asked.

"Let's go, but after that, we're hitting the Pompidou Center."

I grinned. "It's on the schedule?"

"It is."

We went to E. Dehillerin. Aaron bought one copper egg pan. It took him two hours to decide on it and the stool in flatware was gone. In the end, Chuck said that if he didn't pick a pan, he'd pick one and beat him with it. A pan was picked in three seconds flat.

Chuck persuaded us that he'd suffered enough and we skipped the linen store. Instead, we hopped on the metro and went to the Pompidou, spending the rest of the day there. Modern art wasn't my thing, but Aaron and Chuck had to look at every single piece, usually from several different angles. We left at closing and went to a restaurant that specialized in mussels. Since it wasn't crab, I survived, but just barely. I ate mussels in white wine cream sauce. Chuck and Aaron were so happy that they barely looked up from their wide cast iron pots. You know dinner's going to take a while when everyone is served with their own pot.

Chuck dripped big hunks of bread in the juices and groaned with pleasure. "I love Paris."

"I can see that," I said as my purse vibrated against my rear, where I'd wedged it between me and the chair back. "Excuse me. I'm going to find the bathroom."

"Dessert?" he asked.

"Can you order me the waffle with hot chocolate sauce?"

Chuck nodded and went back to dipping. I found the bathroom at the bottom of a set of stairs that looked like they'd been built in the middle ages. The ceiling was barely higher than my head and I had to crouch to get through the door into the bathroom stall that was so small I could've rested my forehead on the sink if I actually had to go.

I checked the Fibonacci phone and saw Spidermonkey's number. I was afraid it was Calpurnia asking for an update, but I guess Spidermonkey was the only early riser.

"Sorry this took so long," he said. "Loretta wouldn't let me escape. We ended up in a hot tub until midnight."

"Are you all pruney?" I asked.

"Very, but I've got the information on your Monsieur Huppert."

"Lay it on me."

Spidermonkey gave me a short list of facts. Emile Huppert was the son of a Burgundy winery owner. They were a very wealthy family and he did work at the Musée d'Orsay in acquisitions. Divorced twice. Three sons. He did have an apartment in Place des Vosges.

"I can't believe he lives there and nobody recognized him. What a pain."

"You were unlucky there, but you identified him anyway."

I grumbled and Spidermonkey laughed. "It can't always be easy."

"I'm waiting for it to be easy one time, just once."

"Don't be greedy."

"It's not greed. It's laziness."

"I wouldn't call you lazy. Are you ready for the rest?" he asked.

I was ready and he told me that Monsieur Huppert was, as I suspected, very active socially. Gina's woman could be one of many he called and texted. Huppert worked with a lot of women. He was a member of a wine club and a dining club with female members that he connected with less often.

"Are there any Americans or Canadians?" I asked.

"Four," he said.

"Are they the right age?"

"Three are within six years of Angela's age. One is sixty-three."

I laughed. "Forget her. What have you got on the other three?"

"Sandy Henderson is in his wine club, married, one daughter."

"How old is the daughter?"

"Ten."

"Leave her for now. What about the other ones?"

"Corrine Sweet, thirty-three, single, works at the Orsay bookshop."

"She sounds good. What's her address?"

"Not really good. She doesn't have a French driver's license, but her passport and Canadian license don't match Angela. She's a blue-eyed blonde, according to them."

"Give me her address anyway."

"I haven't got it yet. The address in her work file is for a building undergoing renovation. She may be staying with friends or renting short-term. But I'll get it."

"Can you see her work schedule at the Orsay?"

"Give me a second."

I checked the time. Chuck was going to start to wonder what happened to me.

"Got it. She works Tuesday to Saturday from opening to 1:30. Same for the rest of the week."

"So she's off today and they're closed on Monday. Who's the other one?"

"Jennifer MacDougall aka Sabine Suede."

I groaned. "Not a porn star."

"Nope. Prostitute, high end. She's twenty-seven and has been here for about eighteen months."

"Any pictures of her?"

"Passport photo isn't Angela, but it's close. She's got the dark, curly hair and blue eyes. Angela obviously used a fake passport to get to Paris, so this one's a good candidate. The only other picture is a mug shot. She got into a fight with a client and they beat each other bloody. Her face is so distorted, it could be my own mother and I wouldn't recognize her."

"I'll start with her. Address?"

"She goes from hotel to hotel. I'd try the Grand Bleu in the first arrondissement. According to my source, the bar is a hot spot for women like Sabine Suede and the management tolerates it."

"I'll try it tomorrow night if I can figure out how to get Chuck over there. I don't know what else to do with the rest of the day. Calpurnia wants her answer quickly."

"You'll have to find something else to do. It is Paris. You're there with Chuck," he said with a chuckle.

"I know," I said. "We'll go interview Paul Richter's daughter."

"That's not what I meant."

A knock rattled the bathroom door.

"Mercy? Are you okay?" asked Chuck.

"I'm fine," I said loudly and then whispered into the phone, "Gotta go."

I opened the door and laughed when I saw Chuck hunched over with his head pressed against a low beam. "Finally, being short pays off for me."

"You've been down here a long time," he said, taking my hand.

"Sorry. I got a little dizzy. Must be the jet lag. I think I need to sleep."

"The dessert's here, but we can skip it and go home."

"Not a chance. I ate mussels. I deserve dessert."

"Are you sure?" he asked. "I think I should get you to bed."

I did a little hip swish and gave him a saucy look. "With you?"

He dropped my hand. "It would be weird with Aaron in the apartment."

"What's going on?" I asked, attempting to recapture his hand, but he avoided it, kissing me lightly on the lips. "Nothing. I'm a gentleman. Get used to it."

"No, you're not. You're Chuck. I've known you practically all my life. Something's wrong."

"I don't know what you're talking about." He went up the stairs and I had the sense that he did it to hide his face.

# CHAPTER TEN

I woke up the next morning with sunlight in my face. I'd forgotten to pull the curtains and I wasn't the first to discover it. An elderly man, holding a frying pan and smoking a long cigarette, waved to me from his window. Thank goodness I didn't sleep nude.

I slipped out of bed, waved back, and closed the curtains. That's when I realized the apartment was completely silent. No snoring. Chuck and Aaron had been doing a duet the night before. Chuck warned me that too much wine made him snore, but I had no idea the levels to which he would rise. Two doors weren't enough to stop the onslaught. No more wine for him. I would get him beer if I had to brew it myself. For the first time, I was grateful not to be sharing a room. I would've ended up in the tiny bedroom for sure.

My door opened with a creak and I sniffed. No snoring and no cooking smells. That couldn't be right. If Aaron was awake, he should've been cooking.

"Aaron," I called out as I trotted down the hall. His bedroom was empty as was the kitchen. I checked Chuck's room and it was empty. A chill went through me. I'd slept like a rock and the Fibonacci phone was under my panties in the dresser. Could Chuck have come in without waking me and found the phone? No. He wouldn't search through my stuff. Another chill went up my spine. Who was I kidding? Chuck was Dad's protégé. He would absolutely search through everything I owned if he thought something was wrong. It was the Watts way. Means to an end and all that. Chuck had been suspicious about my staying in the bathroom so long in the restaurant.

"Oh crap!"

I ran back to my room and yanked the drawer open. The phone was exactly where I left it. My panties didn't seem like they'd been disturbed, but Chuck was a pro. He could search without a trail. Hell. Even I could pull that off.

Multiple clicking noises echoed through the apartment and Chuck called out, "Mercy! Wake up!"

I grabbed the Fibonacci phone and stuffed it under my mattress. "I am up. Where've you been?"

Chuck walked in covered in sweat and still huffing and puffing. "Running. What'd you think?"

"I didn't think you'd keep up exercising on vacation. You're seriously disturbed."

"You can come with me tomorrow."

I poked his hard chest with my finger and pushed him out the door. "I can't. It's against everything I hold sacred."

"Like what?"

"Enjoying my life, for one. Go shower. You smell like Skanky when I bought him from that homeless guy."

Chuck waggled his eyebrows at me. "You can have me for a lot less than a cold latte and a twenty."

My heart leapt. That was kinda sleazy. I'd never have thought I'd miss it so much. "Oh really? I like the sound of that."

Chuck instantly stepped back and grabbed my doorknob. "I'll shower and we can get breakfast." He started to close the door and I stuck my foot out to stop it. "What happened? What did I say?"

"Nothing. You said I stink," he said, avoiding my gaze.

"I take it back. You smell like healthy exercise and I have a big shower. We could put it to good use."

There was a time when that offer would've had him running into the bathroom, stripping as he went, but not anymore. Chuck shook his head. "No French shower is that big." He nudged my foot out of the way and closed the door before I could launch a counter argument.

I stood there, staring at the door with tears stinging my eyes. This wasn't the way it was supposed to be. I never felt further from Chuck than that moment. He'd bothered me senseless since we were kids, but I'd always felt connected, even when I was trying hard not to be.

I bit back a sob and got my regular phone and called Nazir.

"Mercy?" he said. "I thought you were in Paris."

"I am. You have to tell me what's wrong with Chuck right now," I said.

Nazir hesitated and I could hear his wife in the background asking what was wrong. "What happened?" he asked finally.

"Nothing and that's what's wrong. Tell me. I think he's really upset or something."

"What makes you think I have the key to the inner workings of Chuck Watts?" he asked.

"Because of what you said at Kronos before we left. I know you know," I said.

Nazir gave out a weak laugh. "You give me too much credit."

"Fine," I hissed. "You won't tell me. I'll get Spidermonkey on it."

"I swear to God, you better not do that," he said in the same tone he used at Kronos.

"Give me one good reason."

"Because I'm telling you not to. You know me. I'm your friend and I'm Chuck's. Don't do it. If he wants to tell you, he will."

"Nazir..."

"No, Mercy," he said. "Don't be a Watts. Not this time."

I went into the bathroom and turned on the shower. "What am I supposed to do? He's not Chuck—not the Chuck I know anyway."

"Be patient. I know that's not your thing, but this time you have to be," said Nazir before he hung up.

I tossed the phone onto the bed and got into the lukewarm shower. I should've waited until the heater had a chance to catch up. There I was, not being patient, and I paid for it by dropping my body temperature a good ten degrees. My teeth were chattering by the time I got out and pressed my frozen body against the towel warmer.

That was France in a nutshell: enormous towel warmers, tiny water heaters.

Chuck banged on my door. "Are you ready yet?"

"Hell, no!" I yelled back. "I can barely feel my feet."

He came in, saw me suctioned to the towel rack, and burst out laughing. "Why didn't you wait a little?"

I glared at him, all clean and warm. "How could I wait? You're already in here, demanding that I be ready, you giant hot water hog."

He got a couple more towels and wrapped me up like a burrito. "Sorry. I wasn't thinking. Will a latte help?"

"Extra hot," I said.

Chuck made me a steaming hot latte and I drank it before attempting to un-burrito. My hair was dry by that time and had curled into weird ringlets that for some reason all curled forward. Had to be the Seine air. It was not a good look. After getting dressed, I tried brushing it out and managed to make my hair look like Buckwheat from *The Little Rascals*.

Chuck came back in with a second latte. "Holy crap! What happened to your hair?"

"I'm being punished," I said with certainty.

"For what?"

"Lack of patience." I silently promised to be better in the future and tried applying a smoothing serum. That just angered it. Now it was frizzy and sort of greasy at the same time.

"I think you need a hat," said Chuck.

"You hate my hat."

"Today, I'll make an exception."

That's when I knew it was as bad as I thought it was. Groan. I jammed my hat on and asked, "Where's Aaron? I assume he didn't run with you."

"Cooking school. Something about produce. It's you and me," said Chuck.

He didn't sound too happy about it, but I decided to take Nazir's advice and ignore it. "Are you hungry?"

"Oh yeah. Is there any place where we can get an American breakfast?"

"Not so that you'd recognize it," I said, grabbing my purse and heading out the front door.

"I'm going to starve to death."

"In Paris? Puhlease."

"A man can't live on yogurt alone."

"I'll find you an omelet."

"Southwestern?"

I rolled my eyes at him before jogging down the stairs. "What do you think?"

Chuck grumbled his way down the street about how men had to eat and he needed real food. What a whiner. I found a café that agreed to make him an omelet, even though they heartily disapproved. Eggs for breakfast was wrong and in the waitress's opinion might cause vomiting if eaten so early. When she brought out Chuck's omelet, she held the tray as far from her nose as possible and gagged a little when she walked away.

"What's the big deal?" Chuck cut into the fluffy omelet. "Hey. Where's the cheese?"

"No cheese," I said. "Just eat it."

"What's this green stuff?"

"Herbs, you weirdo." I bit into my crusty croissant and washed it down with a café like a good girl.

Chuck polished off the omelet in three minutes flat. "You know, that was pretty good. Maybe I'll get another one."

I pulled his arm down before he could signal the waitress. "No, you don't. We aren't gluttonous Americans."

"Speak for yourself. I want another one."

"Today, I speak for you. I'll get you a crepe later."

Chuck looked around for a creperie. "Where?"

"Oh, for crying out loud. I'll find one." I finished my café and watched him scrape minuscule bits of egg off his plate.

*It's a good thing I love you.*

"I think you got it all."

"Hold on," he said, trying to get the last crumb off the edge.

I paid the bill while trying not to pretend that I didn't know Chuck, who wasn't giving up on that crumb. "Please get up. You're killing me here." The kitchen staff had come out and were watching Chuck, perplexed at this person who would act in such a manner. Omelet in the morning. Trés horrible!

"If you lick that plate, I will murder you with a fork," I said, tugging on his arm.

"Now I want to do it to see what'll happen." Chuck grinned up at me.

"Get up."

He didn't get up. He just had to act like a weirdo. Instead of forking him, I did the right thing. I slung my purse over my shoulder, nodded to the staff, and marched out of the café. Chuck was on me in three strides. "I was only joking."

"Hilarious."

"I thought so."

"Would you burp at the table in Japan?" I asked.

"I don't know. Would I?" Chuck laughed and grabbed my hand.

"Don't make me take off my hat."

He put up his hands in horror. "No, no. Anything but that. I'll be good."

"Alright then. Are we doing this interview today or what?" I asked.

"Right after we find a crepe stand."

Groan.

We found two creperies on the way to the Richter residence and Chuck had to stop at both. He declared that Nutella and bananas were awesome on crepes. Only the threat of hat removal kept him from stopping at a third creperie to try another version, like Nutella was going to be different a block away.

"What was that address?" I asked, steering him away from the cook ladling out a generous amount of batter onto the griddle.

"There it is." Chuck pointed down the street at a striped awning. The family fromagerie had a line out the door—always a good sign. Too bad we were in the market for information, not cheese. I started to cross the street, but Chuck held me back.

"What if they don't speak English? Do you know enough French for this?" he asked.

"No idea," I said. "Come on."

He still didn't let me go. "We should have a plan. Never go in without a plan."

"We're not storming an Al-Qaeda stronghold. They're cheesemongers. We'll figure it out," I said.

"That's not how I do things," he insisted. "We need a Plan B."

"I hate to break it to you, but I rarely have a Plan A and they never work out when I do."

Chuck stared down at me with a look of confusion on his handsome face. I don't think I'd ever seen him have that look. It was familiar. I remember my calculus teacher having it when I got a B on my final exam. Then he sent me to the office, claiming I must've cheated. The nurse searched me for evidence and found nothing because I didn't cheat. I studied. That shocked everyone, including me.

"How have you solved anything?" he asked.

"It's a mystery." I grinned up at him.

"You wing it?"

"Pretty much. Are we going or what?"

He shook his head. "I have to have a plan or at least an idea of a plan."

"You actually read all the police manuals, didn't you?"

"What do you mean by that?"

The light changed and I pulled him across the street in a swarm of businessmen heading to the metro. "Nothing. Here's your plan: if we can't communicate, we'll bring Aaron back with us. Good enough?"

"What's Aaron going to do?" Chuck tried to hold me back. I never knew he was such a worrier.

"He's fluent."

Chuck peppered me with questions, trying to figure out whether my Plan B would actually work when we reached the apartment door next to the fromagerie. The name, Richter, was written in faded black ink next to one of the door bells. "Don't push that button," said Chuck. "We have to discuss—"

I pushed the button.

"Mercy! You have to listen to me," he said.

"I really don't," I replied and turned my attention to the little speaker that gave out a screech.

"Oui?" said a woman's voice.

*Yes! We've got a Richter.*

"Mercy," whispered Chuck.

I shushed him. Then I told the voice who I was and that I needed to speak to Nadine Richter about her father and uncle. The voice asked me who I was and I told the truth, which Chuck didn't look too happy about. The voice was suspicious. I explained in my halting French that I was looking into a case that her uncle investigated in 1963 not that long before his death and I wanted to know if she might have anything that pertained to the death of Jens Waldemar Hoff in Berlin.

The voice didn't answer and Chuck squeezed my hand. "I told you—"

The door buzzed.

"We're in," I said and flounced through. I didn't need a plan. Plans were for wussies and cops with the last name of Watts.

Chuck charged in after me and blocked the rickety staircase. "We should discuss how this is going to go down."

"Go down? She isn't a suspect. She's a fifty-year-old mother of three. I'll ask for her help and we'll see what happens."

"Mercy, you can't flirt your way to every answer."

I kicked him in the shin, the dirtbag. Chuck gasped and I darted past him up the stairs. "Then I'll ask the questions and leave the flirting to you, Rico Suave."

"What did you call me?" Chuck took the stairs three at a time, but I still beat him to the Richters' door on the second floor. He ran up beside me as I straightened my skirt and took off my sunglasses.

"Mercy, what did you say?" he asked, trying to pull me away from the doorbell.

"Like I don't know your squadron nickname. There's a reason you interview eighty percent of the female witnesses that come through the door."

"I hate that name," he growled.

"Well, get used to it, because it's not going away any time soon." I rang the bell and Chuck put on what I assumed was his game face, somewhere between *This is business* and *I'm all about you, baby*. It was weird to watch and I wondered if Dad had the same look when he interviewed women. He was said to be charming, but it was hard to imagine. Chuck was hot without trying. Dad reminded me of a scarecrow. I might not have been the best judge, though.

The door latch clicked and the door opened. An older woman with thick, greying hair looked out and smiled. "Mademoiselle Watts?"

"Oui, ma'am." I introduced Chuck and he gave her his most charming smile. One side of her smile lifted wryly. I think she'd seen his ilk before, but she wasn't put off. She introduced herself as Nadine Richter Roche and invited us in.

I asked her if she spoke English and she nodded as we sat down in her small but neat living room.

"Yes. I speak a little," said Nadine.

In my experience, that meant she was fluent but not perfect, but we'd never know the difference.

"If you don't mind, Madam Roche, English is better. Chuck doesn't speak French," I said.

She nodded and her artfully-cut, asymmetrical bob swung into her face and she tucked it behind her ears. Her large brown eyes stayed on us, alert but not wary and I wondered why she let us in. I'm not sure I would've.

"Of course, I don't mind. You wanted to know about my uncle?" she asked.

"Yes. Werner Richter. Did your father perhaps inherit anything from his brother? Case books? Files from Berlin?"

"Not that I know of. What are you looking for?"

Chuck leaned toward her. "Anything to do with Jens Waldemar Hoff?"

Mrs. Roche puzzled over the question. "I don't recognize the name. It's unusual, non?"

I smiled. "It is unusual. That's why we were able to find Hoff in the first place."

"What did he do, this Hoff?" She was growing more interested but tried to hide it by leaning back and forcing her hands to go slack in her lap.

"He's connected to a group we're attempting to trace," said Chuck. "Have you ever heard of The Klinefeld Group?"

Mrs. Roche smiled reflexively when Chuck spoke and I decided to let him go. She was a woman, after all, and not many were immune to his charms. None come to think of it.

"I'm sorry. I have not. Are they German?" she asked.

"It looks like it. Your father never mentioned them? Your mother, perhaps?"

"Non. They rarely spoke of Uncle Werner. It made my father sad. He was papa's twin. I think he always thought part of him was missing after his brother died." Mrs. Roche did begin to relax, to trust. "It is hard for me to say. I was four when Uncle Werner died."

"Do you remember him at all?" asked Chuck.

Her face lit up and her eyes sparkled. "Oui. He would be my horse. We would gallop around the room, knocking over Maman's lamps and causing her to shriek. He was such fun for a little girl to play with. My papa was much more stern."

"He sounds wonderful," I said.

Mrs. Roche turned to me and asked, "Do you have an uncle like him?"

I thought of Uncle Morty and he was nothing like Werner Richter. I couldn't imagine Morty letting me ride around on his back, but he did spend hours playing games and sneaking me food Mom said I couldn't have. "In a way. My uncle is a game player, though."

She sat up straight. "Oh, yes. The games. My father kept uncle's games. Would you like to see?"

"We'd love to," said Chuck.

She led us back into a spare bedroom filled with packing boxes and piles of clothes. The light went out of Mrs. Roche's eyes. She apologized for the mess. They were going through the things her mother left behind when she left Paris to live with her brother in Brittany.

"I'm sorry about your father," I said. "This must be a difficult time and we're intruding."

"Non, non. We knew papa would be going. He was sick for a long time with the...I don't know the word in English."

"Leukemia," I said. Spidermonkey had told me the diagnosis after Paul Richter died.

Mrs. Roche jerked a little at the word and looked suspicious.

Chuck said quickly, "When we were trying to find your father, his diagnosis came up."

I shot Chuck a grateful look.

"The word is the same then," said Mrs. Roche.

"Yes," I said. "But I shouldn't have said it like that."

"Non, it is fine. It is what happened." She rooted through the boxes and had Chuck help her carry a couple out into the living room. Uncle Werner had liked games, vintage ones from the '20s in particular. Most were European, but there were a few in English. We went through each box and found nothing. I didn't think a cop would hide case evidence in a zoo game from Austria, but you never know.

Mrs. Roche found some paperwork in her father's files—her uncle's death certificate, a police report in German, unfortunately.

"There is nothing else. My uncle was not married. I don't believe there was much for my father to inherit," she said.

"Thank you, Mrs. Roche," said Chuck. "It was a long shot."

"Long shot?"

"Not likely that you'd have anything after all this time."

She sat back down in her chair and drummed her fingers on her knee.

"Is there something else?" I asked.

"I don't know if it is something," she said. "You know that my uncle was run down in Berlin two weeks after he visited us here?"

Chuck and I looked at each other. A little zing went through me and, if I went by the look on Chuck's face, he felt it, too.

"We knew he was hit by a car in Berlin," I said.

"Your father thought that was significant?" asked Chuck. He said it like he knew the answer. I did, too.

"Maman didn't like for him to speak about the accident. She said it would bring us bad luck."

"Like the bad luck your uncle had?" I asked.

"She was...frightened."

"Of what?" asked Chuck.

"My father always said Uncle Werner was murdered because he was a policeman. He said it wasn't an accident."

Chuck picked the accident report up off the table, his eyes searching for a familiar word. "What do you think?"

"It wasn't an accident," she said. "The report said so."

He held out the report. "Can you read it?"

She took the paper and scanned it. "I speak a little German, but I cannot read it so well. An accident late at night. No one saw. The rest..." She threw up her hand.

"What else did your father say about it?" I asked.

"Nothing...but I think he was nervous about something. To me it was a great mystery. I always wanted to know what happened and why someone would do that to my uncle. To Maman, it was frightening. She told me not to speak of it to anyone, but then you came asking and I think perhaps it is time to talk."

"I'm glad you did," I said. "It's a big help."

"Do you think this Klinefeld Group that you are investigating might have something to do with Uncle Werner's death?"

Chuck reached over and took her hand. "I don't know, but we'll do everything we can to find out."

She patted his hand and stood up. She went into the other room and we could hear her talking to someone on the phone in French.

She came back in and said, "I think I may have something to help you."

"Really?" I asked. "Who did you ask?"

"Maman. I persuaded her that now that papa is gone, it will be safe to find out what happened," said Mrs. Roche.

"What did she say?" asked Chuck.

She offered us coffee and said, "It may be nothing, but she said that when my uncle came to visit, the two of them would go out to see someone. They wouldn't tell her who it was. After Uncle Werner died, Papa told her it was to do with a case in Berlin. He told her never to go there."

"How would she go?" I asked. "Did he tell her the address?"

Mrs. Roche dropped another sugar cube into her cup and gave us a sly smile. "Non. She followed them a couple of times. Papa caught her and was very angry."

I laughed. "I like your maman."

"She was always a nosy woman."

Chuck glanced at me and smirked. What was that supposed to mean?

"Does your maman still remember the address?" Chuck sipped his coffee. He appeared cool and calm for the most part, but his right foot was jiggling with excitement.

Mrs. Roche saw it, too and smiled. "Oui. She wrote it in her diary. Papa never knew. He was not nosy." She wrote down the address, a nice one in the Marais, and gave the slip of paper to me.

"Did your father ever go to this address after your uncle died?" I asked.

"He told Maman that he didn't, but she didn't believe him. Will you go there and tell me what you find?" she asked, standing up.

I wrote down both our phone numbers for her and she accompanied us to the door. We shook hands and assured her that we would tell her everything we found out.

I walked into the hall, but Chuck didn't follow. Mrs. Roche held him back to ask, "Do you think like my papa that my uncle was murdered?"

Chuck patted her hand. "I think it's a possibility, but I'd like you to keep that to yourself for now."

She nodded. "Oui, of course."

We walked down the stairs and ran right into the fromagerie line. It was even longer than before and wrapped around the building.

"That must be some cheese," said Chuck. "Do you think we should get some?"

I waved the slip of paper at him. "I thought we were going straight to the Marais."

"We are, but it wouldn't hurt to have some snacks for the trip."

"How can you be hungry again?"

"I ran twelve miles."

I grabbed his hand and dragged him away from the line. "I can't believe I'm the one who wants to check out this apartment."

"You're not. I'm saying we could make a pit stop."

Chuck and I bickered all the way back to the metro, on the metro, and right into the lovely Marais. It was going to be a long day.

# CHAPTER ELEVEN

Lucky for Chuck, the Marais stopped me from clobbering him. Once we'd gotten a few blocks in, the music started. Quartets played everything from jazz to Beethoven. Chuck couldn't stop smiling. We stopped in front of the Carnavalet museum and watched a string quartet play "Dream a Little Dream of Me." A little old lady danced beside the bass player, a little soft shoe. She wore a flapper-type outfit in emerald green satin with a cloche hat pulled down tight over her silver curls.

Chuck leaned over to me. "Is she crazy? They seem like they know her."

"She's part of the performance." I put my arm around his waist and folded myself into him. He was so entranced by the performers that he didn't pull away or make an excuse. I breathed in his scent and wished it could last forever. It didn't, of course. Nothing perfect ever does. The quartet finished their set and the violinist introduced each member of the group, including the lady, who opened a velvet-tasseled bag for donations.

"How much should we give?" Chuck whispered in my ear, his warm coffee-scented breath tickling my cheek under the brim of my hat. I smiled up at him, afraid to break the spell.

"What?" he asked.

"Nothing," I said, finally. "You just looked so happy."

"I'm always happy when I'm with you."

I didn't contradict him although I was aching to find out why that wasn't true. Instead, I gave him five euros and he dropped them in her bag, receiving a cheerful "Merci" in response.

"When do you think they'll play again?" asked Chuck.

"He said a half-hour, but there's no shortage of musicians in the Marais," I said.

"Is it always like this?"

I scanned the crowded street. It was summer, but the crowds did seem bigger than I remembered. "Kind of. We usually come in the shoulder season, so I'm not sure."

"I want to see them again," said Chuck. "Let's get to that apartment."

He yanked on my hand as I dug in my heels. "There's a tea shop. Maybe a cup before we go to the apartment."

"Are you crazy? Let's go."

"I was thinking maybe an ice cream. I think Amorino might be open," I said.

"What the...are you trying to piss me off?" Chuck asked, frowning.

I couldn't suppress a grin. "What? You don't want a snack to carry you through the next ten minutes?"

He dragged me down the street, laughing. "You are a pain in my ass."

"You love it."

He swung me around the corner and I ended up in his arms on a cobblestoned street, surrounded by flowers with music in the air. Paris at its most romantic.

"I do love it," he said.

I gazed up at him, so handsome yet flawed in just the right way. I pursed my lips, waiting for the kiss that had to happen. Every romance novel ever written demanded it.

"Let's go find that apartment." Chuck spun me back out again and dragged me down the street, taking his long strides so that I had to jog to keep up.

"Slow down!" I panted.

"We're almost there."

"I'm almost passing out."

Chuck waited for a car to pass before charging across the street to a building that tourists dreamed of living in. It sat on the corner with a turret rising to a black-tiled dome high above the street. The creamy stone set off the black iron balconies, dripping with red blossoms. The entrance was in the turret, a pair of over-sized golden oak doors with vintage, wavy glass and a keyhole the size of my thumb.

"Did you expect this?" asked Chuck.

"I didn't think about it." I stared at the numbers on the small brass panel. No names. It wasn't that kind of building. These people didn't want to be known.

Chuck held out a finger. "Here goes nothing?" He pushed 3A and we waited.

Nothing.

Another push and then another. Chuck's finger went to hover over another button.

I pulled down his arm. "Wait. What's your plan?" I asked.

"Plan? I thought you didn't believe in plans," he said with a smirk.

"This is different," I said.

"Oh, yeah, Why?"

I let go of his hand and crossed my arms. "Because they're not home. If you get in there, what are you going to do? Pick the lock?"

Chuck went all bright-eyed. "Did you bring your picks?"

I did bring them in case I found Angela Riley and had to get in her apartment. "Yes," I said, slowly. "You aren't really going to break in, are you? You're a cop. Don't they frown on that kind of thing?"

He nodded. "You're right. You break in."

"Are you kidding?"

"You brought it up."

"It was a question, not a suggestion," I said.

Chuck jiggled the door handle. "Too late. Do you think we can push buttons until someone lets us in?"

"And say what? This isn't New York. They don't have pizza delivery."

He cupped his hands and looked through the etched glass. "You know Paris. Think of something."

"I know Paris, but I've never committed a crime here."

A man wearing heavy black glasses and a grandpa sweater that accentuated his paunch strolled by. The hipster movement was alive and well in Paris, much to my dismay. The man smoothed his scraggly beard and gave me a scathing look as if he knew what we were up to. Maybe he did. We obviously couldn't get in and I had to admit that we didn't exactly fit the building.

I gave a winning smile when the man glanced back at me as he crossed the street. Then I poked Chuck. "Stop looking like you're casing the joint."

"There's no doorman. If we get through this door, we're all good," he said. "How do you get into a fancy apartment in Paris that you have no business being in?"

I got out my regular phone, careful to keep my Fibonacci phone under a bunch of crumpled tissue. "I have an idea."

"Oh yeah?"

I held up my phone. "Apartment 2C is a vacation rental and it's unoccupied."

"This place is pretty sweet. I wonder why."

"It costs 6,500 euros a week."

"Holy shit. They're proud of their apartment."

I called the agent handling the rental and spun a yarn about how we hated the apartment we'd rented and we wanted to get a look at 2C before we committed. Monsieur Rey would be right over.

He showed up ten minutes later, typed in a code on the brass keypad, and the door made a tiny delicate click. We were in. That was the upside. The downside was that we had to take a tour of 2C and seem like we could possibly rent an apartment for 6,500 euros a week.

I could lie with the best of them but acting was another skill and Chuck had it. He praised the building, the street and Monsieur Rey's suit, saying that we were on our honeymoon and our parents wanted us to have the time of our lives. By the time we arrived at the door of 2C, Monsieur Rey believed I was the daughter of a soap opera actress and he was the son of a retired baseball player, who'd invented a special kind of athletic cup. I winced at the cup reference, but Monsieur Rey didn't blink. Maybe it was so weird that it seemed real. Who would say their father invented a something special for protecting testicles, if it wasn't true? Oh, that's right. My boyfriend.

Monsieur Rey opened the rosewood door carved with lilies and we were wowed. If I had 6,500 to spend on a rental, I would've totally spent it there. The apartment was a Belle Époque gem with its original flooring, woodwork, and ceilings. The furniture was modern but fit perfectly. There were four bedrooms and five baths and Monsieur Rey claimed there were three water heaters so we would never have a cold shower. Oh, to dream.

We spent a half-hour in the perfect Parisian apartment with Chuck taking pictures every five seconds to show our parents and then he gave Monsieur Rey his number and we left to skulk around the corner until the realtor left. I don't think I said more than three words the entire time. I'd tried to slip away several times to go up to the third floor, but Monsieur Rey was too attentive. If I could get away, I could let Chuck in later and we, or shall I say *I*, could break into 3A, but he didn't even try to distract the realtor, so the whole thing was pointless.

I poked Chuck in the side after Monsieur Rey crossed the street and was out of range. "That's fabulous."

"I know. Genius," said Chuck with a wicked grin.

"Genius? Are you cracked? That was a huge waste of time. We're no closer to getting into that apartment than we were an hour ago."

Chuck peeked around the corner and then dragged me back to the building's front door. "Aren't we?"

"We aren't," I said.

"I can't believe how little faith you have in me or...maybe you're just short."

"Huh?"

Chuck punched in a code and the door made a little click. "How do the French say it? Voila?"

"How'd you do that? Rey stood in front of the pad when he did the code," I said.

"Monsieur Rey is about five foot seven," said Chuck, opening the door. "I could see it over his shoulder."

I elbowed him as I went through. "I heard you were good at this."

"Did you ever doubt it?"

"Maybe a little."

We rode up the tiny elevator, nose-to-chest, and found that 3A had an identical door to 2C with one glaring exception. It was padlocked and had large screws driven into the lovely wood to attach the ugly steel latch.

"This is weird, even for France, right?" asked Chuck.

"Definitely. We can't pick that."

"We could take a bolt cutter to it."

I wrinkled my nose at him. "Yeah, that won't be obvious at all." I jiggled the ornate brass knob. "It's locked, too."

"Someone wants to be very sure," said Chuck.

I swiped my finger across the top of the padlock and came up with a light layer of dust. "No one's been in for a while."

Chuck rubbed his hands together. "Time to canvass the building."

"I guess so, but not many people are home. We've yet to see a single resident."

"Maybe they're all writers like Morty and never go out."

"I'm sure that's it."

My phone rang and it was Aaron, texting that my dreaded pastry class started in forty-five minutes.

"I've got to get to class. Maybe we can do it tomorrow," I said.

"No," said Chuck. "You go to class. I'll canvass."

"You don't speak any French."

He waggled his eyebrows. "I speak other things fluently."

*Well...you used to.*

"What if they're all men?" I asked.

"I'll wing it the way you taught me." Chuck kissed me on the forehead and shooed me down the hallway. I heard him pounding on his first door as the elevator closed. He wasn't intimidated by the French and that was more than I could say for most people. If anyone had a shot, it was him, but if he got into that apartment without me because I had to make stupid pastry, I would scream.

I stumbled out of Atelier Guy Marin three hours later, covered in flour and sugar. My arms ached from beating the choux dough and whipping cream by hand. By hand! They had mixers—lots of mixers, the freaks. I'd been lectured on proper method—something about wrist movement—and belief in one's pastry. Oh, I believed in pastry. I believed I'd never willingly go back and make it.

"Put on your hat," said Aaron as he turned me around toward the metro stop.

"Now I can put on my hat. Thanks a lot." I jammed my floppy hat on my head.

Chef Jacqueline, the pastry Nazi, said no hats in the kitchen and, of course, I couldn't wear a chef's hat because, as she helpfully pointed out, I wasn't a chef. I had to remove my hat and reveal my bizarre Buckwheat hair to the world. You may say that it wasn't the world, it was just an exclusive pastry class. No. It was the world. Everyone had cellphones and they all had to take pictures of me and post them to their Twitter accounts, their blogs, and websites. Did everybody have to have a website? Chef Jacqueline was very helpful when she used my full name every time she spoke to me. Every time. In case someone missed it. It was the pastry class from hell. My choux sucked. My raspberry gastrique congealed for no good reason and my custard broke all four times I made it. Now I was being demoted to beginning pastry. I looked like an idiot and I turned out to be one.

To improve the situation, I got five irate texts from Mickey Stix asking why the hell I looked like a demented pastry chef instead of a sexual fantasy. I wasn't their cover girl to make men cringe. Now I was trending on Twitter and not in a good way. I had no answer, so I didn't reply.

"You shouldn't take that off," said Aaron.

"You think?" I marched down the steps into the metro and a huge gust of wind came up from the tracks, sweeping my hat off my head. It disappeared over a mob of people coming down the stairs. They carried Aaron and me with them to the platform. People were giving me sidelong looks and I crossed my arms. If anyone pulled out a phone, I would harm them. My regular phone was ringing like crazy. I ignored it. If Mickey wanted to yell, he could do it through texts.

We got back to the apartment and I collapsed on the bed.

"You hungry?" asked Aaron.

"This is the worst vacation ever."

"Chocolate?"

I buried my head under my pillow. "I'm going to sleep. When I wake up, that class will not have happened. Got it?"

"Huh?"

"Sleeping, Aaron."

He finally left after three more attempts to get me to go out to find food. I wasn't fooled. He wanted to go to that vintage linen shop. All the restaurants he mentioned just happened to be on that street and it was way too late for lunch.

I fell asleep, only to be jolted awake after what felt like five minutes. "It is not!" I opened my eyes to see Chuck staring at me from the end of my bed and, for some reason, my arms were in the air. I dropped them and tried to pretend that didn't happen.

"I think you were dreaming."

*Oh no! Oh no!*

"Did I say anything?" I asked.

*Please say no.*

"You said, 'My god damn cream is whipped.' I guess you didn't like the class."

"It was a freaking nightmare and I couldn't wear my hat."

He sat on the edge of my bed. "I heard."

"From who?" I said slowly.

"Pretty much everybody I know. You're trending, hot stuff."

I flipped over and buried my head. "Go away. You can't be seen with me. I'm a Halloween mask waiting to happen."

"That would be hilarious," he said, rubbing my foot. He probably didn't want to get too close to my hideous head.

"No, it wouldn't!"

"Okay. Funny to me," he said. "Get up. We've got a reservation."

I sat bolt upright. "Are you kidding?" I pointed to my head. "My hat is gone. Gone, I tell you."

"If you wash it, it'll go back, right?"

"In theory." I didn't bring up my scuba hair in Honduras. It took a month before my hair calmed down. My hair wasn't like other hair. It had feelings and I think I insulted it.

"Take a shower then. You smell like butter. On second thought, I like butter, all oily and slippery."

For a second, he seemed like Chuck. I moved in, all ready for him to start kissing me all over, but the second I did, his face changed and he leaned back.

"There's plenty of hot water," he said. "You can soothe the savage hair. I booked a dinner cruise at eight."

"I'm not going if this keeps happening," I said, pointing to my head.

"Deal."

I went into the bathroom and left the door cracked just in case Chuck decided to join me. Fat chance. I got into a boiling hot shower and lathered up my frizzy mop. "Did you get in the apartment?"

"What apartment?"

"Chuck Watts, I'm not in the mood."

He laughed and said, "No. There were only three residents at home."

"Men?" I asked.

"Yeah. My bad luck and they were ancient. They couldn't have heard me even if I could speak French."

I rinsed out the suds. So far so good. "We can try again."

"Absolutely. But first we'll go to dinner," said Chuck.

I finished up and came out wrapped in a towel. "How does it look? I was afraid to try the mirror."

"Normal for wet hair, I think."

"Thank goodness."

"You want another hat?"

"I'll have to. Where's Aaron?"

Chuck headed for the door, leaving so he wouldn't see me naked. Gasp. What a nightmare that would be. "He's going out with cooking cronies."

"Where's he going?" I wanted to get a plan together on the whole Angela thing.

"I don't know. Aaron's a big boy."

I raised an eyebrow.

Chuck grinned. "Metaphorically speaking. He'll be fine. He lived here for years."

"I can't tell you how weird that is. Aaron doesn't look like a world traveler."

"Looks aren't everything."

"Clearly. Can we talk about what's going on with us?"

"No. We can get ready. We have to be on the boat at eight sharp. Get ready."

I sighed. This was going nowhere fast.

*Patience, Mercy, patience.*

## CHAPTER TWELVE

The boat slid through the Seine silently, heading for the brightly lit dock next to the Pont de Arts. I leaned against Chuck's shoulder and gazed out at the twinkling lights of the Louvre.

"Did you like it?" he asked.

"It was perfect." Perfect wasn't an exaggeration, even with my frizzy hair stuffed under a cheap, rather misshapen fedora I bought off a street vendor. Chuck had chosen one of the oldest boats still afloat on the river, an Art Nouveau masterpiece of brass and polished teak with portraits of nubile women intertwined with lush foliage. We sat on original love seats angled to see out of the wide glass windows. None of the cheaper touristy boats done in glass and shiny white for us and I felt warm and grateful for it. This was the way The Girls saw Paris. They ignored the commercial places and saw only what had been and would always be.

The captain announced that we'd docked and wished us a pleasant evening. We wove through the love seats and elegant booths to the gangplank and trotted down the creaking wood path to land on solid, gravely ground.

"Should we go home?" asked Chuck. "I don't know what people do in Paris after dark."

I laughed. "Neither do I."

"You've been here a dozen times."

"With elderly ladies. Sometimes we went to the Louvre when it was open late, but that's about it." I was playing it cool, but I knew exactly where I wanted to go. Chuck couldn't figure it out or I was up a creek. "You know, I heard about a lovely bar where we could get a drink, maybe see a little Parisian nightlife."

"Was it in the guidebooks?" Chuck and those guidebooks. If it wasn't in a book, it didn't exist.

"No...Ellen's mom went there. She said it was nice and very Parisian."

"Which way?'

I led him up stone stairs that were suspiciously sticky and smelled of urine to the Pont des Arts. We passed the thousands of love locks fixed to the bridge, walking over toward the Louvre and possibly Angela Riley in the form of Sabine Suede.

"God, it's beautiful at night. Totally different. There are so many people out and it's a weeknight."

"That's Paris for you. Always something happening." I tugged on his arm when we passed the Louvre and went down a little side street. I'd memorized the directions to Grand Bleu, Sabine Suede's hangout, but that meant nothing when it came to me. I could get lost anywhere and frequently did.

That time was no different. We ended up in an alley next to a bunch of trashcans that smelled like three-week-old shrimp.

"Let's have a seat," said Chuck with a wide grin. "That smell rocks. I can feel it seeping into my skin. It's my first souvenir."

"Shut up," I said, looking at the map on my phone. It wasn't helping.

Chuck took the phone. "Okay. Left at the light. Then right, right, left, right, and a left. Got it?"

"What do you think?"

We made it to Grand Bleu fifteen minutes later. The hotel was upscale—not Bled family upscale, but it was pricey. The bar looked like it could've been used as a set for *Midnight in Paris*, very Art Deco with lots of geometric shapes and polished walnut paneling. I missed the Art Nouveau ladies of the boat and their sensual take on nature.

"This is more like it," said Chuck, taking a look at a pair of women at the bar, chatting up the bartender. The place had more customers than I expected. They were mainly businessmen, looking for a good time. From the looks of it, they'd find it easily, but Chuck didn't have to know that. We'd stay for an hour or so. I'd look for Sabine Suede, maybe ask the waitress or bartender to point out Sabine Suede if I could manage it, and we'd go.

Chuck ordered us martinis because it seemed like a martini kind of place and I chose a table at the back with a view of all the action. And there was plenty of action. I'd never seen so many hot girls in one room since I'd been backstage at one of the DBD concerts. Even though the guys were members of AARP, they could still lure the young ones in.

The waitress brought our drinks and I sipped my martini, making a face. Too strong. I needed to keep my wits about me with the steady parade of women coming through the bar. The bartender caught my eye and I saw instantly that he thought I was one of their ilk, using the Marilyn fantasy to get customers. I gave him a slight shake no and he frowned.

Chuck scuttled to the edge of his seat. "Mercy, it's time to go."

"Huh?" I was scanning the room.

"We need to go now."

I pulled my hand out of his. "Why? We just got here." I couldn't leave. Sabine hadn't shown up yet.

"This isn't a place I'd bring you. Let's go," he said.

*Oh no! I should've known the cop would figure it out.*

"What are you talking about? It's nice and the drinks are good."

"The drinks are strong for a reason."

"And what reason is that?" I asked, still scanning.

He pulled me closer. "These women are hookers."

"No," I gasped. "How can you tell?"

"When's the last time you saw a guy like that"—he pointed to a balding man in his sixties with a serious paunch—"attracting not one, but two twenty-five-year-olds?"

"Maybe he's famous," I said.

Chuck pulled me out of my chair. "He's not famous. He's a John." He tossed some euros on the table and tried to push me to the door.

"I have to pee."

*Smooth, Mercy.*

"Sorry. I...um...need to go to the ladies'. Be right back." I dashed toward the hallway to the hotel before Chuck could protest. There was a sign for the bathroom pointing down another hall. I had no plan, as usual, and hoped something would come to me.

Something, or rather someone, did. One of the women came out of the bathroom, pulled on her extremely short skirt and plumped up her breasts so that they threatened to pop out at any second. She didn't strike me as French with her almond eyes and darker skin.

I pulled fifty euros out of my purse, waved it at her, and pointed to the bathroom. She sized me up, shrugged, and followed me in.

"Do you speak English?"

She looked me over and leaned languidly on the bathroom stall. "Yes." She had an Eastern European accent and looked about seventeen, if you bothered to look past the heavy makeup. "You like?"

*No in so many ways.*

"I'm in the market for some information, not...that," I said.

"Information? You like watch?"

*Ew.*

"No, no. I want to ask you some questions. I'll pay if you give the right answers."

"What is right answer?"

I got out my Fibonacci phone and showed her Angela Riley's picture. "Have you ever seen this woman?"

She shook her head. "No. Who is woman?"

"I'm just looking for her."

The girl pouted. "I prettier than her."

"That doesn't really matter. This woman is missing. Do you know someone called Sabine Suede?"

She puzzled over the question. "I hear name. Not know her. How much you pay?"

How much did I have? Two hundred. That would work for words. Her other services were probably much pricier than that. I waved the fifty euro. "Can you get ahold of Sabine Suede?"

"No. I not here long." She pouted again. I assumed she did this with men and it worked. I couldn't imagine why. It was seriously odd.

"Do you know anyone who could get ahold of Sabine?" I asked.

"I can do."

"Now?" I waved the fifty.

She called someone called Cashmere and held out her hand. "She at bar."

I gave her the fifty and Cashmere came in a few minutes later. Cashmere was probably at the end of her career, at least thirty-five but probably older. She was much more wary than the other girl and eyed me coldly, then adjusted her sequined dress over her implants. They were so large they put me to shame and I wasn't a small girl by any stretch. The nurse in me wanted to ask her if they were painful, but I caught myself. I was there to cross Sabine off my list. Nothing else.

"Do you speak English?" I asked.

"Yes. How much?" she asked.

I crossed my arms. "It depends on what you have to say."

She calculated my worth. Since her outfit obviously cost more than mine, it wasn't much. "How much do you have?"

"Look. I don't have a lot of time. Do you know Sabine Suede or not?"

"Is she in trouble?"

"Not from me. I only want to figure out if she's the woman I'm trying to find," I said.

"What woman?" she asked.

I held out my phone. Cashmere gave Angela's picture a careful look, but she gave nothing away. "One hundred euros."

"Do you have a picture of Sabine?" I asked.

She nodded and I gave her a hundred euros. It was painful, but I could tell Cashmere wasn't any pushover. Plus, I didn't have time to argue. I expected Chuck to pound on the door any second.

"Let's have it," I said.

She showed me several pictures of a woman with Angela's dark curly hair and a jagged scar from her mouth to her ear.

"From her customer last year?" I asked, indicating the scar.

Cashmere was caught off guard and nodded before she thought about it. I showed her Angela's picture. "Have you ever seen this woman?"

"No. Who is she?"

"The one I'm looking for," I said. "Thanks."

I went for the door, but Cashmere grabbed my arm. "I can do anything she can."

"I have no doubt." I opened the door right into Chuck, who was in the hall and had a sheen of sweat on his brow.

"Are you okay?" He hustled me out of the building.

"I'm fine. I'm not so sure about you," I said. "What's wrong?"

We turned right and Chuck's stride lengthened so that I was jogging.

"Nothing's wrong. What happened in there?"

I dug my heels in and he dragged me three feet before stopping. "Nothing happened. It was a bathroom. I went to the bathroom. What is up with you?"

"I don't want anything to happen to you." He hugged every ounce of breath out of me. I struggled in his arms and ended up having to pinch him to get free.

"Sorry. Sorry," he said, his voice husky.

I kissed his cheek. "Nothing's going to happen."

"Things have happened before and I wasn't there."

"You can't always be there."

"You wanna bet?" He laughed, but I think he meant it.

"Yes. Let's bet. Ten bucks says you can't be with me every second."

He hugged the breath out of me again. "You know what I mean."

"I do, but it's pointless to try."

We walked home hand in hand. Chuck wouldn't say anything else about the bathroom incident and I forced myself not to push. Not an easy thing given my lineage. I wondered what Mom would've done in my place. The right thing, undoubtedly. Whatever that was.

My thoughts strayed to Angela Riley. I was getting closer. If she really was in Paris, could she feel me closing in or would I come as a surprise? I supposed it didn't matter. I was coming. I'd had a taste of success and I wouldn't give up and Calpurnia expected nothing less. Six days left in Paris. Sabine was off my list and it was on to the Orsay. Time to call in a favor.

## CHAPTER THIRTEEN

The favor was easy to obtain, even at midnight. I called Myrtle and Millicent's connection at the Orsay, Monsieur Dombey. I knew from what The Girls said that Monsieur Dombey would just be getting home from dinner and drinks. He was wide awake and remembered me from our previous visits. I asked to be allowed into the museum before opening and he said he'd be honored to accommodate a Bled. That's what he called me, a Bled. I didn't correct him and I felt a little bad about that. I wasn't a Bled and I didn't usually let that mistake stand. I did need to get into the Orsay early to position myself for my next target, so I let it go with a silent apology for my impersonation.

Chuck and I walked up the wide stones to the Musée d'Orsay entrance with Aaron lagging behind, muttering about duck fat. He'd gotten up at five to roast a Brest chicken and potatoes in duck fat. The results weren't to his liking, but I had no clue why. Tasted great to me, although I think I could hear my arteries hardening as we walked. He was so fussy, I thought we were going to be late and that would be a faux pas, to say the least. Monsieur Dombey was never ever late and he wasn't that morning. We cleared the last step and found him standing beside the queueing maze outside the Orsay's main entrance. Monsieur Dombey spotted us and clapped his hands before hurrying over.

"He's young," said Chuck with astonishment.

"What were you expecting?" I asked.

"Well...I guess Mr. Burns from *The Simpsons.*"

"Why in the world—"

Monsieur Dombey held out his big hands to me. "Mademoiselle Watts, it is my pleasure to see you."

We gave each other cheek kisses like old friends, which I guess we were. I met Serge Dombey years ago when I was thirteen and he was twenty-one, fresh out of the Sorbonne and adorably terrified at being ordered to accompany Bleds around the museum. The Girls made it easy on him with their charming ways and genuine love of art. I had a huge crush on Serge. He wasn't like any other Frenchman I'd met, big and bulky with the hands of a farmhand, not a painter, which was what he was in his off-duty time.

"Please," I said. "Call me Mercy."

"And you must call me Serge."

It took us five minutes to go through the dance of politeness that was required given our respective positions. When we agreed that it was acceptable to call each other by our first names, I introduced Chuck and Aaron. They would be called by their formal titles. No way around it. They hadn't known Serge for ten years.

"Right this way," said Serge with an arm sweep toward the reserved entrance.

"Where is everyone?" asked Chuck.

"I told you we're getting a special tour because of The Girls," I said as we went through the doors and past ticketing.

"This is pretty special."

*Pretty special* didn't cover it. The Girls were VIPs. The Bleds had a relationship with the Orsay since its inception. They'd been huge supporters of the idea of turning the train station into a museum and donated generously. The Orsay was the only museum in the world that they loaned pieces to and it was all because of Elias Bled. Few outside the family knew about him. Elias was that kind of secret.

The Bleds, while being geniuses at business and brewing, also had a streak of insanity running through the family. Elias had been one of those. Born in the mid-1800s, he fancied himself a painter. No one knew how he got that idea, since he couldn't draw a stick. The family tried to convince him that he was better at business, but he knew better. He moved to Paris and bought an apartment on the Île Saint-Louis. There, he created terrible paintings and even worse sculptures, but he became friends with the soon to be great artists of the day, Pissarro, Monet, and many more. Elias had no end of money and he supported many of the artists by commissioning works. All the work he'd purchased was found in his apartment after he'd been missing for a couple of weeks. Elias's close friend, the artist Jean-François Raffaëlli, telegrammed the family saying he couldn't find Elias. There was something about a woman, possibly a prostitute, that Elias had fallen in love with. Whoever this woman was, she ran off and Elias was distraught. Several friends saw him on the Pont Marie near his apartment, gazing into the water. Elias's brother, Constantine Bled, was dispatched to Paris to find Elias, but he never turned up. The art community supported the family and the search and the Bleds always felt a special connection to the art and artists of the period.

The Orsay never tried to dictate to the Bleds. Other museums did, trying to say that they must do this or that for the good of the public. The Orsay knew how to handle the rich and eccentric better than anyone else in the art world and they were rewarded for it. The Bleds didn't even want credit for what they did for the museum. The works they loaned weren't attributed to them, neither was the influx of cash that came every so often. The Orsay loved the Bleds and consequentially me.

"Can I get you anything before we start?" asked Serge, ready to make us coffee with his own hands, if necessary.

"I think we're fine," I said. "Thank you."

"Would you like to begin at the beginning?"

Chuck grinned. "Is there a better place?"

"Not in my opinion. Shall we?" Serge led us into the main gallery. The glass arched ceiling made everything feel light and airy. The grand hall's creamy stone set off the sculptures, making them seem small until you were standing next to them.

"Nice," said Chuck, his head swiveling like crazy.

"We'll start with early Romanticism and go through all the periods," said Serge. Chuck got a little stony-faced at the idea of multiple periods, but Serge knew his business. He said just the right amount for me, someone who'd seen it all before, and for Chuck, whose interest in art was in its infancy. We saw Monet, Gauguin, and Toulouse-Lautrec. Chuck blushed at *The Origin of the World.* Aaron didn't blush or appear to think anything was remotely interesting about the work that shocked pretty much everybody who saw it for the first time. He stood in front of that famous crotch and asked, "You hungry?"

Serge raised an eyebrow and I gave him a little eye roll. Aaron was weird. He might as well know it. I glanced at my watch and at the museum staff starting to arrive. We had an hour left before opening and Corrine Sweet, my next possibility, would be in the bookshop.

"Not yet," I said. "Let's finish the tour."

We worked our way through the rest and I could see Chuck starting to sag. Art did wear people out, even with an excellent guide like Serge. The clock on the top re-energized him. There's nothing like that clock to make a person feel separate from Paris yet a part of something special at the same time. The face was clear with black Roman numerals and hands. Chuck and I posed for a picture, careful not to obscure Sacré-Coeur in the distance, its white domes gleaming in the morning sun.

We toured the main Impressionists gallery and I fell in love with the faces once again. Renoir's veil over Mme. Paul Darras's face entranced me as always. How did he do that? The faces didn't do it for Chuck. He bypassed the sunny scenes of luscious ladies topless in fields and went right to the winter scenes of the sea or icy villages encased in thick snow.

"You like Sisley?" I asked.

"Who?"

"Alfred Sisley, the artist."

He stared at a figure walking down a lane between two snow-covered walls to what looked like a dead end. "It's very..."

"Lonely," I suggested, taking his hand.

"You think so?" he asked.

"I prefer the sun."

He kissed my forehead and chuckled. "Of course you do."

Serge had been allowing us to explore on our own, interjecting tidbits now and again. He always did have perfect timing. "Several of the artists enjoyed the winter. Monet was often observed, half-frozen, studying the constantly changing appearance of snow. Perhaps you will like *The Magpie* as well."

Chuck did like *The Magpie* and every other chilly work he showed him. I strayed to the faces of people long dead and wondered about them. Did they know or have the smallest hint that a great artist had captured them for all time and they would someday be seen by millions and admired? I supposed a woman sipping absinthe in a café couldn't possibly know what Degas would do with her ordinary face. Still, I wondered.

We finished the Impressionists and headed to the room installations of Art Nouveau furniture and Aaron said, "You hungry?"

"Yes," I said. "And I think we've seen it all."

"Indeed you have," said Serge. "Would you like to repeat any galleries?"

Chuck grinned. "I think I'm good."

"You said you wanted to see everything," I said.

"I didn't know how much everything was."

Serge guided us back into the gallery and asked, "Have you been to the Louvre yet?"

"Not yet," said Chuck.

"Best to go on the late night. The crowds will overwhelm on the first visit."

"When's that?"

"Wednesday and Friday. The summer is crowded as one would expect," said Serge.

Serge led us to the first floor restaurant and sat us at a table on whimsical, colorful plastic chairs that didn't go at all with the baroque interior of gold-painted woodwork and chandeliers. He hurried off to find a member of the staff since the restaurant wouldn't actually open until 11:45.

"They don't do anything small here, do they?" asked Chuck, looking at the twenty-foot windows.

"Clearly, you haven't been to any of the café bathrooms yet."

"I'm blessed with a big bladder."

"Showoff."

"Always." He took my hand and kissed it. "When was the last time you were here?"

I kissed his hand in return. "In the fall after Honduras."

"I thought you went to Venice."

"We did."

He shook his head. "Being a Bled is a whole other world."

"I'm not a Bled," I said.

"We're in a restaurant that doesn't open for another three hours and getting the grand tour. You're a Bled. Face it, baby."

"It's more like two hours," I said as the manager hustled over and asked what we'd like. He looked nervous, for some reason, and Chuck gave me a look. We ordered café crème and éclairs. I was afraid Aaron would turn up his nose at museum pastry, but he was good, eating in silence. Serge came back and sipped an espresso. He wanted something, but he was having a hard time asking for it.

"I can't stand it, Serge," I said after listening to him beat around the bush for five minutes. The museum had opened and he glanced repeatedly at the growing din through the doors to the main gallery.

"You know the director does not like to ask anything of your family," he said after a protracted hesitation.

Chuck cocked an eyebrow at me and I gave him a gentle kick. The big snot.

"I know, Serge. What is it?"

"You must understand this is my idea alone and I am responsible for this query."

"Now I'm intrigued."

He finished his espresso and it gave him caffeinated courage. "I have been recently made aware that there are certain pieces in The Bled Collection that the museum and, indeed, the world have never seen."

I dabbed a bit of chocolate icing off my lip instead of licking it off.

The Girls would be so pleased. "What pieces?" I feared he would say something about the Holocaust pieces that Stella had smuggled out. There were several works the museum would love to get ahold of, but there was nothing I could do for Serge when it came to them. The Girls didn't consider the pieces to be theirs. They were only caretakers until their owners claimed them.

He cleared his throat. "Early sketches of several master works, possibly some Degas, Monet and others."

"Huh?"

A breath whooshed out of Serge. "You aren't aware of these pieces?"

"Well...no. They have sketches, but I can't remember any by Degas or the Impressionists." I thought Serge would cry, he looked so disappointed.

"My information must be incorrect. I was hoping to mount an exhibit focusing on the artist's planning stages."

"Where did you hear that the Bleds had them?" I asked.

Serge pulled a slim sheath of paper out of his breast pocket. "These are copies of letters between Paul Durand-Ruel to Alice, Monet's second wife. He wanted to buy some early sketches and Alice says that Elias Bled had bought them when Monet wasn't selling."

"Oh, that's a different story," I said. "Elias's collection is separate from the Bled Collection. I don't know what it includes."

"Then there's hope." Serge gave me the sheath and I opened them to squint at the letters written in French. I could read it to some extent, but I wasn't seeing any titles.

"Which ones did Elias buy?" I asked.

"That is unclear. I believe they were from the period of Monet's first marriage to Camille."

I glanced at the visitors outside the door of the restaurant, scanning the menu before eyeing us, sipping our coffee well before opening. The book shop would be open for business but not too crowded. I could hopefully get a good look at Corrine Sweet. "Serge, I don't know exactly what's in the Elias Collection, but I can find out."

"Thank you, Miss Watts. Such an exhibition would be a triumph for the museum."

I smiled. "Especially if the sketches have never been seen before."

"Indeed."

"And a big deal for you," said Chuck, giving Serge a critical look, but Serge was unfazed.

"This would help my career. Yes."

The men eyed each other. If I didn't know better, I'd say Chuck was jealous, but I couldn't imagine why. Serge and I had zero chemistry. Any fool could see that. He was gay, for crying out loud. Maybe I should've mentioned that to Chuck, although it hardly seemed relevant to a museum tour.

"So...maybe we could have dinner together while we're here and discuss the Elias Collection," I said.

Chuck scowled down into his cup and Serge's smooth brow furrowed. Then he darted a look at me and I shrugged one shoulder. A little light went on in Serge's eyes, and being ever so helpful, he said, "Oh, yes. I would enjoy that immensely and so would Roman."

"Roman?" asked Chuck.

"My partner. He discovered a new bistro in the seventeenth that I would like to try."

Chuck straightened up and was all smiles. "That'd be great. What night would be good for you two?"

"Perhaps Saturday or—"

I cut Serge off. "Okay. You guys work it out and I'm going to hit the ladies' room."

They barely glanced at me as they bonded over the bistro that cooked their chicken by hanging them from strings in front of a fireplace. They thought it was cool. It sounded like a mess to me.

I excused myself and went out into the crowded corridor. It'd been forever since I'd been to Paris in the high season. I'd forgotten how many tourists there could be. I wove between strollers, walkers and people who were too busy looking at the view to watch where they were going and headed for the stairs. That was the one place nobody else was. The elevators had a line though.

The book shop sat in a corner on the ground floor and had about six times the people in it than I expected. What the heck, people? You buy stuff first before actually looking at the art? Seriously? I squeezed through the door between two Austrians with their babies in backpacks and worked my way around the tables stacked with art books and biographies. Two employees assisted customers, recommending different titles. Either could've been Corrine Sweet, except that they both had light French accents. Where was she? I didn't have much time. Chuck was going to think I was up to something and I couldn't afford that. I leafed through a history of Impressionism, casually glancing around and checking my phone for the time. Going on twelve minutes. Not good. Come on, Corrine. We need you. Five Asian ladies, laden with enormous purses, came in, each with a look of needing assistance and taking up half the space.

A third male employee came out of a nondescript door with a stack of Pissarro bios and put them on an already over-burdened table. I squeezed between the Austrians toward the door. Corinne could be back there. I wasn't quite sure if I had the nerve to open the door. Explaining that wouldn't be easy without claiming to be an idiot and I hated to do that as a general rule. I looked like an idiot often enough without doing it on purpose.

Still, the shop was getting more crowded and no one else came out to help. I had to give up or come back with Chuck, which wasn't ideal. I had every faith that the detective in him would pick up my intentions. Obviously, I didn't need any art books. The Girls had cornered the market and I had a bookshelf full of them. He wouldn't buy it. Never. No way. I had to try the door and plead ignorance.

I reached the door and went for the knob when a voice said, "Mercy?" My hand snapped back so fast that I punched myself in the stomach before I turned around with a fixed look of innocence on my face. Chuck wouldn't buy it. I was so screwed.

Serge frowned at me between two of the Asian ladies. I glanced around frantically, looking for Chuck. He wasn't there and I blew out a breath as Serge came over. "I thought you were going to the toilette."

"I was," I said. "I got...distracted."

Serge only watched me.

"What?"

"You got distracted from the need to go to the toilette?"

"Er...well...you know, books. I like books."

Serge blew a raspberry at me but with only one cheek. Very French and very 'I don't believe a word that you're saying to me.' Great.

"Really," I said. "You've got some great stuff in here."

"Do you approve of our remodel?" he asked, all ready to raspberry me again.

"Er...sure," I said.

Serge took my arm and led me into a corner behind the Austrians. "What are you doing here in Paris?"

"I'm showing Chuck the city."

He blew his raspberry again.

"Really. What else would I be doing here?" I asked.

"Your godmothers called me three days ago."

I stopped breathing. Crap. Double crap. "What for?"

"To ask me to assist you if you were to call," said Serge.

"You are assisting me. Let's go back to the restaurant. I sure could use another café."

Serge didn't move. "I will assist you with whatever you are really doing in Paris."

"What did The Girls say exactly?" I asked.

"Only that this trip was unexpected and something that you could ill-afford. They did not say that you were up to something, but that is what they think. What are you doing here?"

I grabbed Serge's arm and looked through the glass walls that separated the shop from the museum. "Where's Chuck?"

"In the restaurant. I told him I'd find you and that"—he made a little telling cough—"the ladies' rooms are hard to find, so it would be easier for me than him."

"Thank goodness."

Serge's eyes roved over the tables. "Do you need a present for Chuck? Perhaps I could help."

"You can help, but it's not a present that I want. Can we keep this between just us? You can't even tell my godmothers." I tilted my chin down and batted my eyes. I couldn't resist. I always wanted to try that on Serge back in the days when I thought I had a shot if I could just get him away from my godmothers for thirty seconds. Predictably, he laughed, causing everyone in the room to look at us and crushing my thirteen-year-old self.

"Shush," I hissed.

"You are charming, my dear Miss Watts. In another life, perhaps...if you always wore a hat. Where is your hat? The curling has begun."

"Never mind that. Will you keep quiet or what?"

"You have my word."

I tugged him down my level. "I need to see Corinne Sweet and she can't know that I'm looking."

Serge whispered back. "The Corinne Sweet who works here?"

"Of course."

Serge didn't ask any more questions. He went straight through the grey door. I went to the kids' table and picked up a childrens' guide to the Orsay in English. My friend, Ellen's, girls might like it and I might need it if Corinne was Angela.

Serge came back into the shop with a woman behind him. He smiled broadly and swept his arm toward me. "This lady is in a rush, Corinne. Can you help her"—he saw the book in my hand—"with her purchase?"

The woman said she would in a soft voice and turned to me with a polite smile, asking if I was done selecting my books. My breath got snagged in my throat. Angela Riley in the flesh.

"Ma'am?" she asked in her Missouri accent.

"Yes, yes," I said. "I'm finished."

Serge said he had someone to attend to and left us heading to the counter. Angela aka Corinne took my book, holding it by the spine, I noted, and scanned the code. I gave her my credit card and studied her face as she ran it and bagged the book. One of the other employees asked her a question and she answered in nearly accent-less French. If I hadn't studied the pictures so hard, I would never have known it was her. But the changes didn't fool her sister. She knew her instantly. It made me think about what Dad said about our other senses, our intuition. Corrine Sweet wasn't recognizable unless you were really paying attention. But Gina felt who she was. Her heart told her.

The reality of this so-called missing woman standing in front of me made me a bit woozy. I looked again, almost unable to believe it, but it was absolutely her, standing in the Orsay bookshop, handing me my credit card slip. She'd highlighted her straightened hair with auburn and given herself bangs and wisps of hair to frame her face. The brown contacts were a nice touch and her nose was smaller and upturned. Whoever did the surgery did an excellent job by not making it too small or obviously altered. The thing they didn't and couldn't change were the uneven lips and shape of the eyes. It was Angela Riley. I wanted to jump up and down. Yes! Yes! Yes!

"Is that all, Ma'am?" she asked.

"Yes," I said automatically. "Thank you."

She turned away and nodded to the customer behind me. I moved out of the way and walked into the now packed museum.

The crowd surged around me, pushing me toward the exhibits. I had to fight my way back to the stairs. I trotted halfway up and then slipped my hand in my purse. The Fibonacci phone sat at the bottom under a scarf and a bunch of tampons to discourage snooping.

*Crap and double crap.*

I didn't have a plan for if I actually found Angela. I'd only thought about the search, not the aftermath. I didn't know until that moment that I didn't expect to find Angela in Paris. In my heart, I'd believed her dead. I could call Calpurnia and unleash the Fibonaccis on Angela, but then they would decide her fate. I leaned on the black hand railing. No. Not yet. Angela Riley had pulled off the perfect disappearing act, leaving the children she reportedly adored, her sister, her parents, not to mention her husband. She left with nothing, but somebody paid for that nose. Who and why? I had to know. There was a lot more to this story than a dissatisfied housewife who did a runner. This was orchestrated and I was going to find out why.

# CHAPTER FOURTEEN

I slipped into my chair across from Chuck with no plan, as usual, hoping something came to me. Nobody goes to the bathroom that long. I could say I had cramps, but I'd rather die than say that in front of Serge, who was watching me with amused eyes.

"What are you guys doing?" I asked.

Chuck looked down at his cup. "We were having coffee."

"Oh, yeah. I mean..."

*What do I mean? What do I mean?*

"You hungry?" I asked.

Aaron actually looked at me and that never happens.

"No," said Chuck. "I had three croissants while you were gone. I get that you haven't seen him in a while, but that was a long time."

"Um..."

Serge signaled for another café and said, "Emilio does like to talk and the Bled family is here so rarely."

I clutched my book. "Emilio?"

Chuck narrowed his eyes at him, suddenly hyper alert.

Serge accepted a fresh cup. "I don't believe you made the trip to *Restorations* last fall."

It took me a second. Sometimes, I'm so damn slow. "Oh, you mean Mr. Mazzagatti. I never call him by his first name." I touched Chuck's hand. "I'm sorry. I saw The Girls' favorite restoration artist by the bookshop and I had to say hello."

"It's okay. I was a little worried you were sick or something."

"Not sick, just thoughtless. I got a book for Ellen's girls."

Chuck wanted to look at the book, but I distracted him by saying that Serge had to be getting back to work. Serge agreed and waved away Chuck's attempt at paying the bill. It was on the house.

We said goodbye and I told Serge that I'd definitely find out about those sketches. We did the cheek kisses and he whispered, "Merci," in my ear and I in his.

Aaron led the way outside. The wind was kicking up and the whole city had a grey cast to it. My hair reacted instantly to the moisture. Fabulous.

Despite the dreariness, a quartet of musicians played romantic standards on the walkway at the edge of the wide stairs.

"They have a lot of guys that play the bass here," said Chuck.

"I bet you've never seen so many accordions in your life," I said.

"No kidding. Does anyone play the accordion in the States?"

"Not that I've noticed." I sat down with the crowd on the steps, weighed down by Angela's fate being in my hands.

"What's wrong?" asked Chuck, sitting next to me.

"Nothing. I miss Myrtle and Millicent."

He put an arm around me and I reveled in the feeling. He touched me so rarely. "I'm no substitute."

"That's not what I meant."

He laughed. "I know. I was teasing you. Why are you so serious all the sudden?"

*Better change the subject.*

"What do you think is in that apartment?" I asked.

"That's a switch. What made you think of that?"

"The Girls. It might have something to do with The Klinefeld Group."

"Do you have a feeling?"

I leaned into his warm body as a breeze blew off the Seine. "I think so. What about you?"

"I don't get feelings. I get facts," said Chuck. "I called Spidermonkey. He's going to find out who owns it."

"That doesn't tell me how you feel."

He looked away at the musicians playing their hearts out. "I feel hungry. Let's get lunch."

"What about all those croissants?" I asked.

"I'm a guy. Pastry doesn't last long. Let's get something on the way to the Louvre."

I stood up and dragged him to his feet. I had to get moving. Angela was in there and I needed to find the truth about why. "It'll be packed. We'll go on Friday."

"What should we do then?" he asked.

The Fibonacci phone vibrated in my purse and I pressed it against my hip. "I think I'm supposed to go to the cooking school again. Aaron?"

"Huh?" the little weirdo said while chewing on his super short nails.

"The cooking school. Don't we have class today?" I asked.

"You hungry?"

I punched him in the shoulder. "Focus. Cooking class. We *have* to go to the cooking class."

"Okay." Aaron trotted down the stairs.

"What about me?" asked Chuck.

"You'll go back to that apartment and see if you can find someone who speaks English and isn't hearing impaired. I'll go roll dough until my forearms ache."

"Dough again?"

"It's a different dough."

Chuck's phone dinged. It was Spidermonkey, but what he said didn't make Chuck happy. Spidermonkey couldn't find out who owned the apartment. He could only tell that it hadn't been sold for the last thirty years.

Aaron turned left into a narrow street packed with tourists. I was going to lose him. I dragged Chuck behind me. "What's the plan?" I asked.

"He wants us to contact a guy named Novak."

*What the hell? Novak for both cases. How's that going to work?*

"What's he going to do?" I asked.

"He lives here and speaks French. He can get the tax and utility records. Sorry, but you'll have to deal with it."

I spotted Aaron turning left. How did those little legs move so fast? "Sorry about what?"

"Spidermonkey says this Novak won't like me. It's better for you to handle him."

*Thank god.*

"No problem," I said. "Aaron! Slow down."

Aaron stopped and began eyeing a menu posted on a café window. His expression didn't change, but he didn't approve. I could tell by the set of his shoulders. Even I could tell it wouldn't be decent. There were pictures of the food on the menu. Never a good sign.

We caught up to him and he said, "Class in twenty."

Thank goodness. An out.

"Got to go," I said. "You'll go back to that apartment?"

"I don't have anything else to do," said Chuck, sounding put out.

I went up on my tiptoes to kiss his cheek. "Sorry."

Chuck grumbled.

"Aaron, when will we be done with class?" I asked.

The little weirdo had wandered over to the next tourist trap and was staring at a garish placard of sandwich pictures that looked like it'd been made before I was born.

"Aaron!"

He held up four fingers. I hoped that meant what I thought it meant.

I hugged Chuck before he could step back and avoid it. "How about we meet at Patrick Roger at five? I promised Mom I'd get her a box of chocolate pralines."

I must've made a face involuntarily because Chuck asked, "What's wrong with him?"

"Not him. Them. The shop ladies always treat me like a low-rent hooker."

A change came over Chuck's face. He went from strikingly handsome to demonically angry in a split second. "They treat you like what?"

*Oh god! I've released the beast.*

"Nothing. It's fine," I said.

Aaron had spun around and he, too, had an expression. Almost. He said something in rapid-fire French. My French isn't great, but I think he said something about rude prune butts. Not sure what that meant, but I never should've mentioned Patrick Roger.

"Alright then," I said. "Forget about the chocolate. Mom can order online."

"Oh no," said Chuck. "We're going to that shop and, if those women don't treat you with the utmost respect, I'll—"

"Go batshit crazy?" I asked.

"It's a possibility."

"Were you always this nuts?"

"Only when it comes to you," he said, still demonic.

I gathered my overprotective males and herded them to the Solférino metro stop. "How come I never noticed this part of you before?" I asked as we went down the stairs.

"You never let me date you before," said Chuck.

I didn't know what to say about that. Clearly, I had a lot to learn and there were some surprises in store for me. From the expression on his face, they wouldn't all be pleasant.

We got on the metro and split up at Concord. Chuck went grumbling to the Marais district on the One line to try for more information on the mysterious apartment. If he didn't wipe that expression off his face, he'd get nowhere fast. I tried to lead us in the opposite direction on the One, but Aaron trotted off in the warren of tunnels to the Eight. I chased him down and grabbed his sleeve. "Wrong platform. We have to go to the Champs-Élysées for class."

"No class," he said.

"There's no class?"

"No."

"Where are we going then?" I asked.

Our train pulled up and the doors ratcheted open. Aaron wormed his way on through the crowd and I had no choice but to follow. The doors closed and I ended up in yet another armpit. There were fifty percent women on that train and still I managed a male armpit. Aaron was next to a group of teenagers that looked like they spent hours dressing to get the perfect look. My guy was an American wearing a tank top and had never trimmed anything on his body, including nose hairs.

I prayed we'd get off at Madeleine. We didn't and neither did Mr. Pit. He stuck with me all the way to Strasbourg Saint-Denis. I should've worn my crappy fedora, instead of crossing my fingers that this would be the time that my hair would behave. At the very least, I'd have to scrub the hell out of it to get the pit stink out.

Aaron rocketed off the train at Strasbourg Saint-Denis without checking to see if I followed. Before I could question our destination again, we were on the number Four. We got off at Château d'Eau and emerged from the depths into a solid drizzle. I could feel my hair getting angrier and angrier. I had no clue why we were in the tenth arrondissement. Food could be the reason. The tenth had lots of great ethnic restaurants or so I'd heard. The Girls didn't have much interest in Middle Eastern food and we'd spent almost no time there. From the fabulous spicy smells wafting around the metro stop, they needed to rethink.

Aaron spun in a circle and then headed off down the street on a mission, trotting past nail salons and little shops selling food I couldn't readily identify. I had the weird sense that we'd gotten on the train in Paris and gotten off in some other country.

I chased Aaron down and tugged on his sleeve. "What are we doing?"

"Novak."

"How do you know where to go?" I asked.

"Spidermonkey."

"He called you?"

"You didn't answer."

I pulled out my Fibonacci phone, held my breath, and looked at the screen. Aaron was right. It wasn't Calpurnia demanding answers. It was Spidermonkey asking for an update.

Aaron stopped and I ran into his back. "What the..."

We stood in front of a narrow little shop called Urfa Dürüm. Under the red and gold sign hung a canopy with "Sandwich Traditionnel Kurde" printed on it. The smells coming out of that shop were straight up amazing. A pretty young woman with dark hair knotted up in a bun worked in the window, flattening out little dough balls into disks. Aaron stood there in silent reverence.

I elbowed him. "Novak lives here?"

"You hungry?"

"What about Novak?"

He ignored me and got in the line that was rapidly forming at the door. Food was the reason. Dammit. I had stuff to do, mysterious disappearances to solve. I sat down at the low wooden table in front of Urfa Dürüm and called Spidermonkey.

"I found her," I said the second he answered.

"Sabine Suede?"

"Angela Riley." I was suddenly very proud of myself. Not bad for an amateur.

Spidermonkey hesitated and asked, "You're sure?"

"Very. She's Corinne Sweet at the Orsay."

"I thought you were checking out Sabine Suede first."

This was an unexpected reaction. "I did. It wasn't her. We went to the Orsay this morning and there she was with a new nose and hair."

"I don't know what to say," said Spidermonkey.

"How about congrats, Mercy. You rock."

"You're positive?"

"You don't believe me? What the hell? I'm telling you it's her," I said, beyond miffed.

Spidermonkey sighed. "I believe you. But I can't believe it, if you know what I mean."

"You can't believe she's alive *and* we found her?"

"I didn't think she was alive. There were no indications, other than the sister. This isn't exactly good news," he said softly.

"Because now I have to tell Calpurnia and wreck people's lives?"

"I don't think you should tell Calpurnia. This is a delicate situation. Angela Riley left for a reason. It could be dangerous for more than just her if we let the cat out of the bag."

"You're right. I need to find out why she did it before I decide," I said.

Aaron leaned out of the doorway and held up a finger. I shook my head no. I wasn't very hungry before and I definitely wasn't now. He crooked a finger at me and I got up anyway. My mind was swirling with possibilities, none of them good.

"First, we need concrete evidence," said Spidermonkey.

"I got her prints on a book," I said.

"Excellent. Where are you?"

"A Kurdish sandwich shop."

"So Aaron's with you."

I squeezed past a couple of patrons and joined Aaron at a skinny wooden counter stacked with puffy baked ovals of flat bread. The woman would slide dough in and out of the oven between her and two men working at a barbecue with amazing speed. Aaron asked what I wanted again and he ignored me as usual.

"Of course I'm with Aaron. How else would I end up at a Kurdish sandwich shop in Paris, of all places?" I asked. "I didn't even know there was such a thing as Kurdish sandwiches."

"Is it Urfa Dürüm?" asked Spidermonkey with a chuckle.

"How'd you know?"

"Novak lives across the street."

"Seriously?"

"There's a method to his madness. Give Novak the book and he'll run the prints. Once we confirm her identity, you can decide what you want to do."

"I don't want to do anything," I said, now sounding as peevish as Chuck had.

"Not an option. Call me when you have results." Spidermonkey hung up and Aaron gave me a rolled up sandwich stuffed with seared meat and some sort of slaw.

"I told you I'm not hungry."

"That's for Novak. You get this." Aaron gave me a roll of plain flatbread.

We left the shop and found the line going down the block. I started to rethink my "no." Kurdish sandwiches must be pretty good. Aaron picked a piece of crusty meat off his sandwich and popped it in my mouth without asking. He always knew what I wanted before I did. The meat melted on my tongue and had exotic spices that lingered long after I swallowed.

I eyed the sandwich in my hand. I could eat that, Angela situation or no. "How do you know Novak wants it?"

"He wants it." Aaron led me across the street to a rundown building that looked unlikely to house anyone as savvy as Spidermonkey. I doubted Novak was up to par. Aaron pushed an unmarked button on the cracked plastic panel next to the door that had greying plywood nailed over the bottom half. Nice.

"Oh, well," I said. "He's not here. Bummer."

Aaron didn't move. He stared at the speaker and the spiders making a nest in it.

"Come on. You must have the wrong address."

The speaker squawked to life, startling both me and the spiders. "Oui." The voice was less than friendly and also less than French.

"Watts," said Aaron.

The voice didn't answer, but the door clicked. Great.

Aaron opened the door to reveal the dingiest foyer I'd ever seen and that's saying something. I'd been in a crack house once, trying to get information out of an addict. This foyer was worse. I think I saw hepatitis on the floor. Aaron didn't care. He trudged over broken bottles and wads of material with questionable stains, kicking boxes out of the way to get to the elevator.

The doors clanked open after a five-minute wait and a smell came out of that tiny space that made even Aaron step back.

"It should go without saying, but I'm not taking that elevator," I said, looking for stairs or an escape route, which ever I found first.

Aaron snagged my sleeve. "We gotta go up."

"There's a dead rat on the floor. With maggots. I don't know who this Novak is, but I'm fairly certain he's a freak."

"Take the stairs," said the same voice from the speaker.

I spun around, searching the ceiling for a source.

"Miss Watts, turn to your left. Walk ten paces and open the door on your right," said the voice.

"Novak?"

"Yes."

"Your building is a health hazard."

"Yes." And that was all he had to say, so we did as instructed. The door in question was one I'd never have opened otherwise. Graffiti covered it and the walls surrounding it. There were penises and I never open doors with penises on them. It's just a bad idea. Instead, I called Spidermonkey and told him to call the cops if we didn't get in touch in five minutes. He laughed, but I wasn't amused. Every alarm bell I had clanged in my head. Everything about that place said do not proceed.

On the other hand, I didn't want to be a wussy. I gave Aaron Novak's sandwich and a second before my hand touched the knob, it clicked. I opened the door, sweeping away a used hypodermic and a container filled with something that could've been urine. It certainly smelled like urine.

I held my breath that it wouldn't knock over. It didn't. Thank god. My breath whooshed out when I saw the staircase. It was as clean as the foyer was filthy. And I don't just mean clean. I mean sterile with white walls and a gleaming stainless steel handrail.

"Go up to the fourth floor," said the voice and I happily did.

The door clanged shut behind us and a bolt slid back into place. We were locked in now, but, for some reason, it didn't bother me. Getting out of the filth was a huge relief.

On the fourth floor, another door clicked, letting us out of the stairwell. We walked into another, wholly unexpected world. Thick Turkish carpets dotted the shiny hardwood floor of a narrow hall painted a rusty orange and covered in family photos and artwork.

"This is really weird, right?" I asked Aaron.

He shrugged.

"Any idea which door?"

The hall had four doors, none marked.

"Second door on the left," said the voice.

I still couldn't spot a camera and it creeped me out. I texted Spidermonkey about the creep factor and he sent me an emoji rolling its eyes. Thanks a bunch.

Aaron ignored my texting and had trotted to the door, knocking loudly. It occurred to me that I'd never seen Aaron nervous. As far as I could tell Aaron has two emotions—hungry and excited about food.

"Go to the door, Miss Watts," said the voice.

I sucked it up and went to the door, seriously worried about exactly what we were going to find on the other side. I'd had experience with two hackers, Uncle Morty and Spidermonkey. Neither of them prepared me for the man that opened the door.

Novak had Chuck's height but weighed fifty pounds less, at least. He wore a bicycling outfit so garish that my mouth dropped. It was skintight and electric blue with pink polka dots and epaulets printed on the shoulders. For a second, I thought we were in Italy. I'd seen some outfits that rivaled it there, but nowhere else. To top it off, he sported a man bun the size of a cinnamon roll on the crown of his head. Brown strands had come loose and framed his face, accentuating his large hatchet-like nose and small brown eyes.

"What happened to your hair?" he asked, sounding much more friendly in person.

My hand went up automatically. Shit. The curls were back and in corkscrew form.

"It's raining," I said.

"You should wear a hat."

"Thanks for the tip."

"Or carry an umbrella."

I resisted the urge to throw my flatbread at him and crossed my arms. "I should wear sunglasses."

"What?"

"You're blinding me."

Novak's narrow face went blank.

"The outfit," I said. "You could be seen from outer space."

He looked down and laughed. "Spidermonkey said I'd like you. Come in."

Aaron gave him his sandwich, which was exactly what Novak liked, and we went into Novak's apartment. Or maybe not. The room was a chilly sixty degrees and was so clean you could make microchips in there. Two walls were covered in electronics so sophisticated the NSA would be jealous. Another wall had multiple monitors. All of them were on, but they had a screen scrambling thingy going so that I couldn't tell what was on them. The fourth wall, opposite the monitors, had a metal desk with an exercise ball for a chair and multiple laptops. Novak got us two metal folding chairs and he sat on the exercise ball, steepling his fingers in front of his mouth.

I sat on the icy chair and shivered. "What is up with your foyer? It's seriously disgusting."

"Yes."

"You don't seem to like disgusting," I said, glancing around and trying to find a speck of dust and failing.

"I don't. The foyer is only an additional level of security," he said.

"Security? It looks like a crack den."

"Exactly. People believe what they see. A phenomenon you should be familiar with." Novak watched me with a level gaze, unnerving at best. He was very different from Spidermonkey and Uncle Morty. They achieved their level of intrusion with laptops and serious smarts. Novak was a whole other animal.

"Who do you work for?" I waved at the wall o'equipment. "This isn't for background checks or snooping in people's bank accounts."

"I won't ask you who you're working for," he said without blinking.

I snorted. "I doubt you have to."

A smile broke out over his face, lighting up his eyes and relaxing me. "No, I don't. I rarely have to ask those kinds of questions."

"Well, I do. What kind of work do you do?"

"All kinds. All levels."

I shifted in my seat. I wanted to confirm Angela's identity, but this guy might be a gateway to people I shouldn't know. People that nobody in their right minds would want to know. "Which side are you on?"

"A wise man once told me that there are no sides. Only results."

An electric zing went through me. I'd heard that, too, in the not so distant past.

"That sounds familiar."

"I'm not surprised, considering your recent...misadventure."

He knew about Cairngorms Castle. I'm not sure why, but the thought settled me down. Novak knew Leslie, and Leslie was on our side. I'd met him at the castle. He was a former operative for the US and had been put out to pasture in an isolated spot in the country where he couldn't cause any trouble.

"Tell me you don't work for terrorists," I said.

"Terrorists by whose definition?"

"What the—"

"Terrorism is in the eye of the beholder," said Novak, clearly enjoying the subject. Me, not so much.

I crossed my arms. "Fine. My definition. The commonly-accepted definition. Guys that commit crimes in order to terrorize people to get what they want."

He shrugged. "They pay well."

"Oh my god!" I rocketed out of my chair and went to the door, then turned around to tell Novak that he was a world-class piece of crap when I discovered he was grinning ear to ear, an expression I was intimately familiar with from more than one quarter. "Are you just bothering me?"

"I wanted to see what you'd do," he said, still grinning.

I waved my bread cone at him. "I have bread and I'm not afraid to use it, dirtbag."

"You are a formidable woman with your...what would you call it? An afro?"

I patted my hair. Yes, it was curly. Beyond curly. Dear lord. I'd done something to deserve this. I wished I knew what it was so I could never do it again. "I kind of hate you."

"You aren't the first woman to say that to me. So tell me, Miss Watts of the bread weapon, why are you here?" he asked.

During this whole exchange, Aaron hadn't moved, other than to chew. I wasn't sure if he'd even notice if I left. Some partner he was. I sat down next to him and glared. He didn't notice.

"Spidermonkey said you'd help me out," I said.

"Yes. I owe him a favor," said Novak.

"Two favors?"

"Two?"

"He said you'd help on the apartment thing, too," I said. "Spidermonkey told you about our Klinefeld Group investigation?"

Novak nodded and another lock fell out of his bun. "Yes, he did.

Two favors to pay back. Your priority is Angela Riley?"

"Yes. I actually found her this morning."

"Which one is she?" he asked.

"Which one?" I asked.

"Sabine Suede or Corinne Sweet?"

I could barely hear him over Aaron munching on his sandwich and groaning. I shot him an irritated look and inched my chair closer to the desk. "Spidermonkey told you about them?"

"He did. Which one?" He peeled back the white butcher paper on his sandwich and began to eat as loudly as Aaron, giving me a mocking look. I'd known the man for a total of three minutes and he was already bothering me. What is it with me and men?

"Corinne Sweet," I said, ignoring the moans of pleasure coming at me in stereo. I gave him a quick description of my encounter with Angela.

"What do you want me to do then?" Novak asked.

I laid the Orsay bag on the desk. "I want you to confirm. She held this book in the middle on the spine side."

Novak got out a blue paper towel and gingerly laid his sandwich on it before snapping on a pair of latex gloves and taking the book out of the bag. "Excellent."

I stood up. "When will you be able to get me the results?"

"Two minutes." He went to the wall of equipment and pulled out a slender wand. "Here?" He pointed to the spine.

I nodded and he pushed a button on the wand. It glowed blue and he ran it over the area I'd indicated. He turned off the wand and put it away. Then he put a wireless keyboard on the desk and began typing at phenomenal speed. One of the monitors unscrambled, but the only thing it revealed was code. I couldn't even tell what language it was.

"Did you scan the prints?" I asked.

"Yes," Novak said without a pause in typing.

"You don't need the powder?"

"No."

I squinted at the monitor. "Do you have Ang—"

"Stop talking," said Novak.

Now *that* I recognized, a crabby hacker. Novak's eyes switched back and forth between two laptops. I assumed he was comparing prints, but I wasn't going to risk asking, so I buttoned my lip and glanced at Aaron to see if he noticed. He didn't. His mouth was stuffed with meat chunks and the groaning had increased. Weirdo.

"Confirmed," said Novak. "Twenty-point match."

The monitor now showed two fingerprints with little red dots at various points on the swirls and ridges.

"No wiggle room there, I guess."

Novak sat with his long fingers poised over the keyboard. "You wanted wiggle room?"

I leaned back and an icy chill went up my back. "Not really. But now I have to decide what to do. Where'd you get Angela's prints from?"

"She worked for your postal service before she was married."

"Did you find out anything else about her? Anything I don't already know," I said.

Novak smiled and ran his fingers over the edge of the keyboard. "I don't know what you don't know."

"What do you know?"

"I did a background on Corinne Sweet."

"Lay it on me," I said.

And he did. Novak might be totally different from Spidermonkey and Uncle Morty, but he was just as thorough. Corinne Sweet signed an apartment lease five days after disappearing in Chicago. She paid the deposit and first month's rent in cash. The apartment was out in the boondocks near La Défense. She got a job at Les Cahiers de Gibert, a bookshop in a non-touristy area. She had one credit card under her alias and a bank account with Barclays, which seemed a little weird. Why did she have an English bank while living in Paris? Her accounts weren't interesting though. She had only the money she earned at Gibert as an accountant. She opened the account on the same day she signed the lease. Since then, Angela/Corinne had lived a quiet life. She loved the chain restaurant, Frogburger, and shopped mostly with cash. Her email was just as quiet. She didn't date and had few friends outside her work. No clubs or religious affiliation. She had grown more comfortable over the years, slowly moving from the nosebleed section of the city to an apartment next to the Pompidou Center. She left the bookshop after four years in favor of the Orsay, tourist central.

"Bold for a woman in hiding," said Novak, "or reckless."

"I don't think she was either," I said.

"No? How do you explain it then? She moved herself to two areas where she was more likely to be recognized and she was. Perhaps she wanted to get caught or the cat and mouse game excited her."

I stared at the fingerprints and shook my head. "She wasn't likely to be recognized. No one in her family had passports until her sister got one for her honeymoon. No one she knew intimately was a world traveler. The Fibonaccis only go to Italy and Greece. No. Angela wasn't playing chicken."

"Playing chicken?" asked Novak.

"Flirting with danger," I said. "It's an American thing."

He pushed his keyboard away and lowered the zipper on his top like he was hot. That wasn't possible. It was freaking freezing in there. My goose pimples had hypothermia. "What's your answer for the move?"

"She was lonely."

Novak's eyebrows shot up. "Lonely?"

"How many Americans would she have had contact with at the bookshop or out in La Défense?"

"Few," he conceded. "Interesting notion. I took a look at your Angela Riley. There's little difference between her and Corinne Sweet."

I glanced back at the fingerprints, the same person but not, at the same time. "But Angela did abandon her family," I said.

"She did," Novak agreed with little interest.

"But I can't imagine why. It's not like Corinne's been a party girl for the last few years. She's basically lived the same life she lived in St. Louis, unremarkable. What's the point of leaving if nothing much changes except your city?" I asked.

"Perhaps she hated her husband or her children."

"It doesn't look that way. This was an elaborate plan that cost a bundle, but she has no one special here. How'd she even get the job at Gibert?"

Novak tugged the rubber band out of his hair and it tumbled to his shoulders. He ran his fingers through the thick mop and his forehead creased in thought. "She had help, but I cannot find who gave her the help. She's received no money unless it was cash. Perhaps your country's witness protection program? She may have had something on the Fibonacci family."

"I don't think so. She wasn't involved with the business at all and nothing happened to the Fibonaccis. Not a single indictment. Nothing."

"A housewife doesn't seem to be a good candidate," said Novak.

I glanced at the fingerprints again. "Did Angela fly into Paris?"

"Not with her new name or her old one. She may have taken a train or car."

The Fibonacci phone buzzed in my purse and my chest constricted. Calpurnia hadn't been bugging me and she was well overdue for an update. "Why did Angela do this? What was the point?"

"That's a mystery I suspect only she can solve for you," said Novak.

The phone stopped buzzing and I took a deep breath. "There has to be another way."

"Not from where I'm sitting. If you can find me a new lead, I can follow it."

"You need another name," I said.

"That would be helpful."

Aaron crumpled up his sandwich paper and smacked his lips. "You hungry?"

My flatbread lay in my lap untasted. "Not really."

Aaron took it and started dissecting it like a scientist. Novak and I watched him for a minute before getting back on task. Novak seemed to accept the oddness without question, but then again, he was fairly odd, so maybe it was easy to accept one of his own. I wanted to tell my partner to knock it off. I didn't because it wouldn't do any good, like telling Chuck to stop being tall. Not going to happen.

"How good is the security on Corinne's, I mean Angela's, apartment building?" I asked.

"Standard. Lock to enter the building and a lock on the door."

"Any idea what kind of lock?" I asked.

"No," said Novak. "You'll have to go and see."

I sighed. "I doubt I'll be able to pick her lock. I'm not that good and Parisian locks are a pain."

"They are, but there are other ways if you're creative. Her building's under construction, so she's staying at a Novotel. You may be able to use that to your advantage."

I batted my lashes at him to see if I could get a reaction. Nope. "If you have any ideas, I'm all ears."

"I love your American expressions. But I have nothing to tell you, other than things you should already know. There will be workmen there and you are beautiful. You can talk your way in." He raised an eyebrow. "If you wish."

"Why wouldn't I wish to?"

"It is my understanding that your job was to find this woman and confirm her identity. You have done that. You can tell your client and go back to your vacation."

I stayed quiet.

"Unless you don't want to," he said.

"I don't know. This doesn't feel right. Something is up, big time," I said.

"Does it have to as you say feel right? You did your job."

"No, I can't reveal her without knowing why she left. There are other people to consider." I turned to Aaron like an idiot to ask his opinion. I wanted him to say I was right, that I shouldn't rock people's worlds just because I owed Calpurnia Fibonacci a favor. "What do you think, Aaron?"

"This bread is perfect." He held up a shredded piece. "Look at the structure."

*Ask a stupid question.*

"Never mind," I said.

Novak cocked an eyebrow at me. "This is your partner?"

"He's more useful than he looks."

"I hope so."

I leaned forward, feeling a flame of anger in my chest. "Look, you don't—"

"Quiet." Novak sat bolt upright and began typing furiously. The monitors all unscrambled and, in a second, they showed live feeds from around the building.

"What is it?" I asked.

"We have a visitor or...no..." He looked at me, his eyes glittering. "You do."

# CHAPTER FIFTEEN

"Me?" I asked, jolting out of my chair. "What kind of visitor?"

Without pausing in his typing, Novak said, "Someone is trying to break through my firewall." He shrugged one shoulder. "They're not very good."

"What's that got to do with me?"

"They're tracking your pings."

"Huh?"

He stopped typing and held out his hand. "Give me your phone."

I handed over my regular phone after unlocking it. Novak gave me a look that said, "Like I need your help." He examined my phone for about thirty seconds before putting it on the desk. "Give me your other phone."

My stomach went queasy. "Er...what other phone?"

"The one in your little red bag."

I looked at my little red bag. "You think two phones would fit in there?"

"I think this phone," he pointed to my regular phone, "is entirely secure and encrypted, done by someone very good. Morton Van Der Hoof is my guess. He doesn't know about your other device, does he?"

"Well...I..."

Aaron woke up and said, "Give it."

"Dammit, Aaron."

"Give him the phone."

I gave Novak my Fibonacci phone but not without a wave of nausea. That phone linked me to Calpurnia. I lived in fear that someone, namely Chuck, would get ahold of it. I gripped the edge of the desk, itching to get it back like some nutty teenage girl who just had to Instagram her entire life to strangers.

"Relax," said Novak, examining the phone with his thumbs in a blur. "I will take care of it."

"By doing what?"

Novak answered by taking a hammer out of a drawer and smashing my Fibonacci phone to bits. I didn't make a sound, not a peep.

*Oh god. I am so screwed. Calpurnia is going to be pissed.*

Novak swept the debris off his desk into a trash can.

"We good?" asked Aaron.

That got my vocal cords going. "No. We're not good. How am I supposed to contact Calpurnia?"

He shrugged. Very helpful.

"I have her information," said Novak. "The bigger problem is that man." He pointed at a monitor, showing a grey building, fifth floor. I didn't see anything.

"What man?" I asked.

"He's in the right window, trying to reacquire you," he said. "Now he can't."

"No kidding. How's he trying to reacquire me?"

Novak tapped a few keys and the camera zoomed in on the window. There were lacy curtains and I could make out a figure and a glint of something metallic. "He's using a Stingray to mimic a cell tower to get your location. My system noted the appearance of a new *tower* and alerted me.

"You still don't know it's me," I said.

"Once he got you, he tried to access your phone through your carrier. He succeeded."

"Oh crap."

Novak gave me my regular phone back. "He got little data. I jammed him and wiped your texts."

"You can do that?"

"That's why I am who I am."

I wasn't sure who he was, but it seemed to be a good thing. "What's he doing now?"

"Trying to break back in. Have you noticed anyone following you?" he asked.

"No." I turned to Aaron. "Have you seen anyone?"

"When?" asked Aaron.

"Whenever."

He shrugged.

Novak rummaged around in his desk and came up with a phone and a stack of euros. He messed with the phone for a few minutes and then slid it across the desk to me. "Take this one. I'll only communicate with you on it. I don't want your uncle to know our connection. Calpurnia Fibonacci's number is in there as well as mine. It's clean and encrypted."

"By clean, you mean..."

"No spyware, tracking software or anything else."

"You're not going to track me?" I asked.

"Why would I need to?"

"Seems like something you'd do just because you can."

He grinned again. "It does, doesn't it?"

That made me suspicious, but I figured I didn't care. I needed the phone and he knew what I was up to in Paris anyway.

"What's with the cash?" I asked.

"No using your credit or debit cards. Those have been accessed, too."

I slumped in my frigid chair and looked at the ceiling. "Fantastic."

"So have the cop's," he said.

My eyes jerked to his. "Chuck's?"

"Yes."

"Who's doing it? And when did you find out? In the last two minutes?"

"I knew before you arrived. I checked you out." His expression darkened and he ran his fingers through his hair again. "I didn't expect this." He pushed the cash over to me.

The stack was high and hefty. Thousands, if I had to guess. "I can't pay this back. Not any time soon."

Novak scowled at the monitors. "Don't concern yourself. It's my pleasure. He will pay me back."

"He?"

"The interloper. I will find him and extract my payment."

A chill went down my back. It competed with the chair and won. I had no doubt that Novak would get his money and whoever that guy was, he'd regret trying to breach Novak's system.

Novak glanced at the laptop. "You better go. He's on the move. It took him a while, but he knows we're onto him. He won't want to lose you now that he can't track the phone. I'm not picking up any other surveillance. You can go out the back exit."

I made a face.

"I would've thought from your background that you wouldn't be bothered by filth," said Novak.

"Paper's different than the real person."

"Like Angela Riley."

Novak stood up and led me to the door. "She can't be what she seems. I'll take a closer look."

"You're not done?" I asked in surprise. Novak was obviously super pricey. I didn't think a favor to Spidermonkey would stretch so far.

"I finish what I start." Novak towered over me, bent slightly, like a reed in the wind. "I believe you are the same."

"I am, but what about the apartment in the Marais?"

"The apartment is on my list. It may be the source of the interest in you."

I looked back to see what was keeping Aaron and the little weirdo had gone to sleep in the chair, uncomfortable as it was. "That's a lot of work to pay back Spidermonkey."

Novak grinned. "Then Spidermonkey will owe me. A useful exchange."

I tucked the cash in my purse "Works for me. When will you have something?"

"Hard to say." Novak slammed the door and Aaron jumped.

"Huh?"

"We're leaving."

Novak led us down the hall into another apartment filled with rich fabrics and antiques of an exotic variety. Definitely not French. More like Turkish. An older woman, dressed completely in black, sat in an oversized armchair, knitting an afghan that could've covered a king-sized bed. She nodded at me as we passed through.

"Who was that?" I asked.

"My mother," said Novak.

"Do you own the whole building?"

"And the ones on either side."

We went through multiple rooms, entering a different building, until we reached a heavy metal door with a keypad. Novak typed in a complicated code made of letters and numbers and had his thumb scanned before it opened to a staircase, a nice clean one.

"Is it gross at the bottom of this?" I said.

"Not at all. This is my brother's domain. He wouldn't have it so. You will go to the bottom of the stairs and take a left." Novak continued with the directions. I was lost after the first left, but I didn't want to look stupid, so I nodded and said, "I got it."

Aaron and I hoofed it down the stairs, made the left, and then my partner took over, following Novak's directions with ease. We went out through an alley and ended up back on the same street three buildings down. Success.

I checked out the street to see if anyone was interested in us. A few people were, but I think it was my heinous hair that they were looking at. Even Aaron noticed and bought me an adorable little fedora with the right shape and everything at the shop next to the exit and we headed off down the street, feeling safe as could be.

It didn't last long. I saw him when we crossed the street. A man with blond hair wearing a light grey plaid suit crossed the street a moment after we did. I noticed him immediately because of the suit. Not exactly stealthy. Nobody else in that neighborhood was wearing a 3000-dollar suit. I wouldn't have noticed him in the first arrondissement or the seventh. Maybe that's where he expected us to go.

I stopped, grabbing Aaron's arm and looking at my phone like I was lost. The suit stopped, too, and pretended to look at a butcher's window with goat legs hanging from the ceiling.

"We're being followed."

"Yeah," said Aaron.

"There's a bulge in his waistband and I don't think he's just happy to see us."

"Huh?"

I pointed down the street in the opposite direction from the metro stop. Aaron shook his head and pointed to a corner café. Out of the corner of my eye, I saw the suit take note. Aaron dragged a protesting me into a café. We wove through the tables as fast as possible, knocking into people sipping cafés and watching the world go by.

A waitress saw us and called out, "Arrêtez!"

We didn't arrêtez. Aaron let out a stream of French so rapid it seemed like one long word. He tossed fifty euros on the last table and said something like, "For your trouble."

Aaron grabbed my arm and wheeled me into an alley. We dashed through a warren of narrow back streets and came out, to my surprise, at République, another metro stop.

We ran down the stairs and through a series of fast turns ended up on Platform Eleven exactly one minute before the train was due. There were only seven other people heading South and none were wearing suits or were remotely interested in us. Such was the politeness or perhaps disinterest of the Parisians. I totally would've been interested in us. I was panting and sweat dripped off Aaron's chin, staining the front of his tee. My partner swayed and I grasped his shoulders. "Aaron, are you okay?"

"It's here," he said.

The train zipped in and a prickle of fear went up my spine. The doors ratcheted open and I glanced back in time to see a pair of shiny shoes come into view on the stairs and another pair directly behind them. The kind of shoes you wear with snazzy suits.

Aaron started for the nearest door, but I grabbed his hand, dragging him to the last car. "Come on." We slipped through the doors a second before they closed and I caught the tiniest glimpse of grey plaid going in another car.

We squeezed in and I found my required armpit, this time an older gentleman that inexplicably smelled of fresh-cut grass and carried a cello. The doors closed and I whispered to Aaron, "He's on the train. Could be two."

Aaron nodded.

"Off at Châtelet. It's big. We can lose them."

*In theory.*

"We'll have to be fast off the mark," I said.

Aaron stared out the window, disinterested at best. My stomach felt like I'd been forced to eat andouillette. The cello man jostled me and he really shouldn't have. The mere thought of intestine sausage was enough to make me hurl.

The train stopped at Arts et Métiers and I squeezed the pole so hard my hands hurt, but nothing happened. People piled in, creating a protective barrier between us and him if he chose to get in. He didn't show his face and by the time the doors closed I was panting again.

At Rambuteau, half our car emptied out in a rush and he was there. The suit forced his way through the exiting passengers without politely waiting, getting him many angry looks. He didn't notice. His intense green eyes were on me. A tourist with an enormous black backpack rammed him, yanking open his jacket. The black butt of a compact handgun was visible for a second as he rushed to the doors. The door buzzed to signal closing and he dove between two women. I spun around my pole and kicked him in the lower intestines. I was aiming for his junk, but it still worked.

"Ahhh!" He stumbled backward and my red flat flew past his head. The doors closed and he was gone.

"Mademoiselle," exclaimed the cello man, inching away from me.

"Ex-mari," I said, making a face.

He nodded sagely, like kicking one's ex-husband was a reasonable idea. I'd never had one. Maybe it was.

The train rolled through the next stop without incident and I began to relax. I was pretty good. Too bad Dad wasn't there to see it. All those years of self-defense were finally paying off. But then again, he'd probably critique my performance. Points off for missing the junk and losing my shoe. Never mind. No witness was good. Aaron didn't count. I nudged him. "Did you see that? I nailed him."

"Huh?"

"What do you mean, 'huh?' I saved us."

"There's a second one," he said without blinking.

"Way to pee on my parade."

He glanced around, the most interested he'd been in anything all day. "What parade?"

"Never mind. You're hopeless."

The train announced Châtelet and I grabbed Aaron's hand. The doors opened and we ran off. The platform was packed, of course. Was there a second suit? I didn't know. Two exits.

*Which way? Which way?*

Aaron yanked me to the left and we ran up the stairs. I glanced back down and saw him, another suit. Suits in Châtelet weren't unusual, but this one was looking right at me, brown eyes boring into my green eyes. There was something about him. Vaguely familiar. Aaron pulled me around a corner and I lost sight of him.

"Number two, beige suit, double-breasted," I gasped.

Aaron didn't answer. We ran through tunnels and then up the escalator, yelling, "Pardon!"

The crowd helped us, but beige suit was never far behind. We crossed through the station and ran down another escalator with more yells of "Pardon!" Once in the tunnels again, music welled up ahead of us. "Non, Je Ne Regrette Rien", the song that Myrtle and Millicent said had lyrics to live by, echoed off the concrete and tile. The instrumental version drew me toward it, saying this way, this way.

I refused Aaron's next turn and made him go my way, kind of stupid in retrospect. I could get lost practically anywhere and Châtelet was confusing even if you had a sense of direction, which I didn't. But Aaron let me choose and we came into a crossroads with a large open area containing the string quartet, playing their hearts out to passersby, and a fruit and vegetable stand. We could hope to outrun the beige suit or try something else. Since I was missing a shoe, I was all about something else. I started telling the vegetable guy that we needed help. He stared at me blankly until Aaron took over, saying that there was a man who groped me on the train chasing us. I pointed to the table his wares were piled on in decorative arrangements. He nodded, and we dove under the skirt. The heavy felt didn't quite reach the floor and I could see shoes hurrying past as we crouched underneath, thighs burning.

Then he came, the beige suit, with his gleaming mahogany shoes. He went past, tapping on the concrete and then doubled back, spinning around. Then he approached the vegetable stand. I squeezed Aaron's arm so hard it had to hurt, but he didn't wince. I held my breath as the suit asked the vegetable guy if he'd seen me. He spoke French with an unusual accent. Beige suit described me as an American with a sneer. I didn't have to see his face to recognize the expression.

*Bastard!*

Then he said I was fat with horrible hair. Typical American.

*I will—*

Aaron held me back from lunging at his leg, teeth bared. I think I might've bitten him if I'd had the chance. Fat! I don't think so. I was more like festively plump, curvy, if you will.

I growled with frustration under the table and the vegetable guy raised his voice to cover it. Aaron squeezed me tighter in case I completely lost it, which was a possibility, I have to say.

The veg guy said I had gone to Line Fourteen, but there was something in his voice that made me forget all about my supposed fatness, a little quaver, a doubt. Beige suit heard it, too. He pushed, questioning if veg guy was lying and saying he was a member of the Paris police and I was a fugitive. I noticed no noise of him pulling out a badge. Veg guy shuffled his feet. Now he was nervous.

*Crap!*

The song had led me astray. I was starting to regret hiding under the table when another voice interjected, a strong male voice with a Parisian accent saying that I had gone to Line Fourteen and to basically bugger off unless beige suit wanted to show some identification. The quartet started playing "Fuck You" by CeeLo Green with a vengeance. Beige suit hesitated until veg guy asked for his badge, then he did bugger off, walking away with hard, dare I say angry, taps on the concrete.

Aaron and I waited, hoping he wouldn't double back again. I went to settle my new fedora more firmly on my frizzy head and discovered it was gone. Two hats lost in four days. It was a record.

Veg guy knocked on his table and Aaron climbed out. I came into the light more slowly. My hair was weighing me down. Aaron thanked him profusely. I said that we weren't criminals and the suit definitely wasn't a cop. Veg guy nodded sagely. I broke into Novak's cash and pressed a hundred euros on him. He tried to refuse, but I wouldn't let him. He offered me fruit in exchange, but I picked out five perfect pears and paid for them, too.

Then Aaron asked who the other voice was. Veg guy nodded to the bass player of the quartet, who smiled at me. He was an older, slight man, who hardly looked strong enough to hold up the bass, much less carry it.

I thanked him and the rest of the quartet, giving them a hundred euros, too. They thanked me and the bass player crooked a finger at me. I leaned in and he said, "Il avait une arme."

"Oui, monsieur. Je sais."

I kissed the bass player on the cheek and we dashed off. Now that was courage. He stood there, holding his bass as his only protection, and lied to a man claiming to be police with a weapon in his waistband. He didn't have to. Nobody asked him. I never loved Paris more or bass players, in particular.

Aaron tried to take me to the Line Four, but I dragged him to the Seven. My heart was still pounding when we got on the train and no suits ran down the stairs to stop us. The doors closed and we plunked down on two seats, not an armpit in sight.

I looked up at the Line map above the door and put my head on Aaron's rounded shoulder.

"What are you looking for?" asked Aaron.

"Our destination. We can't go home again."

# CHAPTER SIXTEEN

We got off at Pont Marie and walked up the stairs into a thick mist wafting off the Seine. The drizzle had stopped, but my hair didn't care. If anything, the curls got tighter. I could hear them mocking me. It was going to take a village to straighten my hair.

I took Aaron's arm and tried to fix a dignified expression on my face.

*I don't care that I'm in Paris, looking like an idiot. I just don't care. It doesn't matter. Maybe nobody will notice.*

A couple of men dressed like they were going to a polo match passed us and gave me quick glances. Not the good kind or even the sleazy kind of quick look I was used to. More like an I'm afraid to look at this woman too long. I might burn my eyeballs off kind of look.

We reached Pont Marie and its five graceful arches over the Seine. I tugged on Aaron's arm to cross, but he couldn't be moved.

"You hungry?" he asked.

"Aaron, we were just chased by armed men through the Paris metro," I said. We're soaking wet and I'm missing a shoe."

He shrugged. "They didn't catch us."

I stared at him for a second until it dawned on me that he was right. We hadn't been caught. That deserved a pastry, at the very least. "I could eat."

He tried to turn me off the bridge, but I refused. "First, the apartment, then food."

We crossed the Seine to the Île Saint-Louis. Aaron didn't question where we were going. I got the impression that he didn't much care as long as there was food in our near future. I hadn't spent much time on the island, so I didn't know what restaurants were good, but I was sure Aaron either knew or would sniff out the best spots before I had a chance to kick off my remaining shoe.

I found the building easy enough from memory. It would be hard to forget that entrance even if I tried to. The double doors were well-worn bluish-green and eighteen feet high, rising to an arch with a weeping woman's face carved over them in stone. I couldn't imagine all the work that went into making the wood carvings, from the enormous wreath at the top to the multitude of panels, circular, square, and rectangular. Whoever made it really knew how to cook up a door.

My memory wasn't much help when it came to getting in. I didn't have a key or a code. Monsieur Barre would be in residence. He was the building manager. I hated to let him see me like that. Monsieur Barre wore suits 365 days a year and his three hairs were never out of place. Not one of my three million hairs were in place and he would let me know it.

"I have to call Myrtle and Millicent. I hate to wake them up, but Monsieur Barre is a stickler. We need permission to stay here," I said.

The question was what to say. What were the right words to keep The Girls from getting alarmed and calling Mom and Dad? The last thing I needed was Dad showing up and sticking his long, freckled nose in my business. I'd be able to keep Angela Riley a secret for about fifteen minutes at the outside. "I don't know what to say."

"Okay." Aaron got on his phone and began searching restaurants on the island. We all have our priorities.

The Girls were awake and having a *Thin Man* marathon with their best friends, Magdalena and Ruth. It had run into the early morning hours.

"Mercy, my girl, how are you finding Paris?" asked Millicent with a cocktail shaker going like mad in the background.

"Are you drinking?" I asked to stall. Maybe I should start having plans. No. That would mean Chuck was right. No plans.

"Of course, dear. We're watching *Song of the Thin Man.* One must have cocktails when watching William Powell."

"Martinis?" I asked.

"With extra olives," she said with gusto. "Did I ever tell you that I met Mr. Powell? On Martha's Vineyard."

"New York City," I said.

"What was that?"

"You met William Powell in New York, not Martha's Vineyard. You met John Wayne in Martha's Vineyard."

There was a slight pause. "Well...they're not the same at all."

*Holy crap! She's drunk.*

"No, they're not the same at all."

"Mr. Powell was odd. Did I tell you that?" asked Millicent.

I stifled a laugh. "You did. Speaking of odd," *I've got it.* "You know Elias?"

"Elias the Odd?"

"The very same. I was wondering if we could use his apartment instead of the one on Montorgeuil."

Millicent hiccupped and slurred, "It's haunted, dear."

*That's new.*

"Haunted by what?" I asked.

"Elias, of course. He jumped off the Pont Marie. Did I tell you that?"

*Oh dear lord.*

"I heard. Can we stay there anyway?"

"Why would you want to? He walks around at night and makes a terrible racket. The neighbors complain, but there's nothing we can do. He won't listen to reason. He never did, even when he was alive."

"Are you saying you've actually seen Elias...in the apartment?"

*Maybe this isn't such a swell idea.*

"Why, of course. He walks around moaning about that woman."

She put the phone down. "Myrtle, what was the name of that prostitute?"

"I really don't need her name," I said. "I need to get into the apartment."

There was a little scuffle during which the phone was dropped three or four times before Myrtle picked up. "I'm sorry, dear. We don't use the P word."

*Thank god.*

"Myrtle, can we stay in Elias's apartment?"

"That's not a good idea. Why on earth would you want to? Montorgeuil is lovely."

"It is. I...um...um." I scanned the riverbank, searching for an idea. I finally stopped on the Louvre. That made me think of museums, the Orsay, and then Serge. "Serge."

"Serge?" she asked. "What's that about Serge?"

"Er...he asked me a favor. I didn't want to bother you, but he has an idea."

"Dear man. What's his idea?" Myrtle asked.

I told her about the Monet letter and the sketches. I said Serge had been very kind and I wanted to check the inventory to see if they even existed before I asked about the possibility of an exhibition.

"You'd have to stay in the apartment then," she said.

"Why?" It slipped out. What an idiot. I wanted to stay.

"Because I don't remember any sketches on the inventory, but it's not complete. You'll have to search the apartment. Elias was a packrat. It will take some time, dear."

"That's okay," I said. "Can you call Monsieur Barre and ask him to let me in?"

"Right now?"

"Yes, please."

"You won't be frightened?" asked Myrtle.

"I'll be fine. I'm *not* overly-sensitive," I said.

Myrtle took a long drink of something. "Of course not. I don't know why Millicent said that. You're practically a block of wood."

*That's not better.*

"Um...great. Thanks, Myrtle."

"Now if anything happens, you only need to be yourself."

*Block of wood. Got it.*

"No problem. By the way, do you happen to know where Marie is?"

There was a delicate burp before Myrtle said, "Which Marie?"

"*The* Marie," I said.

"Of course. What other Marie is there really?"

"Do you know where she is? I might want to ask her some questions."

"No idea, my dear," said Myrtle. "She could be anywhere at anytime. I'll call Monsieur Barre. Must get back. Ruth is running dry."

I thanked her again and hung up. "We're in."

"Auberge de la Reine Blanche," said Aaron.

"What the..."

"Or Nos Ancêtres le Gaulois."

"Are you talking about lunch?" I asked.

He stared at me as if there couldn't possibly be anything else to discuss. Ever.

"Focus, Aaron. We've got bigger problems. The Girls are under the impression that this apartment is haunted and we've got guys with guns hunting us."

He shrugged and I rolled my eyes as the right door made a thump. My heart went into my stomach. So ridiculous. Elias the Odd wasn't going to open that door or any door, for that matter.

A wizened old hand came around the edge of the door and Monsieur Barre peeked out at me. He blinked and stared. His slightly clouded eyes ran up and down my form and he frowned severely.

"Miss Watts?"

"Bonjour, Monsieur Barre," I said pertly.

He didn't believe me. I had to show ID, two forms. I didn't think I looked that bad, but I guess I did. Monsieur Barre finally opened the door and the smell of expensive pipe tobacco enveloped me. He stepped back, revealing the inner sanctum of the building, a foyer that movies were filmed in from time to time. Black and white marble covered the floor and there were arches everywhere, leading to a staircase with black wrought iron.

"Merci, Monsieur Barre," I said, accepting the heavy brass keys to

Elias's door and a card with the code on it before heading for the elevator.

Sadly, Monsieur Barre followed with the soft patter of his bespoke shoes. He was slow, but the elevator was slower.

"Mademoiselle, you must"—he did a shrug and a wave together—"do something about the appearance. You are a Bled."

I didn't argue. He saw me as a Bled and that was that. "I will. I promise."

"This coiffure is unbecoming."

I poked the up button repeatedly. "So I've been told."

Monsieur Barre smoothed his three hairs and pulled a slim gold case out of his breast pocket. Inside was a neat collection of business cards. He gave them a scan and selected several.

"No, no. I'm fine, Monsieur Barre. It was raining." I pointed to my head. "This isn't normal."

He pursed his lips and held out the card collection. "I agree."

The elevator dinged. "I really don't need any help."

"Have you viewed yourself recently?" he asked.

"Er..."

"I really must insist." He held the cards out. The glint in his eye said he would be calling Myrtle and Millicent one way or the other.

*I'm so screwed.*

"Thank you, Monsieur."

"Madam Ziegler will be happy to...make you more presentable."

The elevator door opened at a snail's pace. So painful.

"I assume she's a private dresser," I said, my heart sinking. How would I ever pay for this?

"But of course. She is the best," said Monsieur Barre with a gentle yet pitying smile. I obviously needed the best since I was such a mess.

Aaron and I got on the elevator and I pushed the button for the third floor. The elevator had to think about it. While it did, Monsieur Barre waited patiently, taking note of my every defect. It was quite a catalog, I'm sure.

The elevator finally decided that it would in fact take us to the third floor and dinged. The doors inched closed and Monsieur Barre nodded before saying, "When you are ready to leave, please ring me to return Monsieur Elias's key. I assume an hour or two will be sufficient."

"Oh, no," I said. "We're staying. I'll return the keys in six days."

Monsieur Barre's face went from calm to absolutely panicked in a split second. "Mademoiselle, that is not wise. Monsieur Elias...he—"

"Monsieur Elias is dead," I said, sounding more confident than I felt. "We'll be fine."

"Mademoiselle, this is Paris and Monsieur Elias was French at heart."

*What's that supposed to mean?*

I put my hand out and stopped the creaking door from closing. "Monsieur Barre, I wouldn't be here if it wasn't an emergency. It is an emergency. Elias will just have to get used to it. By the way, if anyone comes looking for me, you haven't seen me since last fall. Okay?"

Monsieur Barre's forehead wrinkled. "Mademoiselle is in trouble?"

"Yes, I'm in trouble," I said, surprising myself with my frankness. "But that is between you and me. Telling my godmothers will make it worse. Please trust me on that."

Monsieur Barre's eyes went all squinty. "You are investigating in my city."

My jaw dropped a little. "You...uh...know about me."

"I have the internet."

*Of course you do. Great.*

"Then you know secrecy is vital."

"Call Madam Ziegler. She will know how to make you blend in," he said before putting his finger to his lips and stepping back.

I let go of the door and it closed. My last image of Monsieur Barre was of him smiling with excitement. That was new. I didn't know he could get excited.

The elevator crept up to the third floor and my anxiety increased. I'd been in Elias's apartment before, but it was always a short-term affair. The Girls liked to check on it to make sure it was in order. We never stayed there and I didn't know anyone who had, come to think of it. Even when the other Bled properties were filled, we didn't stay in Elias's apartment. We went to a hotel.

*Stop it! It's fine.*

The door opened on Elias's floor. A round foyer with two doors labeled A and B didn't look remotely frightening. The inlaid wood floor with its shiny sunburst in six kinds of wood was warm and inviting.

"Which one?" asked Aaron.

"Both, actually."

Each floor in the building had two apartments. Elias had bought both on the third floor because a single man with zero hope of marriage needed two apartments. Elias was so weird, his father, Balthazar Bled, made him sign a document saying that he wouldn't get married without family approval or he would be disinherited. I'd seen the document. Surprisingly, it was about love, not control. The Bleds loved Elias, but they clearly knew he was nuts.

I opened A and the curved door swung open without sound or encouragement. Elias's apartment proved the nuts theory. It was packed with mismatched furniture. Think early twentieth-century garage sale. Paintings, prints, and engravings covered every inch of wall space. I wasn't sure what color the walls were. When wall space ran out, Elias stacked canvases against the walls.

I dropped my purse on the table in the entryway next to a wood carving of Christ on the cross and entered the living room, marveling at the collection and how little it had changed. Elias's mother, Brina, never bought the suicide story. She insisted that his home be kept just as it was when he left. She believed he would come home. If The Girls were right, he never actually left.

I pushed that creepy thought away and went through the rooms, turning on the lights and opening the shades. The place was spotless. Monsieur Barre personally supervised a thorough cleaning once a month. There were even clean sheets on the beds.

"Alright, Elias. If you're here, I want you to know this isn't forever. Please don't haunt us," I said, peeling off my sopping sweater and flinging it into the claw-foot tub. No shower. Chuck wouldn't be happy.

*Chuck!*

I whipped out my phone and called him. After three tries, I gave up and left a message, saying it was urgent and to call me immediately.

My stomach twisted around into a bow tie. He'd gone to that apartment with the Klinefeld connection. I didn't know who the suits were, but The Klinefeld Group was my first guess. I supposed Calpurnia could've hired them, but why? I reported to her. No, definitely The Klinefeld Group. And where there were two suits, there could be three or four. I called Chuck again and again. No answer.

"Aaron!" I yelled.

He didn't answer and I had to search the apartment, only to find him in the kitchen, staring at what could loosely be called an appliance.

"Stove," he said.

"I guess. Don't try to turn it on. Nobody's lived here in over a hundred years."

Aaron examined the so-called stove. It was a La Cornue, one of the first, if I had to guess. It was blue and resembled an anvil sitting on a low table with three hot plate-looking disks on top.

"It doesn't work," said Aaron.

"You tried it. Are you crazy?" I pulled him back from the stove. "Call Chuck. He's not answering. I'm freaking out a little."

"Huh?"

"Call Chuck." I managed not to yell, but it was close. "We got away. Maybe he didn't."

Aaron called and then shrugged at me before going back to the stove. I didn't know what to do. I called our apartment's land line. No answer there either. I could go over to the building and do what? Ask people if they'd seen a hot guy asking questions about an apartment with a padlock? Yeah, right.

"Aaron." I nudged him in the rump with my foot. "I don't know what to do. Chuck always answers unless he's mad at me. Is he mad?"

"No."

"Maybe I should go down there. I could canvass the building. That's what he was going to do."

"Call Spidermonkey," said Aaron with his head wedged behind the stove.

*Spidermonkey. Of course!*

I called Spidermonkey without a thought to the time.

"We were chased and I can't find Chuck," I said in a rush the second he answered.

"What? Mercy?" Spidermonkey sounded woozy.

"Two guys in suits chased me and Aaron when we left Novak's place. Now Chuck's not answering the phone."

"Where's Chuck?" asked Spidermonkey.

I slapped my forehead. "Are you okay?"

"Loretta's trying to kill me."

"What the hell?"

"She made me eat sushi."

"That's not enough to kill you," I said. "Me, on the other hand..."

"It was bad. I'm in the ER. I can't—" There was a horrible purging noise and I almost horked out of sympathy.

A woman's voice came on the line, "Hello? Hello? Who is this?"

I was so shocked I couldn't speak.

Then she said, "Honey, where did you get this phone? Is it the nurse's? Who are you trying to call? Augusta is on her way." She came back on the line. "Hello? Hello?"

I hung up. Loretta the wife. I knew of Loretta's existence, but I was fairly certain she didn't know about mine and her husband's alter ego of cyber sleuth.

"Poor Spidermonkey."

"Huh?" asked Aaron, still behind the stove.

"He has food poisoning. He's in the ER and Loretta found his second phone because of me." I plopped down in a rickety cane-bottomed chair. "Oh my god. What's she going to think? A secret phone and I hung up on her. An affair. That's what she'll think. Crap."

Aaron popped up. "Where? Who did it?" He was actually looking at me. It was kind of unsettling.

"Nobody did it. Spidermonkey wouldn't have an affair."

Aaron gave me a look and I realized he couldn't care less about an affair. "It was bad sushi."

"Where?"

"I don't know."

"It's a restaurant?"

"One would assume, unless Loretta made it at home and she really is trying to kill him."

He rubbed his hands together. "We won't ever go there."

"There was never any danger of me going to a sushi place," I said, pulling out Novak's phone. Spidermonkey was out. Novak was in. I hoped he didn't start charging me. Monsieur Barre's silence was going to cost me plenty. I didn't need French style. I needed shoes that didn't fly off when I did a roundhouse kick.

I left Aaron muttering about incompetent sushi chefs and went to get Novak's phone out of my purse. He took four rings to answer and I started to get worried about him.

"Miss Watts," he said. "I have information for you."

"Yeah, well, you're not the only one," I said.

"Did something happen?"

I told him about the chase and our new, possibly haunted, digs. Then he got quiet.

"Novak?"

"How do you feel about the Fibonaccis?" he asked.

"Good as you can about a crime family. It's not Calpurnia, if that's what you're thinking."

"Perhaps it's not her."

"There's no perhaps. I work for her," I said. "There's no reason to chase me down."

"Tell me about this apartment you wanted information on," said Novak.

"I thought you were supposed to tell me about it."

He laughed softly. "And so I will. First, I want to know why you are interested in it."

I told him everything about The Klinefeld Group, tracing the trail through the years to the doorstep of the Marais apartment. "I would guess they know about Richter. They have people using Jens Waldemar Hoff as an alias."

Novak began typing. "Maybe they're hoping you'll lead them to whatever they want."

"They have the advantage there," I said. "At least they know what it is."

"You've proved resourceful in the past. I'm betting you'll find it before they do."

"I'm glad you're confident about that. What do you have on the apartment?" I asked.

The typing continued. "Nothing. It's a dead space."

# CHAPTER SEVENTEEN

Dead space, according to Novak, meant the apartment was cloaked. It used no electricity or gas, and mail didn't go into its box. It didn't mean no one was there or that the lights didn't work. It meant that somebody had made it so all usage wasn't tracked by utilities or any other service. The apartment was dead like it wasn't even there, except that it was. Some safe houses were like that. If you were going to tuck federal witnesses away, you wanted them to go into a black hole. I pointed out that nobody would pick a swanky apartment in the Marais. An isolated farmhouse, that I would buy. Novak said that plain sight wasn't such a bad idea. Tourists abounded in Paris. No one would think anything about new people coming and going. I pointed out that there was a freaking padlock on the door. What safe house did that? He reluctantly agreed. Since the apartment hadn't been sold in thirty years, he was going to have to sift through records by hand. He wasn't thrilled. Neither was I. Hand-sifting records took time and I didn't have much, especially if The Klinefeld Group had decided that it was time to take it up a notch and snag me. On the upside, Novak could tell that Chuck's phone was off. He suggested that I go to the chocolate shop as planned. With any luck, Chuck would be there. Novak seemed to think this cured all my worries. It didn't. What if Chuck wasn't there? Novak didn't have an answer for that. I'd have to go and find out.

But not for a couple of hours, and I couldn't go out, even if it wasn't. I had one shoe and was sopping wet. I went back to the bathroom, wrung out my sad sweater, and draped it on the pedestal sink. The tub taps squealed something awful when I turned them, but hot water did eventually come out. I filled the tub and continually checked my phone. Nothing from Chuck and he still wasn't answering. I slipped into the hot water and soaked while staring at my phones. I had to call Calpurnia. If I didn't, she might do something crazy and deploy Fats Licata to Paris to find me or possibly somebody worse. I reluctantly tapped her name and she picked up immediately. It kind of surprised me since she didn't know the number.

"Miss Watts," she said with a relieved sigh after I identified myself. "Where have you been?"

I decided not to tell her about the suits. I didn't want Fats showing up to protect me. I couldn't imagine the kind of attention a guy named Fats would attract. Plus, I was in Paris on Fibonacci business. Calpurnia might not take kindly to my looking into The Klinefeld Group on her time.

"I lost your phone, but I replaced it with another secure one," I said quickly.

"You lost it." She sounded doubtful.

"Well...less lost and more stolen."

She bristled. "Stolen. By who?"

"I don't know. I was at Sacre Coeur and got pickpocketed."

"Why were you there?" she asked suspiciously.

"I have to play the tourist with my boyfriend and Aaron here."

She mulled it over and then seemed to forgive me. "You have a good replacement?"

"From my Paris contact. He's very good."

"Better than Spidermonkey?"

I started, sloshing water on the floor. "You know him?"

"I know of him. He won't work for me at any price."

"Oh, well...Spidermonkey referred me to this guy and I think he's going to be a big help."

"Do you have her yet?" asked Calpurnia.

"I might. I'm waiting for confirmation," I said, wondering how long I could string her along.

"But you think it's Angela."

"It could be. I have to get fingerprints to make sure."

Calpurnia didn't say anything and I heard the juicy glug of wine being poured. I imagined her on her deck, sitting next to Cosmo and watching the fireflies in the woods around her house.

"If it is her," I said, "what do you want me to do?"

"Do?" she asked.

"If Gina's right and her sister's alive, that means she pulled off the near impossible, faking her own death. Why?"

"Do you think you can find out?" asked Calpurnia.

I checked my regular phone. Nothing from Chuck. "Maybe," I said. "It'd be worth it to try. If it's her, this is going to screw up a lot of lives."

Calpurnia's voice went huskier as if she just realized the implications. "I thought this was fruitless. Gina is...an unreliable source."

"She has instincts."

"But you're not certain yet."

"I will be soon."

"When you are, get me all the information," she said. "I knew I chose the right girl for the job."

I smiled. "I'll get it done."

"I know you will."

We hung up and I sunk under the water, running my hands through my tangled hair. There was no shampoo, only a cube of green soap, probably Savon de Marseille, chock full of olive oil. I wasn't sure what that would do to my hair, but, since it was already corkscrewing, I figured it couldn't hurt.

The cube was so old it took a good ten minutes to get a lather off it. After that, it was smooth and creamy. I rinsed and waited. No corkscrewing. I used the cube on the rest of me and my skin felt like room temperature butter.

When I finally got out of the tub, I was so relaxed I nearly forgot to worry about Chuck, who still wasn't answering. I could hear my dad's voice in my head saying that Chuck was a sight more capable than me. Dad pretty much thought everyone was more capable than me. He had yet to get over me setting fire to the Bleds' garage when I was seven. It was an accident, for crying out loud.

The bad part about Elias's bathroom was the towels or rather the weird fabric squares that I found on a shelf. No terry cloth there and no covering my bits either. I found a dressing gown on the shelf next to the clothes and was surprised to find it was a woman's, Japanese style in pink silk with wide sleeves that draped nearly to the floor. Strange. All the stories about Elias said he was a hopeless failure with women.

I slipped it on and found it fit perfectly. Either Elias wasn't very big or he was odder than the family was willing to let on. I opened the bathroom door and Aaron stood there. I screeched, slipped, and would've landed on my rump if Aaron hadn't grabbed me.

"You have got to stop doing that. You're going to...what's that smell?" I asked.

"Stove," he said.

"Oh my god. You turned it on. Are you trying to kill us? Do you want to die?" I rushed past him to the kitchen and found the middle plate red hot and smoking. I threw open the window in a fit of coughing and cracked Aaron on the shoulder. "What the hell?"

"Burning it clean."

"You are insane."

"They're here."

I had a *Poltergeist* moment and sucked in a breath. "Who? What?"

"People," he said, staring to the left of my face.

"Er...living people?"

"Yeah."

I blew out the breath and leaned on the wall. "Don't do that to me."

"What?"

"Oh forget it. Who is it?"

Aaron shrugged and went to stare at the stove, looking for what I couldn't say. There was nothing for it but to go see whoever it was in an ancient dressing gown, shoeless and wet. Mom would be mortified, but I couldn't put on wet clothes, could I?

I crept down the hall to the living room, listening to soft French voices. One of them was Monsieur Barre, the interfering old toad. I sashayed over and whipped open the door. If you're going to look inappropriate, you have to do it with conviction and conviction was all I had. I wasn't even wearing panties.

"Monsieur Barre, what is going on?" I asked, summoning up my inner Aunt Miriam. Nobody is haughty like her.

Four people, in addition to Monsieur Barre, turned around and I instantly wanted to run away. I very nearly did. The people, two men and two women, epitomized Parisian style, uber skinny, lots of black, and impeccable tailoring.

"Mademoiselle Watts?" asked the oldest of the crew, a woman who looked like Coco Chanel at sixty, but with less wrinkles and more pearls.

"Yes."

"We are here for you."

"Who are you and what do you plan to do?"

"To fix you, naturally," she said.

I could use a lot of fixing, but that was still pretty insulting. My face must've shown it because Monsieur Barre quickly said, "This is Madam Ziegler. She consented to come immediately as this is an emergency."

Only in France is bad hair considered an emergency.

"Well, I do need some shoes, but my credit card is...gone. Stolen at Sacré-Coeur." When you pick a lie, it's best to stick with it. Dad is right about some things.

The entire group looked scandalized and apologized like they'd committed the crime themselves. During the apologies, I was measured from head to toe. My hair got evaluated and Madam Ziegler pronounced me, "Not hopeless." I think that was a compliment, coming from her.

Madam Ziegler opened the front door and wheeled in racks of clothing—four to be exact—stuffed with everything from coats to dresses to purses. I could smell the expensive and it was a heady experience.

"But I told you my credit card, it's gone." I didn't say that my credit card probably didn't have enough space to buy one shoe, forget about a whole pair.

"We'll put it on your account," said Madam Ziegler.

"I don't have an account," I said.

"But of course you do."

"I do?"

"Madam Millicent uses it for your purchases."

One of the guys pushed in a cart loaded with curling irons and whatnot. He grabbed a large drawing pad and began sketching. It was me. Sort of. Me if I were six feet tall and a hundred pounds.

"What purchases?"

"Your Valentino suit, for instance. Lovely pieces. You look well in it?" asked Madam Ziegler.

"Oh, yeah. It's gorgeous."

"Then we shall begin."

And they did begin. No amount of protesting did any good. I don't think I even got to finish a sentence. They talked over me and under me and all around. Surprisingly, Frederic thought my hair was perfect and didn't rewash it. He did lacquer it and put it in an updo that took two people to accomplish.

I had to try on bras, skirts, pants, boots, and sunglasses. Pretty much everything you could imagine. I didn't pick out one damn thing. Not one. I bought six outfits with all the fixings. I didn't ask the price. Some things are better unknown. Besides, I had two kidneys. What were the chances that I'd need both? I'd heard there was a market.

This was all done in an hour and they left as quickly as they came, leaving me not with a bill but with strict orders to call a certain tailor who would come and alter everything in an afternoon. I thought it all fit perfectly. The look on Madam Ziegler's face said I was very wrong.

Monsieur Barre kissed my hand, said it was a pleasure watching my transformation, and asked for the pleasure of burning my lone red flat. I gave it to him and he left, holding it at arm's length and leaving the faint scent of pipe tobacco in the air.

Aaron wandered in and I twirled. "What do you think?"

"Huh?"

"I got new clothes and hair and makeup. It all probably cost more than Dad's car, but I'm not going to think about that."

"You hungry?"

"We didn't eat, did we? I forgot. No time now. I have to go to Patrick Roger." I made a face and then realized, for once, I looked the part. Maybe I wouldn't be invited to leave like I was stinking up the joint. "Go turn off that stove. I'm afraid it'll burn down the apartment."

Aaron obediently went to the kitchen while I tried to think of a way not to bring him in the shop. Aaron hadn't dried out well and he didn't look too good to start with. He looked like Aaron and those women at Patrick Roger were guaranteed not to like it. I doubted Aaron would notice the looks and mind, but I would. If those women gave him so much as a slight sneer, I might do another round house kick. Chocolate everywhere.

We arrived at Patrick Roger on Saint-Germain before five. My heart had taken up residence in my throat. I was certain Chuck wouldn't be there and I'd already decided to lump it and call Dad. If Chuck was missing, I didn't care if the whole Fibonacci thing was exposed. I didn't care if Dad found out that we were investigating The Klinefeld Group in hopes of finding out who murdered Lester and exactly what went on when Dad flew Josiah Bled to Paris. I didn't care about anything but Chuck.

The sight of the storefront made me wrinkle my nose. It wasn't the most welcoming of sights, cool and sophisticated in black and mint green. Mom loved it, but Patrick Roger made me feel less than. I took Aaron's arm to cross the street, my little black booties clicking on the pavement. The little peplum skirt that Madam Ziegler picked out fluttered against my herringbone stockings and I straightened my snug little jacket and tossed a purple scarf over my shoulder before reaching for the door handle.

The blonde woman behind the center counter saw me and smiled.

Then she saw Aaron. The smile held but just. I checked my phone for the time. Two 'til. I itched to call Dad and unburden myself.

The attendant asked if she could help us in French, her eyes shifting between us. I started to answer, but Aaron beat me to it, speaking so rapidly I lost interest. Before I knew it, I had a chocolate flavored with lemongrass in my mouth. I'm not sure how that happened. But I can say one thing for sure, it will never happen again. Gag.

Aaron came at me with a little dark chocolate square. I saw the cracked peppercorn on top a second before it hit my lips. "Is that pepper chocolate?"

"Szechuan," he said.

"That doesn't make it better."

The attendant saw my face and went to gather different chocolates for me to try. She did it with a smile and it was freaking me out. I'd been inside for five minutes and she wasn't pointing to the door.

"Why's she being so nice?" I whispered. "I know Madam Ziegler made me look decent, but you kinda look like you live in a gas station bathroom."

"I told her that you're Nina Symoan," said Aaron.

"Nina's old enough to be my mother."

"So?"

"I don't know. It seemed kind of important."

It wasn't. The attendant totally thought I was a fifty-year-old rock star wife. I wasn't sure how to take that. It did keep them from giving us the boot while I waited in vain for Chuck to walk through the doors. We sampled so much I was going to have to buy a pile to satisfy the attendant. I let Aaron choose. He had tastes similar to Madam Ziegler—the more expensive, the better.

My heart got heavier the more we waited. Fifteen after and no sign of Chuck. I wanted to cry, but I wasn't sure what would happen to the fancy mascara Frederic slathered on my lashes.

The attendant started stacking green boxes on the counter. Big boxes.

"How much chocolate do you think my mother wants?" I asked.

"Presents," said Aaron.

"For who?"

"Sisters."

That took me back. For a second, I forgot about Chuck. Aaron never mentioned his family. He didn't seem to have one. He spent holidays with us and nobody questioned it. I'd come to think of him as a singular creature who appeared out of nowhere and belonged to no one but us.

"You have sisters?"

"Yeah."

"How many?"

"Four."

"Holy crap. That's a lot of sisters."

"Yeah."

That was all I was going to get on the subject. Aaron majored in one syllable answers.

I pulled a hundred euros out of Novak's stash and hoped it was enough. "Here," I said. "Tell me if you need more. I've got to tell Dad about Chuck."

*Plus, I'm going to cry.*

"I'll be outside." I started for the door.

"Why?" asked Aaron.

I slapped my forehead. "Pay attention. Chuck's not here. He's in the wind. Something's happened. Since we were chased by a couple of armed suits, I'm guessing it's not good."

"He's in the back."

I froze. "What? Who?"

Aaron licked a speck of chocolate off his lip. "Chuck."

"Chuck's here? Right now? Here?"

"Yeah."

I punched his shoulder hard enough that he fell against the glass display cabinet and the attendant exclaimed in horror. The thing barely shuddered. Chill, woman.

"He's safe and you didn't tell me. Are you some kind of masochist?" I yelled.

"Women like Chuck," said Aaron, completely unperturbed.

"Really? Ya think?" I grabbed his tee. "I'm going to punch you until you pop."

The attendant came around the counter all flustered. "Madam, madam, you will have to leave. You are disturbing the other customers."

I turned to her. "Oh, really? We're the only ones in this snotty joint."

"Madam, I insist you leave."

I let go of Aaron and spread my arms. "Go ahead. Insist."

That stymied her. Apparently, normal people left when she insisted. I wasn't normal just then and it's possible I never was.

I crossed my arms. "I'm not leaving until I get what I came for."

"And what is that, madam?" she asked, taking out her cellphone.

"First, I'd like you to take a good look." My voice went all squeaky. "Do I look fifty?"

She squinted at me. "You are well-preserved. Americans do not age gracefully."

"In my case, I wouldn't have aged at all. I'm twenty-six. Hello, twenty-six."

"I do not believe this to be true."

"What the..." I went for her, chasing the woman around the counter. I would've caught her, too, but Chuck chose that moment to come out of the back with two French beauties hanging on his arms.

"Mercy! What the hell are you doing?" he shouted.

I stopped on a dime and went for him, already in a full-blown ugly cry. I hit his chest so hard, he stumbled backward and barely stayed on his feet.

"What the hell is wrong with you?"

"Ithoughtyouweredeadorkidnapped," I snuffled into his tee. I won't lie. I was snotty and it was gross, but I didn't care.

"What?" he asked, pushing me back. "I can't understand you."

"Your"—I inhaled and my body shook—"phone. I thought you were dead."

"What about my phone?"

I wiped copious amounts of mascara off my cheeks. "You didn't answer."

"Oh shit. I turned it off when I was interviewing and forgot about it." He accepted some tissues from one of the lovely attendants, who didn't look all that pleased to see me, and dabbed my cheeks. "Why in the world did you think I was dead? I'm pretty good at not being dead."

I blew my nose. "There was an incident."

He stiffened. "An incident that made you think I might be dead? What the hell happened?"

My angry attendant came over, making a shooing gesture. "Madam, monsieur, you must leave."

Chuck gave her a look that chilled my blood and it wasn't even directed at me. "Madam, we'll leave immediately. Aaron, settle up."

He took me to a back corner and asked again what happened. I told him about Novak's apartment, leaving out the Fibonacci stuff, and said that he'd caught someone trying to get into my phone, my regular phone. A flush colored his cheeks when I told him about the chase, but he was eerily calm.

"Are you okay?" I asked.

"We can't go back to the apartment. If they found you at Novak's, they know where we're staying."

"We went to Elias's place."

After explaining the apartment, he looked me up and down. "I thought you looked different."

"Good different?"

"Super hot different. You didn't get any more of those red shoes, did you?" he asked.

"No, but I can."

He scowled and I laughed while hugging him. "Thank god. You're okay."

"I won't turn off my phone again."

"Please don't. My heart can't take it."

Aaron poked me in the kidney. "Done."

My partner had three big bags, full up with boxes. The attendant had gone to help some other customers who'd wandered in. They were Americans dressed in workout gear and tennis shoes. She didn't approve of them either. I could tell by the set of her spine, ramrod straight.

"Let's get out of here," I said.

Chuck insisted on going out and checking the street first. It was pointless. The suits could easily hide in the foot traffic. The sidewalks were teaming with Parisians and tourists. Once he decided it was clear, we hoofed it into a cab and went straight back to Elias's place. The cab dropped us at Notre Dame so we could get lost in the crowd before heading over to the Île Saint-Louis on foot.

Monsieur Barre took one look at Chuck and his damp, snotty tee before calling Madam Ziegler. Chuck couldn't talk him out of it. I don't know how he thought we were going to pay, but that wasn't his concern. Style was, plain and simple. Madam Ziegler would be on our doorstep first thing in the morning. Monsieur Barre had it arranged before we walked over the threshold.

Chuck marveled at Elias's place while I apologized. "I'm sorry about the clothes. I'll see if I can do some appearances for DBD to pay for them. Mickey wants me back."

He shrugged. "Don't worry about it."

"Um...these clothes are bound to be crazy expensive."

"I figured." He went through some of the canvases stacked against the living room wall. "They're not all by geniuses, are they?"

I went over to look at a rudimentary nude. The nipples were huge, but not in a Picasso-like way, more like an I-don't-know-how-to-draw way. "No, they're not. You understand what I mean by crazy expensive?"

"Mercy, I'm a single guy that makes decent money and lives in a studio apartment. I can afford it." He led me into the bathroom. That was way more upsetting than the clothes situation. "There's no shower. What the fuck is that about?"

"You can take a bath," I said, suppressing a smile.

"I don't think I can. I'm a guy. It's against the guy code."

"Elias obviously did it."

"He threw himself off a bridge. Enough said. What about the other Bled apartments or a hotel, for Christ's sake?"

"Absolutely not. This apartment is listed nowhere. You'd have to do some serious rooting around to find out about it. If we go to a hotel, we'll blow through Novak's money in three days. This is free." I left and had him following me room to room, crabbing about the lack of a shower. I peeled off my little jacket and flopped on the bed. It made a tremendous creak and I sunk into a hole. "I think I'm stuck."

Chuck leaned on the doorway. "Hotel sounding better?"

"Fine. Three to a bed."

He paled and then pulled me out of the hole. He didn't pull far enough and I slid right back in. "I admit it. This isn't ideal." I clawed my way out and asked, "So you were interviewing when you turned off your phone. What'd you find out?"

"Nothing," he said.

"You turned off your phone for nothing? This day sucks."

"In this case, nothing is something. I interviewed three neighbors," he said.

I frowned. "Women?"

"The best kind, beautiful and chatty."

"Don't make me get out of this bed."

"I'd love to see you try." Chuck laughed and then told me that the *nothing* was quite interesting. According to the beautiful neighbors, the apartment was empty or at least no one had ever been seen going in there. The padlock had been installed more than ten years ago. As far as the ladies knew, it had never been unlocked since. They didn't know who owned it and the building management was mum. It was the subject of many a Christmas party when the neighbors got together for drinks. The favorite theory was that it belonged to some eccentric billionaire who was so busy traveling the world that he or she had forgotten they owned an apartment worth several million. Angeletta, the most beautiful neighbor, owned the sister apartment and told Chuck that it was quite large with several bedrooms. Hint, hint. I didn't like Angeletta one bit.

"So while Aaron and I were being chased through the metro, you were flirting with this ancient woman."

"I never said she was ancient," said Chuck.

"She's as old as your great-grandmother and hag-like in my mind. Let's leave her that way, shall we?"

"You're jealous."

"You're a flirt."

"It's what I do and it works. You've been known to flirt your way to answers," he said.

My nose tipped up. "I don't know what you're talking about."

"Okay, sure," he said with a grin. "Let's go to dinner."

I pointed at the crusty spot between his pronounced pecs. "You can't wear that."

"You got a better idea?"

"Maybe there's something in the wardrobe," I said.

"You want me to wear hundred-year-old clothes when you're rocking the sexy?"

I rolled my eyes. "Oh, puhlease. Men's clothes don't change that much."

Chuck opened the tall walnut wardrobe and rooted around, coming out with, you guessed it, a white-collared shirt. "How big was Elias?"

"Not big."

Chuck stripped off his tee and I very nearly gasped. The abs were crazy, and I hadn't seen them in a while.

"Have you been working out more?" I asked.

He shrugged and tried to put on the shirt. Nope. Not going to happen. Chuck couldn't even get a sleeve on. "Okay, baby. Plan B?"

"We'll buy something on the way," I said, once again trying to escape my bed hole. I think it was getting worse. My rump was touching the floor.

Chuck reached for me and there was a tremendous bang from somewhere in the apartment. He spun around and ran out, leaving me stranded. "Wait! Help!"

I clawed my way out, shredding the mattress. "What is it?"

"It's fine!" Chuck yelled back.

"What happened?" I ran into the hall and was hit with a stinky gas smell. "What the hell?" I made it into the kitchen and found that Chuck had ripped a curtain panel off the window and wrapped it around Aaron's head. There was a cloud of grey soot filling the room and I went into a coughing fit that nearly knocked me to the floor.

"It's fine," said Chuck. "It's completely fine."

I wasn't able to answer, but I threw open the windows and used a skillet to wave out the smoke. Chuck unwrapped Aaron's head. His glasses were intact, but his eyebrows were gone. Only red stripes remained where they used to be.

Once I stopped hacking, I saw the stove still belching out soot. I ran over and started searching for a shutoff valve, finally finding it behind the stove, but it was rusted open. "Chuck!"

Chuck managed to wrench it closed and the belching stopped.

"I got the oven working," said Aaron with a wheeze.

"You call this working?" I asked.

"I can make dinner."

I grabbed him by the tee and dragged him out into the hall, slamming the door to hold in the stink.

"Hey!" yelled Chuck.

I whipped open the door and pulled him out before shutting it again.

"Thanks. You're so kind."

"Oh my god," I said. "The Girls are going to kill me. This apartment was intact."

"Calm down," said Chuck. "It's not that bad."

I poked him in the bulging pec. "Telling people to calm down doesn't change anything. Don't say calm down!" My voice went all squeaky.

"Okay. Don't calm down."

"Don't get smug with me."

"I'm not smug. I'm calm."

"Well, don't do that either. Oh my god. Oh my god."

Chuck took me by the shoulders and gave me a tiny shake. "The Girls don't have to know. We'll clean it."

I blew out a breath. "That's true as long as Monsieur Barre doesn't find out we're—"

A sharp rap echoed down the hall.

*Damn and double damn.*

I pushed Chuck and Aaron back in the kitchen amid loud protests. "I'll handle this."

"I can do it," said Chuck.

"Quiet. You're shirtless."

"That might help," he said.

I booted him through the door. "It's not going to help."

Luckily, I was fully dressed and wearing black and grey. Any soot would be concealed. I straightened my top and glanced in the hall mirror. Even with yellowish glass and peeling silver backing, I looked okay, not good, just okay. I tucked in several loose strands of hair as the rapping got louder and more insistent, and then I opened the door. As I feared, Monsieur Barre stood there, his face all puckered up like a dried apple. He held a fire extinguisher like he was ready to club somebody with it.

"Hi, Monsieur Barre," I said cheerfully. "What's up?"

He leaned to the side and peered around me. "Madam Leibovitz heard an explosion."

"Oh that. We were...playing a game."

*What the what. Game. Crap.*

He frowned at me. "A game where something explodes? What game is this? I insist on knowing."

*No. No. Not the insisting.*

I tipped my chin down and batted my eyelashes. I'm not proud of it, but I was desperate. "It's just an American thing. We're weird, you know. Noisy. Always doing stuff."

"Mademoiselle Watts, you are charming as always, but I insist on coming in." Monsieur Barre's tone said that I wasn't charming and never had been. Maybe I should've sent out shirtless Chuck.

"There's nothing to see." I blocked him as he attempted to dart around me.

"There is something to smell," he said. "Perhaps a gas leak."

"I think it's fine."

Monsieur Barre waved his hand in front of his nose. "Shall I call your godmothers?"

I did more batting. It was reflexive. "Whatever for?"

"Mademoiselle." He gave me a withering look and I slumped. I looked pathetic; I have no doubt. Oddly, pathetic worked. He patted my shoulder. "Let us see the damage."

I let him push past me to the kitchen, where Chuck remained

shirtless, causing Monsieur Barre's eyebrows to hit his three hairs. Aaron looked worse than I remembered. Some of his hair was burnt to a crisp and his hairline was now an inch farther back. Now that the smoke had cleared, the kitchen smelled like burnt hair.

"You used the range," said Monsieur Barre, glaring at me.

"Well, not me personally, but it was used or turned on, I guess," I said.

He surveyed the kitchen with a critical eye. I'm not sure he had any other kind, to be honest. "This is not a disaster," he said at length.

"No?" I asked hopefully.

"No." He turned to Aaron. "This is a disaster. You must have salve for your burns and your hair must be shaved."

*Shaved? Mom's totally going to notice that.*

Chuck looked closer at Aaron's head. "I don't think he's really burned. More like singed."

Monsieur Barre gave Chuck a glance that made him clamp his mouth shut. "You will dress and you"—he gestured to Aaron—"will come with me."

"I need to cook," said Aaron.

"You may cook on my range. It doesn't blow up or set my apartment on fire," said Monsieur Barre. "He may stay in my guest room. You two are on your own. The cleaning staff will arrive promptly at seven tomorrow morning. Have your dinner elsewhere."

Aaron trotted out of the kitchen like an obedient dog and Monsieur Barre followed, telling him he really needed a stylist. I think he meant clothes. Good luck with that. I'd never seen a new shirt on Aaron. He had the well-worn look down pat.

The front door closed with a thump and a clink and I turned to Chuck. "So it's only us tonight."

I was pleased. He wasn't. Chuck looked like I might pounce on him.

"What's wrong with you?" I asked.

"Nothing." He took a step back. What the hell?

"Alright. I'm taking your nothing to dinner and then to the Eiffel. Got it?" I flounced out of the room with him trailing me.

"Why are you mad?" he asked

"I'm not mad. Why would I be mad? De-soot yourself and let's go."

He did and we went without any more questions about why I was mad. Smart man.

The dinner I assumed would be Paris romantic wasn't. We had crepes while walking to the Eiffel. Not that that can't be romantic, moonlight stroll and all that, but with us it wasn't romantic in the least. Chuck didn't want to talk or hold hands or do anything else with me. I ate my crepe and practiced my patience.

By the time we reached the top tier some two hours later, it had worn so thin I could see through it. We stood at the railing, gazing at the City of Light and saying not a thing about it. The only good part about the whole thing was that we weren't followed. I didn't see the suits and I was looking since I wasn't looking at Chuck. It's easy to check for tails when you haven't got anything else to do.

"Are you done?" he asked after a grand five minutes.

*Patience is a virtue.*

"I'm so done," I said.

"What does that mean?" He took my arm and pulled me close. Not too close, I noticed.

"It means let's get in the elevator line."

"What's wrong?"

I yanked my arm out of his grasp.

*Patience nil. Virtue gone.*

"What's wrong with you?" I asked. "Let's have it."

"Nothing."

"Don't give me that. This is the Eiffel, romance central. Something is wrong," I said.

Chuck turned away and stared off in the direction of Sacre Coeur, but not really seeing it. "It's not you."

I leaned against the guard rail as a gentle breeze ruffled my hair and tickled my neck. "That's what people say right before they dump you."

He jerked his gaze to me, his smooth forehead furrowed. "I'm not dumping you."

"What are you doing?" My voice sounded harder than I intended.

"I'm getting used to us." His long fingers wrapped around my bicep and squeezed. He could've hugged me, but he kept his distance. It could be my imagination, but it seemed to be getting worse since we arrived in Paris.

"You're not thinking that I'm not what you expected me to be?" I asked in a whisper.

"God no." He stepped closer and the smell of him enveloped me. I don't know when he had beer, but there it was, beer with wintergreen gum and a hint of ancient soot.

"I miss you," I said.

"I'm right here."

"Are you?"

Chuck bent over me and I thought for a second that the spell was broken and he'd kiss me. Instead, he kissed my forehead and gave me the quickest of hugs. His heart pounded away. I had a feeling. This wasn't excitement or, God forbid, passion. This was fear, intense and unrelenting. Patience couldn't change that.

# CHAPTER EIGHTEEN

I slept in Elias's bed, or more accurately, in the pit in the center of Elias's bed. The pit was more comfortable than it looked, kind of like a hammock.

I fell asleep as soon as I slipped into the hole and dreamt vivid dreams of New Orleans, of black cats and my ancestors in St. Louis Cemetery No. 1. It was the first time I'd dreamt of the city and my grandparents' house without waking up screaming. Richard Costilla had always shown up before, charging up the stairs, blade in hand. But not that time. I was safe in Elias's bed in the beloved city of Paris.

Aaron woke me up by standing at the foot of my bed and staring at me. I was so bleary that at first, I thought it was Elias, thinking I was the woman he loved.

"Don't do that," I said after screeching and cussing.

"Huh?"

"I thought you were Elias. He's supposed to haunt the apartment."

"Why?"

"How should I know?" That's when I noticed his hair. It was still there and that wasn't a good thing. His hairline had moved back another couple of inches, leaving an angry red stripe like a headband over his forehead. The rest of his hair stuck up but not like it normally did. It almost seemed like it was styled but that couldn't be. "How come you didn't shave your head?"

"Cold."

"It's summer."

He shrugged and watched me struggle to get out of the hole. I flailed my arms. "Help."

Aaron hauled me out and stared at the wall, saying, "We got to go."

"Where?" I asked, cracking my back and stretching.

"Class."

"We can't go to class. Chances are the suits are on to that."

Aaron closed the bedroom door. "We'll go the back way."

"There's a back way?"

"I don't know."

I rubbed my forehead. "You're giving me a headache and I've only been awake for five minutes. That's just wrong."

"You got to go to Angela's," he said.

"I know, but I don't think Chuck will let us go alone to Guy's. We'll have to Fike him."

My door rattled and Chuck shouted through the wood. "Are you guys in there? Are you okay?"

"See what I mean?" I whispered.

"We're fine, worrywart." I opened the door to reveal Chuck looking ready to pounce.

"What are you doing in here?" He scanned the room, looking for intruders, I suppose.

Aaron and I watched as Chuck stalked around, every muscle in his lean body taut. "You think I wouldn't know if there was somebody in here?" I asked.

"I don't know," he said. "Would you?"

I crossed my arms. "Don't talk to me like my father. Yes, I'd know. Aaron and I lost two tails yesterday and I kicked the crap out of one of them. I'm not a complete moron."

Chuck did a slight shake and refocused on me. "Sorry. Yesterday shook me."

"Why?" I asked. "It's not like this kind of stuff doesn't happen to me all the time."

"I'm not usually around."

"That makes it different?"

"Hell, yeah."

I wasn't sure what to do with that. If Chuck got the idea that he had to protect me every minute of every day, we were going to have a problem, a big problem. And this whole together thing wasn't going to work out.

Lacking anything to say, I shooed them out of Elias's room. "I have to get dressed."

Ten minutes later, I emerged in another of Madam Ziegler's outfits, a plum-colored dress cut on the bias and a pair of heels she claimed were comfortable. I wouldn't know until it was too late and I had blisters the size of quarters. Madam Ziegler had allowed me three purses and three hats, a twenties-style cloche, a beret, and a brimmed hat straight out of *Casablanca*. I know the hats sounded like they were over-the-top and they were, especially the beret. Is anything more trite than a beret in Paris? I don't think so.

Madam Ziegler swore that I absolutely had to have the *Casablanca* hat to go with the three-piece suit that she insisted was perfect for me. Since she managed to produce a vest that fit my breasts, I agreed to it. I still wasn't sold on the beret, but at least it had the right shape. I put on the cloche instead and it did its job by making me look like a twenties movie star instead of Marilyn. It was kind of amazing. Madam Z was a genius.

I walked into the kitchen and found Chuck and Aaron sitting at the butcher block table on delicate cane-bottomed chairs not designed for their size or weight. A coffee carafe sat between them and they held little eggshell cups with roses and vines on them.

Chuck shot a hawk-eyed glare at me. "What time are your classes?"

I did an affected yawn. "I don't know. Aaron doesn't tell me these things."

"I'm going."

"What for? You have a burning desire to roll pastry?"

"I have a burning desire to keep you from getting killed," he said with a glare.

I helped myself to his coffee, a fabulous fruity blend, and said sweetly, "Why are you mad?"

"You're going to try and Fike me. It's not happening."

*It is so happening, bub. You haven't got a clue.*

A loud knock echoed through the apartment and Chuck jumped to his feet. "Don't move."

"For goodness' sake, Mr. Paranoid. It's not them. The suits aren't the type to knock politely," I said.

Chuck grimaced at me, but he knew I was right. He stalked to the front door and whipped it open. Monsieur Barre stood there, holding another carafe. He walked in without being invited, followed by two ladies, introduced as Madam Ulliel and Madam Gabin.

I leaned on the hall wall and did a finger wave. "Bonjour."

"Wait," said Chuck, putting his hand up. "Who are these women?"

"The cleaners I spoke of. I presume the kitchen is as it was," said Monsieur Barre.

"Absolutely filthy," I said. "This way, ladies."

I showed them the kitchen and after some tsking about the coating of black soot, the ladies shooed us out and we went to the living room. Chuck scowled at me and I rolled my eyes. I drank three more teeny cups of coffee before applying a coating of Guerlain lipstick that Madam Ziegler said went with my dress. The color was Insolence, which seemed appropriate. Monsieur Barre took note of the atmosphere, his dark eyes flitting back and forth between me and Chuck.

"Don't even think about it, beautiful," said Chuck.

I turned up my nose at him. "Ready, Aaron."

"I'm ready," said Chuck.

"You don't need to follow me around," I said. "I'm a big girl or haven't you noticed?"

"I've noticed that you can get into trouble at the drop of a hat."

"And out of trouble just as fast." I spun around. "Where's my purse?"

"Which one?" asked Chuck. "You bought three."

My hands went to my hips. "Bought is a strong word. Madam Ziegler said I had to have them."

"You could've said no."

"I can't wait to see you try it."

As if on cue, another knock echoed through the apartment. This time, it had a distinct female sharpness to it. Madam Ziegler.

Monsieur Barre went to let in the fashion horde and I headed for the bedroom with Chuck's voice ringing in my ears. "I can handle Madam Ziegler."

"Yeah, right," I called over my shoulder.

My purses were on the dresser beside an ancient shaving kit and a framed photo of the Bled family circa 1880. They were arranged on the front gallery of Prie Dieu, the family seat. Most of the faces were familiar, even if I didn't know their names. The Bled face, with its high cheekbones and narrow mouth, were strongly in evidence.

I chose the boho bag in black and stuffed my few belongings in it. My Novak phone had to be dug out of the depths of Elias's bed, the one place Chuck was guaranteed not to look.

Aaron appeared at the door. "Now?"

I smiled. "Oh, yeah."

We headed back into the living room where we found Chuck standing in the middle, surrounded by the horde. They ran their manicured hands over every inch of him and his protests went unheeded. The French was flying fast and thick. I only caught a few words. Handsome, sad, dirty, and fit. They were going to fix Chuck and fix him good.

I turned to head for the front door and Chuck's long arm snaked out and snagged me. "Not so fast."

He attempted to turn me away and failed. Not a surprise since he had three people tape measuring him. One tape was around his neck. I ended up facing the outside wall with its band of ceiling-high windows and the black wrought iron balconies beyond. Someone had thrown back the curtains in an attempt to put some light on the subject so, for the first time since I'd been in the apartment, the view was unobstructed. What I saw sitting on the middle balcony froze me in my tracks. Peering in through the wavy glass was a cat and not just any cat, a skinny black cat with startling green eyes. I squeezed my eyes shut.

*No. Not here. Nope. Can't happen.*

I raised my lids the smallest amount possible and he was still there, Blackie, from my grandmother's house in New Orleans. Actually, my mother called him Blackie. I don't think he really had a name. The cat had come with the house purchased in the 1800s. He wasn't always around. The cat showed up in times of tragedy or great danger. When I'd been in New Orleans on a case, he'd straight up saved my life. He may have been a supernatural presence, but his claws were very real.

"Mercy," whispered Chuck. "What are you doing?"

I swallowed and looked up at his puzzled face and then at everyone else's. The hubbub had stopped and the room was silent.

"Nothing." I glanced back at the window and Blackie was gone. This couldn't be a good sign. "I got a little light-headed for a minute."

"Then you're not going at all," he said. "You should rest."

"That's a hard pass." I peeled his fingers off my arm and slipped around him. He tried to follow but was completely caught up in tape measures.

Monsieur Barre intervened. "Monsieur Watts, this will only take a short time and the transformation will be remarkable."

"I don't need to transform. I need to take care of Mercy." He grabbed a tape and yanked but couldn't get it off his thigh. The measurer would not release him.

Monsieur Barre stepped in front of him. "Monsieur, I must insist. Two hours is all I ask."

"Two hours! Screw that!"

"Fashion is time and effort," said Madam Ziegler.

"Do I look like some kind of pansy fashion guy to you?"

She nodded. "Yes indeed. You are perfect for the styles I have in mind for you." She gave him a stinging slap on the forearm. "Stay still and do as you are told. I will not have you escorting a Bled in a shirt covered with...a substance that shall not be named."

I peeked around Monsieur Barre's well-tailored shoulder. "You did agree to this."

"The timing sucks. Don't leave, Mercy. I'm ordering you," Chuck said.

"If you think you can order me to do anything, you've got another thing coming. I don't take orders. I give orders."

*Where the hell did that come from?*

"I'm leaving and, if you know what's good for *us*, you won't follow," I said, slinging my purse over my shoulder.

Chuck stared at me. "You sound like your dad."

"Get used to it. There's a lot of Tommy Watts in here." Seeing the dismay on his face, I decided to throw him a bone. I did love him, after all. "Les Invalides in three hours. I'll meet you at the ticket counter. Don't be late." I flounced toward the door and tossed over my shoulder, "Enjoy the fitting. See you at Les Invalides."

"I didn't agree to that."

"Nobody's asking you to agree." I grabbed Aaron's arm and steered him around the racks of men's clothing and out the door. I slammed it shut, cutting off Chuck's protests.

Three hours to get what I needed to decide Angela Riley's fate. I prayed it was enough.

Aaron and I stood across from Angela's apartment, unsure how to approach it.

"When Novak said under construction, he meant it," I said.

Angela's building was having a full facelift. Scaffolding covered the entire façade with a company logo on a placard on every level. Heavy construction sheeting draped the top four floors, concealing what they were actually doing. Workmen swarmed over the various levels and a jackhammer wrecked the peaceful air of the avenue, breaking up the sidewalk in front. A small company trailer sat on the sidewalk,. blocking it off completely. The foot traffic had to be diverted into the street with a roped off walkway.

I couldn't see Angela's apartment on the fifth floor, but there were guys on that level. I'd planned on talking to the building management to weasel my way in, but there wasn't any management to speak of.

The front entrance wasn't blocked off. The double doors, huge rough-hewn things, were propped open and two workmen argued, pointing at a bunch of snaggly wires coming out of the ceiling and the walls. What a mess. I couldn't sweet talk them. Even if I did, they'd want to walk me to my door. They were bound to notice me picking the lock, and that might be a tad bit suspicious.

"We need Novak," I said, digging out his phone.

He answered on the first ring. "Miss Watts, are you in the apartment?"

"Not exactly."

"Where are you exactly?"

"Across the street."

"What is stopping you?" he asked.

I scanned the building again, looking for someone in charge and coming up empty. "I need some help."

"Yes."

"Can you call the construction company and tell someone to let me in? There's no way I can just walk in and pick the lock."

Novak laughed. "What do you suggest I say?"

"I suggest that you make the building management company name pop up on their phone so they'll think you're official. Then you tell them that I lost my keys and I need to get in to grab my spare set. They're working on the inside and outside. They have to have keys."

"Is that all?" he asked with a chuckle.

"Can you do it?" I asked.

"Of course I can do it. Do you have a number or do I have to find that out, too?"

I gave him the number and waited a half-hour at the corner café, having breakfast with Aaron. When my phone dinged, I paid the waitress, slathered more Insolence on my lips and sashayed down the street with plenty of swing in my hips.

"Okay, Aaron," I said. "You're my boss, a chef at Guy Marin's atelier. I'm a dingbat and you're helping me out. Got it?"

Aaron shot me a look that suggested that that was exactly what was happening.

I elbowed him. "Don't get any ideas. I'm still the brains of this operation."

"Huh?"

"Never mind. Wow them with your French." I smiled broadly at several workmen that noticed our approach and I gave them a finger wave before trying to turn the wrong way. Aaron snagged my arm and turned me around before we went to the trailer. He knocked on the door and did indeed wow the foreman with his French. Before that moment, I thought I was okay with the language, but the sheer volume of words and musicality of the explanation of who we were and what we were doing made me understand that every French person I'd ever spoken to had been humoring me. I sucked. It was a humbling experience, but all I had to do was look vacant and flirty while saying "Bonjour" with a terrible accent. I imitated Sarah Susanne from my tenth grade French class. She was from South Boston and I could barely understand her English. Her father struck it rich with some kind of invention and that's how she ended up sitting next to me at Whitmore Academy. We were the only two blue-collar girls in that white collar world and we stuck together. Her accent had served me well on several occasions, but never before in French.

Somehow the conversation—what I could follow of it—went to restaurants. The foreman named one. Aaron would counter with another. Roast chicken was a popular topic and it was a strain not to lose my dingbat pose and poke the little weirdo in the ribs. We had a timeframe, but, with the mention of food, Aaron forgot all about it.

Finally, after a half-hour of just about crawling out of my skin, I interrupted and asked in halting Sarah Suzanne French if he had my key. I'm not ashamed to say I flicked my tongue over my lips as I did it. The foreman immediately forgot all about who had the best roast chicken, Chez L'ami Louis or the chicken lady at Marché Bastille, and found my key or rather Corinne Sweet's key on the pegboard at the back of the trailer. I held out my hand and he dropped the key in my palm while looking deep into my eyes. I felt a little sizzle as he did. It's a French thing and an Italian thing come to think of it. Those men, no matter what they look like, can look at you and make you feel as though no one, absolutely no one, has ever seen you before. This guy was older than my father, craggy and lined from a life in the sun, and he smelled faintly of diesel fuel, but I still kissed him on the cheek and loved it.

We left the trailer and the foreman shouted that we were to be let in. The guys with the wiring pulled it back to make way and I smiled my best smile as I passed.

I overdid it and four guys tried to follow us to the stairs since the elevator was part of the jumbled wiring problem. I didn't know when Angela thought she was moving back in, but it was no time soon.

Aaron told the guys that we didn't need any help. I think he may have said something suggestive about me and him, but it was in slang, so I didn't really understand what he meant. The meaning was clear when I saw the smirks on their faces.

When we made it to the third floor landing, I did jab Aaron in the ribs. "That took forever. Why did you have to bring up food?"

"It's Paris," he said, staring to the left of my head.

I turned and dashed up two more flights. "We don't have time for chicken. If we don't make it to Les Invalides on time, Chuck will have a freaking fit and I'll never be able to Fike him again."

Five floors with no elevators suck. I about keeled over when we stumbled into the hall. Aaron kept up with me surprisingly well. I blame the heels, which didn't hurt yet but slowed me considerably.

Three workmen at the elevator jerked their heads up from their own jumble of wiring, blocking the hallway. I did my little girly wave and let Aaron explain that I was très débile and lost my keys. The guys gave me the once over and decided on the spot that I was obviously an idiot and that letting the idiot through was fine. They helped me over the wires and I found Angela's door at the end of the hall. Aaron opened the door to keep up the moron persona and waved me in.

Angela's apartment fit her perfectly, a small studio with the world's smallest kitchen. Kitchenette might've been more accurate. She had two electric burners and no oven, certainly no dishwasher. A tiny microwave was her only appliance. She didn't have room for more. This would be the only apartment I could afford if I moved to Paris. Even then, I'd probably have to sell my blood every so often.

Aaron set about searching the kitchen and I went through the bathroom and living room/dining room/bedroom. Angela didn't have much, but what she did have was neat and clean. I saw a cord for a laptop, but the laptop was gone. In the way of paperwork, she had bills, some sales circulars, and exactly sixteen birthday cards. She must've given Corinne a different birthday from herself. I doubted she'd hung onto the cards for seven months.

"I'm done," announced Aaron.

"Find anything?" I asked.

"She likes Pâté Lorraine."

"Very helpful. Anything to link her with her former life?"

He shrugged.

I guess I didn't really expect to find a glaring clue. Angela had been careful and very well organized. She left with nothing, not even her purse. She was committed. Angela's world made me sad. She left her kids for this. What the hell? Why? The apartment was in Paris, but that's where the awesome ended. It looked like the apartment came furnished with serviceable stuff, blond wood IKEA-type furniture. It said nothing about her. Except...

The artwork. She had three Robert Doisneau prints, not big poster-sized pictures but twelve by nines. The Girls had several signed and numbered prints by Doisneau. He was famous for his shots of post-war Paris. Angela had picked the most famous of his works, *Pipi Pigeon, Un Regard Oblique*, and the kissing one. They were the only pictures to grace her walls. Her only mirror was in the bathroom. It was so small, my rear barely fit in there.

*I sense a theme.*

"What do you think of these?"

"Huh?"

"Only three pictures, all sort of romantic and vintage." I took the kissing one, a staged work that The Girls disdained but that I loved, off the wall. It looked professionally mounted, but the back was messed up. The brown paper had been peeled away and then pressed back into place.

*A clue. A clue. Yeah me.*

I slid my nails under the paper and held my breath as I prayed I wouldn't wreck it and leave my own clue. The paper cooperated and stayed intact, revealing a trio of three pictures, all printed on a home printer, low quality but serviceable. They were all of a man, not Phillip, Angela's husband. None of the pictures were particularly romantic, no nudes or anything like that. Just a man, dark-haired and moderately handsome, sitting in a restaurant, on a park bench, and in a car.

I waved Aaron over. "Check it out."

"Panera," he said without a moment's hesitation.

"What did you say?"

He pointed to the restaurant picture. "Panera Bread."

I looked closer. "Really? Wait. You've been to Panera Bread? That doesn't sound right."

"Had to check out the competition."

"I don't think they're your competition."

"Me either." Aaron lost interest and started chewing on his thumbnails, both, at the same time. He looked especially weird, considering his new hairline and lack of eyebrows, but who was I kidding? Aaron was never going to be normal. I couldn't imagine what his sisters were like.

I laid the three pictures on the counter and took several shots of each, then put them back in the frame and hung it up. Next was the boys at the urinal picture, my dad's favorite. He thought it was hilarious. The back of the picture wasn't as neatly replaced and seven pictures and a couple Mother's Day cards fell into my hands with no effort at all. Angela had looked at the pictures and cards so often that the paper wouldn't restick and I could see why. They were all of her children, two of her holding them as newborns, the same shots I'd seen at Phillip's house. The others were of Christmas mornings and birthdays. The cards had "I love you, Mama" written in uneven block letters.

All the pictures and cards were well-worn. Angela had probably looked at them hundreds of times. My heart twisted in my chest.

"She didn't want to leave," I said, my voice thick. "She does love them."

Aaron glanced at the little mother's horde of love and asked, "How can you tell?"

"If she left because she hated her life, why would she keep these? She's not a sociopath. She cares, deeply."

*My life just got a whole lot harder. Crap on a cracker.*

I took pictures of everything and placed the picture back on the wall. The third print came undone as easily as the second. The back contained pictures of an older couple I assumed were Angela's parents, Gina, various women that struck me as friends, and Phillip. Her husband got one picture, but he was as well-thumbed as the rest. I took shots of each one, replaced them, and stuck the print back on the wall.

I checked the time. An hour until we had to meet Chuck. An hour until I had to look happy and not demoralized at all. Angela didn't want to abandon her babies. That meant she had to. I couldn't imagine what would be bad enough to make her do that. Or maybe I could. My mom drove me nuts practically on a daily basis, but she'd die to protect me. Maybe that's what Angela was doing, protecting her family. But from what or who? Calpurnia? No, that didn't track. Phillip was still with the family and Angela had nothing to do with the business. Calpurnia didn't think Angela was any kind of threat and she had to be a good judge of character or she wouldn't be where she was.

"We better go or the guys in the hall will—" I turned and a poof of white hit me in the face. I sneezed and sputtered. "What the what? Aaron, have you lost your damn mind?"

He stood in the kitchen with a small flour sack in hand. "Got to look the part."

"Why would I have flour on my face?" I sneezed again.

Aaron shrugged. "It's you."

Dammit. He was right. Flour on the face did seem like something that I would do. "But there's a mess. What do you say to that?"

He dug in a cabinet and came out with a paper towel. He wet it and cleaned up the floor before stuffing the dirty towel in his jean pocket. It wasn't a good look.

I held out my hand. "I can't have you walking the streets of Paris like that."

"Huh?"

"Give me the towel."

Aaron gave it to me, but I could tell he didn't get it and I wasn't about to explain. We locked up, said goodbye to the elevator guys, who, unfortunately, noticed the wet spot on Aaron's jeans. They gave me sly, questioning looks and I whispered, "Riche."

They nodded and we jogged down the stairs, returned the keys to the foreman, and hurried away to the metro. No one followed us or, if they did, they were very good.

We actually got seats and I texted Novak and Spidermonkey the pictures that I took. Both wanted to know what I wanted to do. I had no answer for them. Why couldn't Angela turn out to be a soulless, child-abandoning witch who was slutting it up in the City of Lights? I'd turn her over to Calpurnia and let her do whatever she wanted. Now I couldn't. Dammit. All I knew was that I wasn't ready to out Angela before I knew why she did it. I had to know. I was going to be a mother someday and I had a feeling that figuring out Angela might stop me from screwing it up royally like she did.

# CHAPTER NINETEEN

Novak texted me as we walked through the gate of Les Invalides. I didn't look at the text. I looked at the building down at the end of a long cobblestone road with conical trees standing guard. I'd spent an uncountable number of hours in there. For old ladies, The Girls sure did love the army museum. I think they had the armor memorized. On one notable visit, they noticed a mistake in a set of German armor. The armor had been cleaned and put together wrong. It took three hours of arguing, but they finally got through to the head curator and got it fixed. We had to watch it happening. Myrtle and Millicent refused to leave until they saw it properly displayed. That was one of the longer days of my life. I learned more than I ever wanted to know about 800-year-old metal.

I took Aaron's arm. "Don't you just love this building?"

"Never been before," he said.

"But you lived here for five years. What about Napoleon's tomb?"

"Nope."

"What the heck were you doing with your time?" I asked.

"Cooking."

*Ask a stupid question.*

A big group of students with backpacks passed us and flooded the security tent, dropping their packs on the wobbly folding table to have them searched. The female guard in her black uniform and odd hat gave us the stink eye. Loitering wasn't seen the same way it had been in view of the recent terrorist attacks in the city.

"Let's get in line," I said, steering Aaron down the rope aisle and queueing up behind the raucous students.

Another guard with a stern face and a hint of greying stubble stepped out from the little guardhouse, saw us, and waved us past the line. It's good not to carry packs in Paris. My little boho bag barely had enough room for my cellphones, wallet, and lipstick. Despite that, the guard looked through it good and hard, examining my cellphones. He was the first security guy to take an interest in them.

*Thank god Chuck isn't here.*

"Pourquoi avez-vous deux portables?" he asked with an edge in his voice.

"Un pour le travail et un pour personnels," I said.

"Travaillez-vous à Paris?"

"Non. Aux États-Unis."

He asked what my work was and I showed him my ACLS card. My ability to run codes satisfied him, but just barely. He cracked a rusty smile and waved us through. We walked down the long drive and stared up at the enormous building with its Mansard roof and arched entrance that reached all the way to the ridgeline. Louis XIV wanted it to impress and it certainly did. Only the Sun King would build an army hospital to look like a palace. He never did anything small or restrained.

This time, I wasn't admiring the architecture. I was looking for Chuck. Thankfully, I didn't find him.

"You're going to have to carry Novak's cell," I told Aaron.

"Why?"

"Because if security gets nosy again and Chuck's there, I'm toast."

"Why do I have two cells?" he asked.

"One's your backup," I said.

"Weird."

I was surprised he knew that. He didn't seem to know that shaving the front two inches of his hair was weird. "I know, but Chuck'll buy it if it comes from you."

Aaron shrugged and I pulled out the vibrating phone. Novak wasn't giving up.

"Keep an eye out for Chuck," I said. "I've got to answer this."

"Are you okay?" asked Novak in a rush when I answered.

"I'm fine. Why?"

"You weren't answering. I thought the suits caught up with you."

I scanned the building as we approached the entrance arch. We could see clear through to the inner courtyard past two dozen milling tourists. Chuck wasn't there. "No suits. We've lost them."

"Where are you?" he asked.

"Les Invalides. Walking in."

"I'll meet you there."

A zing of fear zipped up my back. "You can't. Chuck's here."

"I work for you *and* Chuck on the Marais matter."

I blew out a breath. "I forgot. Can't you just tell me over the phone?"

"My results aren't digital and I'd like to meet this Chuck who you have to keep in the dark on so many things," said Novak.

"Not so many things," I said, walking through the enormous arched wooden doors.

"Okay. One very important thing. The Fibonaccis."

"He's a cop."

"I know and an interesting cop, too."

"What do you mean by that?"

Novak didn't answer the question. "I'll be there in two hours. I have to confirm something."

"Where are you?" I asked.

"EDF." He hung up and I gave the cellphone to Aaron.

"What's EDF?" I asked him.

"Electric company."

"I wonder what Novak's doing there?" I turned right to the ticket office and trotted up the stairs. An arm shot out and grabbed mine. I screeched and prepared to punch, but it was only Chuck leaning on a pillar, looking much more relaxed than I felt. "Did you say something about Novak?"

"Don't do that. Are you crazy?" I smacked his hand and his cheeks colored.

"Sorry. I wasn't thinking. You knew I'd be here," he said.

"Yeah. You and three million other guys."

"Got ya. No sneaking up. Now what was that about Novak?"

"He's got something for us. He wants to meet here in a couple hours."

"Something on the Marais apartment?" Chuck asked.

"I guess so. He didn't say. It's not digital, whatever it is." I opened the glass door to the ticket office and was amazed, not for the first time, that it was empty. Three clerks looked up and I felt a bit of performance anxiety. French people behind desks always unnerved me even if they smiled, which was rare. I had to remind myself that they were never going to behave like Americans. I wasn't going to get wide smiles and a call across the room asking if they could help us. The trio would stand there, patiently waiting with neutral expressions for us to come up in our own time. No eagerness would be felt or displayed. A hint of a smile would be nice though, a little tension breaker, although I was the only one who was tense. Chuck made a beeline for the brochures and Aaron looked disinterested as always.

"I'll get the tickets," I said.

The clerks spoke English, mercifully, and I got the tickets with a minimum of stress. It was my first time. The Girls usually bought tickets to practice their excellent French. I accepted our tickets and handed them out to Chuck and Aaron.

"What about those?" asked Chuck, pointing to the paper Napoleon hats on display.

I rolled my eyes. "Those are for the kids."

"I want one," he said.

"You're messing with me, right?"

"No way. They're cool. Aaron wants one."

Aaron's expression didn't change. *Want* was putting it a bit strongly.

"I'll ask them if you won't," said Chuck.

"You're going to ask if you can have a paper Napoleon hat?" I asked. "You? Chuck Watts?"

"If *we* can have hats."

"I have a hat," I said.

"You can never have too many hats. Besides, we're on vacation."

*I don't know what to do with this.*

"Okay. Go ahead and ask," I said.

He did. I couldn't believe it, but he did. Chuck rakishly leaned on the desk, flirted shamelessly, which was pretty much the only way he flirted, and he got three hats plus smiles from all three clerks. He did the impossible and I wasn't grateful, especially when he popped a paper triangle into shape and said, "Take off your hat."

"I'm good."

Chuck's face lit up. "Are you worried about what people are going to think?"

"Little bit," I admitted.

"Come on."

"No."

He formed another hat and put it on his head. Sideways, of course. "We're never going to see these people again. Who cares?"

"You're killing me here."

He put Aaron's hat on and it actually improved the little weirdo by covering up the sad hair.

I sighed. "Fine, but if this makes it on the DBD site, you're going to pay."

He laughed and settled the heinous hat on my adorable cloche. "Awesome."

I slung my purse over my shoulder and headed for the door. "I didn't know you were a dork."

"This isn't dorky," he said, catching up with me in two strides. "This is cool."

We looked at Aaron, who trotted out the door. Total dork.

Chuck grinned at me. "Okay. It's different on everyone. You, for instance, are hot and whimsical."

"And you are?" I asked.

"Rakish and charming."

"And humble, too."

"Always. Which way should we go?"

"What do you want to see?" I asked.

"Everything," he said.

*Groan. So much armor.*

"Armor?"

"Abso-friggin-lutely."

We looked at the armor and then we looked at more armor. When we were done with that, there were swords and uniforms. Then Chuck decided we had to double back and look at Otto Heinrich's display. It didn't get much more impressive than Otto on his charger. The horse's armor was particularly interesting. What kind of horse could carry its own armor and Otto in his? That guy was huge. Apparently, Chuck found this question fascinating, too. Pretty soon, he had a docent and pelted the poor guy with questions about weight and individual pieces.

I pointed to some benches at the end of the hall and he nodded, too busy with girth to notice much about me. I positioned myself behind another display so Chuck couldn't get a clear view of me and called Novak on my regular phone.

"Where are you?" I asked when he picked up.

"I'm glad you called. I'm going to be late. What part of the museum are you in?"

"Armor."

"Still?"

"Chuck seems to think there's going to be a test afterward." I groaned and slipped off my shoes, rubbing my soles. Madam Ziegler was right; the shoes didn't hurt. My feet were just sick of being walked on.

"My research says he's not a museum type of man," said Novak.

"Mine, too. When are you going to save me?"

"Give me an extra hour."

"Why do you hate me?"

Novak laughed. "It will be worth it." He hung up and I hid the phone a second before Chuck headed over.

"I'm done."

I stretched. "Really? Are you sure you don't want to count the rivets on that beaky helmet six rooms ago?"

"They didn't have rivets."

"Whatever."

"Let's check out the World Wars." Chuck was bouncing on the balls of his feet like Aaron did when he was waiting for a food opinion.

"The wars it is."

Chuck put my shoes back on after a complimentary foot rub and hauled me to my feet. We climbed the stairs to WWI because why take an elevator when you can march up stairs? We toured the WWI section and the horror of it depressed me as always. Then we went into WWII, an era that seemed so much more exciting and romantic. I'm sure it wasn't if you had to actually live through it. I zeroed in on the Resistance section as I always did. Stella Bled Lawrence was a part of it and I always felt somehow connected to her when I looked at the coded letters and maps. She wasn't there in the displays since her work was still classified, but I knew she deserved to be. Maybe someday there'd be a section on her exploits. The Girls would love that.

Chuck put an arm around my waist and I caught my breath.

"They have an Enigma machine here. Did you know that?" He was so excited and close, I had to say, "Really? Where?" even though I did know.

We looked at the Enigma machine and the code breaking display before working our way to the uniform part. Chuck found my favorite uniform first, a German uniform with giant basket boots for walking in snow.

"I wonder how in the hell he walked in those?" asked Chuck.

"Not very fast, I'm guessing."

The Novak phone started vibrating in my purse and while Chuck looked at other displays, I called him back.

"I'm here at the tomb," he said. "Can you tear them away?"

I wasn't sure. Aaron was scowling at a display of ration cards and I think Chuck might've been counting medals on a general's jacket.

"I'll try." I hung up and tucked the phone away. "We need to go."

Chuck glanced back at me. "Did Novak call?"

"Yeah. He wants us to come to the tomb," I said.

His eyes went back to the display and my hand went to my hip. "He's doing us a favor."

"Fine. Fine. But we're coming back. I don't want to miss anything."

*God forbid.*

"Deal. Let's go."

I dragged Chuck and Aaron down the stairs and out of the building into the courtyard. Dragged is right. Chuck wanted to look at everything and there wasn't even that much to see. I reminded him that Novak had information on the mysterious Marais apartment and it might be a clue to The Klinefeld Group. That got him going and we walked into the monument to Napoleon ten minutes later.

"Whoa," he said. "This is huge."

"I know. Novak's waiting at—"

"Is that him?" asked Chuck.

It was Novak. Did the man own nothing but bizarre biking outfits? This one had orange and green tiger stripes and a little hat to match. No wonder Chuck spotted him from across the wide expanse, standing at the marble railing that overlooked the sarcophagus—or should I say sarcophagi, since Napoleon had six caskets like nesting dolls. One of anything was never enough for the great man, not even in death.

"That's him," I said, handing my purse to security. That guard was much less interested in security and barely glanced in my purse and he waved Aaron through without checking him at all.

"He doesn't look like a cyber expert," said Chuck.

"I don't know what he looks like," I said.

"At least I don't have to worry about the competition."

I glanced up at him, astonished. "Were you worried?"

"It occurred to me, but I'm over it."

I had to lead Chuck around the railing. His head seemed permanently pointed at the dome and he kept bumping into people. "Look where you're going."

"How many tombs are in here?" he asked. "I thought it was only Napoleon."

"There's a bunch of generals and some other Bonapartes," I said as we reached Novak.

"First time at the dome church?" asked Novak.

"How can you tell?" I grinned at him. "It's a good thing there's not a dress code."

"There's nothing wrong with my outfit."

I wrinkled my nose. "Only to the colorblind."

Novak laughed and Chuck tore his eyes away from the magnificence, sticking out his hand. "Chuck Watts. Thanks for taking on this case for us."

"You're welcome. Any friend of Spidermonkey's is a friend of mine," said Novak. "I have some information I'd like you to see."

"Let's do it." Chuck turned and happened to look down into Napoleon's tomb. "Whoa. I thought he was a little guy."

"Only in stature," I said. "We'll go down in a minute."

"We can go down there?"

"Sure." I headed for a bench that some Brits, fully decked out in the red and gold of the Manchester United, vacated. They almost made Novak's orange and green seem reasonable. Almost.

I sat down, chilling my bum instantly, and the guys took the spots on either side of me. Aaron wandered off, probably thinking of the wonders of duck fat.

"What have you got?" I asked.

Novak took an adorable little backpack off his back and pulled out a sheath of papers. "You remember when I told you that the Marais apartment is a dead zone?"

"Yeah. Isn't it?" I asked.

"It is, but that's not the end of it. Dead zones use utilities. It's just not recorded, so no one can track the usage."

Chuck nodded. "I get it. If you're squirreling someone away, like a political prisoner, for instance, you wouldn't want anyone to know how many people you had by how much water was being sucked up."

"Exactly."

"But water is being used," I said.

"And electricity and gas. Usually," said Novak.

"Usually?"

"You got me to thinking with your dates. That address has been dead for the twenty years of records I accessed."

"So?" asked Chuck.

I smiled. "So Werner Richter knew about the apartment in 1963 and his brother thought it had something to do with his death. I bet the apartment was dead even back then."

Novak nudged me. "That's what I thought, too. The apartment was secret. The wife and daughter weren't to go there or know anything about it."

"Are there more records?" asked Chuck.

"Not that I could access online, but I have a friend at EDF. They've been in business since 1946."

Novak's friend was a very good friend and he let Novak into corporate headquarters. Five hours of digging through files in the basement and then more digging into billing gave Novak the info he needed. Well...not the info, but a lead. A very good lead. Electricity was being used in the Marais apartment, but not a lot. Novak's friend said that, in his opinion, no one was living there and there are electric heaters, only used enough to keep the pipes from freezing. And, more importantly, someone was paying the bills.

"Please say The Klinefeld Group," I said.

"Sorry. No," said Novak. "Obsidian Inc."

"Who's that?"

"From what I can tell, it's a shell corporation based in Switzerland."

Chuck put his elbows on his knees and gazed at the marble railing. "Who owns it?"

"I haven't been able to find that out yet. The Swiss are very good at keeping secrets, but I will break through...eventually."

"So what's with the papers?" I asked.

"These are the usage details, gas, electric, and water. I thought you would have to see it to believe it." Novak passed me the sheath and I scanned them. No water used. No gas used. 1999. 1983. 1972. 1961. It kept going and going to 1946. The account was setup at almost the same time EDF was formed.

"Who's Marcel Paul?" I asked, looking at the name at top of the last paper.

"He founded EDF."

"That's interesting," I said, staring at that date in May 1946.

"What is it?" asked Chuck.

"Apparently, the Marais apartment has been a dead zone since 1946," I said.

Chuck stood up and started pacing. "Who would do that? It's crazy. Certifiable."

"Marcel Paul set it up," I said. "It doesn't say why. What do we know about Paul?"

Novak shrugged. "He was a politician, a communist. A little controversial."

"Could he have been a Nazi collaborator?" I asked.

"Not possible. He was part of the Resistance. He tried to assassinate Hermann Goring."

"Holy crap. He was in Valkyrie?"

"I think it was a separate attempt, but I can find out if you'd like. He was arrested and sent to Buchenwald."

I leafed through the papers again. "So he wouldn't have anything to do with The Klinefeld Group, assuming we're right and they have some Nazi connection through Jens Waldemar Hoff."

"Stella was in the Resistance," said Chuck. "I wonder if she knew Paul."

"Stella?" asked Novak.

"Stella Bled Lawrence," I said. "I doubt it. The Resistance wasn't really centrally organized, more like small cells."

"I can investigate her," said Novak.

"I'd rather have you on Obsidian, Inc."

He nodded. "I've already discovered they have been paying the taxes on the property all these years."

"That's a lot of money to pay for an apartment nobody's using," said Chuck. "We have to find out who they are."

"I will do my best to find out." Novak got up and stretched. "And now I will go for a café. Care to join me?"

He was looking at me rather intensely.

"We haven't been down to the tomb yet," said Chuck.

"I'll pass," I said. "I could use a café, not to mention some sitting. You and Aaron go."

"Where is he?"

I stood and spun around. "I don't know. Call him."

Aaron was in one of the antechambers with Louis Bonaparte's tomb. Chuck headed in that direction. Novak and I went out the front door. I couldn't help but notice all the stares we were getting. We were an odd couple, to say the least.

Once we were out the doors and walking down the steps, I said, "I assume you have something else for me."

"You assume correctly."

Novak found a secluded spot on the corner of the café's small wooden deck. I had a good view of anyone coming around the corner of the dome church and he could watch for anyone coming down the gravel lane behind me. We ordered espresso and croissants. I needed it. I'd managed to twist my ankle on the gravel. My shoes were much worse on rocks than cobblestones.

"So," I said, eyeing the nearby tables for eavesdroppers, but no one was close enough to hear anything, unless I shouted, "have you found anything out on the suits?"

The waitress brought our order and gave Novak a disapproving once over. She muttered something about Germans as she walked away. Novak grinned and took off his hat. His long, tangled hair fell onto his shoulders in a clump. "She thinks I'm German."

"Why? You don't sound German."

"Who else would wear this outfit to a museum?"

"I've seen a whole lot of Germans and none of them dress like you," I said.

He took a sip of his espresso. "It is a stereotype, one I like to encourage. The French think the Germans have no taste. The Italians say so, too."

"How does that help you?"

"If someone were to come looking for us and questioned the waitress, she would not remember a Marilyn Monroe lookalike and a Bosnian Serb. You don't look like yourself. I wouldn't think you could be so well concealed."

"I can't take the credit. A stylist did it."

"A good job. About the suits as you call them, I did find one." Novak opened his backpack and put another sheath of papers and his phone on the table.

I took a sip of my espresso and tried to look nonchalant. I was anything but. "How?"

Novak brought up a photo on his phone and pushed it across the table. "Video surveillance on the metro. I got clear shots of both men chasing you."

I flipped through the shots and they were surprisingly clear of the men on the platforms, coming down the stairs, and, my favorite, me kicking the crap out of one. "Can I have a copy of that?" I asked.

He smiled. "Of course. It is impressive."

"Thanks. So you've identified one of them."

He pointed to the second suit. "Jules Henri Poinaré, a Corsican."

"Sounds like a history professor," I said, looking closer at the angular face on the screen, handsome in a hard, unyielding way. His was a face that didn't smile a lot. Why was he so familiar?

"Academics are not what Monsieur Poinaré excels in," said Novak.

"Please don't say he excels in killing people."

"Among other things."

"Like what?"

"Kidnapping, extortion, torture. And he's not shy. Several murders credited to him were executed in public places at close range."

My hands shook a little and I put them in my lap, but not before Novak noticed. "Torture? Who does he work for, the French CIA?"

"He works for whoever will pay him."

"Who's he connected with most often?" I asked.

"He mainly works for other Corsicans. Germani was his mentor until he was arrested in 2014. It's believed that he murdered several members of the Brise de Mer gang in retaliation for the murder of Germani's mentor, Casanova. The other suit may be connected to Germani as well. I'll keep looking, but it seems he's a new face."

I squeezed my hands into fists and then forced them to relax before tearing into my croissant. "That sounds like you're making it up. Casanova? For real?"

Novak nodded. "Movies have been made about these people, but they are quite real and deadly."

"You think this Poinaré wanted to kill me?"

"If he wanted to kill you, you'd be dead. He's not an amateur. Kidnapping is my guess."

"If he works for The Klinefeld Group, that kind of makes sense. They probably still think I know where that box is that they want."

Novak polished off his espresso and signaled the waitress for a second one. "You really have no idea what it is?"

"I really don't, and my godmothers don't either. Have you found any connection between The Klinefeld Group and Poinaré?"

"No. Nothing yet. He uses untraceable portables and never stays in one place too long."

"Does he have a family?"

"Parents and three sisters. He's careful to shield them. Everything they do is monitored by the state in an effort to catch him at something, anything, but they are as careful as he is. I will come at this from you."

"Me?"

Novak nodded. "He's hunting you and someone hired him. Who's connected with you?"

"Well, the Fibonaccis, obviously, but Calpurnia had me in her house. If she wanted to get info out of me, that was definitely a better time to do it."

"I agree. Who else?" he asked.

I sighed and started listing the people I'd helped catch. Most were still awaiting trial, including the mass murderer. Besides the cases I'd personally worked on, there was my dad. He had thirty-five years of enemies racked up. Somebody could be looking to get at him through me.

As I listed the cases, Novak shook his head, took his phone back, and typed the names into his phone. "Your life hasn't been a calm one."

"Not so much."

"I'll see what I can do with this, but Spidermonkey would be better. My connections are mainly in Europe."

"He's still in the hospital. We can't bother him," I said. "Wait. Can I see that picture of Poinaré again?"

Novak handed me his phone and I stared at that sinister face. "I've seen him somewhere."

"In the metro."

"No. Somewhere else, but he didn't look like this."

He nodded. "You have a good eye. Poinaré is a master of disguise. For years, no one knew what he looked like. Even the hair and eye color aren't certain. His bone structure is how I identified him."

"Very James Bond," I said.

"Poinaré would kick Bond's ass."

Those cold eyes came back to me. "The Marais!"

"The Marais?"

"I saw Poinaré when Chuck and I were trying to get into the Marais apartment for the first time." I bit my lip. "I think it was him. He was a pudgy hipster with a beard and glasses."

"Why do you think it was him?" asked Novak.

"The eyes...yes. He's the same guy that chased me in the metro. I recognized him then, too. I just couldn't place him."

"He was following you for a while before he decided to make a move."

I sat back puzzled. "Why then? I'd just seen you. Maybe that was it."

"Could be, but I think it was the unidentified suit who kicked it off. He's inexperienced and it was him that tried to access your phone in my apartment. As soon as you made him on the street, both he and Poinaré were screwed. Poinaré would've checked you out. He'd know that once you knew you were being followed, you'd change up everything and he'd have to reacquire you. He probably thought it would be easier to nab you right then."

"It wasn't," I said with pride.

The waitress brought Novak's espresso and he affected a German accent. It was really good. Bavarian, if I had to guess. "You were better than Poineré expected. I'll do what I can without Spidermonkey.

I checked the time. We'd been gone a while, but Chuck's ability to take forever was well documented. "How about Angela? Did you figure out how she got that job so easy?"

"No, I couldn't get any information on that," he said. "But I got something else equally helpful."

"What's that?" I asked before eating the last of my croissant.

Novak unfolded the papers and pushed them at me. "See if you can find it."

"You're testing me?" I asked. "That sucks."

He smiled. "I just want to see if you find it."

"Swell." I leafed through the papers. They included Angela's first lease agreement, copies of her rent payments, done electronically, her job application at the bookstore, and copies of her paychecks. He had her credit card statements for her first six months in Paris and her utility bills. "You've been busy."

"Don't stall," he said.

"I'm not stalling." I was stalling. Everything looked kosher, the opening of the bank account, credit card. Or...no. "She didn't charge anything for almost three months. That's a little weird. She used it regularly after that. Not a lot of money. Little stuff, like dinner and wine."

"Right," said Novak.

"You're not going to give me a hint?"

"You're the detective. I'm tech support."

I wrinkled my nose. "Yeah, right. That's what Spidermonkey says, too."

"He's right."

"Whatever." I went through the papers again, now concentrating on the dates. Angela might've had enough cash to get her through those first few months, but that was a lot of cash. "She didn't make any withdrawals from the bank during that time either."

"Yes," Novak said with a smile.

"She would've had to have had enough cash to buy groceries and whatnot for nearly three months. That's got to run into the hundreds." I looked again. She was in Paris five days after her disappearance. She signed her lease and got the bank account. She started her work. "Oh my god."

"That was much faster than me. What did you find?"

I pushed the papers back to Novak and pointed to the date on her work application. "The date's wrong. It's two and a half months after she disappeared. She made a mistake. She put the date she actually filled it out, not the date she was supposed to have been here like the other applications. She wasn't in Paris for those first ten weeks. Of course she wasn't. She had a nose job."

"The nose was what made me pay attention to the dates. She was being paid and had an apartment, but she wasn't here," said Novak. "Thanks to Nine Eleven, flight manifests are forever. I believe that Corrine Sweet arrived the day before she filled out that application. She flew under the name Lauren Thomas, a single woman arriving for a vacation from New York. The card she used was never used again in Paris or anywhere else."

"So where was she? A nose job doesn't take that long. Any clue?" I asked.

"Not so far. I don't know where to look."

*Ten weeks. Ten weeks. Doing what for ten weeks? Duh. French.*

"What's Les Cahiers de Gibert like?" I asked. "Do they carry English editions or is it purely a French bookstore."

Novak drummed his long fingers on the table. "Only French. Why?"

"I doubt Angela Riley spoke French, but Corinne Sweet does."

He craned back his head and his Adam's apple jutted out so far it looked painful. "Corinne is fluent. She had to be."

"She spent those missing weeks learning French. That's an immersion program in the States," I said. "There can't be that many programs."

"Spidermonkey would be the one I would go to on this," said Novak. "Can you call him to see whether he's better?"

"Er...no. That's not a good idea. He'll have to call me, which he might never do."

"Why not?"

"I think Loretta thinks we're having an affair. Plus, the only number I have is a secret phone that's no longer so secret. Spidermonkey is out. But maybe it doesn't matter where she learned French."

"What matters is who paid for it."

I shrugged and asked for an espresso. "I don't think so. Angela arrived fully fluent. She had to be to do bookkeeping in French. That kind of program isn't cheap or short. She might've been in it for most of the ten weeks. What's that cost? Ten thousand? Twenty? No lover paid for that."

"The government, but we agreed that she wasn't a witness. Nothing happened to the Fibonaccis."

"Then it's something else. She has to be a federal witness."

Novak groaned and I accepted my new espresso. "It's not so bad."

"You think not."

"No, I don't. You said you have to find out about the suits by looking at me, right?"

He nodded but was obviously unconvinced. "Let's look at Angela. It's safe to say she didn't want to leave her kids."

"Is it? Are we sure of that?"

"I'm sure, so let's go with it," I said. "Someone made her do this."

"Your government," said Novak.

I nodded. "They got something big for putting her in the witness protection program, but right now I'm more interested in the one thing we don't know."

"We don't know a lot of things, Miss Watts," said Novak.

"I think you can call me Mercy at this point," I said. "And we know quite a bit, especially about Angela's life here, except for the identity of the Panera guy. She kept those pictures. He must be important."

"Panera?" asked Novak.

"The pictures of that guy. Aaron says he's sitting in a restaurant called Panera Bread"

"That's not her husband?"

I shook my head. "Nope. Phillip's the blond, plump one with the kids. I don't know who the handsome guy is."

He frowned. "You think he's handsome?"

"You don't?"

"He's somewhat generic." Novak turned and gave me his profile, running his finger down the bridge of his considerable nose. "He lacks character."

I chuckled. "You've got no shortage of character."

His eyes twinkled and I got the giggles. Must be the jet lag.

"I know what you Americans say about men with big noses," he said proudly.

"They use a lot of tissues?" I asked.

He sneered. "That's not correct."

"I think you're thinking of men with big feet."

Novak held up one of his size fourteens. "I've got those, too."

"You're the whole package, my friend. If I knew any women in Paris, I'd recommend you," I said. "Can we get back on point? Chuck might get done sometime this century."

Speak of the devil. My phone rang and it was Chuck asking where we were. I gave my directions and told Novak to put away all the Angela evidence.

"So you'd like to find this *handsome* Panera man," said Novak.

"Can you start with Angela's credit and debit cards to see if she charged anything there?" I asked.

Chuck and Aaron came around the corner and I waved. Novak grabbed a third chair for us and stood to leave.

"You don't have to go," said Chuck, smiling but rather worn out around the edges.

Novak offered his chair to Aaron and said, "I'm afraid Miss Watts has given me a mission and it's time to go."

He headed off and Chuck asked, "What mission?"

I told them about Poinaré, Germani, and Casanova and how Novak thought kidnapping was the aim. "He's going to try to connect The Klinefeld Group with Poinaré and figure out who the second suit is."

"Novak's going to be a busy guy."

*You have no idea. Thank goodness.*

"He's going to try and find out who's behind Obsidian, Inc., too," I said. "Are we ready to go?"

"Abso-friggin-lutely," said Chuck.

I gave him a wary look. "You seem awfully excited."

"Hell, yeah. We've got to finish World War Two and I want to go to the De Gaulle exhibit. I talked to an Aussie and he said it was excellent."

"I think I need another espresso," I said.

We all had espressos and sandwiches. Then we closed down the museum, walking non-stop until six. By the time we got back to Elias's apartment, every joint in my body ached. The only thing on my body that didn't hurt were my feet. They were numb. I popped a couple Tylenols, put on PJs, and fell into the pit. Chuck and Aaron went out to dinner and brought me back some soup. I think I ate it. I'm not sure. I was sure about my dreams though. I was back in New Orleans, running scared, but the man coming up the stairs wasn't holding a knife and he wasn't Richard Costilla.

## CHAPTER TWENTY

I woke the next morning with the unsettling feeling that I was being watched. I peeked out from under my lashes, expecting Elias to be there, but he wasn't.

"Thank goodness," I said, but the feeling didn't go away.

There was a rustle to the right of the bed and there he was, sitting on the dresser with a hind leg in the air. Blackie from New Orleans. That damn cat or whatever he was.

"Shoo. Go away," I said.

Blackie didn't shoo. He was unshooable.

"Please go away. I really don't need this right now."

The cat stopped cleaning and stared at me with those great green eyes.

I waved at him. "Go home, you freak. You belong to Grandma's house. Go home."

A gentle knock rattled my door. "Hey, Mercy," said Chuck. "You up?"

I looked at the cat and he did a big stretch, arching his skinny back and then slinking around the framed portrait of a woman with an enormous amount of hair and a shy smile.

"Yeah, come in." I winced in anticipation of what Chuck was going to say when he got a load of Blackie. Since New Orleans, he'd decided that the cat was just a cat and the family was messing with me. He didn't come with the house because that was looney. I agreed, but I still believed it.

Chuck opened the door slowly, probably afraid that I was nude and ready to pounce. "How'd you sleep?"

"Not great." I glanced at the dresser and Blackie was gone.

*Great. Now I'm losing it and I didn't have much of it to begin with.*

"Help me out, will you?" I asked.

Chuck hoisted me out of the pit. "Are you okay? You looked sort of scared when I came in."

"I'm fine. What's on the schedule for today?"

"I wanted to take a run at the Marais apartment manager. I talked to Novak and he says the guy lives on site, but I think I'd rather wait until we know who really owns it. We're going to be typical tourists today. If we don't get busy, we're going to miss half of Paris."

"Don't I have class?" I had stuff to do on Angela. Calpurnia had texted me three times while we were in the army museum. She wanted progress. I put her off, but she was getting suspicious and wouldn't wait much longer. She mentioned sending Fats Licata over to "help me out". Translation: motivate me. I didn't need Fats on my tail. It was hard enough to keep Chuck out of the know.

"Not today," he said. "I checked."

*Fan-freaking-tastic.*

"Great," I said. "What should we do?"

"The catacombs. It's on my bucket list. Get a move on. Rick Steves says we've got to get there early or we'll be in line forever." He patted my shoulder from an arm's length.

"We're going to be waiting forever no matter what," I said, hoping hours in line would deter him. It didn't.

"I don't care how long we wait. I've got to see it. This is my chance. I might never make it back to Paris." Chuck left the room and the instant the door closed, Blackie was back, staring at me from the dresser.

"This is so disturbing," I said.

He didn't blink. I didn't think he could.

"Feel free to disappear and never come back. That would be nice."

The cat yawned, did a toe spread, and began cleaning each little toe on his hind foot, biting each of the razor sharp claws. Blackie was going nowhere.

"Swell." I found another of Madam Ziegler's outfits on the rack she left me, the high-necked white dress with the asymmetrical hem. It wasn't anything I'd ever pick. It kind of reminded me of Princess Leia's outfit in *Star Wars* without the hood. Madam Ziegler poo-pooed that notion, stuck the beret on my head, and declared me stunning. I chose it mostly because it went with the beret, even though it made me feel sort of stupid. But the cloche had served me well at the army museum. I didn't get one comment about being Marilyn and the looks I got were more about the clothes and fit than me. I really enjoyed that. I hoped the beret would have the same effect.

I slipped the dress on and sat on the bed to put on the low sandals that also matched. The cat leapt off the dresser onto the bed and stalked over to rub on me.

"Knock it off. You're going to get hairs all over me." I checked and he didn't get a single black hair on my snow white dress. I guess you can't shed if you're not actually a cat.

He sat on the bed doing his usual stare and a little zing of fear went up my back. I'd only seen him in New Orleans before Richard Costilla tried to kill me. Mom had seen him when Aunt Tenne had her terrible car accident and when her grandparents were killed in a plane crash, but those were all post-tragedy. I saw him before and after the Costilla incident and everyone else saw him, too. I wanted to call Mom and ask her about it. Had she ever seen him before something happened and not in New Orleans? But I couldn't call Mom. She'd tell Dad and he'd get a feeling and my parents would be all over that. I couldn't have Morty sniffing around my activities in Paris. No, definitely not Mom. The only other person who would know and might be trusted to not tell my parents was Aunt Tenne.

Aunt Tennessee was the kindest, saddest person I ever knew. Scratch that. She was the kindest, formerly sad person I ever knew. The accident that killed her friends and, nearly ruined her life, sent her into a tailspin that lasted forty years. That all changed in Honduras when she made a fresh start and met Bruno, an artist of uncommon talent. Aunt Tenne was the happiest she'd ever been, but she still competed with my mother. Sisters. Some things never change.

Chuck knocked on the door. "Are you ready yet?"

"Not yet," I said. "Where's Aaron?"

"I don't know. I'll call him."

While he tracked down Aaron, I called Aunt Tenne. It was about midnight in St. Louis, but she'd become a night owl since Bruno was going through a phase of painting the Mississippi. He said he was studying the effect of the moonlight on the water.

Aunt Tenne answered with a groggy voice. I guess the night phase was over. "Sorry, it's me," I said.

"Carolina?"

"Mercy. Did I wake you?"

"Yeah, but that's okay. How's Paris?"

I bit my lip and then said, "Good. Can I ask you a question about the cat?"

"We don't have a cat," she said with a yawn.

"Grandma's cat."

"She doesn't have a cat either."

The family, as well as Chuck, had gone back into ostrich mode when we'd gotten home after New Orleans. "Come on, Aunt Tenne. We all know he exists."

She paused and I could feel the tension through the phone. "Has something happened?"

"Not exactly."

"Why didn't you call your mother?" she asked.

"Why do you think?"

There was a faint laugh and then she said something to Bruno about going back to sleep. "Go ahead. Ask away."

"You won't tell Mom and Dad?"

She yawned and said, "No. I won't tell overprotection central. What is it?"

"Have you ever seen Blackie anywhere other than Grandma's house in New Orleans?" I asked.

"Why do you want to know?"

"Can you just answer the question?"

"Yes. Have you?"

"Er..."

"Mercy," Aunt Tenne said, her voice razor sharp.

"Here in Paris. Where did you see him?" I asked.

I heard some rustling, footsteps padding across hardwood, and then a door closing. "I saw him in the St. Louis house."

"Mom's house?"

"No, my parents' house when we lived in St. Louis before my grandparents died. It was right before...my accident. Mercy, if you've seen him, you need to pay attention."

"To what?" I asked.

"To whatever you're really doing in Paris," she said.

"I'm on vacation with Chuck."

"And Aaron, your partner."

I wasn't sure what to say. Lying to Aunt Tenne wasn't on my to-do list.

"Mercy, it's fine. Do whatever it is that you're doing, but be very careful. That cat shows up when something happens to the family."

"Like a warning?"

"And then he sticks around afterward. I don't know why," she said.

I held out my finger. The cat sniffed it and then marked me with his cheeks. "Did anyone else see him before your accident?"

"That was the weird part. Well...it's all weird, but I was the only one who could see him that time. By the way, my grandmother saw him before the crash and nobody else saw him either."

"Did she tell you that?"

"No, I was curious after she died and I read her journal. She'd been seeing him for a week before they got in that plane."

*I think I'm gonna barf.*

"I have to get on a plane pretty soon," I said, my throat hot and tight.

"You're flying commercial. Theirs was a private plane. And it's not like it was an accident."

The cat let out a loud meow and I went stock still. "What did you say?"

"Um...you knew that, right?"

I shook my head no.

"Mercy, I'm sorry. I thought you knew. I thought Carolina told you."

"They were murdered?"

"I'm afraid so. The plane was tampered with."

"Who did it?" I asked.

"Nobody knows. Two men were seen going into the hangar prior to flight. They wore the right uniforms, so nobody challenged them."

"Why would somebody kill them? Was anybody else in the plane?"

"No. Grandpa was a licensed pilot. They were flying to St. Louis. We don't know why. Grandma called my father's office and left a message that they needed to see him. His secretary said she sounded tense. Their house was searched before we got down there for the funeral."

"What did they take?" I asked.

"Jewelry, cash. I don't remember how much it was worth, probably less than 500."

*Nobody sabotages a plane for 500 bucks.*

"Nothing else was taken?"

"Not that I know of. You could ask, but I will say that this still upsets my mother. She never talks about it and I didn't tell anyone about the cat in Grandma's journal or about the time I saw him. My point is that it's not a commercial plane you have to worry about."

"That's not as comforting as you think."

"Tell Chuck."

"About the murder?" I asked.

"About the cat. It's a warning. I wish I'd known you were seeing him when you were in New Orleans. I would've told you then," said Aunt Tenne.

"Mom knew. Why didn't she tell me?"

"I told you that I never told anyone."

Chuck knocked again and opened the door, peeking around the edge. "Are you ready?"

I looked up.

He pushed open the door. "What's wrong? Who's that?"

"Aunt Tenne."

"Is she okay?"

"She's fine," I said.

"Tell him," said Aunt Tenne and she hung up.

I grabbed my purse and dropped the phone in. "Ready."

He grabbed me before I made it out the door. "What happened?"

"I'll tell you later. We have thousands of dead Parisians to see."

"They can wait."

Chuck wouldn't let go, so I broke down and told him about my great grandparents, leaving out the cat who had disappeared the second he opened the door. I didn't want to freak him out.

"I'm not sure what to say. I'm sorry," he said.

"I thought it was an accident my whole life. I remember asking about it. Mom would get upset and leave the room. Dad told me to stop pestering her. He wouldn't say anything either. I thought Mom missed them like I'd miss Nana and Pop Pop if that happened to them."

"Do you think it could be The Klinefeld Group?"

"That long ago? What for?"

Chuck got thoughtful. "Your family has been connected with the Bleds for a long time. Maybe it had something to do with what The Klinefeld Group is looking for. They're capable of murder. Lester proved that," he said.

I took his hand and squeezed. "I really don't want to think about Lester right now."

He hugged me hard for the first time in forever and it felt so good. "We'll figure it out."

I listened to his heart rate go up and said, "We'll figure out a cold case from forever ago?"

"If it's connected to The Klinefeld Group, we will. I think we're getting closer." He pushed me back. "You still want to go to the catacombs? We can skip it."

I smiled. "No way. It's on your bucket list."

"It won't upset you?"

"I've been there before and I'm not the hysterical type."

He kissed my forehead. "Thank god for that."

"Is Aaron here?" I asked.

"No, he does have a class."

*Dammit. I need to check Novak's phone.*

"Is he already gone?"

"Yeah, Monsieur Barre said he left a while ago, but not before making him a traditional English fry up. I think I know why Monsieur Barre offered to let Aaron stay with him. That geezer's been eating like a king."

"Bastard," I said with laugh.

"I'll feed you on the way to the catacombs."

I grabbed his arm. "Aaron went to class?"

"Yeah," Chuck said slowly.

"The Corsican and that other suit probably know about the class. They might be watching."

Chuck shrugged. "It's fine. Aaron said he found out about another way in from one of the chefs."

My racing heartbeat slowed. "So he won't be seen going in?"

"Nope. He's going through another building on another block.

"I guess that'll work," I said.

"I told you it's fine." Chuck hustled me out of the apartment, jabbering like crazy. I think he was trying to take my mind off the Corsicans and my great grandparents. He needn't have bothered. My mind was firmly on the here and now, specifically on two men in suits and the black cat of doom.

I was right. Why am I always right when it comes to lines and so rarely when it comes to other stuff? Rick Steves was wrong and an hour before the catacombs wasn't enough. We got there an hour and a half before the opening at ten. The line was wrapped around the little park next to the small, dark green building that looked appropriately like a mausoleum or maybe a garage if you didn't know what lay beneath it.

I groaned when I saw the line, but it didn't bother Chuck. He was happy to wait and read the tour books he brought for entertainment. If I could've thought of a way to slip away and get the search on Angela's hotel taken care of, I would've done it. Since I wasn't so bright, I stayed with Chuck and the other tourists in line for two and a half hours. It was the worst I'd ever seen it, but Chuck was treated to a special show of a teenaged girl forcing her way out of the entrance in complete hysterics. From what I could tell, she freaked out in the tunnel leading to the catacombs and never actually made it in. Hysterical girl added fifteen minutes to the wait while the staff got the rest of her group up top with her. The line got pretty restless with her screeching on the sidewalk. Chuck thought I should do something since I was a nurse, but the staff handled that kind of thing on a regular basis and it's not like I had a Xanax to give her.

The wait was worth it, though. Chuck had a great time, going down the spiral stairs and through the tight tunnels where he had to duck his head. He even liked the claustrophobia and prickles of fear that came with the ticket. I'd never gotten used to the feeling, but I knew it would stop as soon as we passed under the sign saying that we were entering the Empire of the Dead and got out into the ossuary.

Chuck entertained me with a myriad of facts and pelted me with questions as if I knew whether there were children in there among the adults. The thought really seemed to bother him. Adults were fine, but children were a problem. With six million people down there, odds were children were among them, but I said I didn't think so. They wouldn't stack right and the catacombs were done decoratively. Chuck seemed soothed and we made it through in under an hour, coming out of a nondescript door that you'd never think was connected to a graveyard if you didn't already know. I was ready to hoof it to a café, but Chuck spotted the gift shop, and we had to go. He got a magnet for his lieutenant, a notorious worrywart, that said, "Keep calm and remember you're going to die," a cheery thought that made Chuck gleeful. He liked to bother the man when he wasn't bothering me.

When we got out of the shop, the hysterical girl was now at the exit, hyperventilating and wailing.

"Maybe you can do something," said Chuck. "She's been at it for a while."

"It's a put-on," I said. "You can't wail and hyperventilate at the same time. It's an either-or kind of thing."

"Are you sure?"

"Pretty sure. Ready for lunch?"

"I don't think we should do lunch before," he said.

I steered him away from the growing crowd around the wailing girl and asked, "Before what?"

"The sewer tour. I think it stinks."

"Hell, yeah, it stinks. You never said anything about the sewer tour," I said.

"Didn't I?"

"No, you didn't."

"Aaron wants to go," said Chuck.

My hands went automatically to my hips. "Aaron wants to go? Oh, really?"

"Really. He told me."

"You make it sound like you had a conversation with him."

"I did."

"Nobody has conversations with Aaron. He barely speaks and I would know. He's my partner."

"Call him and ask," said Chuck, pulling out his phone. "I wonder where the closest metro is."

I did call Aaron and we had what apparently counts as a conversation these days. I asked a question and he said, "Huh?" and then when I asked a second time, he said, "Yeah." That was it.

So we got on the metro and headed for the sewer tour. I'd only been once before and once was enough. Millicent said we had to go so we'd be well-rounded tourists. I should've known the guys would want to go. It had engineering and pipes and concrete with a tremendous stink.

Like with the catacombs, the entrance to the sewer tour wasn't all that impressive. The Girls and I passed it three times when we went. I wanted to give up, but The Girls weren't fans of giving up or skipping museums. We only knew we had the right area from the smell wafting around on the breeze from the river. Eventually, we realized the toll-booth-looking building was it.

Chuck didn't need the stink. He zeroed right in on the booth and bought three tickets. He claimed that Aaron's "yeah" meant he was on his way. Chuck kept checking to see if we were followed. We weren't and the area around the booth was so deserted it was easy to tell. We hung out and watched the tour boats heading toward the Eiffel until we heard labored breathing coming up behind us.

"You ready?" Chuck asked Aaron.

"Yeah."

"I got tickets."

"Okay," said Aaron.

"Alright."

Chuck nudged me. "See? We talk."

"Impressive," I said before heading over to the entrance, basically a concrete-lined hole in the ground, and waving Chuck down into the depths first. I got halfway down before Aaron poked me in the back. "What?"

"Novak called," said Aaron.

"What did he say?" I asked.

He shrugged.

"You didn't answer? What the...it could be important."

"Your phone."

I glared at him and held out my hand, not trusting myself to say anything. Aaron wasn't always useless, but he was right then.

"Huh?"

"Give it to me," I said between clenched teeth.

"Hey," Chuck called up the stairs, "are you coming or what?"

"Aaron has claustrophobia," I called over my shoulder.

"He doesn't have to come."

Aaron gave me the phone and I tucked it in my purse. "Oh, he's coming alright." I turned around and smiled. "I gave him a mint. He's fine."

"Mints help with claustrophobia?"

*They do today.*

"Sometimes. Are we all set?"

Chuck gave us our tickets and checked to make sure no one was following us. We gave our tickets to an exceedingly bored young woman who'd clearly lost her sense of smell long ago. We headed in for the self-guided tour and, I have to admit, it wasn't so bad. Chuck kept pointing that out and I held my tongue. A line from some old country song Dad liked kept going through my head, "It's gonna get bad before it gets better."

Chuck was having a grand old time reading about how sewers work and Aaron was right there with him. Then we passed through an arch and it was like hitting a wall of invisible stink. One minute it's bearable, then take one step and it isn't.

I dug in my purse for a tissue to hold over my nose and itched to check the Novak phone for messages.

"Does it smell worse now or is it just me?" asked Chuck.

I horked a little and pressed the lone tissue I had to my face. "It's you."

"Do you have any more tissues?"

"No, and I'd kill you before I'd give this one up. Go read your signs," I said in a strangled voice.

"It's not that bad."

"Don't make me kick you."

Chuck and Aaron led the way deeper into the stink and I tried to remember how much of the museum was left. I couldn't remember. I'd blocked it out or maybe it'd been fumigated out. We walked past arches in the walls where you could see rivers of waste rushing by and then into a corridor where you got to walk over the river. With each fenced-off grate, there was a sign telling the history of the Paris sewer and some artifacts, things like swords and whatnot that had been found in the sludge. Of course, Chuck had to read each placard and I saw my chance.

"I'm going to find a bathroom and vomit a little. Be back in a minute." I hurried away before he could offer to go with me. I went back through the exhibits, ducked around a wall next to a display of a mannequin sewer worker in some sort of iron cart, and got out Novak's phone. No bars, naturally, but I had a bunch of texts waiting. Novak had been busy. Some came in at five that morning and I read them in order. He'd identified the second suit and his instinct was right about the guy. He was new to the mafia game. His name was Michel Colonna, a twenty-one-year-old Corsican with various arrests for assault and menacing. Novak couldn't find any connection between him and Poinaré, so he didn't think they were working together. It was more likely that I had a set price on my kidnapping and both suits were going after it.

Colonna's inexperience was showing. He'd been hanging out on the street outside Novak's apartment while we were at Les Invalides, not exactly stealthy, and Novak got him on surveillance when he came home. Because of his position, Novak got a fix on his disposable cell. The idiot was sexting his girlfriend while hoping to nab me.

Novak's last message came in at eleven thirty, when Chuck and I were leaving the catacombs. Colonna was at the Miromesnil metro stop, the one closest to class. Novak said we shouldn't go back to the cooking school since the Corsicans were watching the metro.

Eleven thirty. Aaron was at the school then. I called him and he came to meet us. He probably used Miromesnil.

*Oh shit!*

A muffled yell echoed through the stone tunnels and I instinctively reached for my purse, but my Mauser was an ocean away. But the mannequin had lots of potential weapons. I grabbed a wooden two by four and ran back through the museum.

I turned into super stink zone and dashed into the display area. Aaron was on the ground, face down next to the second placard on Napoleon. I ran to him and checked his pulse. Alive. A clang echoed off the walls. There were two sets of legs behind the last placard, Chuck and another set in sharply-creased trousers. The men stumbled from behind the placard and around the corner. Colonna had a knife to Chuck's throat. I chased them around the corner and Colonna, despite being a lot shorter than Chuck, had my guy backed up against the railing on the bridge over a river of sewage.

Chuck surged when he saw me. He flipped around and Colonna was against the rail.

"Duck!" I screamed.

I ran for them with the two by four poised like a bat. Chuck ducked at the last possible second and I got a brief glimpse of Colonna's face right before I cracked him in the teeth. His head snapped back and then, in what seemed like slow motion, his head came back up, eyes focused on me with a mouth full of blood. The knife slashed at me as I jumped back.

Then Chuck grabbed him by the legs and flipped him backward into the sewage. There was a sickening thwack as Colonna's head hit a metal bar that extended over the river and his body hit the brown muck with a splash. Chuck and I looked at each other for a second and then we raced to the other side of the bridge. Colonna's body floated past, slowly sinking into the waste of Paris.

*Aaron!*

I spun around and ran back to my partner, crouching at his side. "Aaron. Aaron."

He groaned and I rolled him over. His throat was slightly red and blood flowed out of his nose.

"Can you follow my finger?" I asked.

Aaron followed fine. He was focused and alert. Well...as alert as Aaron gets.

A sleeper hold and Colonna dropped him on his face. Dad had demonstrated it on me when I was fourteen. That was the closest he ever came to Mom divorcing him. He slept in the garage for two weeks before Mom would let him back in the house. I was fine and Dad claimed he was teaching me how to escape the hold. He didn't teach me very well, since I passed out.

Aaron rubbed his throat and coughed before Chuck hauled him to his feet.

"We have to get out of here right now," said Chuck.

"What about the body?" I asked. "What about the police?"

"It's self-defense." He grabbed my hand and pulled me past the placards. "Did you touch anything?"

"Are you kidding?"

"Good."

We turned the corner and my weapon and Colonna's knife were lying on the bridge. Chuck kicked the knife over the edge and tossed my two by four after it.

"We can't just leave," I said.

Chuck spun me around and held me by the shoulders. "I don't want anyone to know that guy's dead. Whoever hired him will bring in a replacement. Somebody better."

I pointed at what looked like a camera up in a corner. "It's probably on video."

"Good. That proves self-defense."

"You're bleeding."

An open, still-bleeding slit extended from Chuck's ear to just under his jaw. He touched it and looked at the blood on his fingers. "I didn't feel it."

"We can't hide that," I said.

"Sure we can. Don't you have a scarf in your purse?"

"It's a girl's scarf."

"I don't give a crap."

I tied the scarf around his neck and it didn't look half bad. It was a good thing his button-up shirt was navy. It hid the blood well. Aaron had a black tee on, but blood was all over his face. I whipped off my beret and wiped it away before stuffing the hat in my purse.

We walked out of the museum like nothing happened. I have to give it to Chuck. He actually flirted with the bored girl as we left. He went up the stairs first to see if anyone was lying in wait. The area was clear, so we went to the nearest metro. I briefly considered telling Chuck about Novak's text. But there was no point and it would've led to Novak's phone and Aaron not looking at the texts. Aaron was just being Aaron and Novak didn't expect either of us to be at the school that day. If he had, he would've called me on my regular phone.

I glanced up at Chuck's neck and saw the blood oozing through my scarf. I got out my regular phone and googled the nearest hospital or clinic.

"What are you doing?" asked Chuck.

"Looking for a hospital."

"Are you crazy? We're not going to a hospital. They'll report a knife wound to the neck and put me in the system. I'll have to give an address and somebody could track you through me," he said. "Besides, I've got a nurse on retainer. Don't you have stuff?"

"I don't have sutures and that definitely needs suturing."

He grinned at me. "So improvise. Isn't that what you do best?"

"Stop using my own words against me and stop smiling. This is serious. You could've been the one floating in Parisian poop."

"With you around? No way." Chuck became thoughtful. "You know, I should've gone on vacation with you sooner."

I wrinkled my nose at him. "'Cause this is so much fun?"

"Hell yeah, it is. We stuffed a guy that probably works for the Corsican mob. I call that a good time. If I came here with anyone else, we would've toured museums and eaten great food and then gone home. Boring."

"There's something wrong with you. That was not fun."

Chuck elbowed me. "Come on. There's one less bad guy in the world and I didn't even have to fill out any paperwork."

"What about Aaron?" I asked. "Sleeper holds do kill people."

We looked at Aaron, whose nose had taken on a Shrek-like appearance.

"He's fine and I'm starving," said Chuck. "Where to for lunch?"

Before Aaron could take over, I said Tribeca on Rue Cler, but not until I'd worked on Chuck's neck. Aaron agreed with a shrug. Maybe he felt guilty about not looking at the texts. I'd never know. I bought supplies at a pharmacy on the way home, cleaned and butterflied Chuck's neck wound closed, and then we went on to Tribeca, the restaurant where Gina had seen her long-gone sister and started me on a wild goose chase that turned out to be plenty wild and where the geese just might kill you.

# CHAPTER TWENTY-ONE

Blackie sat on Elias's bed, purring away almost like a real cat, while I got dressed the next morning. I'd dreamt of that unknown man in New Orleans again, but it hadn't frightened me. I didn't know who he was and I didn't much care. I felt oddly safe with the cat there, staring at me with his green eyes. He'd saved me in New Orleans and I was pretty sure he'd protect me in the apartment if it came to that. Outside the apartment was another story, but Chuck had convinced me that we'd handled the sewer situation just fine and that the suit wasn't trying to kill anyone, not originally, anyway. He'd done the sleeper hold on Aaron and then tried it on Chuck. Not a great plan, since Chuck was so much taller. He failed and that's when the knife came out. Chuck, like Novak, didn't believe that killing was on the menu. They wanted me for information. The suits showed up after we found out about the Marais apartment, but if The Klinefeld Group murdered Werner Richter in '65 after he visited it, presumably they knew about it, too. What in the world did they think I knew?

Nothing was the answer, but they'd come for me again if that was really the intent. At dinner, I'd expected my old aversion to food to rear up, but it didn't, surprising me immensely. Colonna was just as young as Costilla and just as dead, but I didn't feel a bit guilty. What I did feel was anger. He attacked Aaron. He could've killed the little weirdo. A person didn't get much more defenseless than Aaron. Attacking me or Chuck was one thing. Attacking Aaron was quite another. I didn't wish I found another way. I was glad Colonna was dead. He deserved it.

Novak agreed. When we'd gotten back the afternoon before, I holed up in the bathroom, filling the tub and telling Novak what happened. It warmed my heart to hear him get upset. I assured him we were fine, which was more than I could say for poop guy as we'd started referring to him. Novak checked his sources and found, to his surprise, that the body hadn't been found yet. If the surveillance had been working that day, nobody had seen fit to check the footage. We had left a couple of clues to our identity, blood from Aaron's nose on the concrete and Chuck's prints on the cash he used to pay for the tickets, but they had to find the body before they started looking for us. Novak didn't think the Paris police would exactly bend over backward to find out what happened to a dirtbag like Colonna. It wasn't unusual for dirtbags to show up in the sewer and they might not even realize where he went in. If that happened, they might never connect Colonna to us.

Novak agreed that a discreet disappearance was good. It would probably take days before anyone realized Colonna was gone and what were they going to do? Report him as missing and say, "Hey, he was in Paris trying to kidnap an American. Somebody must've killed him." I don't think so. Hopefully, by the time his employer knew he needed another guy, we'd be back in the States and on Calpurnia's turf.

While we'd been dealing with poop guy, Novak had been busy. He'd broken through the Swiss firewall and found out that the equivalent of 50,000 dollars was put into an account for Obsidian in 1946. The electric bill and taxes on the apartment were taken out of the account once a year. The interest on the account had sustained it since then and the payments were sent out automatically. Novak couldn't find anything on Obsidian. The money wasn't a bank transfer. Someone had personally arrived at the bank with cash and opened the account. That would've all been done on paper and he didn't have access to that. Someone did check in every five years. A bank employee named Claus

Sterner had been assigned to the account for the last twenty-five years. Sterner checked the balance and made a notation that the account was in good order. He must be doing it for someone and Novak thought he could find out who if he dug into Sterner.

He'd made progress on Angela, too. He found her language school in Maryland and the U.S. Government did pay for it. She stayed on campus for eight weeks, not the entire ten, and was, by all accounts, an excellent student. The other weeks were a blank, but she probably spent them getting a nose job and testifying about whatever it was that she knew.

I asked about Panera guy, but all he had was charges at a local Panera Bread near Angela's house. He hadn't had time to do more, what with the Obsidian stuff and figuring out the identity of the second suit. I asked him to send me Angela's financial records so I could look through them and the rest of what he had. Spidermonkey still hadn't contacted either of us, but Novak hacked the hospital and found out that he was stable to be released tomorrow. That was a relief, but I really needed him. Novak sent me the files but looking at them on the phone gave me a screaming migraine. I didn't really get anywhere before the water got cold and Chuck came banging on the door wanting to go out. We had dinner at Monsieur Barre's apartment because Chuck was right. Monsieur Barre recognized Aaron from his Paris cooking days and was living the sweet life of constant food that was usually mine. After dinner, Chuck finally admitted that his neck hurt and I gave him some Norco, which knocked him out cold for the night.

I'd gotten plenty of sleep without Norco and managed to get myself out of the bed pit on the third try. I got dressed quickly and pulled on the cloche before checking Novak's phone. No messages. Chuck was still sacked out in the other bedroom. I could leave him a note and dash over to Angela's hotel room for a quick search, but Monsieur Barre said Aaron was still asleep. Normally, I would just do it alone, but I did need a partner with Poinaré after me. Instead, I ventured as far as Monsieur Barre's apartment and stole his coffee, curling up on his comfy fainting couch and going back to Angela's life on the small screen, complete with headache.

Monsieur Barre left me alone as he did his rounds in the building, taking care of the more normal inhabitants. When he came back, he brought almond croissants and fresh fruit. He sat opposite me, drinking coffee from a little espresso cup and watching me.

"Thanks for the croissant," I said.

"You're welcome. When will you be telling me what you've been up to?" he asked.

*Hello. Never.*

"I have no idea what you're talking about," I said, avoiding his penetrating gaze.

"Miss Watts, I've been a part of this building for fifty years and we've had all sorts of people here and they've done all sorts of things. There's nothing you can say that will surprise me."

"I seriously doubt that." I took a second croissant. They were so good; I felt all melty and peaceful.

"Herr Licktenfeld killed two men in his bathroom by exsanguinating them."

*Wrong again.*

"When was that?" I asked.

"1972. He was a drug addict and he owed them money."

"How'd the cops catch him?"

Monsieur Barre smiled and took a small sip of his coffee. "As I said, he was a drug addict and not the most intelligent of men. Inherited wealth often has that effect on a bloodline. Not the Bled family, obviously. Herr Licktenfeld tried to flush one of the heads down the toilet and it didn't work out very well for him."

"I can imagine. Did he flood the apartment?"

"He did."

I poured myself some more coffee. "Well, I haven't exsanguinated anyone."

"I certainly hope not." He looked at me over the rim of his cup. "I may be able to help."

"I don't think so."

Monsieur Barre took a croissant for himself. "I can keep a secret, as most of the men in this building could tell you."

*Ew. I don't want to know that.*

"I'm sure you can," I said.

"You have the look of the overwhelmed."

I sighed. "I guess I am. Thing's aren't going the way I thought they would."

"Do your plans usually work well?"

"No. I'm not a huge planner. This time, someone who usually helps me is sick. I'm a little lost without him."

Monsieur Barre went to his little stove and poured another mini cup of espresso from his Moka Express pot. It made the best espresso, in my opinion, but I wouldn't be mentioning that to Chuck or he'd buy one. As little as they were, I didn't have the room.

"What does this person do for you?"

"He looks at data."

"The data you have on your phone?"

"Yes, unfortunately. It's so much. I don't know how to approach it," I said.

Monsieur Barre sat down and took a long sniff of his espresso, swirled his cup, and then took an evaluating sip like a wine connoisseur would. "Ask me how I know when one of the tenants of this building is doing something they ought not do."

I smiled. Anything to distract me from the task at hand. "Alright, I'll play. How do you know?"

"I know them, their patterns, their likes and dislikes. When those change, I know something has happened."

"You're telling me to look for a change in pattern. I already know to do that," I said.

"Then why aren't you doing it?"

"It's...so much on this little screen...and I don't want to." I didn't know until that moment that I wasn't doing what I should because I was mad. This was Spidermonkey's wheelhouse. I wasn't supposed to have to sift through data. I hated that crap.

Monsieur Barre smiled. "Make it small. What do you know?"

"She went to a certain restaurant and there are some pictures of a man at the restaurant, but I can't identify him." I shouldn't have said that much, but talking was a nice way of avoiding the data.

"Monsieur LaFeche began an affair last August. Before last August, he came home at seven o'clock in the evening every night. After August, that changed. He came later on Fridays and then Wednesday as well. Then it became Thursdays and meetings on Saturday afternoon. Madam LaFeche noticed in November and caught him in December, on the eleventh. I changed the locks for her on the twelfth. This was a short period, but when Madam asked me about his comings and goings, it was easy to pinpoint when the affair started."

"You think my subject was having an affair?"

"Yes."

"I hate to tell you that she's not the type," I said.

"You don't want her to be the type, but there is no type. People are illogical. They do what they shouldn't."

I sighed and looked at the screen, tapping a few times to look at credit card charges in St. Louis the day before Angela disappeared. Nothing. No Panera. Then I moved back through time, searching for Panera and found zero in the last two months before Angela disappeared. What the heck? Novak said there were lots of Panera charges. I did a universal on the account and found he was right. Angela went to Panera a lot, but apparently not in those two months. I returned to the timeline and worked backward. For two months before she disappeared, Angela never went to Panera. In the three months before that, the charges were twice a week. Prior to five months before she disappeared, the charges were once a week for a solid two years. So something dramatic happened at five months before and two months before her vanishing act in Chicago. That's when Angela's pattern changed.

"You found something?" asked Monsieur Barre.

"Maybe, but the changes could be a coincidence," I said.

"You think so?"

My queasy gut said no and I shook my head before texting Gina to ask why her sister went to Panera Bread so much, thinking she would answer when she woke since it was the middle of the night in St. Louis. But Gina was a light sleeper, anxious for news about Angela, and she came right back. Gina said that Angela liked to get out of the house, do the bills, and write her poetry. I took a shot and asked why only once a week. Gina answered that that was all the time Angela had. She volunteered in each of her kid's classes every week, had a book club, and all the other stuff wives and mothers do. I thanked Gina and said I would hopefully know something soon.

As Monsieur Barre suggested, I went over what I knew and then jumped into Angela's email, looking at specific dates the ones where she added a Panera trip and low and behold, there it was. A clue. A clue. Angela, at five months before she disappeared, began skipping her book club and telling teachers she couldn't make it to the class. She was very good at lying. I should've known she would be, given the way she handled herself in that Chicago bar. Angela spaced her excuses so that no one thought anything of it. She didn't drop all the kids' classes, just one, here and there. She went to book club but missed three meetings in the five-month period. Those excuses didn't cover all the times she went to Panera. I assumed she fit in the other times when she was supposed to be doing other stuff, like grocery shopping or whatever.

I checked the police interviews and it was as I suspected. Nobody, from the teachers to the book club ladies, said anything about Angela dumping her obligations. They didn't notice. Her excuses were too good and she didn't overdo it. The woman was good. I had to find out who the Panera guy was and there was only one person in Angela's life I could safely ask. Gina. She wasn't totally stable, but she was all I had. I texted her that I needed her to look at a picture, but not to tell anyone about it. She promised and I sent one of the Panera pictures, crossing my fingers that she would recognize him and not tell a single soul about it.

"I don't know him. Seems familiar," Gina texted.

"Familiar how?"

"Saw him somewhere."

I sucked in a big breath and texted, "The bar in Chicago?"

It took a couple minutes before she answered. "No. Don't know where."

*Damn.*

"Call me if you remember," I texted.

"No affair. Angela wouldn't."

I'd bet the farm that everyone who knew Angela would say the same thing. She wasn't the type. Of course, she wasn't the type to fake a kidnapping and leave her family either and she did that. Monsieur Barre was right. There was no type.

"Okay," I texted. "Trying to figure out who he is. Do you remember Angela being sick or the kids being sick in the months before she disappeared?"

"No. Why?"

No one else mentioned the illnesses she used as excuses to get out of book club or volunteering either.

"Just checking," I said.

Then I told her that she absolutely could not tell Angela's husband, Phillip, or Calpurnia about this guy. No asking around about him. It would hurt my investigation.

"You found her," she texted. It wasn't a question.

I hated to lie, but I couldn't confirm it yet. Outing a government protectee was a very bad thing. "Maybe. Still checking on leads. Paris is huge."

Gina agreed on the hugeness of the city and had to go. I hoped to god it wasn't to go show everyone she knew the picture of the Panera guy. Calpurnia thought she was a nut, but Gina loved her sister. I only hoped she could stay on her meds and keep herself to herself.

Aaron walked into the living room, yawning. "You hungry?"

"We had croissants," I said.

He went into the kitchen anyway and started banging pots. Not sure if that was a rebuke for eating without him or what. Monsieur Barre raised his eyebrows at me. "He likes to make breakfast."

"And every other meal, snack, and beverage."

"Your friend is a genius. I met him when he was Chef de Cuisine at Guy Savoy. Wonderful."

"I have no doubt." I went back to the phone and then jerked my head up. "What was Aaron like back then? I assume they didn't let him cook in Batman tees and jean shorts."

"You would assume incorrectly," said Monsieur Barre.

"Seriously?"

"He is much as he ever was."

"Really?"

Monsieur Barre smiled and lifted one shoulder. “He didn’t need to change to cook magnificently.”

“I thought there were rules,” I said.

“It would be foolish to be a slave to the rules.”

*Or to plans.*

“Excuse me,” I said, standing up. “May I use your bathroom?”

Monsieur Barre shook his head in dismay and his few remaining hairs waved at me. “You still don’t trust me, a loyal servant to your family for many years.”

“For the last time, I’m not a Bled, and I trust you.”

“I see you are taking your phone with you.”

I looked down at my hand like I was surprised. “Oh well, I’m attached. You know my generation. We’re over-connected and over-share.”

His mouth tightened around the edges and I knew I’d disappointed him, but there wasn’t any choice for me. Monsieur Barre was loyal...to the Bleds. If he told The Girls what I’d said so far, I could weasel my way out of it, saying it was some generic investigation for a friend. The minute I said Angela Riley, I was so done.

“Thanks.” I went down the little hall with two sets of eyes on me. At least I could tell Aaron what I was up to later. I found the bathroom, scrupulously clean and not much more modern than Elias’s bathroom, old tub and all. I turned on the water and tucked myself into the corner farthest from the door.

“Novak,” I said. “It’s me.”

“Did you find something?”

I scooted down the wall and hugged my knees. “I think Angela was having an affair with the Panera guy.” I explained about the credit card charges and the changes in her schedule.

“Perhaps she was sick.”

“Her sister says no.”

Novak made a humming noise and I could hear keys clicking in the background. “What do you want me to do with this information?”

“Can you find other charges at that Panera at the time Angela was there?”

“Of course,” he said.

I gave him a particular week in which Angela was there three times and he said he'd get the charges around the hour Angela bought her coffee. If we could find the same card being used during those times or a Panera Rewards card, we'd have him. I was excited. Novak wasn't so much.

"He could've used cash," said Novak.

"Don't pee on my parade."

He chuckled. "I will keep that saying. It's a good one."

"Well, good. Enjoy."

A knock sounded on the bathroom door and Monsieur Barre said, "Miss Watts, your other phone is ringing. Shall I answer it?"

*Ah crap!*

"What are you going to say?" I asked.

"That you are indisposed."

I sighed and told him to go ahead.

"What was that?" asked Novak.

"I got caught having a second phone by a friend of the family."

"This will be trouble?"

"I have no idea," I said. "I think I want to get into Angela's hotel room today. There might be something of interest there. Is she working?"

Novak typed like mad and then said, "Yes. Tell me if you find a new lead."

"Same to you."

I hung up and forced myself to walk out and face Monsieur Barre, but there really wasn't any facing to do. Aaron had made him the fluffiest omelet known to mankind and he barely looked when he told me that Chuck was up and awaiting me at Elias's. I gave Aaron the Novak phone and tucked my regular one back in my purse. Aaron gave me a cup of thick hot chocolate with a beautiful, shimmering swirl of raspberry puree in the middle.

I didn't think I had the time, but Aaron bounced up and down on the balls of his feet, awaiting my judgement. Why I made one ounce of difference to him was a mystery. The best palates in the world had tasted his food. I was me, a girl that refused seafood and was grudging in my praise because he bothered me.

"You need it," he said.

"I suppose I do." I took a tentative sip. Raspberry is a classic pairing with chocolate, but I never liked it. In my opinion, chocolate should be unsullied by flavorings. Aaron managed to change my mind. It was fabulous and the strangest word came to mind: unctuous. People use that word to describe food like it's a good thing, even though it really means fatty or false earnestness and some other less than good things. But unctuous came to my mind for the first time ever. The hot chocolate was so rich and luscious, it was almost fatty, but in a good way. I couldn't say unctuous out loud like some snotty prig, so I said, "It's amazing, Aaron, and I don't even like raspberry so that's saying something."

Aaron clapped his hands, poured Monsieur Barre his own cup, then whipped off his apron and said, "I'm ready."

"Alright then." We said goodbye—actually, only I said goodbye. Aaron just left. Monsieur Barre didn't notice since he was in ecstasy.

Back in Elias's apartment, Chuck wasn't waiting at the door as I expected, tapping his foot. I tapped on the bathroom door and heard a splashing. "Don't come in."

I rolled my eyes. Heaven forbid. "How's your neck? Don't get it wet."

"It's okay. Healing pretty good. I'll be out in a few."

*A few too many. Sucker.*

"Take your time. Aaron and I are going to class."

"What?" Big splash. "No. I'll go with you."

"You're too busy."

"Doing what?"

"Talking your way into the Marais apartment. Novak gave you the info," I said, giving Aaron a thumbs-up, which he stared at like he'd never seen one before. Weirdo.

"I'll have better luck with you there. You can flirt with the manager," said Chuck.

"Maybe he'll like you better. You never know until you try."

"Mercy, I'm getting out."

"See ya," I called out. "I'll call when we're done. Get into the apartment."

A string of cursing rang out behind the bathroom door. Some-body'd been listening to Uncle Morty and learned his lessons well. I closed the front door mid-curse and hurried to the elevator, dragging Aaron behind me. "To the hotel. We're close. I can feel it."

"Close to the hotel?" asked Aaron.

"To an answer."

The elevator opened and Chuck yelled down the hall. "Mercy!"

I laughed and we got in.

*Better luck next time.*

# CHAPTER TWENTY-TWO

We were close to the hotel, a Novotel at Gare de Lyon. Aaron and I went down into the metro for the short trip and were shocked at the amount of people. It was absolutely packed and at ten o'clock in the morning, too. We couldn't wedge ourselves on the first train that came in, but I forced us into the second and ended up in my usual armpit. This pit was dressed, thankfully, and scented with the now familiar Savon de Marseille olive oil soap and belonged to a man carrying what looked like an oboe case. He apologized for whacking me with his oboe several times. That didn't trouble me at all. What were a few bruises? What bothered me was the sense that someone was watching us. Little prickles kept going up and down my back. I searched for the culprit, but, in the crush of humanity, couldn't catch anyone at it.

Aaron and I squeezed out at Gare de Lyon and I asked as we walked up into the enormous station, "Did you see anyone suspicious in there?"

"Huh?"

"Never mind." I glanced over my shoulder and found no suits or anyone who resembled Poinaré with his angular face and cold eyes. Maybe I was crazy, but I didn't think so.

We went into the main part of the train station and, instead of going out the door, Aaron trotted off toward the food stands.

"Where are you going?" I called out after him. "You can't be hungry."

Aaron ignored me as he always did. I chased him to a little stand selling tiny, delicate pastries so beautiful they looked like they were for a magazine shoot, not for real eating. Aaron threw up his hands and shouted, "Baptiste!"

A rotund man with a pointy corkscrew mustache ran out from behind the counter and they embraced. I'd never seen such emotion from Aaron. He was smiling and waving his arms around. So was Baptiste. They embraced again and I was so transfixed I didn't see the rush of travelers headed my way. In a second, I was swept up and carried away toward the trains. I got turned around, pushed this way and that. Trains were coming in and dropping their passengers at an incredible rate. The little prickles got stronger. I had to get back to Aaron. I caught several men looking at me, but I couldn't tell what they were up to, Corsican mafia or just guys who liked breasts.

The station seemed abnormally busy and by the time I got back to the pastry stand, Aaron and Baptiste were gone. I asked the girl left in charge where they were and she didn't know. She thought they may have gone for a café since they were friends from the old days. Aaron might go for a café and leave me. I called him and he didn't answer. My heart started pounding. I shouldn't have ditched Chuck. I shouldn't be in Paris at all. Stupid favor owing.

I wasn't sure what to do, but I did have a timeline. Besides, the station was packed. Witnesses galore. I didn't let myself remember Dad saying that busy places are places where no one is paying much attention. I clutched my purse to my chest, glanced around, and headed for the exit. I'd go to the Novotel. Maybe Aaron would, too. I passed by nooks and crannies, trying to avoid any place I could be snagged and dragged away. About two blocks from the station, the crowds thinned and I caught sight of him, a man dressed like an American tourist with khaki shorts, white tennis shoes and socks, a fanny pack, and a floppy canvas hat that concealed much of his face. I'd seen him before on the train. He'd looked like he was in a group, but there was no group now. It had to be Poinaré.

Instinct told me not to go to my goal. Instead of turning for the Novotel, I hung a left onto a shopping street and spotted a likely shop, a boulangerie. I went inside and dithered over the choices of pre-made sandwiches while keeping an eye on the street outside. Sure enough, five minutes after I entered the shop, Poinaré aka the tourist passed the window with a discreet glance inside. I had a tail, but a curious one. He could've separated me from Aaron on the train. Aaron got off first and the tourist must've been behind me. He could easily have pulled me back and the doors would've shut, cutting me off. The train was crazy busy, though, and I would've screamed my head off. This was a pro. He must have a plan. What was he up to? Just following? Why? I wasn't that far from the Marais apartment, but not that close either.

I bought a sandwich and texted Aaron. Who didn't answer. Great. I called the Novotel and asked if a little guy wearing jeans shorts and a *Transformers* tee had come in and was wandering around the lobby. Nobody had seen my partner. That's when I started to get worried. I never imagined Aaron as a target. I thought they were after me. Maybe I'd gotten it all wrong.

I left the shop, digging out my pepper spray and palming it as I walked down the street. Poinaré was behind me, so far back he must've been very confident of his tracking skills. I almost wanted to take the long way back to the station going down side streets, looking confused, which I would've been if my phone hadn't been telling me exactly where I was, to see if he'd make a move. But I remembered my mother and decided on safety instead, heading straight back to the station.

The station teamed with even more people when I got back to it. People were streaming out of the doors with small suitcases for a weekend in Paris. I squeezed back in past musicians carrying guitar cases and went straight for the little stand and Baptiste. I saw him at a distance and he saw me, frowning instantly. He came out and began speaking in ultra-rapid French. I barely caught a word other than Aaron and gone. I told him he had to slow down and if he could speak English that would be swell.

"Excuse me. Of course, you are American," said Baptiste. "Where is Aaron?"

"Last time I saw him, he was with you," I said, my voice squeaky.

"You disappeared and he went looking for you. He said you might be in trouble. That you often are in trouble."

*Too true.*

"Which way did he go?"

Baptiste pointed in the direction the crowd had taken me, but where the hell was Aaron? I called him again and so did Baptiste. No answer.

"Call the police," I said.

"Is it that serious?" asked Baptiste.

"I hope not, but we have to find him."

Baptiste heaved a sigh and blew a kiss over my shoulder. "There he is. My dear friend. Where have you been?" he called out.

I spun around and saw Aaron coming through the crowd with a trio of soldiers with their Famas assault rifles at the ready. I wanted to run to Aaron, but it didn't seem like a good idea with all that firepower and the wary eyes of the soldiers scanning the crowd.

They walked up and I said as casually as I could, "Where were you? I was freaking out."

The ranking soldier answered in clipped English. "He was robbed and locked in a storage room."

My mouth fell open, I'm not ashamed to say it. I thought it was a possibility that something had happened, but logically that something was more likely to be something involving food.

"Robbed?" I couldn't think what Aaron had worth stealing. He had the travel wallet I'd given him, but he kept that in his front as instructed.

"His mobile phone."

*Oh my god. Novak's phone.*

"They locked you in a storage room for a phone?" I asked Aaron, trying to sound less panicked than I felt.

"Yeah," he said, looking past my left ear.

"We heard him banging on the door. He will have to make a complaint." The soldier gave me directions to the security office and I pretended to follow what he was saying instead of having my mind spinning.

The soldiers apologized for the inconvenience and went back to their rounds. Baptiste clapped Aaron on the back and said he needed a tarte au citron. The baker dashed back behind his stand and I waited until the soldiers were out of earshot before hugging the little weirdo. "Are you okay? Did he threaten you?"

"No."

"What happened?"

Aaron shrugged.

"Use your words. I need to know what happened," I said.

"Pushed me in. Took my phone."

*Crap and double crap. How will I get in touch with...wait.*

"Did you say your phone?" I asked.

"Yeah," said Aaron as he started chewing on a hangnail. No big deal. Just a minor incident in a train station.

"He didn't get Novak's phone?"

Aaron patted his left front pocket. "No."

I bent over and breathed deep while Aaron patted my back. "Oh, thank god. Novak's not perfect. They could've broken the encryption. Are you sure you're okay?"

Aaron shrugged.

"Who was it?"

"Poinaré."

Baptiste came out, beaming and holding two perfect little tarte au citrons.

"Are you sure? What was he wearing?"

Aaron took a tarte before answering. "Tourist stuff."

I described the guy who'd been following me and Aaron nodded before eating his tarte. Baptiste bounced up and down like Aaron did, waiting for a verdict.

Aaron embraced him and proclaimed it to be perfection. He was spot on. It was best tarte au citron I'd ever had and they're hard to get right despite being simple. I thanked Baptiste and said we had to go. The two friends made plans to get together before we left Paris and we headed off.

"Do you want to fill out that report?" I asked Aaron.

He lifted one shoulder.

"We can, if you want."

"Phone's gone." He glanced up at me. "You hungry?"

"We just ate...never mind. I could stand some coffee. I assume you have something in mind." Aaron went on to describe three different places he wanted to visit and I told him to choose. We hopped back on the metro with eyes peeled for Poinaré, although I wasn't sure I'd know him. That disguise was a good one and he might've changed it. I thought about the pictures that Novak had sent me. Maybe I could spot the sharp jawline and thin lip if he wasn't wearing another hat. Maybe.

Aaron and I took the metro back to Châtelet and dashed through the complicated tunnels to lose anyone who might be following before back toward Gare De Lyon on Line One. I didn't see anyone and I had the feeling that Poinaré knew when he was made and would try a different day. And why not? He knew about Elias's apartment. He had to. It was the only explanation. Maybe he'd followed Aaron from the school to the sewer like Colonna and then followed us home. He might've been able to triangulate our location using our regular phones, even though Uncle Morty had encrypted them. It didn't matter. Poinaré had definitely followed us to the Gare de Lyon, but the purpose wasn't nabbing me, not anymore. He wanted Novak's phone. Somehow he knew about that. And he wanted to follow me. He could've nabbed me if he tried harder, but he didn't. Why?

Aaron found the place he was looking for in the Marais district, a tiny café in a back alley. It wouldn't be in any of Chuck's tour books. It didn't have a name or a sign out front, only a small chalkboard propped up against the wall next to the steps, listing the day's specials. We were early for lunch, since it was not yet twelve, but the elderly owner welcomed us in and gave us a table by the dusty window. Vintage pots and pans hung from the black-beamed ceiling and doll furniture was pinned to the walls around the five tables. The whole restaurant could've fit into my apartment back home, but it smelled delicious, like wine, fresh herbs, and slow-cooked meat.

The lady tried to give us handwritten cards and Aaron declined, saying that we'd have whatever she recommended. She beamed at us and her husband brought a decanter of red wine. Aaron poured and I glared.

"If it's crab, you will pay," I said.

He wasn't worried. I sipped the house red and discovered it was lovely. Then I called Chuck and told him that class was done and we were already in the Marais for lunch. He was at the metro, getting ready to go back to Elias's apartment. I gave Aaron the phone for directions since I had no clue how to get there and I asked for Novak's phone.

"It's me," I said to Novak.

"What did you find?"

"Nothing and something."

Novak chuckled while continuing to type. "It's the same here."

I told him about my aborted trip to the Novotel and Aaron's misadventure.

"He's changed his tactics," said Novak. "I'm going to put one of my people on Elias's apartment."

"You have people?"

"Naturally. I'll have someone watch for Poinaré. It seems he knows where you are staying. If we catch him there, we can tail him to where he's staying and it will be easier to track him through pings."

"Sounds good to me, but what if Chuck sees your guy? It won't be pretty," I said.

"He won't."

"If you say so. Anything else new?"

He told me about the Panera guy or at least who he thought the Panera guy was. Someone had used a stolen credit card on all three of the dates I'd given him and within fifteen minutes of Angela's purchases. Novak had gone back and checked other dates randomly. Some had nothing and others had more stolen credit cards.

"Any idea who stole the cards?" I asked.

"Not yet. That's the nothing."

I sagged in my seat. If I didn't find out what Angela had done before we had to leave Paris, I'd have to blindly lie to Calpurnia, a bad idea if I ever heard one, or tell her I found Angela and hope for the best. "No offense, but I think we need Spidermonkey. He has the American angle."

"None taken and I agree. I called and left a message on his voice mail."

"Nothing?"

"Not yet, but I heard angry wives are quite a deterrent."

"My mother is. So that's it?" I asked.

More furious typing. "The charges definitely belong to your target, the Panera guy, as you call him."

"How can you tell?"

Novak made a tsking noise. "He orders the same thing every time. Kale salad and coffee."

"A health nut," I said.

"I assume so."

"Are you trying to trace the stolen credit cards?"

"Without luck. They are part of a batch of stolen numbers. It will take time. I got a little more on the Marais apartment," said Novak.

"Please say the owners," I said.

"Sadly, no. I found out that Marcel Paul was the one who checked on the account in Switzerland until 1970."

"Really? So he was super involved."

"He was."

"Who took over after him?" I asked.

"An American law firm in New York, Dietzel and Ford. Do you know them?" asked Novak.

"Not even a little bit. Who are they? Not litigation."

"No. It's corporate and huge."

I groaned. Huge wasn't good. We needed small. "It sounds like Marcel Paul was personal, a favor to a friend or something. But a big firm is business. Who got billed?"

"This arrangement only lasted until 1985. I didn't see any billing."

"There has to be billing. Those types don't do anything for free," I said.

"They don't, but I didn't find any record of billing. Perhaps Spidermonkey..."

I thanked him and hung up, reaching for the wine when my regular phone started vibrating.

"Maybe Chuck's lost," I said.

Aaron made a noise of derision before looking at the screen. "Spidermonkey."

I snatched the phone out of his hand. "Are you serious?" He was. It was Spidermonkey's number on the screen. I'd imagined the angry Loretta stomping on his second phone, but I guess he managed to calm her down, meaning lying to the wife effectively. I gave Aaron Novak's phone and answered, unable to keep the relief and joy out of my voice.

"Hello. Thank god. I've been so worried," I said.

"Who is this?" said a woman's voice, not an unfamiliar one.

*Oh crap!*

"Er..."

In the background, I heard what sounded like Spidermonkey explaining something. I couldn't quite make out what.

"Hello," she said. "Who is this?"

There was nothing for it but to tell the truth and hope it would be okay. "Hello," I said. "It's Mercy Watts."

"What is your association with my husband?" asked Loretta, very businesslike.

"He didn't tell you?"

"Don't mess with me, young lady. How do you know my husband?"

I sighed and sipped my wine. It helped as wine always does. "I can't tell you that."

"You refuse to tell me? You absolutely refuse?" She was now breathless. I didn't know what Loretta looked like, but I imagine hair standing on end and a bright red face.

"I can't. But if you're thinking it's something...er...sexual, you're completely and utterly wrong. Your husband is lovely and he would never ever in a million years betray you."

Loretta was silent for a few minutes and then said, "He says he works for you. Prove it?"

"I would if I could," I said.

"He says he was working for you when we were in Austria."

"Well, yes, he was. We're kind of partners."

"That's what he says. I want to know what you're working on. The truth."

"I can't out your husband. I can't. Ask him."

Spidermonkey and Loretta bickered in the background before she said, "What's his code name?"

"You tell me," I said.

She did a delicate little snort. "He says Spidermonkey. I never heard anything more ridiculous. My husband isn't a...hacker. He plays golf and builds forts for our grandchildren."

"Are you really Loretta?" I asked. "The real Loretta."

"Naturally. Who else would I be?" she asked.

"You just went on vacation with your husband. Where did you go?"

"Germany and Austria."

*That's too easy.*

"What did you do every afternoon?" I asked.

She paused. "I took a nap. I get tired. I'm not as young as I look."

"You made your husband take a side trip, a dream of yours. What was it?"

"Dream of mine? You don't mean the *Sound of Music* tour, do you?"

I laughed. "Hello, Mrs. Spidermonkey. Nice to meet you."

"Are you completely serious? What he said...it's outrageous."

"It's true. Your retired golfing husband is a super hacker and super cool, in my opinion. Why are you calling at this hour anyway? It's the middle of the night."

"I caught my *super cool* husband creeping down the stairs. I presume he was trying to get to this phone."

"Probably. He tends to work at night after you go to bed," I said.

"I don't know what to think about all this. He's sitting there, looking smug. I'm going to smack him," said Loretta.

Aaron tapped the table and pointed out the window. Chuck was across the street, looking for a sign and, of course, not finding one.

"Go ahead and smack, but first tell him to call Novak. It's critical."

Loretta got all sharp and interested. "Critical, you say?"

"Absolutely critical. I've got to go." I waved to Chuck and he smiled in relief.

"I'll tell him," said Loretta and I hung up right before Chuck came in.

"This place isn't easy to find, even with directions." He plopped down and drank my much-needed wine. "Who was on the phone?"

"You'll never believe it." I told him about Loretta and he was suitably astonished.

"I can't believe he told her the truth."

"I don't think he had a choice if he wanted to stay married."

"So he's back on the job?"

"Let's hope so."

I crossed my fingers under the table.

*Please, Loretta. Be cool.*

Chuck asked me if Novak had called and I gave him a quick rundown as our appetizer arrived. I should've known, rillettes and foie gras. I wasn't a huge fan of either, but, lucky for me, Chuck was starving and ate everything on his plate and mine so I didn't insult the couple, who kept checking on our progress. Next was amazing roast chicken made with duck fat. The crispy potatoes that came with the chicken were so good I got teary-eyed. I didn't know that could happen with the lowly potato. Aaron informed me that it was the duck fat. Best not to think about the calories.

I had to defend my plate from Chuck's fork. He stole one potato and I very nearly stabbed his hand before I remembered I wasn't the only one who'd been up to something that morning. "Did you get in the apartment?"

"If I had, I would've sent you pictures. That manager wasn't playing. I get the feeling he was lucky to get the job and he's not going to give me a damn thing," said Chuck.

"Fabulous." I resisted the urge to lick my plate. Instead, I smiled at the lady who was welcoming more customers, people who look like they'd been coming to lunch for years. There was much cheek kissing and exclamations of joy.

Her husband came over and asked about dessert. Aaron took charge and I got a mini cherry clafouti with crème anglaise. Delicious. Chuck inhaled his strawberry napoleon and then asked for a round of coffee, in French. He got a little bit sexier when he said it, which wasn't great, since there didn't seem to be any sex in my future.

"Don't look so down," he said. "That guy started the job a couple months ago. I say we try the former manager. If he's anything like old retired cops, he won't give a crap what anyone thinks."

That was both a cheerful and a frightening thought. We could get info out of the old manager so that was good. But eventually, Chuck was going to be a retired cop who didn't give a crap. I could barely handle when he did.

"Do we have the address?" I asked.

"I got it from Novak."

"Do you want to try the old guy after lunch?"

"Nope," he said. "Not today."

"Why not?"

He leaned back in the little wooden chair he was perched on and stretched. All his muscles flexed under the perfectly-fitted silk polo Madam Ziegler picked out for him. It was so soft, it molded into the curves of his six pack, and I was momentarily transfixed. "Because we're going to the Louvre. You said Friday is the best day."

"Oh yeah. Uh huh."

"What?"

I sipped my café crème to clear my head. I wanted to say how good he looked and perhaps purr a little, but by now I knew better. It would only make him uncomfortable. "I was thinking about what we should see."

He rolled the cup between his hands and gave me a boyish grin. "Everything."

I checked the time. "Everything in seven hours...in the Louvre."

Chuck pumped his fist. "We can do it."

"Everything it is."

## CHAPTER TWENTY-THREE

We didn't see everything in the Louvre. Not even close. Chuck didn't realize the immensity of the museum until we got off the metro and entered the mall beneath it. The crowds were insane. The line for the bathrooms started at the elevator. Chuck had to use his long arms to push our way through.

"I thought you said it wasn't going to be too bad today?" he asked.

"Wait for it," I said.

We made it through the entrance area into the long corridor filled with swanky shops, Lalique and the like.

"Do we need tickets?" Chuck asked.

"Museum pass," I said. "We're good."

He squeezed my hand and said, "There it is. There it is," as the inverse pyramid came into view.

I glanced back at Aaron, who had a hint of a smile. I squeezed Chuck's hand back. "Pretty awesome, huh?"

"You know, I never thought I'd come to Paris," he said, dragging me over for pictures next to the point.

I asked the group ahead of us to take our pictures and we posed with Aaron for a few shots. Chuck was grinning like mad. I thanked our picture taker and quickly emailed the best pic to The Girls and Mom.

"Alright then," I said. "What do you want to see first?"

"The Islamic section."

I blinked. Didn't see that coming. "Not the *Mona Lisa*? *Winged Victory*?"

"We'll get to that." He took me over to the information desk, searched for a map in English among the many languages and then studied it intensely. "Okay. I think we go in through Richelieu. Where's the gate?"

"We have to go through security first." I led them over to the line that Chuck thought was long, but it was minuscule compared to what it would've been that morning. The line went fast and we were through and headed for the Islamic section before I knew it. To my dismay, Chuck and Aaron were serious about Islamic art and we spent an hour and a half in the new building designed to look like a sand dune from the top. I ended up sitting on a chair and watching them read placards while thinking about Angela and the identity of the Panera guy. He was the key and I feared, not a good guy at all with his stolen credit cards. What had she gotten herself into?

From Islamic art, we went to the showstopper, the *Mona Lisa*. We hit it at the right time and the room was nearly empty. We went to the Egyptian section, and my guys moved so slowly, I was pretty sure the rest of the day would be in there. The collection was huge, no, ginormous. Chuck wasn't really an art person, but he knew a lot about the Egyptians, dynasties, and whatnot. My favorite section of the museum was the Dutch masters, so I knew almost nothing.

I must've looked bored, because after two hours with the Egyptians, Chuck asked, "Are we taking too long in here?"

"Not at all. I was thinking about where the closest bathroom is," I said.

Chuck consulted the map and gave me a set of hopeless directions that I pretended to understand and then headed off in the wrong direction. Aaron spun me around and pointed past a case of coffins.

"Got it," I said, somewhat surprised that they were letting me go alone. We hadn't seen anyone suspicious, but I wasn't convinced that we'd know Poinaré if we saw him. There was security in every other room and I found myself feeling safe and secure in the former palace. Poinaré didn't seem like the type to waste his time. If he was following me in hopes of finding some mysterious destination, there wasn't much point in tracking me around the Louvre.

I wandered around aimlessly, going the wrong way every time until I finally figured it out. I was always wrong. If I thought that I should go left, right was the correct way to go. Once I decided to do the opposite, I found the bathroom. I used the same plan going back, although I started second-guessing myself and made several wrong turns. Chuck texted me, asking if I was okay.

"I got lost," I texted back.

He sent me a laughing emoji. Smug, good sense of direction having bastard.

I did find my way to the Egyptians again and made it back to the coffin case, but they'd moved. No surprise there. My phone vibrated again and I answered tersely, "I'm coming."

"To where?" asked a raspy, almost unintelligible voice.

"Who is this?" I asked, the hairs rising on the back of my neck.

"Spidermonkey."

I looked at the screen and it was him. I blew out a breath and leaned on the icy cold archway next to the coffin case. "Does Loretta know you have the phone? You don't sound so good."

"She's forgiven me," he said. "She had to."

"Had to doesn't sound likely."

"She had two very good reasons," said Spidermonkey.

"Oh really? Two good reasons to forgive you for hiding a second, somewhat illegal, occupation and lying to her a lot? Do tell."

"Loretta made the sushi that nearly killed me."

I smiled in spite of myself. Salmonella poisoning was no laughing matter. "That's a good reason, but not nearly enough."

"That's what she said. You did the rest of the convincing."

"Me? I hardly said anything," I said.

Spidermonkey hesitated and then said, "It was enough."

"Come on. There's no way. She thought you were having an affair with me."

"Well...it wasn't so much what you said."

"What else is there?" I asked.

"You. Loretta googled you," said Spidermonkey, sounding dejected. I'd never heard that in his voice before.

"Oh, no. Now she'll think I'm a brazen hussy, a slut, or worse. Why'd you let her?"

"Good grief. Do you think my wife asks my permission? She googled you and she doesn't think you're a slut. More importantly, she doesn't think we're having an affair."

I rubbed my forehead. "I don't see how that's possible."

"She saw you and...decided that a woman who looks like you would never have an affair with an old goat like me. She used the word "goat". Goat. I'm her husband. I was handsome back in my day."

"It's still your day and you are handsome." I could picture Spidermonkey, lower lip poking out. His feelings were hurt. "She's just upset."

*And right.*

Spidermonkey was about the same age as my grandpa. Ew.

"I'm not that old," he said.

"You're not," I replied, hoping this thread was at an end.

"So you'd date me if you weren't attached?"

*Er...*

"I never thought about it." Time to change the conversation in a big way. "So is this why you called? To ask me out?"

"I'm not asking you out, Mercy. Have you lost your mind?" asked Spidermonkey.

There was a burst of laughter somewhere in the vicinity of my cyber sleuth.

"So why are you calling?" I asked.

Spidermonkey told Loretta to pipe down. She didn't and he continued amid laughter.

"I have information for you. Are you alone?" he asked.

"For the moment."

Spidermonkey wasn't allowed to get out of bed, so he'd been working my cases with a vengeance under Loretta's direct supervision.

"Brace yourself. You aren't going to like this," he said.

"Lay it on me. I expect nothing good," I said.

Spidermonkey was right. I wasn't happy. The credit cards the Panera guy used were from a military data breach from something called AAFES, basically the military's version of Wal-Mart. The numbers belonged to soldiers killed in Iraq and Afghanistan. Whoever had stolen the data was smart. They used the numbers after the member was killed—right after, before the family could cancel the cards or pay any attention. Hundreds of thousands worth of charges had gone through, causing no end of trouble for the families. Angela's affair was that kind of guy. Fabulous. She really knew how to pick 'em.

"So can you trace those particular cards?" I asked.

"I can follow the charges and get a picture of the guy who used them. Identity? I don't know. Security camera footage from that long ago is a no go."

"But you'll be able to figure out the family?"

Loretta said something about the Fibonaccis. When Spidermonkey answered me, he sounded harassed, "You're worried it's Calpurnia?"

"Not really. She seems to have some standards," I said.

"Don't romanticize the woman, Mercy."

"I'm not. You're the one who told me that she got out of the sex trade."

"This is credit card fraud."

"Preying on dead soldiers. It's pretty freaking low. I don't see Calpurnia doing that and I doubt anyone with the Fibonaccis would start something up with Phillip Riley's wife. You'd have to have a death wish."

"I agree with you on that."

Chuck and Aaron came around the corner.

"Here comes Chuck," I said, loudly.

Chuck's grin changed to the frown. "Who is it?"

"Spidermonkey," I answered and then said into the phone, "Have you got anything for us?"

Spidermonkey laughed. It sounded painful. "I do."

"Am I going to like it?" I asked.

"It's disconcerting at best," he said.

Disconcerting was right. Spidermonkey made short work of the New York Law firm, discovering pretty quickly that United Shipping and Steel was a client and had been for a hundred and fifty years. United was the client behind the check on the Marais apartment once a year.

"Why does that name sound familiar?" I asked.

"Because it's owned by the Lawrences"

I went blank for a second. "The Lawrences...who...wait. You mean Nicky's family."

"Yes. That's how I knew who to look at. I saw the company on the client list. Novak didn't know the name. It would've taken weeks to sift through client files."

The Lawrences. Stella Bled Lawrence's in-laws. If I'd been thinking of the last thing I expected, that would've been it.

"Do they own the apartment? The Lawrences, I mean," I said.

Chuck poked me and I held up a finger.

"Not as far as I can tell." He paused again and then said, "It gets stranger. Guess who's keeping an eye on the apartment now."

"Not my parents," I said. "That would be weirder."

"Close."

"Seriously?"

"Big Steve."

Big Steve Warnock? What did he have to do with anything?

"Did he work at United or something?" I asked.

"No. Never. But he knows the Bleds and we know the apartment has something to do with them."

I shook my head. "We don't know that. There's no evidence, just these tenuous connections."

"It's a big coincidence."

Chuck poked me again. "Tell me or I'm stealing that phone."

"Big Steve's doing the watching on the Marais apartment."

Chuck put his hand over his mouth and walked away.

"Mercy?" asked Spidermonkey. "Think. Have you ever seen any closeness or connection between Big Steve and the Bleds?"

"He doesn't work for them, but they know each other socially," I said.

"Have you seen him at the mansion?"

I searched my memory. I'd spent half my life in the Bled mansion.

People came and went. There was nothing odd about it. The Girls were social. "Sure, but they know each other."

"How? Through your mom?" asked Spidermonkey.

"That can't be it. Big Steve started on the apartment in 1980."

Spidermonkey said something to Loretta before coming back to me. "That's right. I think we can surmise one thing."

"What's that?" I asked.

"The apartment is the key. You have to get in there, but you'll have to lose the Corsican first."

I looked at the ceiling. "He must know by now that I don't have access to it. If he works for The Klinefeld Group, what's he after? They clearly know about the apartment. What do they need me for?"

"Maybe they can't get in."

"Maybe. But if they killed Werner Richter over the apartment, that's a long time to wait."

Spidermonkey attempted to clear his throat and failed. His voice was getting so bad I could barely make out his words. "You're there, trying to get in the place. Maybe they think that means the box, or whatever it is, is in there."

There was a tussle on the other end of the line and Loretta took over. "That's enough. He needs to rest."

"Thanks, Loretta. I'll call you if anything happens." I hung up and looked at Chuck pacing in front of a display of funerary tablets.

"We have to get in there," he said. "Tomorrow."

Aaron took my arm and started to lead me away from the Egyptian celebration of death.

"Where are we going?" I asked.

"Chocolate."

"Did you see everything?"

Aaron shrugged and Chuck caught up with us but stayed silent. I wondered what he was thinking, but I didn't ask because I didn't know what I was thinking. As we walked out of the Sully wing back into Richelieu, I started to feel more and more uneasy. Something wasn't right. We were missing something. I was missing something.

We went to Angelina and ordered the famous hot chocolate. Aaron watched me like a hawk and garnered some teasing. I made little moans of pleasure and sniffed my cup repeatedly, making Aaron wiggle in his seat and fidget. He deserved it. If he had a cooking show, it would be *The Needy Chef.*

Finally, Chuck broke up and couldn't stop laughing. "Stop. You're being mean."

I pushed Aaron's shoulder. "You know yours is better. Do I really have to say it?"

"Yes," he said.

I rolled my eyes. "Yours is better."

"How?"

*Oh dear lord.*

I proceeded to explain the betterness of Aaron's hot chocolate. At a certain point, I ran out of adjectives and resorted to really good. It did take my mind off the uneasiness. When we left, Chuck decided to throw me a bone and we went to see some paintings. We worked our way from Holland through all the French works. I got lost in the faces, the stories that I would never know. Battle scenes, landscapes, and fruit had no thrall for me. It was the people I loved. We reached a portrait of a wealthy French family of three by de Largillierre. The parents and their daughter were unknown and I always wondered about them, rich, handsome, and years before the revolution would destroy their world. I couldn't stop looking and thinking about the mysteries behind their smooth faces. There was a point when Chuck started sighing. He was long done. Portraits weren't his thing.

"One more minute and we'll go to the moats," I said.

He brightened up and clapped Aaron on the back. I heard Aaron ask about dinner when they exited the section. Dinner was much more interesting than the medieval foundations to Aaron. I turned back to the painting for one last look. The mysteries remained, but all their troubles were over. Mine were just beginning.

# CHAPTER TWENTY-FOUR

Leaving the portrait gave me an uneasiness that stayed with me through the Medieval Louvre and a late dinner at Le Boui Boui on Rue Marie Stuart. A fabulously perfect meal, but even the aligot couldn't ease my mind.

When we got back to the apartment, Blackie was waiting for me in Elias's bedroom. He sat on the dresser next to the shy woman's portrait, looking imperious. I tried in vain to shoo him. Instead, he followed me into my dreams. New Orleans in Nana's house, crowded with people and one black cat in the center of the party. No, it wasn't a party. Some of the people were dead—not gross, rotting dead, just no longer alive. My great-grandparents were there and some of the Bleds that I only knew from pictures. Among the living were my parents, Nana and Pop Pop, Uncle Morty, Aaron, and The Girls. Chuck wasn't there. I wove through the crowd, avoiding sloshing champagne flutes and unwanted hugs, to look for him. I caught a glimpse of a broad shoulder outside the glass wall, but someone grabbed me and pulled me back.

I woke up with a jolt and lay cuddled in the pit under the unblinking gaze of Blackie, still on the dresser. There was no going back to sleep, so I went through everything that had happened since we'd been in Paris. I didn't dwell on the incident in the sewer. Monsieur Barre said no one had come looking for us and a quick check of the news confirmed that the body hadn't been found yet. I couldn't afford to think about it. My therapist said I was doing well, but that anything could spiral me back into starvation and self-recrimination. No, I wouldn't be thinking about the guy who would've happily killed Chuck and Aaron. There'd be no thinking and no mourning for the wicked.

My thoughts led back to the soothing portraiture. Just as I was drifting off, my eyes flew open. "Chuck."

I dug Novak's phone out from under my rear. "It's me. I got it."

Novak sounded woozy. "Got what. Who is this?"

"It's Mercy. I got it. The Corsicans were after me, only me."

He yawned. "We know that."

"We thought we knew, but we didn't know. Ya know?"

"It's three. Go back to sleep. I'm having a nightmare."

Click.

My Serbian snoop hung up on me. The nerve. I wasn't crazy or a nightmare. I was right.

I tried again. "Novak. Listen to me."

He groaned. "You again. What do I have to do?"

"Listen, obviously. The Corsicans were after me, not Chuck. That's the important thing and we were ignoring it."

"The Klinefeld Group thinks you have information."

"Chuck and I are working together on the Marais apartment. Poinaré saw us together there. It's pretty obvious. Chuck should, in theory, know what I know."

Novak started to sound more awake. "Yes. This is true."

"But they went after me when Chuck was off doing apartment stuff and I was chasing Angela. Chuck could've gotten in the apartment and found the box or whatever The Klinefeld Group wants, but Poinaré didn't care. It's not about the apartment. It's Angela they want. Poinaré was hoping I'd lead him to her."

A flurry of typing started. "Budala" he muttered.

"Huh?" I asked.

"I'm an idiot. Of course, he's after Angela. It's the reason you are here in Paris."

"Yeah, well, it seems obvious now, but the Corsicans didn't show up until we found out about the apartment. It made sense at the time."

Novak groused and continued typing. "He's in his room. No activity."

"You found where he's staying already?" I asked, astonished.

"Simple. Poinaré was outside Elias's when you got back tonight. He stayed until the lights went out and then returned to his hotel. George V."

"Holy crap. Crime really does pay."

"He has a standard room, not a suite."

"Still, that's high class," I said.

"Yes. The price on Angela must be very high. My information says Poinaré is very good, and therefore, very expensive. Now that we have his location, I can warn you when he leaves in the morning and keep tabs on his internet activities."

"I thought he was encrypted."

"He is, but I have his room. He's using the hotel server. I can't see what he's doing on the websites his room is accessing, but I can see what they are. He's the only one in the hotel who is interested in Corsican news. Have you told Spidermonkey and his lady yet?"

"So you talked to Loretta?" I asked.

Novak laughed and then yawned. "Yes. His life is going to be more difficult in the future."

I agreed and hung up before calling Spidermonkey, ready for a grilling by Loretta. I didn't get it. Spidermonkey answered and was wide awake, fueled by buckets of coffee. He was thrilled by my revelation. It made his life easier. He could look for a crime family with Corsican connections instead of looking at anybody who was into credit card fraud, which was pretty much everybody.

"I got it narrowed to the East coast before this," he said. "The cards were primarily used in Maryland, Jersey, and New York. St. Louis is an aberration."

"So definitely not anyone from Calpurnia's crew?" I asked.

"I'd say no. Go back to sleep. I've got a connection to find."

"Say hi to Loretta for me."

"I will."

I cuddled down into the pit, going to sleep straight away. For the first time since sleeping in Elias's bed, I had no dreams. Knowing Poinaré was sleeping in his luxury linens was a good thing.

Chuck was on fire. He had me up and out of the apartment by nine. I wasn't thrilled. He didn't care. We were getting into the Marais that very day. He was certain of it and he wanted to get out to interview the old apartment manager before he went out for the day and we lost our chance.

It was Chuck that insisted I wear the three-piece suit and *Casablanca* hat. I felt like I was wearing a costume, but he said I looked hot so I went with it. I think he was just trying to get me out the door and would've said I looked hot if I'd been wearing footy pajamas.

He tried to skip getting Aaron because he was afraid it'd be a class day and he was done with me baking. I insisted because I had to hand over Novak's phone.

Aaron answered the door and said we didn't have class. I ducked into the kitchen to say goodbye to Monsieur Barre, but he was in a stupor over being fed New York-style cheesecake for breakfast and could barely nod. We walked down the stairs instead of squeezing into the tiny elevator. Chuck started to unlock the building's front door and Aaron grabbed my arm.

I stepped behind Chuck's back and Aaron flashed me the screen on Novak's phone. 112. Huh? I didn't get it. Aaron mouthed, "911."

"Oh," I said.

Chuck opened the door and turned around. Aaron hid the phone behind his back and I'm sure we both looked guilty as hell.

"Oh what?" he asked.

"I...uh...forgot to tell Monsieur Barre a...um...message from The Girls," I said.

Aaron and I took a step back.

"Leave it," said Chuck. "You can call him."

"I could do that," I said.

Chuck frowned at me. "So call him."

I glanced out the door at the bright sunshine slanting down through the trees. "Um...you should check outside. You know, in case Poinaré's out there waiting."

"He doesn't know about this place."

"I think he might. He followed Aaron and me yesterday somehow."

Chuck stepped out with one foot. "Yeah, you've got a point. I'll take a look."

I pushed him the rest of the way out the door and closed it. "Thank god."

Aaron gave me the phone and I've never dialed so fast in my life. "What happened?"

Novak's voice came through tight and fast. "He's on the move as of three minutes ago."

"By on the move, you mean..."

"Left his room," he said.

I heaved a sigh. "Dude, you scared me. So he's still in the hotel, nowhere close to me."

"Where are you?"

"At Elias's. About to walk out the door. We're going to the old Marais manager."

"Good, you're closer. You've got to ditch Chuck now."

"Did I miss something?" I asked.

"I told you I was monitoring Poinaré's internet use?"

Aaron bobbed up and down, pointing to the door. Chuck would be back any second.

"Yeah, yeah," I said. "Get to it."

"He checked out the Conciergerie this morning about five minutes before he left."

"So?"

"So that's where Angela is volunteering this morning."

My heart started pounding and so did Chuck on the door. "He doesn't know who she is."

"We didn't think he knew about Elias's apartment, but he found out. Get over there and warn the woman."

"He's going to kill her," I said breathlessly.

"Yes."

*Shit. Double shit.*

I saw the code being put into the security system. Chuck was coming to get me. I had to lie or tell the truth. No truth. Truth bad.

He opened the door. "What the hell, Mercy? We've got to go. We could miss this geezer."

"I know," I said, pushing between his bunched pecs. "So you have to go right now."

He grabbed my wrist. "You're coming with me."

"I can't...family crisis. The Girls and Barre, the sketches. I have to deal with it."

"You can do that later," he said.

I pushed again. "No, no. I can't because..."

*I've got nothing. Say something. Something now.*

Aaron came to my rescue and peeled Chuck's fingers off my wrist. "Mercy owes The Girls."

Chuck relaxed. "Sorry. Of course you owe them. Hell, I owe them. Maybe I should stay, too."

Aaron and I pushed together. "No. Not necessary. You go. This won't take long. Be there asap. Bye."

Chuck went out the door and I closed it firmly behind him. "God that was a pain."

"You could tell him the truth," said Aaron.

"Yeah," I said. "I'll get right on that."

I took Aaron's hand and dragged him top speed through the building and out into the inner courtyard that was surrounded by all the buildings on the block. There was a service entrance two buildings down from Elias's. We squeezed out past a plumbing van and two flower delivery trucks and peeked out onto the street. Chuck was nowhere to be seen. Thank God.

We ran left and dashed over cobblestones and through narrow streets across the Ile de Saint Louis to the Pont de la Tournelle. We sprinted across the arched expanse to the left bank. It was too far to run, especially in my kitten heels. Poinaré would beat me. George V was much farther, but he'd be in a cab. Cab. I needed a cab.

I looked up and down the street, packed with cars and scooters. "We need a cab. We'll never make it."

Aaron didn't shrug or say, "Huh?" He stepped out into the middle of the street and flagged down a scooter.

"What are you doing?" I yelled.

He waved me over. "He'll take you."

"He'll take me?"

"Yeah."

The scooter guy flipped up his visor and his blue eyes widened. He was about eighteen and couldn't believe his luck.

"Conciergerie?" I asked, praying he wasn't a freak.

He looked me up and down. "Êtes-vous une actrice?"

I said yes. I didn't give it a moment's consideration. I could be an actress. Why not? He held out his hand and I perched on the back of his seat, sidesaddle with my skirt hitched up. The Girls were right again. I did need to know how to ride sidesaddle and it did come in handy. Who would've thunk it?

Scooter guy revved his engine and we peeled off, weaving between cars and a couple of buses, but he was fast, super fast. That seven-minute ride took at least three years off my life. The roads were incredibly crowded and there was, in the distance, an odd, booming sound like music, but not that good.

We cut off a cab and zipped onto the Pont Saint-Michel, then braked so hard I cracked my nose on my driver's shoulder.

"Pardon!" he yelled before hitting the accelerator and racing onto the wrong side of the road. I pictured my un-helmeted head hitting the concrete. This was such a bad idea. We drove onto the island and the crowds got worse. There were musicians everywhere and scooter guy drove up onto the sidewalk, scaring the crap out of a tour group. Their flag bearer dropped her flag and screamed at us in German.

"You're going to kill us!" I yelled.

I could feel him laughing through his leather jacket. "We get there, Mademoiselle."

He jolted to a stop to avoid ramming a gelato cart. The rear wheel popped up and I screamed. He laughed again and we zoomed around the cart. I could see the black spires of the old prison up ahead.

Almost there. And that's when I saw the source of the boom, a freaking parade float right in the middle of the street. We had to stop. The crowd was huge, surrounding the unmoving float and band behind it. All I could see was a pyramid that looked like it was made of gold tinfoil.

"What is it?" I yelled.

"Futbol," he yelled.

*What the...*

I hopped off the back of the scooter, hugged him, and ran into the crowd. Everything was at a dead stop. I pushed my way through the crowd, none too gently, and got a load of what was so exciting. I should've known. Girls in scant bikinis danced on a platform. I couldn't see any connection in the Mayan theme to futbol, but that wasn't bothering the transfixed crowd. I shoved my way past, marveling that the cars stuck behind the float weren't honking. They sat there patiently as I squeezed past them. I was concentrating so hard on going fast that I went right past the ticket office and didn't realize it until I was in front of the Palais de Justice courtyard.

"Shit!" I spun around and ran back to the office. They hadn't opened yet and I pounded on the tall glass door, shouting, "Emergency! Help!"

People were staring at me.

*Oh right. Wrong words. What are the right words?*

"Urgence! Nécessité!" I shouted at the door. Angela should be there. She was supposed to volunteer at nine-thirty.

The doors rattled and an older woman opened the right one. She was shocked at my barrage of bad French.

"You can speak English," she said.

"Thank goodness. I'm looking for Angela...I mean, I'm looking for Corinne Sweet. I understand she volunteers here. It's an emergency, a family matter. I have to find her. Is she here?" I asked, all in a rush.

"Come in. Come in," she said, waving to the ticket desk and the security guard behind it. They fought about letting me in for a minute before he relented.

"Mademoiselle Sweet should be here," she said. "But I don't know where she is."

"You have to buy a ticket," said the guard.

"Fine." I dug in my purse.

"Not now. When the museum and chapel is open."

"I can't wait," I said, giving him the big eyes before looking over my shoulder in case Poinaré had caught up with me. He hadn't.

"Laurie," said the woman. "Let her in. It's only a few minutes."

He grumped and insisted on rummaging through my purse and giving me a pat down. I bet none of the other tourists would be getting that. The woman smacked him with a brochure until he sold me a dual ticket for Sainte-Chapelle and the prison. I grabbed my purse off the counter and rushed for the courtyard door, only to double back.

"I'm sorry," I said to them. "There might be a man coming, a Corsican. He's looking for Mademoiselle Sweet, too, and he'll probably have a gun. Don't let him in."

They both exclaimed and I ran into the courtyard before they could stop me. The door to the prison tour was already open and I darted inside. My heels clicked on the stone steps as I ran down into the Men-at-Arms hall, an enormous area with graceful stone arches where they used to keep condemned prisoners during the revolution. It was eerily empty and my footsteps echoed off the giant fireplaces and attacked my ears.

At the end of the hall, I dashed up the stairs to the bookstore. A woman jerked upright from behind the counter at my sudden appearance.

"Corinne Sweet? Ou est elle?" I gasped.

"Corinne?"

"Oui."

She pointed to the door to the rest of the tour and I ran up more stairs, past the memorial plaque to the cells. There was a man there, sweeping and getting ready for the opening.

"Corinne Sweet." I could hardly get it out.

He told me she was in the cell down the stairs. I assumed he meant Marie Antoinette's cell and went for it. Lucky for me, there was only one way to go or I'd have gotten lost. I ran into the small chapel where prisoners prayed for a reprieve and then looked into the Queen's chapel, built where the Queen spent her last day. Its walls of silver tears were barely visible in the dim morning light.

Empty, of course.

Poinaré would be coming. I screeched in rage and a head popped up in the window to the women's courtyard. Angela. She looked right at me and her eyes widened. She recognized me from the Orsay. Damn my face. Even with the hat, it was memorable.

She ran for it and I dashed out the door to the courtyard in time to see her enter the far door to the Queen's recreated cell.

"Wait!" I yelled. "Angela!"

I chased her back through the prison, into the bookstore, and down into the big hall, past the fireplaces and dodging pillars. She was fast and wearing flats, not teetering on heels. Our footsteps bounced off the stone walls and she hit the stairs at full speed.

"Angela! No! Don't go out there! He's out there!" I screamed so loud it hurt my ears, but she didn't stop. She ran full steam up the stairs and disappeared. I followed, but not fast enough. By the time I got outside, she was running past the gate guard. She was supposed to stop and be checked, but it happened so fast, they let her blow by. I wasn't so lucky. The first guard grabbed me and the other pointed his pistol at me. If I'd had any sense, I'd have stopped. I didn't, so I stomped on the guard's foot and slipped past the other one through the gate. I guess he wasn't prepared to shoot an unarmed woman.

The guards yelled after me as I went straight into the parade madness on the street. The float was still there and the girls were still dancing. I spotted Angela when she looked over her shoulder for me. I yelled for her, but nobody could've heard me over the din of the band.

She ran past the ticket office and a man stepped out. Poinaré. This time he'd replaced the fanny pack with snug jeans, a fitted tee, and a bulky backpack. He had tattoos up his arms, black hair, and bushy sideburns, but I knew him instantly, not so much by his looks but by his tense manner. The grumpy security officer came out behind him and said something. Poinaré ignored him and went for Angela full throttle. She saw him. There was no mistaking that look. I'd seen it when he tried to nab me in the metro and on Michel Colonna's face on the sewer tour. She turned into the crowd with Poinaré right behind her and the officer behind him.

"Arrête-le!" I had nothing. Just freaking pepper spray, and I was too far away.

Angela darted into the band, ducking behind a tuba player. The startled musician turned and blocked Poinaré and the security officer grabbed his arm, spinning the assassin around. The men were face to face. Poinaré's shoulder jerked and a jolt of surprise came over the officer's face. He staggered back into the crowd, still clutching Poinaré's arm. I ran past them and chased Angela's bobbing head through the rest of the band into the stopped traffic.

I didn't remember that boulevard being so long. It seemed like miles with the crowd and the cars. Angela zigzagged past the float and shoved her way through the line at the Berthillon stand on the corner before the bridge. People yelled and shook their fists at her as she knocked ice cream to the ground and crepes went flying. She glanced over her shoulder at me, a look of sheer terror on her face and then something happened. Her face changed. In that glance, I saw it. Angela Riley changed her mind. She had cornered around Berthillon and was positioned to run down the length of the Ile de Cité toward Notre Dame. Instead, she did a U-turn and ran onto the bridge, weaving through the dense crowds and bumper-to-bumper traffic.

I was so close; I could hear her ragged breath. "Angela! I can help you!" I screamed. She hit the side rail of the bridge and a zing went through my heart. I kept running for her. She stopped and turned to look at me one last time.

"No! We lost him!" I screamed, dashing for her, arms outstretched.

"They know I'm alive!" Angela turned and went over the side a second before I got there. Her foot brushed my hand and I hit the low stone rail with a thump screaming, "Angela!"

My mom, usually when lecturing me about something stupid I'd done, always said, "Look before you leap." As usual, my perfect mother was right. Angela Riley didn't look before she leapt and it didn't work out for her any better than it did for me.

I leaned over the railing, a couple hundred people screaming in horror all around me, and saw Angela, not sinking into the Seine but lying on the roof of a tourist boat. She was facedown and not moving, but I'd take it.

"Thank you, God!" I looked heavenward and then heard yells of protest and then panic. Poinaré shoved his way onto the bridge and he carried a handgun at his side. No. Not a handgun. It looked like a mini machine gun, a Škorpion. I peed my pants a little. He looked at me and then did a sweeping motion with the weapon. I've never seen people drop to the ground so fast. I didn't. I froze.

Poinaré stalked across the bridge between a Mini Cooper and a Fiat, his cold eyes fixed on me. He made a little motion with the gun. He was telling me to get out of the way. He knew where Angela was. Hundreds of people pointing probably helped.

He stepped over a crouched man and aimed at me.

*I don't know what to do! I don't know what to do! Shit! Yes, I do.*

I followed Angela's example. I went over the side. It was a little harder, since I had on a skirt, but the tiny delay gave me a second to think.

*Bend your knees. Roll.*

Jumping from a height when chasing a suspect was one of Dad's lessons, one I had to pay attention to because he made me jump off our ten-foot fence and the garage, until Mom caught him and he had to sleep in the garage again.

It worked. Burning severe pain shot through my feet all the way to my eyeballs. I rolled twice down the sloping wooden roof and caught myself inches before I fell off the edge. I hopped up and did a scrambling crab-like run down the length of the boat toward Angela at the bow.

There was a staccato burst behind me and someone screaming my name.

*Faster! Go faster!*

Another burst and the sound of wood splitting at almost the same time. I dove for Angela, a real diving for home plate kind of dive, and shoved her body off the roof as a spray of blood hit me in the face. I jumped off the roof onto a set of deck chairs and an unconscious Angela. If I thought the screaming was bad on the bridge, it was nothing to the tourists on that boat. I looked through the etched glass windows and realized I was on the boat that Chuck and I had our dinner cruise on or one exactly like it. The interior was filled with potted palms and terrorized people diving under tables.

I pulled Angela off the chairs with my right hand. My left hung uselessly at my side. I felt no pain and I wasn't even concerned. I noted it and kept on moving. Angela was bleeding from the mouth, but she was breathing. The gunfire stopped and I stood up, bracing myself on the glass with a bloody hand. That's when I saw the other boat, one of those big glassed-in jobs with three times the number of tourists. It was going toward the bridge and the staff was in full on panic mode. The tourists were screaming and pointing at me.

*Stop pointing at me, idiots!*

One of the boat's staff crept around the side and asked me in French what was going on. He held a champagne bottle up, ready to crack me with it.

My French wasn't working, so I said, "Terrorist." It was the first thing that came to mind. I was certainly terrified.

His young face went white and then became determined. "No more shooting. They must have them."

"I hope they—"

There was a loud thump on the roof and then a clatter.

"One is on the boat," whispered the sailor.

"I know." I peeked around the edge of the cabin and saw that we'd cleared the bridge. I didn't see Poinaré, but the other boat's tourists were now pointing at our stern and yelling. I think I heard, "Get it!" amidst the multitude of languages.

*Get what?*

I couldn't see anything with all the deck chairs and plants. A side door opened and a man with an enormous fanny pack and a man bun crept out. He grabbed something and flung it over the side to a chorus of cheers.

"He dropped the gun," I said.

"We're safe," said the sailor, his shoulders relaxed.

I shook my head. "He'll have a spare. We have to hide her."

The sailor looked at Angela. "Inside?"

"No, not close to the others." I scanned the deck, but there was no place to hide a grown woman. There were life jackets. "Are there any police on board?" I asked. "Military?"

He shook his head.

"Help me." I grabbed a life jacket. This was a terrible plan, the worst plan, but I couldn't think of another. I'd have to throw a bleeding, unconscious woman overboard and hope to hell I could distract Poinaré long enough to get her out of range.

We had the life jacket on Angela in a flash and I yelled to the passing boat. "Where is he?"

Several yelled back in English. "Back deck."

I faced the back and motioned, right or left. Right. That's when the captains of both boats hit the throttle. There was such a surge in speed that I hit the glass so hard, I was momentarily dazed. When I peeked around the corner again, the helpful folks on deck were pointing at our stern. Then they screamed and hit their own deck.

I looked in the cabin again and saw Poinaré at the door. Somebody had thought to lock it. Good idea, but it was glass. He shattered the door with a wine bottle and reached in to unlock it.

"Ease her over the side," I said to the sailor.

He didn't question my insane decision, carried Angela's limp body to the port side, and put her over. He did it so quietly, there wasn't even a splash. Poinaré had the door open. He stepped in and I ran to the starboard side, picked up a chair, and started whacking a wooden column between two windows. The glass cracked and shattered as I caught a pane with a chair leg. Poinaré saw me and I flipped him off. I'm not a big fan of flipping people off, but there'd never been a more appropriate moment for it.

Poinaré headed for me and I looked at the sailor. "Run."

He shook his head. His hands were shaking, but he was with me. Totally nuts. I stepped sideways out of the shelter of the cabin. Poinaré was at the other end of the boat. He smiled at me and shook his head. "You can't change this!"

"I already did!"

The other boat was past us and starting to go under the bridge. Out of the corner of my eye, I saw somebody jump off the bridge and land on their boat. The screaming went wild and Poinaré's smile widened.

"Friend of yours?" I yelled.

"I have no friends."

I glanced at the other boat's roof and almost peed again. It was Chuck, running the length of the roof. If Poinaré saw him... I was careful not to look at Chuck or react as he dove off the end of the other boat. He came so close to our boat that for a second I thought he might hit the side.

The assassin started for me, seamlessly reaching down and pulling a small revolver out of his boot. Damn spare.

*Stall. Stall.*

"I'm not surprised," I said, backing up slowly as he advanced. "You are..."—I waved up and down—"whatever this is."

A thick rope that hung over the end of the boat slid to the right. Chuck.

"Where is she?" he asked.

"Who?" I asked, picking up a chair as a shield and he smiled. His disguise was so complete, even his teeth were different, crooked and stained.

"I won't hurt you unless I have to."

"That's reassuring," I said.

"This is nothing to do with you."

Chuck came over the side, slow and stealthy. He didn't make a sound as we passed under the Love Locks bridge and were momentarily cast into shadows.

"I beg to differ. I led you to her." I bumped into the broken window on purpose.

Glass came crashing down, but Poinaré didn't flinch. "You did."

Chuck was five feet away. Four. Three.

"You can't have her." I forced myself to smile with a gun pointed at my chest. "She isn't here."

A look of concern flashed in Poinaré's eyes as a heavy 35mm camera flew out of the broken window and hit him in the shoulder. I ducked to the right as he looked in the cabin and Chuck pounced. He kicked

Poinaré behind the knee and buckled the assassin's leg. Chuck hooked his left arm around Poinaré's neck and his right grabbed the revolver. It went off and hit the wooden overhang, spraying splinters. The tourists started screaming again, but with a new ferocity. Everything but the kitchen sink came out of that window. Cameras, wine bottles, plates, glasses, steaks, and duck legs. A pair of false teeth hit Poinaré on the nose as he wrestled with Chuck, trying desperately to break free. Tourists rock.

Or maybe not. The wine bottles increased. Poinaré took a glancing blow to the head from an empty red. So did Chuck, but his was a big champagne bottle and it was corked. It knocked him to the right and he hit the deck. I threw my chair at Poinaré, but he dodged it and a roast chicken smacked him in the mouth. He fired into the cabin wildly, but the hits just kept on coming. The sailor ran around me and took a swing at the assassin. He knocked the revolver out of his hand and that was it for Poinaré. He ran straight at me, shoving me to the deck. I clutched at his leg, but he shook me off. I grabbed the revolver and jumped to my feet, chasing him to the bow, where he dove off and began swimming to shore, doing a freestyle that would've made Michel Phelps jealous.

It really is hard to hit a moving target, especially when you're on a boat and can't use your left hand for support. I wasted the two rounds I had and they didn't slow down Poinaré one bit. He made it to the Right Bank and clamored up the smooth stone bank, his feet slipping on the algae. A few people were on the lower sidewalk. They stared at Poinaré while some of the tourists screamed at them to stop him. But everyone on shore was too astonished to do anything. Swimming in the Seine wasn't an everyday occurrence. Poinaré ran down the walkway and up a stairway to the tree-lined avenue unmolested. He never looked back.

# CHAPTER TWENTY-FIVE

"Son of a bitch," said an old man who'd come hobbling out and waved his four-pronged cane. "He got away." He looked over, seeing me for the first time. "You are something. That hat. Are you an actress?"

I touched my head. Holy crap. The hat was still on. It belonged in the Hall of Fame for hats.

"I'm a nurse," I said.

"Good," he said. "You're gonna need one."

"Huh?"

He pointed to my shoulder. "You've been shot, honey."

I touched the spot and came away with a mess of blood. "Well, that's not good."

"Shot? Who was shot?" Chuck hurried around the corner with the support of the sailor. Behind them, the boat came alive with the tourists and the rest of the crew emerging, some stunned and others weeping.

"Nobody," I said, rushing to his side. He had a slit on his temple and streaks of blood down the side of his face. I checked his pupils and they were equal. Thank God.

Chuck touched his temple. "My head is killing me." Then he felt the wetness and looked at his bloody hand. "What the fuck?"

I pulled a chair up behind him and eased him down. "You got hit with a champagne bottle."

"Somebody threw a champagne bottle? Why in the hell?"

The old guy and I exchanged worried glances.

"I think you have a concussion."

Chuck snorted. "Concussion. Bullshit. I've had concussions before. This isn't a concussion." He frowned. "What did you say?"

*Crap on a cracker.*

"We need to dock, like now," I said to the sailor. "How far?"

"I'll check for you." He ran into the cabin and then spun around. "You are a nurse?"

"Yes," I said.

"We have injured people."

I stared at him for a split second and then told the old man to stay with Chuck. "Don't let him stand up."

"I can stand if I want to," Chuck growled.

"No, you can't. Just do what I say." I ran into the cabin, slipping on broken glass and ignoring the growing burning sensation in my shoulder. "Who's hurt?" I yelled.

Eight hands went up and one of the crew waved at me frantically. "This one is shot."

Of the three bullets that Poinaré had fired into the cabin, only one had connected. A teenaged girl with big eyes and a blood-soaked abdomen stared at me from her mother's lap on the far side of the cabin. I knelt beside them and assessed her. Rapid pulse and breathing. Plenty of blood loss and a hard, distended abdomen. If I had to guess from the angle of the entry wound, the bullet had perforated her liver, an amazingly unlucky shot since most of her liver would be hidden under her ribcage because she was so young. But maybe it missed the bowel. That would be good. Maybe it was lucky, after all.

"Can you tell me your name?" I asked.

"Trudie," she whispered with a strong accent.

"Are you visiting from Germany?"

"Austria."

I nodded while pulling her shirt down over her wound. "I love Austria. So beautiful." Then I held up my hand to the crew member. He hauled me to my feet with difficulty. I was light-headed and nauseated. "Give me your jacket?"

He slipped it off and I folded it before putting it on Trudie's abdomen. "Firm pressure. That's all," I told her mother and she nodded.

"Where's your captain?" I asked the crew member.

He led me to the back, where the captain was applying pressure to a head wound. It took me a second to see the bloody oar on the deck next to him. The patient wasn't fully conscious, but his eyes were fluttering. "He tried to stop him," said the captain, his eyes flooded with tears.

Poinaré had hit the man several times, but he was still in better shape than Trudie.

"We have a gunshot wound. How fast can we dock?" I asked.

The captain looked into the wheelhouse and a crew man yelled out the window, "Two minutes, mademoiselle."

Two minutes. Not ideal, but what was?

"Have you radioed for emergency services to meet us at the dock?"

"Yes."

"How many wounded did you report?"

The captain looked confused. "Multiple wounded."

"Good. I need you to get back on the radio and tell them we have a gunshot wound to the abdomen."

My helper got the radio and said exactly what I said in French. Then he said, "They have told the trauma unit to expect the critically wounded girl."

The boat slowed and turned astern before they killed the engine. Multiple sirens pierced the air. I returned to Trudie and checked her vitals again. She was weakening. The crewman lifted me to my feet and I asked if he could translate what I said quickly to the ambulance staff. He put me to shame by saying he spoke six languages fluently and could do whatever I asked.

Police and medical staff swarmed over the dock as the staff lowered the gangplank. It barely hit the dock before the EMTs were at Trudie's side and putting her on a backboard. The crewman told them what I said and they had her off the boat in less than five minutes. The crewman with the blows to the head was next. He was talking and complaining about how he could walk, so that was a good sign. Chuck was next and he flat out refused to be strapped down and transported off the boat like, and these are his words, "A damned wussy." The fact that he was seeing double and nearly pitched himself headfirst off the gangplank made no impression on him whatsoever. The rest of the injuries were cuts from the glass and bruises from falling.

I stood out of the way, having stuck my left hand in my pocket, determined to sneak away before the police could question me. I'd assessed my own wound when nobody was looking and it was a flesh wound through the meat of my shoulder. Extremely painful and swelling like crazy, but not life-threatening.

When all the wounded had been removed, the police started their questioning. It was a cluster. About forty tourists and fifteen crew remained on board and they all had something to say and all at the same time. I snuck out of the cabin and circled around the deck to try and get off without anyone noticing.

"There she is!" yelled someone behind me and I flinched.

Three cops and two EMTs surrounded me.

"I'm fine," I said, trying to push past them.

"Mademoiselle, you are injured," said an EMT.

"What is your name?" asked one of the cops.

His face swam in front of me and someone took me by the waist.

"Mademoiselle, your name?"

*Lie.*

"Boba Fett," I said.

*WTF. That's not even a girl.*

"Ellen Ripley."

*Better. They'll buy that.*

A cop held up my purse in front of my face. "Is this yours?"

*I cannot catch a break.*

He frowned at my lack of an answer and dug through my purse. I couldn't remember having anything incriminating in there. "Her identification says Carolina Watts."

Except that.

They attempted to sit me in a chair, but I wouldn't bend my legs. "Mademoiselle, please."

"No, I have to go. They took—" I faked wooziness and I did it so well I got carried off the boat. They didn't even wait for a backboard. They stuck me in the back of an ambulance and examined me despite my protests. Oh well. Maybe they'd think my sad attempt at an alias was a result of blood loss. I certainly thought it was. Boba Fett? I'd spent too much time with nerds.

The next two hours at the hospital were a painful blur. I kept trying to escape my gurney and they kept not letting me. Nobody would tell me anything about Chuck or Trudie or the crew member with the head wound. I had no idea what had happened to Angela. I was afraid to ask and give away our connection. In the snippets of conversations I caught and understood, the consensus was that the boat had been attacked by a terrorist, likely more than one.

Once I was in an exam room, the police descended. I'd been named as the one who tried to distract the terrorist on the boat and fired at him in the water. Apparently, my outfit was unforgettable. Stupid style.

An officer named Malraux glowered at me from the end of my bed. He was so tense, the hairs on his hands were sticking straight up. The word *terrorist* had that effect on first responders and I regretted saying it, but I wasn't the only one. The gun Poinaré had pointed at me on the bridge was identified as a Škorpion machine pistol and witnesses thought it looked like a terrorist weapon.

"Why did you lie about your name?" he asked for a second time.

"I didn't lie. I was out of my head. Who in their right mind would say they were Boba Fett?"

"You were concealing your identity."

"But Boba Fett? Get real."

"The name isn't important," he said, putting his hand on the footboard and clenching.

I laughed. "Have you looked up Boba Fett?"

He grimaced and another officer came in. Malraux asked him, "Avez-vous entendu parler de Boba Fett?"

The other officer's eyes went wide. "*Stars Wars* Boba Fett?"

"*Star Wars?*"

"Oui. Boba Fett est un personnage de *Star Wars*."

Malraux looked at me and I shrugged my good shoulder.

"You said you were Ellen Ripley as well," he said.

The other officer started laughing and left.

"She's the main character of *Alien*," I said.

Malraux slapped his forehead. "Why do that?"

"I don't know. I'd been shot."

"Why did this man,"—he held up his phone with a picture of Poinaré pointing the Škorpion at me—"threaten you? Who is he?"

I shrugged again. "How should I know who he is?"

"He threatened you."

"He was chasing that woman and I got in the way," I said.

Malraux pursed his lips and twisted them to the side. Not buying it.

"You put her in a life jacket and threw her overboard."

"He was going to kill her."

"How did you know that?"

I snorted. "He shot at her."

"And you." Malraux straightened up and crossed his arms.

"If he wanted to kill me, he could've done it on the bridge," I said.

"He knew who you were. You spoke on the boat."

My doctor, a young Briton, came in and told Malraux he had to leave. Malraux told me in no uncertain terms that he didn't believe me and that he'd be back. I said, "Okay," like I didn't care. I did care and I didn't know what to say to get him off my back.

The doc examined my wound and declared it non-life-threatening. No surprise there. I tried to get out of bed and failed. The doc took off and a couple of nurses came in, thwarted another escape attempt, and prepared to clean the wound.

"I need my phone," I said. "Do you know where my purse is?"

"No, mademoiselle," said Elaine. "Lie back and relax so that we may care for you."

*Relax. Right. That'll happen.*

"I really need my phone."

"You have been shot. This wound must be cared for."

"Rub some dirt on it. I've got to go."

"Dirt?"

"It's an American thing. It means I'm fine."

She frowned and said, "You had much blood loss. We will keep you overnight."

*No, you won't. I'm so out of here, sister.*

"I'll pass on the overnighter," I said and winced as she gave me a shot of lidocaine. While it was kicking in, the nurse tried to wrestle me out of my clothes and I'm happy to say that for once, I won. If they got me into a gown, I was going nowhere.

"Mademoiselle, please," said nurse two, Sandrine.

"Please, yourself. Tell me about Chuck Watts. How is he? Nobody will tell me anything," I said.

Sandrine glanced at my chart. "Watts. Is he your husband?"

"Er...why, yes he is, and I demand to know his condition." I would've crossed my arms in defiance, but I could barely move my fingers on the left one.

"Monsieur Watts is in stable condition," said Elaine.

"I could've told you that. I assessed him at the scene. Does he have a concussion? Did he have a CT?"

She sighed. "Lie back. Do not get yourself excited."

"Too late. Don't worry. I'm a nurse. I can take it."

"A nurse?" Both of them brightened up. Suddenly, I wasn't just a pain-in-the-ass patient. I was one of them.

"I could prove it if I had my purse," I said.

Elaine made a call and then told me Chuck did have a concussion and they were keeping him overnight in case a bleed turned up. Other than that, he was fine and complaining as much as me. Since I was a nurse, they also told me that Trudie was in surgery. Her liver was perforated and her bowel nicked, but she was expected to survive. The crew member was enjoying chocolate mousse. He would be released that evening.

*Thank you, Lord.*

Angela remained a mystery. Nobody mentioned her, even when I hinted about other victims. I was about to break down and ask when Aaron ambled in, eating a sausage. Elaine and Sandrine tried to hustle him out, but I promised to be good if they let the little weirdo stay. They agreed out of desperation and I was good with it.

"You hungry?" he asked.

"I'm nauseated."

Aaron stared at me.

"No, I'm not hungry," I said with an eye roll.

"I can make you hot chocolate."

"We're in a hospital."

He shrugged and I held out my good hand to him. He took it with his sausage grease-covered one and sat with me through the cleaning and bandaging. I yelped, but he never wavered, telling me all about his latest incursions into Empire territory in the game. I had no idea what game he was talking about, but it helped to distract me from the insistent poking.

When we were done, I promised to not run away and they left me alone with Aaron and a call button. They said they'd try and locate my purse, but I doubted it. It was a busy day.

"Did you tell the cops anything about Angela?" I asked as soon as the door closed.

"Jango Fett crossed the border and I—"

"Aaron!"

"Huh?"

"We've got a situation here. Did the cops question you about me?"

"No."

I pushed the *up* arrow to get me into the seated position. "How'd you get in here?"

"I walked."

"Nobody stopped you?"

He shrugged. I couldn't believe it. They let a little weirdo eating a sausage walk right in and I couldn't get out of bed without alarms going off. "Do you have Novak's phone?"

Aaron handed it over and started in on Jango again.

"Novak, it's me," I said, keeping an eye on the door.

"Finally. How's the lidocaine?"

"It sucks...wait. Did you hack the hospital?" I asked.

"Naturally, how else would I keep an eye on you? Spidermonkey sends his love. Your parents talked to your doctor and are trying to get on a plane."

I glanced at my hat on the rolling table beside my bed. "Damn. I thought the hat might've concealed my identity."

"It did. Chuck was less concealed and he's very popular," said Novak.

"What do you mean?"

"He already has Facebook fan pages and there's a campaign to give him the Légion d'Honneur like the Americans on the train."

"He was pretty impressive." I smiled. "Like James Bond."

"In this case, I agree. It was very Bond," said Novak. "Why don't you ask me about Angela?"

"Where is she?" I squeezed my eyes shut. "Is she alive?"

Angela was alive. According to Novak's information, she'd clammed up good. The fall onto the boat roof had knocked her out and the gunshot to her chest had lodged in a rib with no significant damage, thanks to me.

"Me?"

"Your dive saved her. The bullet passed through your shoulder and into her chest. You took the brunt of it, from what I can see," said Novak.

"From what you can see?"

"It's all over the internet. You did this in front of a crowd."

"I didn't exactly pick the place. That was Angela. She was trying to kill herself."

Novak laughed. "She hasn't been in Paris long enough then. The fall wouldn't have killed her. La brigade fluviale has to fish many jumpers out of the Seine every year."

"They don't drown?"

"They're usually found clinging to pylons. Sometimes the current gets them, but the survival instinct is strong. Listen to me now. Have the authorities interviewed you yet?"

"Yes, but I didn't really tell them anything," I said.

"They will get more insistent. Don't tell them anything about me."

"I would never," I said, flexing my fingers.

"You must ask to talk to Jean-Yves Thyraud at DGSE and talk to no one else," he said.

"What's DGSE?"

"The French CIA, if you will. Don't tell him about Calpurnia. Tell him you were hired by Gina to find her sister. Leave Spidermonkey out of it. He knows me. You found her through the picture Gina took and then recognized her at d'Orsay."

"Should I identify Poinaré?" I asked.

"Yes. Tell him about the metro and the Novotel."

I got more nauseated. "What if he arrests me?"

"He won't. You can give him the trail. You just won't tell him who found it. He doesn't want this to be a terrorist action. Corsican mafia is much more palatable."

"He can still arrest me for withholding evidence," I said, picking up the pink emesis bag the nurses left me.

"Arrest the heroine who kept her head and held off a killer? No. He won't. You are a heroine. With a record like yours, the public won't want that questioned."

"Have I been identified on the news yet?"

"No, but Chuck has. It won't be long."

I sighed. "No. Not long." Why couldn't Angela have kept on running, gotten in a cab, or thought of something other than a very public suicide? What did she say before she jumped?

"Before Angela jumped, she said that now somebody knows she's alive. It was enough to push her over the edge. Literally."

"Ah yes. That. Spidermonkey found the link. He believes the Bombellis hired Poinaré to track you and kill Angela Riley."

"Why? Who are the Bombellis?"

"Too much to explain now. Call Calpurnia and tell her the plan. She must be kept out of this."

"No kidding. My parents cannot find out about her."

"Or Chuck."

I groaned. How I could lie well enough to fool him? "Should I tell Calpurnia about the Bombellis?"

"It's up to you. Angela hasn't been identified yet."

I groaned again and hung up.

Aaron swallowed the last of his sausage and then said, "You hungry yet?"

"Not quite." I called Calpurnia, my stomach twisting into a complicated knot.

"Miss Watts," said Calpurnia. "I was wondering when I'd hear from you."

"You've seen the news?"

She laughed her throaty laugh. "This wasn't the ending I imagined."

"What did you imagine?"

"That you wouldn't find Angela, of course. It would've been much simpler."

I agreed. Much simpler. "I have a plan and I hope you'll go along with it."

Calpurnia made a sound of disapproval.

"I want to keep you out of this completely. I want to say that Gina hired me. That Oz gave her my name because I helped with his sister and I couldn't say no."

"I can do that."

"Really? Thank you."

"I'd rather protect your reputation than not."

*Uh oh.*

"Why?" I asked, so afraid of the answer that I stopped breathing.

"I may need you again," said Calpurnia.

"And if you cover this for me, I'll owe you again."

More throaty laughter. "You catch on fast."

*I'm so screwed.*

"You'll tell your people and Gina what the deal is?" I asked.

"I will if you tell me why?" she asked.

"Why what?"

"Why Angela did it?"

"I don't know yet, but I will." I told her about Poinaré and the Corsican connection to the Bombellis. Calpurnia got quiet, very quiet when I said Bombelli.

"Are you still there?" I asked.

"I am."

"So who are the Bombellis?"

"A rival family. A former rival family."

"Former?"

The Bombellis were definitely a former family. There wasn't much left of them. Four years ago, the patriarch, Antonio Bombelli, was arrested on multiple charges, including racketeering and human trafficking. Two of his three sons followed him. They were all convicted and given long consecutive sentences. Antonio had his throat slit in the prison shower. His son, Tony, was beaten to death with a broom and Sammy, an epileptic, had a seizure and died in his cell in the middle of the night. Only Marius, the youngest son, was left and he was without the organization his great-grandfather had built. Marius had been taken in by the Gravano family but was nowhere near the top.

Convictions two years after Angela disappeared didn't give us an obvious connection.

"Was...your family involved with the Bombellis?" I asked.

"You know better than to ask that, Miss Watts," said Calpurnia.

"I guess so. Do you happen to know what Marius looks like or is that off limits, too?"

Her voice got sharp. "Why do you want to know?"

"My source says the Bombellis hired Poinaré. Marius is the only one left," I said.

"Poinaré isn't Marius, if that's what you think. I've seen the video from the bridge," said Calpurnia.

"I know. Humor me."

Marius matched the description of Angela's Panera guy, but thousands of men could. He wasn't that distinct. "Do you have a picture you can send me? I can't really do a Google search easily right now."

"I'll find one, but I want to know how this came about. Are you saying that Angela was in the witness protection program?"

"Yes. She was," I said.

"Then she gave up the Bombellis."

"Looks like it. The question is how did she have anything to give up?"

"Leave that to me," said Calpurnia.

I shook my head, even though she couldn't see me. "I can't. It's gone too far. I have to know everything."

"Miss Watts, you don't want to know everything."

"I said, 'have to' not 'want to'."

"I see," she said. "When you know *how* it happened, I'll tell you why."

We had a deal and hung up as the door opened. I stuffed the phone under the covers and Malraux walked in with new determination. Before he could open his mouth, I said, "I want to talk to Jean-Yves Thyraud at DGSE."

Malraux stopped short and gaped at me. His partner, the laugher, came in behind him and glanced between the two of us. "Has something happened?"

"She wants someone at DGSE," said Malraux.

"Who?"

"Jean-Yves Thyraud. Do you know him?"

The partner paled and turned to me. "You know Thyraud?"

"Not at all," I said. "We have what I would term as a friendly connection and I'm not saying another word to anyone else."

"Mademoiselle Watts, that will take some time," said Malraux.

"I'm sure it won't. He's here in Paris. Make a call." I picked up my water pitcher and sipped on my straw. Aaron stood up and made a shooing motion at them.

"Who are you?" asked the partner.

"Aaron," said my partner.

Malraux flipped open a notebook. "And your surname?"

No answer.

"Monsieur, your surname."

"Give it up," I said. "He's not a talker."

Just to prove me wrong, Aaron began talking in French and told them to take a hike.

"Who is he?" asked the partner.

"Family friend."

"What does he do?" Malraux asked it with a sniff like he expected the answer to be dung shoveler or something equally repugnant. I had to admit, dung shoveler did look more likely than chef.

"He's a chef," I said, surprising myself with the pride in my voice. Aaron, my partner, was awesome, even if he smelled like hot dogs and looked like hell.

A change came over both the detectives' faces. "Where does he cook?" asked the partner.

"He has a restaurant in St. Louis now, but he used to cook at Guy Savoy," I said.

Surprise registered on both their faces. "We'll be checking into that."

"Go for it. But, before you do, I have a couple questions."

It was their turn to cross arms. "You want to question us?"

I suspect they thought it was going to be about national security or how bad they were doing their jobs. It wasn't. "Did you catch him?" I asked. "The man on the boat, I mean."

They shuffled their feet. I guess it was about how they did their job.

"No," said Malraux.

"Are you serious?" I asked. "There were hundreds of people watching him run away. Where the heck did he go?"

"He blended into the crowd."

"He was soaking wet."

"Nevertheless."

I groaned. "That isn't going to look good."

"We are well aware of the implications. A terrorist on the loose in Paris. The people are alarmed." Both detectives seemed to feel the failure keenly, but it wasn't their fault. Poinaré was a master.

"You found nothing?"

"A black wig, sideburns, and false teeth in a dumpster," said the partner. "We were lucky there. A maid dropped her bracelet in when taking out the trash and saw the pieces."

"That is lucky. Nothing else?"

"No. We think he had his getaway well planned."

I decided to help them out. Not just because I didn't like police detectives looking bad. I didn't want Paris in an uproar when it needn't be. "I think I can help you calm the situation."

"Can you? How?"

"Get Thyraud and we'll see," I said.

"You know who the terrorist is," said the partner. "Tell us now."

"Thyraud or nothing."

They hesitated and then left, promising to find Thyraud. I pulled out the Novak phone and found a text from Calpurnia, a mugshot of a moderately handsome man staring smugly at the camera. Angela's Panera guy, Marius Bombelli. Holy crap, Angela. What were you thinking? First, you have an affair and then that's the guy you choose? I'd grown sort of fond of Angela, but this was testing my regard.

I texted Novak for Angela's and Chuck's locations. Happily, we were in the same hospital on different floors. Neither was in ICU and they weren't under guard. Next, I took a deep breath and called Spidermonkey.

"Hello, Mercy," said Loretta.

"Hi. I have a name for Spidermonkey," I said.

"He has one for you, too."

"What is it?"

"Marius Bombelli."

*Dammit. He beat me.*

Spidermonkey knew all about Marius and I didn't bother to hide the phone when Sandrine came back with painkillers. I palmed them when she wasn't looking and drank the water out of the teeny cup she gave me. I nodded when she told me the pain would be better soon. She frowned at the phone and I whispered, "My mother. She's upset."

She gave me a commiserating look and left. I settled in for Spidermonkey's info as told by Loretta. Spidermonkey figured out the Panera guy hours before and had begun digging with Loretta's help. He found an unindicted co-conspirator in the Bombelli case. That was Angela and she kicked off the government's whole case.

Marius Bombelli had targeted Angela. After I heard his plan, I realized she didn't stand a chance. According to the federal investigation, Phillip Riley kept a lot of Fibonacci files in his house. He had a state of the art security system that the Bombellis had tried to breach and failed. Antonio Bombelli wanted to take over the Midwest territory that Calpurnia controlled, but he needed information and he wasn't above pimping out his son to get it. He gave Marius the assignment and Marius had spent six months formulating his plan to get in with the wife of Riley. He hacked her Facebook account and studied her likes and dislikes. He knew about the cologne her beloved high school boyfriend wore and he bought it. He listened to the music she liked and watched *Chocolat* until he could quote it. He bought the clothes she looked at from Gap and Banana Republic online. He stopped smoking and started drinking martinis because Angela thought martini-drinking men were sexy. He gave himself a heartbreaking back-story that mimicked her favorite romance novel. Marius became an orphan with a wife, dead from breast cancer. The Bombellis had no shame and I began to think a broom beating was too good for them. Loretta got terse as she told me how Marius had seduced Angela, a woman with a cold husband and a boring little life.

The affair didn't last long, a couple months. Marius weaseled some information out of Angela and then blackmailed her with it. Then Angela did the last thing Marius expected. She went to the Feds and cut a deal where she gave them everything Phillip had on the Bombellis' operation, which was considerable. Calpurnia had been gathering information herself to make a move on Antonio's Vegas operation. So that was the deal. Angela gave them everything on the Bombellis and nothing on the Fibonaccis. Then she went into protection. It was an extreme solution, but Angela must not have felt she had a choice. So now I knew, but I didn't know everything. Since I was as nosy as my mother, I had to know. I had to talk to Angela.

"I can't believe he didn't go to prison," Loretta hissed. "He is pond scum."

"Why didn't he?" I asked.

"His father cut a deal so he could stay out and the charges weren't much, compared to the other brothers: blackmail and menacing."

"I guess he never believed Angela was dead."

"No. He's been watching the whole time. Marius's security isn't as good as it should be. My beloved got into his laptop. He knew Gina went to Paris and he figured something was up when you were summoned to Calpurnia's house. When you flew to Paris, he hired the Corsicans to follow you."

"So that's it," I said, feeling more and more tired. The lidocaine was wearing off and my shins weren't made for high impact. I felt like I'd been beaten with a broom.

"That's it," said Loretta. "My beloved has fallen asleep at his keyboard and I'm going to put him to bed. May I suggest you get some rest?"

"No rest for the wicked," I said.

"It's for the weary."

"Not in my world."

"Well, since you won't rest, go talk to Angela and make sure she doesn't fling herself out the window."

"It's too late for that now. The whole world knows she didn't die six years ago or will shortly."

Loretta sighed. "You know nothing about motherhood. Having your children find out that you betrayed their father and his boss and then abandoned them is a fine reason for flinging oneself out a window."

I didn't know stink about motherhood, but I suspected Loretta was right.

# CHAPTER TWENTY-SIX

Jean-Yves Thyraud was in no hurry to see me. He didn't show up for three hours, during which I broke down and took my painkillers. I went to sleep and woke to find Aaron holding my hand and gnawing a stinky andouillette sausage. He chewed noisily as his teeth bounced off the coiled intestines.

"Oh my god. Where did you get that?" I asked, reaching for the emesis bag.

"Mathieu Torres."

"He was here? Anybody else?"

"Chuck." Aaron took a big bite and made a slurping sound. My stomach flipped like the first time I rode the Screaming Eagle at Six Flags. I was six and spewed in Dad's lap.

"I think I'm going to hurl. How mad is he?" I asked.

"Huh?"

I poked my partner. "Focus. Chuck. How mad?"

Aaron shrugged. "He's okay."

The door opened and a man looked in. "You're awake." His voice was slangy and drew out vowels in unexpected places, what Monsieur Barre would call a peasant's accent, maybe from northern France.

"Yes," I said. "Come in."

A small man, no bigger than Aaron, came in, carrying a fat briefcase. He wore a cheap off the rack suit that was rumpled and smelled of cigarette smoke, but his round face beamed at me, jolly and open. "Mademoiselle Watts. It is a pleasure to meet you." He held out a hand with stubby plump fingers with buffed nails, an odd combo. Then again, he was odd all over.

I shook his hand and asked, "And you are?"

He smiled and laughed. "Can you not guess?"

*It can't be.*

"Um...Monsieur Thyraud?"

He bowed slightly. "At your service."

I tried to wipe the look of astonishment off my face but it wouldn't go.

"You were expecting perhaps Daniel Craig or Sean Connery?"

"Well...you don't seem like a—"

"Spy?" Thyraud pulled up a chair and nodded at Aaron, who kept munching away. "That is rather the point."

I sat up and folded my legs underneath me. "How do I know it's really you?"

"Ask me anything...anything I'm willing to answer, that is," he said.

"Okay. How did I get your name?"

"Novak, a Serbian living in our beautiful city."

"What does he like to wear?"

Thyraud laughed hard, his face turning bright pink. He looked exactly the way I pictured Mr. Fezziwig from *A Christmas Carol* to look, generous and jolly, but he couldn't be if he was who he claimed to be. "Novak wears the most atrocious biking outfits, the more garish, the better." His arm swept through the air, indicating my clothes. "Nothing like what you are wearing."

"I didn't pick it out."

"Ah yes, Madam Ziegler. She has exquisite taste," he said.

"How did you know it's from her?"

"I'd recognize her work anywhere. The hat, the little shoes with bows. Madam Ziegler has a way with women. And men, from the look of your *husband*."

"Er..."

"Never mind your fib. It was necessary. Mr. Watts is doing quite well and will be released shortly."

I relaxed back on the bed. "Thank God. How is the girl, Trudie?"

"Out of surgery. She's expected to recover fully," he said. "Are you satisfied that I'm Thyraud?"

"No," I said, smiling at his surprise. I pulled the Novak phone out from under the covers and texted Novak for a description. He texted back instantly and it matched the man sitting by my bed. "Alright," I said. Where do I begin?"

"With why you are in Paris and proceed from there," said Thyraud.

And so I proceeded, leaving out Spidermonkey and Calpurnia. Thyraud texted while I talked and it was unnerving. "And that's it," I said. "I ended up here and Angela Riley is upstairs, outed to the world."

He finished texting and looked up, a hard, focused look in his warm eyes. "You must stick to that story to everyone, including your illustrious parents and your boyfriend."

"It's not a story. It's the truth," I said.

He nodded. "I believe it is the truth, but not the whole truth."

I stayed silent.

"It doesn't matter. Poinaré is what's important. We will catch him this time."

I must've looked doubtful, because the jolly look came back. "I'm optimistic."

"Why? You don't even know what he really looks like," I pointed out.

"Optimism is essential in my business. I must believe that we can win or what's the point in trying?" asked Thyraud.

"I see what you mean. What happens now?"

The jolly spy stood up. "I will inform our people what has happened and the press will be briefed."

"But what's the story?"

The story was just crazy enough to be believable. Poinaré was a Corsican mafia member, known for his terrible temper, who got into an altercation with an American woman. He decided to track her down and kill her. Angela Riley would remain Corinne Sweet and I was an innocent bystander that got caught up in what happened and decided to act. Chuck went into action to save me. There were no terrorists and the general public was safe. All's well that ends well.

"What about the security guard at the Concergerie? Oh my god. I forgot about him. Is he okay?"

"Poinaré stabbed him. He will recover," said Thyraud.

"Oh good. But he knows I was looking for Angela before Poinaré showed up," I said. "He's going to wonder how I knew he was coming."

Thyraud opened his briefcase and said, "He and any other questioners will be made to understand what really happened."

"That sounds ominous."

"Not at all. National security and the public confidence are a priority. They will do what is right for France." He pulled my purse out of his briefcase. "Nice encryption work on your phone."

My eyebrows shot up. "You didn't get in then?"

"Miss Watts, be realistic. Mr. Van der Hoof is one self-taught genius. I have a slew of those behind me."

"Oh no. Uncle Morty won't be happy," I said.

"I wouldn't tell him. We left no trace of our incursion, but I may be contacting him in the future. He's very talented. It took ten of mine to overcome one of him."

"That's good, but I think I'll keep that to myself for now." I took my purse from him and looked at my phone. Mom was freaking out. She must've sent a thousand texts.

"Call your mother," said Thyraud. "Mothers do worry."

"And yell," I said.

"That, too. And may I suggest that you enjoy the rest of your visit to our city and not do anything that causes more trouble?"

I grimaced involuntarily, thinking about The Klinefeld Group and the Marais apartment. That wasn't done and I only had a few days left to get in there.

Thyraud closed his briefcase and gave me a cheerful look. "I can see you're not done causing trouble."

"I don't cause trouble. Stuff happens and I'm there. That's all."

"Am I going to be getting another call?"

"Not unless you know something about The Klinefeld Group," I said.

The spook hesitated. It was slight, but he hesitated before he opened the door.

"You know about them," I said. It wasn't a question.

Thyraud stopped and looked back at me. "I know about the welfare of my people. If you have anything to say on the matter, I'll always take your call."

"How am I supposed to call you?" I asked.

"You have a phone, do you not?" He winked and was out the door.

Yep. Sure enough, I had a new contact in my phone and I couldn't help but smile. Sean Connery. Nice choice.

I flung my feet over the side of the bed. "Alright, Tonto. We're out of here. Can you grab my shoes?"

Aaron stared at me, mouth full of smelly sausage. "Tonto?"

"You know *The Lone Ranger*. You're my sidekick."

"No."

"No, you're not my sidekick? Come on. You can't be the ranger. Get real."

"I'm Spock. You're Uhura."

I slipped out of bed and put my one available hand on my generous hip. "What the what? Uhura never does anything. She answers the freaking phone. I do stuff. I'm the queen of doing stuff."

Aaron stood up and picked a meaty crumb off his shirt. He ate it. Ew. "You're Uhura."

"Okay. If I'm Uhura, who's Captain Kirk?"

He grabbed my shoes and squatted in front of me, shrugging as if it were obvious. "Chuck."

"Chuck? Are you kidding me? He didn't do as much as I did. Kirk goes places, gives the orders, and has sex with all the hot women."

Aaron nodded. "That's Chuck."

Dammit. He had a point. Chuck had practically made a career of getting hot women like Kirk did.

"Alright. But I still think it's sexist. Just 'cause I'm a girl doesn't mean I have to *be* the girl. I want to be somebody cool. It can be a man or a woman."

"You can be Nurse Chapel."

"I will kick you."

Aaron buckled my shoes. He wasn't worried. Nobody ever kicks their sidekick; however they might deserve it. I asked him to help me put on my blood-soaked jacket, leaving it loose over my arm in its sling. Then I put my everlasting hat on with a rakish tilt before opening the door and peeking out into the deserted corridor. "The coast is clear. We're going to see Angela. By the way, just so you know, I'm Tauriel in *The Hobbit*."

Aaron trotted beside me down to the elevator. "She's not real."

"None of them are real. You're missing the point."

"You're still not Kirk."

*Dammit.*

I had Spock distract the nursing staff while I slipped into Angela's room on the fifth floor. I found her hunched over, clinging onto an IV pole and looking out the window at the skyline of Paris, her refuge that no longer was. The window was a single pane of glass. No way to open it. Thank goodness.

"Angela," I said softly.

She turned and looked at me with swollen eyes, tears soaking her gown. She said nothing and I wasn't sure she even recognized me.

"I talked to...someone and your name will be Corinne Sweet for the media and the world. The assassin will be identified. They're going to say that you and he had some sort of altercation and that's why he went after you. I'm going to be someone who got in the way.

"It doesn't matter," she said, looking back out the window.

"I think it does. Has anyone been here from the embassy?" I asked.

She made a mocking snort over her shoulder. "The embassy. The CIA."

"They haven't got anyone on your door."

"Where would I go?"

Nowhere was the answer, but I couldn't bring myself to say it. Nowhere on her own, anyway.

"Have you seen my children, Phillip?" she asked with a fresh flood of tears.

"I saw Phillip. He was doing okay. The kids looked good in their pictures."

She braced herself on the glass. "They probably don't even remember me."

I shook my head. "That's not true. Phillip has pictures of you up. You're still there. They see you every day."

Angela turned. "Phillip left the pictures up? I can't believe it."

"It's true." I described the pictures to her and she gave me a wan smile.

"What are you going to do?" I asked.

Angela pushed her pole to the bed and lay down. "She'll have me killed, so there's not much to do."

"Who?" I asked. "Calpurnia?"

"She sent you, didn't she?"

I pulled up a chair, making a terrible screech, and fiddled with my sling. "Well, yes. She called in a marker. Why would she have you killed? You testified against the Bombellis, not the Fibonaccis."

"She'll figure out why. Calpurnia is no fool, but I can't figure out how she knew to send you."

"Gina saw you," I said.

Angela gasped and put her hand over her mouth.

"She got married and came here on her honeymoon."

"But...but...this city is huge and she never travels." Her voice went squeaky. "My family goes to Branson, not Europe, not here. Gina has problems. She could never get in a plane for eight hours."

"She has medication for anxiety. It helped her cope. I think the new husband helped, too."

Angela twisted her gown. "My sister got married again? Is she happy?"

"As far as I can tell."

"Where did she see me?" she asked.

"Walking down Rue Cler. They were having lunch in Tribeca.

"How did she recognize me?"

"I think she just saw you and she knew. The way only someone who loves you can. Angela, why would Calpurnia kill you?"

I didn't know Calpurnia well, but what Angela had done didn't seem like a reason to kill anyone. She'd suffered enough, in my opinion. The affair with Marius happened pretty much the way I thought. She met him at Panera and he was perfect. He was everything Phillip wasn't, handsome and charming. He liked what she liked. Phillip mostly watched sports and worked. He barely talked to his wife about anything except the kids, and Marius was interested in her. He liked her. At least, he made a good show of it.

It started innocently enough. He asked about her life and her family. Then he asked about Phillip and his work. Information about the Fibonaccis leaked into their conversation. Angela knew more than Calpurnia or Phillip ever imagined. They'd made the mistake of thinking a stay-at-home mother didn't have much going on upstairs. Just because Angela was great at raising kids didn't mean she wasn't paying attention. Phillip left Fibonacci files open on his home computer. There were files all over the house. He worked wherever he was and never picked up anything. Angela knew what deals were going down, how far the Fibonacci reach was, and their plans for the Bombellis.

Marius got a few salient details out of Angela and that was the thin edge of the wedge. He had enough to blackmail her. If she didn't provide details of the Fibonaccis' plans for the Bombellis and whatever else he wanted, he'd tell Phillip about the affair. That Angela could've handled and Marius knew it. He'd also go to Calpurnia and tell her what he knew about her operation and where he got it. Angela knew more than enough to realize that that would be it for her and Phillip. People disappeared for less. What would happen to the kids? It was all her fault.

Angela put him off and his threats increased. He showed up at her daughter's school and gave the child an envelope to give to her mother. When Angela opened it, she made up her mind. She'd go to the Feds and then disappear. Marius had given her newspaper clippings of children who'd been sold into sex trafficking. He had the power and will to do it. She had no choice. She waited until the kids and Phillip were out of the house to go to the Federal Building. The FBI was more than happy to take what she had and disappear her. Phillip made it remarkably easy. She scanned all the documents pertaining to the Bombellis and copied the files off the computer. She kicked off international investigations of not only the Bombellis but of other families. The Fibonaccis were shielded and Calpurnia ended up expanding her family's influence, but she never knew where her good fortune came from.

When Angela finished her tale, she shrunk down into the bed and gazed at me, her eyes hopeless and now dry. "So she'll kill me, and probably Phillip, when she figures it out. And Marius is still out there. He was willing to destroy my children before. If he can't get to me... all this was for nothing."

"Not for nothing. You took down the Bombellis and a bunch of other nasty bastards."

Her face hardened. "I was trying to save my family. I failed."

"Not yet, you haven't. I have to call Calpurnia. I'll explain it to her. You were targeted and you sacrificed everything protecting the Fibonaccis."

"She won't see it that way."

"I'll make sure she does. Calpurnia isn't unreasonable. Her family came out of this better than they went in. That should buy your lives."

*And end Marius's.*

I called Calpurnia and gave her the abbreviated version of Angela's story. She wasn't as surprised as I thought she'd be, so I decided to be blunt. "Are you going to kill them?"

"Who?"

"Angela and Phillip."

Calpurnia went silent and I started to sweat under Angela's hopeless gaze.

"Are you still there?" I asked.

"I think not," she said.

"Er...you're not there?"

"I think that Angela and Phillip will pay in other ways," said Calpurnia.

The sweating increased. "Oh yeah?"

"Nothing to concern you, Miss Watts."

"I doubt that," I said.

She laughed her throaty laugh. "No physical harm will come to them. There will be a change in responsibilities, pay, etc."

I smiled and nodded at Angela, who didn't react. "You promise?"

"Are you asking me a favor?"

*Ah crap!*

"Er..."

Calpurnia laughed again. "A favor isn't needed. Besides, you already owe me. Gina understands the situation and has agreed to say she hired you. Phillip knows as well as the rest of my people. I've never met you, Miss Mercy Watts. You were asked to help Gina by Oz and you felt sorry for Gina. That's the story and it will not change. I made a mistake with Phillip. I inherited the man from my father and I didn't question how he handled my business. That's about to change."

"So, how are they? Phillip and the rest of Angela's family?" I asked.

Angela sat up, for the first time with hope in her eyes.

"They're stunned." Calpurnia chuckled and I heard her uncork a bottle. "I'm not certain what has surprised them more. That Angela is alive or that Gina was right about something."

"I imagine it's a combo." I watched Angela as I spoke and tried to imagine what I would want me to ask if I were her. "Do they...want to see her?"

"Yes, of course. Her parents have already been to see me to ask for my influence to bring her home."

That was a bit uncomfortable. "You have influence in the government?"

"I have money. It's the same thing."

"If she comes back...what about the Bombellis?" I asked.

"Tell Angela that I will take care of it. She needn't worry. She has my word."

I thanked Calpurnia, hung up, and told Angela what she said. She began weeping in relief. She would go home. It was only a question of when.

"One more question," I said.

Angela blew her nose and asked, "What's left?"

"Why'd you keep Marius's picture after what he did to you?" I asked.

"I needed a reminder of why I was here and what I'd done, what I'd fallen for." Angela began another spate of weeping. I patted her shaking shoulder and left.

Aaron stood outside Angela's door, snarfing on a pastry stuffed with meat.

"Where'd you get that?" I asked.

"Sandrine."

"The nurse?"

"Yeah."

Sandrine waved at me from the desk and came around the counter with a determined look on her face.

*Ah crap!*

"Mademoiselle Watts, you must return to bed," said Sandrine, grabbing a wheelchair from along the wall.

I held up my hand. "I'm good."

"The doctor will decide that."

Malraux and his partner stepped off the elevator. "Where do you think you're going?"

"I'm not a prisoner," I said.

"You're a patient," said Sandrine, putting the wheelchair behind me.

"Not if I don't want to be." I took Aaron's arm and turned to the stairway door, which promptly opened. Chuck walked out, looking like a suspect who got away with murder. "I thought I'd find you here."

"I was having a walk."

"To the jumper's room," he said.

Malraux stepped between us. "Mademoiselle Watts, I have more questions."

"I'm done talking."

"No, you're not," said Chuck, nearly yelling. "What the hell were you thinking?"

I stepped to the right and eyed the stairs. My legs were killing me, but I could still run, if necessary. "I jumped because Angela jumped."

"Angela?" asked Malraux.

*Oops.*

"Corinne. Whatever her name is," I said quickly.

"Is that what our lives are going to be like? Other people jump off a bridge so you jump. What the hell, Mercy?"

Anger came bubbling up inside me like lava. "What the hell yourself. You jumped off the same bridge."

"I was saving you."

"I didn't need saving," I hissed.

Chuck got in my face. His cheeks were a burnished red and his blue eyes glittered, icy and pale. "The hell you didn't. Is it going to be like this when we have kids?"

I sucked in an astonished breath. "Kids? Who said anything about kids? Maybe I don't want kids. Did you ever think of that?"

"Get real. You were made to have kids."

I poked him in his rock hard chest. "Why? Because I have birthing hips? I'll kick you so that you can't give me kids."

"It's because you're so damn maternal!" Chuck yelled.

The detectives and Sandrine all took a step back.

"Are you nuts? I jumped off a damn bridge!"

He grabbed my good arm. "To save somebody. You're always saving people, taking care of people. This can't go on. You're going to get killed."

"I'm a nurse. Taking care of people is what I do," I yelled back.

"You're a mom. You just don't have a kid yet. You've got to stop this and stop keeping secrets."

I peeled his fingers off my arm. "You should talk, Mr. Arm's Length."

Chuck stepped back to get the much needed distance between us as I knew he would. "What?"

"You've got secrets. Something happened and you won't tell me what it was. You barely get near me. You'll jump off a bridge, but you can't bear to get in my bed. What's up with that?"

Chuck glanced at the detectives, who were suitably shocked. Chuck blushed harder. "Nothing happened."

I put my nose in the air and spun around, going for the elevators.

"Okay. Great. Then nothing happened today. I'm going back to Elias's."

Malraux chased after me. "Mademoiselle Watts, I'm not done with you yet."

"Well, I'm done with everything. You've gotten all you're going to get. You have my number. I'm outta here."

I must've looked like I meant it, which I did, because Malraux simply stepped back and let me get on the elevator with Aaron. I turned around and glimpsed Chuck's face as the doors closed. Distraught was the only word that fit his expression. But in that moment, I didn't care. I was going to Elias's to see a black cat that wasn't there and have a stiff glass of whiskey. I didn't even like whiskey, so that's saying something.

# CHAPTER TWENTY-SEVEN

Monsieur Barre met us at the door to Elias's building. I don't know how he knew I was coming. Maybe Chuck called. But for whatever reason, he was there and in a tizzy. I couldn't handle tizzy. I really couldn't. He wanted to know who the woman who jumped was. Was this the case I was working on? How many stitches did I have? Why didn't I get stitches? Shouldn't I be in the hospital? The news reports said I was in the hospital. Why wasn't I in the hospital as reported?

He chased me to the elevator and, despite its tiny dimensions, squeezed right in with Aaron and me.

"Your mother has been calling. Madam Bled is beside herself. Why haven't you called your godmothers?" he asked, his espresso-scented breath ruffling my hair.

"I didn't think of it," I said.

"Do you have your phone?"

"Yes." I was so tired, I sagged against the gleaming paneling.

"Mademoiselle Watts, you are not well."

I put my head on Aaron's shoulder. "I'm fine. I just need peace and quiet."

"Shall I call your mother and Madam Bled for you?" Monsieur Barre asked.

"Please do. I need a bath and a bed. Tell them I'm completely fine."

"You've been shot." He pointed at the stiff red spot on my jacket.

"Other than that, I'm fine."

The elevator dinged and we went to Elias's apartment. Blackie sat in the entryway, his green eyes glowing in the dim interior. Monsieur Barre bustled in ahead of us and walked right through the cat. It was startling, although I expected it. Aaron did the same and didn't notice my maneuvering around nothing.

I went straight for the bath. Unfortunately, Monsieur Barre and Aaron followed me in. "What are you doing? Privacy, please."

"Can you undress by yourself?" asked Monsieur Barre.

"You hungry?" asked Aaron.

"Er..."

Monsieur Barre took charge. He excelled at that. He helped me off with my crusty jacket and informed Aaron that I was indeed hungry and that steak frite was in order.

"And chocolate," said Aaron.

"Très essentiel."

I struggled to unbutton my blouse and said, "Steak medium, Aaron."

"Non, saignant," said Monsieur Barre. "You need the blood."

*Gag.*

"The last thing I want to see is blood. Medium, Aaron," I said.

"À point," said Aaron and trotted off.

"No blood," I called after him and then let Monsieur Barre undress me down to my underwear. I know that sounds creepy, but it wasn't. He was caring for me and I needed some caring. He was matter of fact, draping my wrecked suit over the chair by the tub and telling me he would be in with hot chocolate directly.

"That's my favorite," I said.

"I know." I stripped the rest of the way and slipped into the steaming tub. Ten minutes later, Monsieur Barre was back with an oversized tray that I'd seen in the kitchen and a pink bowl of hot chocolate with a pile of whipped cream on top. He ignored my squeak and attempts to cover myself, fitted the tray onto the tub, and placed the bowl on it with a starched linen napkin.

He watched me with a critical eye as I hunched over so my breasts would be under the tray and took a heavenly sip. I didn't recognize the chocolate and there was something else that was different.

"What's in it?" I licked my lips slowly. "It's...something...I don't know."

"Crème d'Isigny. It adds a depth of favor."

"And you had this stuff on hand."

"Absolument."

I took another sip and enjoyed the warmth as it spread down my throat and filled my chest, making me forget my pain, my irritation. Aaron brought me dinner in the tub. The steak was perfect as were the frites. Crispy, perfect potato flavor. I refilled the tub twice and then got out reluctantly, going straight to bed after taking a couple Norcos from my stash.

I dreamt I was in Paris in 1938, being led by the hand through the streets by a man I didn't know. I saw Stella Bled Lawrence and her husband, Nicky. They sat in a small café, talking with my great-grandparents. Then I was in an antique shop with an obsequious little man, buzzing around and attending customers. Something was familiar about it. The man led me around, having me touch pieces of elegant furniture. I could feel the grain under my fingertips and I smelled something, peach schnapps. I kept asking what I was supposed to find. But the man didn't answer me and then the schnapps changed to the richer smell of chocolate and melting cream.

I opened my eyes to see Aaron by my bed with a new bowl of hot chocolate and a croissant. Behind him was Blackie, once again watching from the dresser, his tail twitching and coiling around the woman's portrait. "Is it morning?" I asked.

"Yeah."

"Am I going somewhere?"

"Yeah."

"Where?"

Aaron shrugged and offered a hand to help me out of the pit. I drank my hot chocolate while he rooted through the wardrobe. He came out with the pink silk dressing gown and took my arm out of its sling before he helped me into it.

Aaron poured me a second bowl of hot chocolate and it dawned on me that as small as Elias was, he couldn't have fit into that dressing gown. The shoulders were way too narrow. I opened both doors of the wardrobe and looked through the clothes. "There are a lot of women's clothes in here."

"Yeah," said Aaron.

"But Elias was supposed to be in love with that prostitute that wouldn't have him."

"Yeah." He refitted my sling and brushed the hair out of my eyes.

I picked up the portrait of the shy woman. I'd assumed she was a Bled, but she didn't have the look of a Bled now that I was paying attention. Whoever she was, her Edwardian dress was lovely with a high neck and plenty of lace. Not exactly typical dress for a prostitute. "I get the feeling there's more to that story," I said, giving Aaron a quick hug and smelling the smell of andouillette. I didn't even mind.

"Yeah." He handed me the croissant and left without another word.

I took a bite and let the buttery flakes of crust rain down and get stuck in my cleavage. Normally, that would've bothered me, but the day before had been such a disaster, I didn't mind a bit of mess. I glanced back at the cat before heading to the door. "Are you coming?"

He leapt off the dresser, stretched like a real cat would, and slinked out the door beside me into the hall. I sidestepped to make way for him at the entrance to the living room. I don't know why. If Aaron and Monsieur Barre could walk through him, presumably I could, too.

"What are you doing?"

I looked up as Blackie brushed by my leg to see Chuck sitting on the Victorian settee directly in front of me. I made sure I didn't glance at the cat, who'd jumped onto the arm of the settee and began cleaning his rear. "What?" I asked.

He frowned at me, making his bruised face look angry and almost demonic. "You moved aside like there was someone there."

"There's no one there."

"I know that."

"So are you still pissed at me?" I asked.

"Are you still pissed at me?" Chuck asked.

"I don't know."

"Me, either."

We stared at each other for a moment and that's when I realized that he shouldn't be facing me. The settee shouldn't have been there, blocking the entryway to the apartment. He'd moved it to block the exit.

"That's a fire hazard," I said.

"I was willing to risk it," said Chuck, sitting back and putting his long, sinewy arm across the back of the settee. Blackie trotted across the back, right through his arm and sniffed his head. I caught my breath and stared until Chuck looked, directly in the face of the cat, and then looked back at me.

"What are you looking at?" he asked.

"Er...nothing," I said, wanting to cross my arms so bad. "So what were you doing, trying to keep me from escaping?"

"I wouldn't put it past you."

"I might have a hole in my shoulder, but I can still push a settee out of the way."

"Not with me sleeping on it." Chuck stood up and pushed it back to its place on the wall. "Are you going to tell me what really happened yesterday?"

"Didn't the cops tell you?" I asked.

"They told me a version of the truth. I want the whole thing. That woman wasn't some stranger you happened across. I knew you were up to something, so I followed you yesterday. Who is she?"

"Corrine Sweet." I spun around and marched back to the bedroom.

He followed me. "I can't believe I bought that bullshit about you going to cooking school with Aaron."

*Me, either.*

"I did go to cooking school," I said, looking through the rack of Madam Ziegler's outfits.

Chuck pushed the rack away from me. "You were on a case. Why didn't you tell me?"

"Because it was none of your business. Get out of the way."

He got in front of me. "No. I won't get out of your freaking way. I never will. You are my business."

I snorted. "Like you're mine. Puhlease."

"Let's not start that again."

"I agree. Go away."

"I'm not going away. You may as well tell me. Your dad's on it already. He's going to find out what the hell you were doing."

I was going to have to tell him. I knew I would have to, but I still didn't relish the thought. The words 'shit storm' came to mind. "Her name is Angela Riley. She disappeared six years ago in Chicago and was presumed dead. Happy?"

"Thrilled. Go on."

I gave him Novak's cover story, how Gina hired me and whatnot, but I could see he wasn't buying it. I'd have to give him a better reason why I'd lie to him and hide what I was up to.

He crossed his arms and stared at me. "You expect me to believe that this is a simple missing person's case?"

*I was hoping you'd never find out anything at all.*

"I did a favor for a friend. It was the right thing for Gina and I didn't actually expect to find Angela. The very idea was ridiculous."

"Who is this Gina? I've never heard of her. How much of a friend can she be?"

"She wasn't the friend." I turned away and pulled up the covers on the bed so he wouldn't see me swallow hard and brace myself for the onslaught that was sure to come.

"Who was the friend?" asked Chuck, his voice now hard.

"Oz Urbani, if you must know."

"Calpurnia Fibonacci's nephew? Are you crazy?" Then he went into a stream of consciousness rant that went on for at least ten minutes. I was bored by the time he stopped, panting at the foot of Elias's bed.

"Are you done?" I asked.

"Your dad's going to flip. What am I going to tell him?"

"I don't care what you tell him. I'm an adult," I said, selecting the bias cut dress to wear. "Do I have someplace to be? Aaron acted like there was an appointment."

"Huh? What? God dammit, Mercy," yelled Chuck.

"It was a simple question. Do we have someplace to be?"

"Yes. Dammit."

"You can stop swearing. It won't change anything. Uncle Morty has provided ample proof of that."

"We're supposed to be meeting a guy," he said, softening up.

"Who is it?"

"The old Marais apartment manager. The Paris cops helped me out."

I flashed a smile at him. "Because you're a hero that attacks terrorists without a weapon."

He flexed and gave me his fabulous rakish smile. "I could be considered a weapon all on my own."

"You're just trying to win me over."

"Is it working?"

I pondered him and our future. "Are you going to tell me what happened with you?"

"Nothing happened," he said.

"Then it's not working." I pushed him to the bedroom door. "Get out."

He put on the brakes. "What for? What are you going to do?"

"Climb out the window and escape with my arm in a sling," I said with a sneer.

"Fine. What are you doing then?"

I shrugged off my robe and revealed my nightie and a good amount of breast. "Getting dressed. Wanna help?"

Chuck practically ran out the door.

"That's what I thought!" I yelled after him.

# CHAPTER TWENTY-EIGHT

Chuck and I arrived in the Marais a half-hour later, having not spoken three words to each other. I think he believed that Gina hired me to find Angela, mostly because I admitted that Oz was my friend. He obviously wasn't going to give up what was going on with him. Try as I might, I couldn't see a way forward. He wasn't alright, at least not with me. It was galling to know that Nazir knew what was up and I didn't. Dad probably knew and, if he knew, Mom knew. The whole thing made me tired.

At least my parents hadn't been able to get a flight to Paris and had settled for hearing my voice and yelling about jumping off bridges, as if I hadn't heard that before.

When we were three blocks from the Marais apartment, Chuck said, "There it is."

A small café sat on the corner, packed with people sipping coffee, reading papers, or just watching the world go by. And there was a whole lot of world to watch that morning. I'd thought the streets had been busy the day before, but it was even worse that morning. The metro had been nuts and I ended up under not one but three armpits and none belonged to Chuck, who was the best-smelling thing in the whole car. He got a lot of looks that morning with his bruised face and dour demeanor. He wore mirrored sunglasses in a vain attempt to cover up, but they couldn't begin to conceal the purple and red bruises that decorated the side of his face. I wore sunglasses and the cloche. It was the only hat I had left that didn't have blood on it. I was able to tuck all my hair up inside, so the blonde wasn't visible.

Chuck took my elbow to lead me across the street and I resisted the urge to snatch it away from him. We walked into the café and a large man at the back stood up and waved to us. He was a big man, bulky and muscular with dark hair and a weathered face. He looked much younger than his seventy years and tougher, too. If someone put him and Poinaré in front of me and asked which one was a Corsican mafia assassin, I'd have picked the manager.

"Bonjour. Bonjour," he called out, beaming at us with a gap-toothed grin. Maybe not so assassin after all.

We wove through the tightly-packed tables to the back. "Monsieur Masson?" asked Chuck.

"Oui," exclaimed Monsieur Masson before pulling Chuck into a bear hug and kissing both his cheeks. Chuck was so astonished; he didn't even react.

Then Monsieur Masson turned to me, looking at my arm. It wasn't in a sling. That would've been a dead giveaway to my identity. I'd put my hand in my jacket pocket and that was enough support. "Mademoiselle," he said, "I am honored with your presence."

We exchanged cheek kisses and he offered me the most comfortable chair at the table. It had pads and I was grateful for them.

"So you know who we are," said Chuck.

"Everyone in Paris knows who you are. The incident on the Seine will be part of our history and we do not forget our history. There is a call to give you both the Legion of Honor, which, of course, you must receive."

*More publicity. Exactly what I need.*

"We would be honored," said Chuck. "Did the officers tell you why we wanted to meet you?"

"They did not, but I have been waiting these many years for you to come," said Monsieur Masson with complete confidence.

"You've been waiting for us?" I asked.

"For someone." He gestured to Chuck. "You are police." Then he looked at me. "And you are a detective. What else could it be? I managed the mysterious and I've been waiting for you to come to ask me about it."

"The apartment?" asked Chuck.

"Oui. What else?"

The waitress brought us café crèmes without being asked. She recognized us but was too polite to say anything. I warmed my good hand on the golden cup and said, "Have you been inside?"

"No, no. That was not my place."

I slumped. "So you don't have a key."

He laughed and thumped the table. When his big hand moved, a small silver key ring remained with a big, tarnished brass key and a small padlock key.

"But you never went inside?" asked Chuck. "Why?"

"I was waiting for you and I was the manager, sworn to do my duty," he said, leaning forward, his bulky form casting a shadow. "Now I'm retired, free to do as I like."

"So you'll let us in?" I asked.

"But of course. What else have I got to do? Play boules all day? Non. Let us see what is in there." He held up a finger. "But first, tell me why you have come."

Chuck and I exchanged glances. I wasn't sure what to say, but it appeared that Chuck wouldn't say anything, so I went ahead and told Monsieur Masson that we were investigating the death of a policeman in Berlin in the '60's. He'd had an obsession with that apartment and we wanted to know what it might have to do with his death.

"This apartment has never been opened in all my years," said Monsieur Masson. "This policeman didn't enter it. I would've known."

"We don't think he got in there, but he wanted to. We need to know why it was so important to the man."

Monsieur Masson finished his café and pondered us quietly. "Many people have come over the years. Every few years, someone would come and I would say no."

"Really?" asked Chuck. "Who came?"

"Mostly people who wanted to buy the place and others who couldn't give me a reason to go in. I pretended not to have the key."

"Why tell us that you have it?" I asked.

"You fought for France. Malraux said I could trust you."

"I'm glad," I said.

"I think I saw that policeman and another man. This was 1965, yes?"

"Yes."

"He came several times, but he couldn't give me a good reason why he wanted to know about it."

I sipped my café. "I can't believe you remember them."

Monsieur Masson went on to describe Werner Richter and his brother, Paul. His descriptions matched the pictures Spidermonkey had dug up. We finished and Monsieur Masson insisted on paying, but the waitress quietly said it was on the house.

"Shall we go find out?" asked Monsieur Masson, offering his arm to me.

I took it. "I think we shall."

The padlock came off easily, but the big brass key took some force. It ground and groaned in the old lock before there was a click and thump. Monsieur Masson turned the knob and pushed. There was a grinding creak and the door opened, revealing a dim interior. I couldn't make anything out, but the apartment wasn't empty. I could tell that much.

Monsieur Masson went in first and turned a knob on the wall. Nothing happened.

"There is electricity," he said in consternation.

"But really old light bulbs," I said.

"Ah yes." He and Chuck went through the main room and threw open the windows and then the shutters. The room flooded with light and my mouth fell open. The apartment was intact. Not intact like Elias's apartment, but completely intact. It hadn't been cleaned or cared for in any way.

"I can't believe it." But it was true. The room was filled with vintage furniture covered in a layer of thick dust. It was good furniture, too. Elegant sofas and mahogany tables. Heavy silk drapes and thick Turkish rugs. There were papers and books scattered on the floor and a woman's coat lay on the arm of a heavy Victorian chair. It was like we'd stepped back into the 1940s and the owners had only left for a minute and they'd be right back.

"It's been searched," said Chuck.

I looked more closely and I saw what he saw. Drawers in the tables were hanging open. Books had been pulled off their shelves. I walked in, smelling the smell of very old dust, and looked at the papers on the table. "Holy crap."

"What?" asked Chuck.

"I was thinking the 1940's, but these papers are dated from November 1938."

Chuck joined me and, forgetting himself, he put his hand on the small of my back. "I'll be damned."

"Do you mind if I touch these?" I asked Monsieur Masson.

He gave me a one-shouldered shrug. "Whoever they were, they are gone forever."

I leafed through the papers. All from the first two weeks of November 1938. Nothing after that. We all stood in the middle of the room and gazed around in wonder at the dusty woodwork enrobed in spider webs, the beautiful antique furniture, but most of all at the delicate porcelain teacups on the table. There were two with gold rims. I picked one up and showed it to Chuck. "They left in the middle of tea." The dried remains of the drink marred the cup. It was full when they left.

Chuck nodded at me and we wandered into the next room, the dining room. It had been searched, too. Drawers in the china cabinet were open and linens tossed on the floor. The china and crystal had been rifled through. Next was the kitchen. Dirty dishes sat in the sink, but the trash bin had been emptied as well as the refrigerator, a small, boxy thing that looked more like a washer.

The beds were made in the three bedrooms, but the dressers and wardrobes had been gone through. I looked at the empty hangers and the spots on the top shelves where suitcases would've been. They'd had time to pack, but they'd been in such a rush they'd left dirty dishes.

"In here, Mercy!" called out Chuck from another room.

I followed the sound of his voice to a small office. The heavy leather desk chair lay on its side, blocking part of the door. The books had been thrown, leaving dents in the striped wallpaper. Papers were scattered about. Somebody had been in a real temper.

"Check this out." Chuck held up a letter.

I hopped over some books and took a look. "What does it say?"

"It's in French, but check out the name." He gave me the letter and its envelope.

Raymond-Raoul Sorkine.

"Do you recognize the name?" asked Chuck.

I shook my head. "Not a bit."

"You've never seen it before?"

"No. Never."

Monsieur Masson came in and said, "I can translate the letter."

I gave it to him and he quickly scanned the pretty copperplate writing.

"It is an ordinary letter. Family news from Belgique, a city called Charleroi."

"What's the relation?" I asked.

Monsieur Masson read the letter again. "Marie-Élise Sorkine is an aunt to Raymond-Raoul."

I turned to Chuck, who was typing furiously into his phone. "Got it."

"Let's see how many names we can find."

Monsieur Masson and I went through all the correspondence. Unfortunately, most of the letters didn't have their envelopes. We got a lot of first names. Going through the drawers, we found files that were supposed to have birth certificates, but they were gone. We did find bills and college tuition receipts from the Sorbonne. The owners of the apartment were Raymond-Raoul and Suzanne Charlotte Sorkine and they had one daughter, Lucienne, who was college age in 1938.

Chuck and I gathered up all the paperwork and organized it by date while Monsieur Masson turned the chair upright, sat, and read the letters in French. It seemed the Sorkines were multilingual. They received letters in English, German, Swedish, and Dutch. Monsieur Masson was fluent in English and could understand a smattering of German, but that was it. I set about taking pictures of the letters for future translation. I had to use my bad hand to do it, but I found the more I used it, the looser my shoulder got.

While I did that, Chuck dropped to the floor, feeling under the desk.

"What're you doing?" I asked.

He held up a thin, delicate rectangle of paper. "I saw this underneath the desk."

I took it and the French was so elementary, I could read it easily.

1938 Oct. 14

Aunt

Have arrived Rome. Am safe and well. Have package. No contact.

A

"A," said Monsieur Masson and he began shuffling through the letters.

Chuck raised an eyebrow at me. "Package."

I nodded. "What's the date on the last letter again?"

"November the fifth," said Monsieur Masson. "1938."

"Are there any A names in the letters?" asked Chuck, hopping to his feet.

Monsieur Masson and I went through the letters one by one. The Sorkines seemed to keep their letters for two years. There was nothing beyond late 1935.

"We have an Alphonse in The Netherlands," I said.

"What's the date?"

"June, 1936."

Chuck picked up the telegram off the desk. "It could be him."

"No," said Monsieur Masson.

"Why not?" I asked.

"Alphonse was seventy-three in 1936. The letter detailed his birthday party."

I groaned. "Probably not running around Italy in '38. Seventy-five was pretty old back then."

"And he was not well."

"So not Alphonse," said Chuck, dropping back down to feel under the desk again. "Maybe I missed something."

I watched him root around and Monsieur Masson continued to read the letters. Chuck found nothing new and was visibly disappointed.

"I know why they left and did not come back." Monsieur Masson looked up at us, his face sad for the first time since we'd met.

"Why?" I asked.

"The Sorkines were Jews."

None of us said anything for a couple minutes.

"But..." said Chuck, "nothing was happening in 1938."

Monsieur Masson laughed a bitter laugh. "It had begun. Our people were harassed in the streets. The Germans weren't the only ones to hate us."

"You're Jewish then?" I asked.

"Yes."

"How did your family escape deportation?"

Monsieur Masson put his eyes on the letters and didn't raise them to meet mine. "Not all of them did. My grandparents sent my father and his sisters to the free zone with forged papers in 1940. What we now call Vichy. He was fourteen. My grandparents owned a small printing shop. They thought they had to protect their property. They were deported in La Grande Rafle."

"I'm so sorry," I said.

He looked up. "My father and his sisters survived." Then he looked down again. "The Sorkines didn't."

I joined Chuck at the desk. "Well...they never returned from wherever they went, but the Nazis didn't invade until 1940."

"You don't think it was the Nazis?" Monsieur Masson's face reddened.

"It probably was," I said. "But November '38 was pretty early. I want to know what happened to make them abandon their home."

Monsieur Masson shuffled through the letters. "They had friends in Berlin. Perhaps they went to them after the Kristallnacht."

I clapped a hand over my mouth and then said, "The Kristallnacht. I totally forgot about the date."

"Kristallnacht?" asked Chuck. "What's that?"

Anger flashed across Monsieur Masson's face. "The Night of Broken Glass, when the Brown Shirts attacked us. They destroyed synagogues and shops. Men were rounded up and sent to camps. The Nazis released most of them, but many died."

"When was that?"

"November the ninth, 1938."

Chuck looked at me. "A lot of things were happening that November."

I nodded. The Sorkines abandoned their elegant home forever. My great grandparents met Stella and Nicky in a café. The Kristallnacht. There had to be a connection, but I had no clue what it was.

Monsieur Masson looked up and frowned. "I don't understand what this has to do with a German policeman murdered in Berlin twenty-four years later."

"I don't know," I said. "But Werner Richter knew about this apartment. It was important to him."

"Perhaps he knew what happened to the Sorkines."

"Or perhaps he knew about 'A' and the package."

"That's a leap," said Chuck.

"This whole thing is bizarre, so why not?" I asked.

Both men shrugged at me and then Monsieur Masson stood up, "I will help you."

"To do what?" asked Chuck.

"If they were deported, I will find the evidence," he said. "I know the correct people."

"Who are the correct people?" I asked.

"I have a dear friend with the Mémorial de la Shoah. He will know what to do," said Monsieur Masson. "Do you know the Mémorial de la Shoah?"

He sounded doubtful, but I did know it. Of course I did.

"I've been several times," I said. "But not on this trip."

His eyebrows shot up. "That is unusual, unless you have a...connection."

"She does have a connection," Chuck said quickly before I could deny being a Bled.

I bowed to the inevitable. "My godmothers' cousin was involved with the Resistance. We always remember those who were lost."

He took my good hand in his rough one and his grey eyes reddened. "It is good to remember. Who is this cousin?"

I glanced at Chuck, unsure how much we should divulge. He gave me a slight nod and I said, "Stella Bled Lawrence, but I don't think you'll find much, if anything, on her. I've looked myself. Her activities during the war are still classified by both our governments."

"Memories are not classified," said Monsieur Masson. "Thank goodness or much would be lost. Are there any other names you would like to know about?"

I shook my head. "Monsieur, I don't know. You could be putting yourself in a dangerous position helping us."

"1965 was a long time ago," he said.

"Yes," said Chuck. "But like you said, the memories are still around."

Monsieur Masson got to his feet and smiled, his eyes lighting up as he gestured to the mess. "This is a mystery that begs my attention." Then he frowned. "Whatever happens, it will be nothing compared to what the Sorkines must have endured."

"It will be safer for you if you don't tell anyone about this," said Chuck.

Monsieur Masson put his finger to his lips. "I will tell no one about you or this apartment. I learned from my father how to keep a secret."

He put the stack of letters back on the desk. It felt kind of strange to leave it neater than we found it, but we could hardly toss the letters into the air. Chuck took a picture of the telegram and then placed it where he found it, under the desk. We went through the rest of the apartment, looking for more names, diaries, anything, but, if there was anything, it was long gone. I did find one thing. A slip of paper under one of the teacups. If I hadn't been putting the other cup back into position, I wouldn't have noticed it. The yellow paper with curling edges had a list of times and numbers.

I held it out to Monsieur Masson and Chuck. "Train schedule?"

"Could be," said Chuck. "I don't think they stayed in Paris, considering the rush to get out."

"No destination," said Monsieur Masson. "That would have been a help."

I smiled. "It can't be easy."

He patted my shoulder as we went out of the apartment. "My father said to me that an easy life is a boring life."

*I could stand some boring right about now.*

# CHAPTER TWENTY-NINE

We didn't say much on the way back to Elias's apartment. I don't know what was going on in Chuck's head, but my brain was in a whirl. I couldn't imagine the reason to keep the Marais intact for seventy plus years, but it had to be the Bleds. Who else would have the will and the money to do it? Nobody. That's who. Who were the Sorkines? Did they know Stella and Nicky? Or maybe my great-great-grandparents, Amelie and Paul?

I pushed through the metro exit gate and the wind from above made me glad I had sunglasses on. Chuck put his hand on my back as we jogged up the concrete stairs. Pont Marie was a pretty small stop in the scheme of things, but even it was bustling. The traffic was bumper to bumper and the tour boats were churning up the Seine. The Angela incident hadn't slowed down trade one bit.

"I don't remember it being this crowded before," said Chuck.

"It wasn't. There must be something going on and it is summer in Paris," I said.

We crossed the street and stepped onto the bridge. Its pleasing arches extended over the Seine and a tour boat glided under the center one with a dozen people pointing at a man leaning over the low railing on the bridge. The man didn't make a move, but the tourists ran for cover anyway.

Chuck took hold of my arm and held me back. "Don't even think about it."

"Think about what?" I asked. "He didn't do a single thing."

Chuck stared straight ahead. "Look at him."

I looked and he did seem odd and out of place. He wore a heavy, black, knee-length coat more suited to the dead of winter than Paris in June, even it if was a high of seventy that day. There wasn't anything particularly odd about the rest of him. He was fairly young with brown shoulder-length hair brushed back from his pale face, decorated with a short, rather thin beard and mustache.

"Knock it off," I said. "He's just a guy and I need a painkiller."

The man heard me and turned in our direction. Our eyes met and I gasped. It was the man from my dreams. He smiled wanly, waved, and turned to walk away across the bridge.

Chuck squeezed my arm. "What is it?"

"I've seen him before." I watched the retreating back.

"Where?" Chuck looked from me to the bridge. "Hey, where'd he go?"

The man was gone. I didn't see him disappear. It was like he waited for me to blink and then he wasn't there anymore.

"Mercy?" asked Chuck.

*Did that just happen?*

I started walking again and Chuck kept trying to pull me back. "Mercy, who was that?"

"I don't know," I said.

"Yes, you do."

"No, I don't."

"Tell me," he demanded.

"I think that's my line," I said, stepping onto the sidewalk and looking left and right in case I was wrong. I wasn't. He was gone.

I trotted across the street, putting on speed, but Chuck caught me easily with his long legs. "How about please tell me?" he asked.

I thought about making some kind of snide comment about how I'd say please if it'd get the info I wanted, but I didn't. Being petty takes so much energy and the Marais apartment had taken most of mine. "Elias."

"Who?"

I hung a left to walk beside the elegant apartment and he matched my pace. "You don't mean..."

"I do and don't say it's crazy, because you saw the cat in New Orleans."

He laughed nervously. "That was just a cat."

I jolted to a halt and looked up at him, my eyes boring into his. "Don't even."

"Okay. How do you know it's Elias?"

"I just know. I can feel it." I headed down the street in silence, not seeing anything but Elias's face or maybe I was crazy. I'd have to see a picture of him to know.

"Holy crap," said Chuck. "What is up with that?"

"Huh?"

Chuck pointed ahead at a limousine parked up on the sidewalk next to Elias's building. The back half stuck out into the road and the front bumper was up against a lamp post. Chuck and I looked inside. No one was in the driver's seat and the limo was locked.

"Did they hit it?" I asked, peering at where the bumper touched the lamp post.

"I don't think so. There's no dent," said Chuck.

"Weird."

"Somebody's getting a ticket and a tow."

"No kidding. What kind of chauffeur would do that?" I went to the big door and typed in my code and unlocked it with the enormous black key. Before I could open it fully, Monsieur Barre flung the door open. "Mon dieu. Mademoiselle Watts, thank goodness you are here."

I stepped back. "Why? What happened?"

Monsieur Barre glanced over his shoulder like a hunted man and there was a sheen of moisture on his wrinkled forehead. I'd never seen the prim little man sweat before. I didn't know he could. Sweat wasn't in his job description.

"She's here," he said in a breathy voice.

"Who?" asked Chuck.

"Madam." He said 'Madam' like it was a name, not a title. He ushered us in to the empty foyer and then looked out at the limo. "Mon dieu. You must get her to go and take that thing with her."

"But who is it?" I asked.

Monsieur Barre was so flustered, he ignored the question and practically ran for the elevator. He pounded on the button, it opened, and he literally pushed me inside and reached in to push the floor button.

"Make her go. Things happen when she is here." The doors started to close. "Mon dieu. She talked to me. She wants to go to dinner."

"But who—" The doors closed and the old elevator creaked upward.

"Any idea?" asked Chuck.

"Not a clue."

"It has to be a Bled. Who else would come here?"

I shook my head. "None of the Bleds are scary."

"I guess we'll find out."

The doors opened and I peeked out. The circular foyer was empty as expected. Then he took the key from me. "I'll go in first."

"Monsieur Barre wouldn't send us up if she was dangerous," I said with an eyeball.

"You never know." He opened the door and we crept in.

I was wrong. I'd completely forgotten about the one Bled relative that was scary and she was sitting in the living room with Blackie on her lap. She stroked the cat and he twitched his tail as he stared up at us, unblinking.

"Marie." Now I understood Monsieur Barre's reaction and he was right. Things did happen when she was around.

She smiled at us, wrinkles turning her face into an origami of age. "I heard you wanted to see me."

I glanced at Chuck, who stared at her hand rhythmically running down Blackie's back. I could see him, but Chuck didn't. He was going to think she was crazy and he wouldn't be the first.

"Who told you that?" I asked.

"The Girls, naturally."

Marie held up a thin hand to Chuck, laden with large rings of emerald and ruby and a set of diamond bangles that clinked together loudly. "I don't believe we've met," she said. "I would get up but you know..." She gestured to Blackie and Chuck took ahold of my arm like Marie might leap out of the chair and bite me.

"Mercy," said Marie.

"I'm sorry." I took her hand and we exchanged cheek kisses. She smelled lovely, like Provence lavender and buttery pastry. "It's great to see you. I can't believe you're here. We had no idea you were in Paris."

Her wicked old eyes twinkled. "And who is this handsome devil?"

I stepped back. "This is Chuck Watts, my Uncle Rupert's adopted son. Chuck, this is Marie Galloway Laurence Morris Huntley Huntley Smith."

"Stella's..." Chuck trailed off, trying to think of the familial connection.

"Sister-in-law," said Marie. "Briefly."

"Forever," I said automatically.

Chuck looked back and forth between us, confused.

"My Lawrence died during the war. Our marriage was short lived," said Marie.

"I'm sorry," said Chuck.

"It was long ago." She extended her hand to him and he took it, clearly unsure of what to do. In the end, he exchanged cheek kisses like me. "Pull up a chair and let's have a talk," she said.

Chuck and I obediently sat on the settee and waited as she fussed with the red cape her thin body was swathed in.

"Have you seen Elias?" she asked. "You have the look."

"Elias?" I asked.

"Ah, now I know you have." She laughed and twisted a heavy emerald ring into its correct position.

"What makes you say that?" asked Chuck.

"The expression in your eyes. Shock, dismay. Seeing a ghost has that effect on people. Let me guess ...he was on the bridge?"

"Er..." I bit my lip, unwilling to admit anything. "It could've been someone else. I mean...ghosts don't interact, do they?"

"Who told you that rubbish?" Marie cocked her head to the side. "He spoke to you?"

"He waved," said Chuck. "But it could've been anyone."

"Anyone who looks like that?" She pointed at a small portrait on the wall in a plain frame. I hadn't noticed it before amidst all the bigger ones with their brighter colors.

I got up and took a closer look. It was him, the man from the bridge. A shiver went down my back. It was definitely him.

Chuck came up behind me. "Holy crap."

"It's him," I said.

Marie waved us back to the settee. "Of course it is. Did you think you'd be the only Bled not to see him?"

"I'm not a Bled."

She snorted and tugged on Blackie's tail, making him twitch. "There's no use in arguing. I'm right and you're wrong. Elias communicated with you."

"He waved," I said.

"That's more than I've gotten."

"How many times have you seen him?" asked Chuck.

Marie scratched the cat's head and Chuck elbowed me. Marie gave me a look as she realized he didn't see the cat and she shooed him off her lap. "I've seen Elias every time I've been in this apartment or on the island. Dozens of times. He's hardly discreet." She narrowed her faded brown eyes at us. "But that's not what's troubling you. Elias is just Elias. He won't bother you."

I was bothered by seeing a man dead for over a hundred years, but the woman in front of us would scoff at such weakness. After the horrors she'd been through, I could hardly blame her.

"Why did you want to see me?" she asked.

I glanced at Chuck and he shook his head. I ignored the 'No' and said, "Can you keep this between us?"

"You mean, don't tell The Girls," said Marie.

Chuck put his elbows on his knees and rubbed his face. "Or anyone. This is sensitive."

"Sensitive is my favorite kind of secret and the answer is yes. I can keep secrets. My life once depended on it."

"Have you ever heard the name Sorkine?" I asked.

She thought about it for a moment and, to my great disappointment, said, "No. It's not familiar."

"Never? Not even during the war?"

"If I did, I've forgotten it. Why?" she asked.

I took a deep breath and told her about Werner Richter, his death, and the suspicious death of Jens Waldmar Hoff in Berlin.

"We got into the apartment today." Chuck gave her his phone and showed her the pictures from the apartment.

Marie swiped through the pictures, her long red nail tapping the screen. "Fascinating. It's a time capsule. November 1938. A terrible month. Grynszpan murdered Von Rath and then Hitler took revenge on the Jews with the Kristallnacht."

"What murder?" asked Chuck.

"A young Jew named Grynszpan murdered a German diplomat, Vom Rath, right here in Paris," said Marie. "Perhaps there is a connection, but that doesn't explain why the Bleds would preserve it like this. It must be something to do with Stella."

I agreed, but I asked, "Why do you say that?"

"She was in Europe on her honeymoon at the time," she said.

"We have evidence that she was here in Paris in November of '38," said Chuck.

Marie grinned at us. "The plot thickens."

"You didn't know she was here at that time?"

"Stella was very good at keeping secrets, too." She tapped her chin. "The best at secrets, I would have to say, which was why she was so valuable to the Allies."

I got my phone out and showed her the pictures of Stella and Nicky with Amelie and Paul.

"Ah yes," she said. "The couple from New Orleans."

A thrill went through me and Marie told us about a time during the war when she and her first husband, Theo Lawrence, met with Stella and a British operative. Stella had orders to go into Germany. It was extremely dangerous and her survival wasn't certain. Marie and Theo were returning to England for some training and Stella made them promise to contact her family and Nicky's family about a couple in New Orleans, Amelie and Paul. She said that they had done her and Nicky a great service, regardless of their own safety. Amelie and Paul should be looked after and helped, if it were ever needed. Stella had written to Florence, The Girls' mother, but she didn't know if Florence got the letter. Mail wasn't a sure thing during the war.

"What was the great kindness?"

"She was evasive on that point and we had bigger things to worry about." She gazed off into the distance. "I imagine it had something to do with Abel."

Chuck grabbed my thigh and squeezed. It was such an intimate gesture that I sucked in a sharp breath and held it. Marie noticed. Chuck didn't.

"Who's Abel?" he asked.

Marie looked away from us. "I never met him. I saw him once at a distance, but don't ask me about that. I won't talk about that."

"Alright then," I said. "What was his last name? Could it have been Sorkine?"

"No, I don't think so. I knew his name. Stella told me I'm sure, but I can't remember it at the moment."

"They were friends?"

Her eyes switched back to me. I expected them to be teary, but I should've known better. Marie was the least teary person I ever met. "Yes, but it was more than that."

"Oh," said Chuck in a knowing voice.

Marie shook her head. "Do not be ridiculous. It wasn't an affair. But it was a bond between the three of them, Stella, Nicky, and Abel."

Marie didn't remember a lot about Abel, having seen him only the once. Abel served as the couple's tour guide on their honeymoon trip through Europe. A grand tour, she called it. He was tall, handsome, and a Jew. My heart sank when I heard that. Being a Jew in Europe in 1938 wasn't an easy thing to survive.

"She was looking for him," said Marie. "That's how we first met. She was in London with Nicky, banging on doors, trying to get information. There was an ambassador who helped her. I think Abel had been arrested."

"In London?" asked Chuck.

"He should've been so lucky. Abel was arrested on the continent by the Nazis."

"In 1938?" I asked.

She tapped the screen of the phone again. "I don't remember, but I met her in 1940, so before that."

Chuck went over to her again and pulled up the photo of the telegram he found. She raised the phone and squinted at it. "A could be Abel, but there are a lot of As in the world."

"Did Stella and Nicky go to Italy on their grand tour?" I asked.

Marie gave Chuck back his phone. "It's not a grand tour unless you go everywhere. Italy was high on the list and they did go. Stella was very knowledgeable about the country. They were there before..."

"Before what?"

"I don't know. She always said before, but we all did with the war on. *Before,* I was a debutante. *Before,* I was a bricklayer. Things like that. At the time, I assumed she meant the war, but now I think it was something more. Stella said to me once about Italy, 'If only I had understood. We would've stayed and the whole business wouldn't have happened.' I asked her what business and she brushed me off. Typical of Stella."

"Do you know if they went to Italy before Paris? My great great-grandparents met her and Nicky in Paris."

"I believe their anniversary was in September so this would've been at the end of their honeymoon time wise." Her eyes bored into mine. "And Abel isn't in the picture."

"Would he have been?" asked Chuck. "He was kind of a servant, wasn't he?"

"You know the Bleds," she said. "What do you think?"

"He'd have been in the picture if he was there," I said without any doubt. I did know the Bleds, but I was beginning to realize that I had a lot to learn.

"Let me see that picture again." Marie studied the picture, zooming in on bits of it to get a better look. "Those clothes are off the rack. Stella hasn't got any jewelry on. Where are her engagement and wedding rings? She married a Lawrence. She would've had a pricey set."

I shrugged and said, "I thought that was odd, too."

Marie tapped her chin. "It's odd, alright. What could make a bride give up her rings? Stella adored Nicky. She treasured everything the man ever gave her."

"So if we assume 'A' is Abel, something big happened between Italy and Paris."

None of us had any clue what that event could've been, other than possibly Abel's arrest, but that didn't explain Stella and Nicky's condition. We asked Marie if she knew anything about Jens Waldemar Hoff, The Klinefeld Group or Werner Richter. She didn't.

Marie stood up, flung her cape over her shoulder, and marched to the door. "I have to go or I'll be late. Any more questions?"

"Are there any names you remember that might help?" asked Chuck.

"Classified. I can't talk about operations or information gleaned from operations."

I smiled at her. "I can't believe you followed the rules then or now."

"Look at you, trying to schmooze information out of me." She winked at me.

"Sorry," I said, trying to look abashed, which was difficult, because I wasn't, not one bit.

"Don't be sorry. It worked," said Marie before exchanging cheek kisses with us. "I'll give you one name, because I didn't get it through an operation."

"Really? Thank you so much," I said.

"Don't thank me yet. This was just a rumor going through the ranks. Stella had an enemy in the SS, a man named Peiper, or so they said. He had it in for her. It might be a load of codswallop, though."

Chuck and I walked her to the door. He opened it and said, "I'll walk you down."

"Don't bother. You've got other fish to fry and she's a pretty fish, too."

Chuck looked away, not at me, not at anyone, and Marie reached up and patted his cheek. "You've been to the wars, haven't you?"

"I'm a cop, not military."

"There are all sorts of wars," she said.

Chuck blushed and then tried to step away, but Marie held him by the arm. "Time won't heal your wounds, but they will fade."

Chuck didn't speak but shook his head.

"Trust me," said Marie. "I know."

"Has Ravensbrück faded for you?"

She laughed and patted his cheek. "Let's say I have beat those memories into submission. They don't rule me. I rule them. You can do the same."

"If you say so."

"I do and I'm right. Must go or I'll be late." She checked her watch. "I have to pick up some things first."

"Late for what?" I asked.

"Sarah's granddaughter's family's flying in. I have to pick them up."

"In that limo?" asked Chuck. "Where's your driver?"

"I don't need a driver. How old do you think I am?"

"Seventy-two," said Chuck with conviction. Marie and I exchanged cheek kisses again. "He's a smart one. They're always the most trouble, but well worth it. You two go out tonight. Enjoy the music. It only happens once a year."

"What happens?"

"Fête de la Musique. Vive la France." Marie swept out the door, calling out, "Monsieur Barre, I know you're here. You can't hide from me, you old rascal."

I closed the door, laughing. "That's why it's so crowded. I totally forgot about the Fête de la Musique."

"Poor Monsieur Barre," said Chuck.

"He probably is lurking out there, waiting for her to leave. She does tend to wreak havoc wherever she goes."

"Like somebody else I know."

"Who?" I asked.

"You."

"I hardly think so. Other people wreak havoc. I just get in the way."

"You've got to stop that."

My hand went to my hip. "Don't start with that again."

"I'm not starting anything. You should go to bed and rest."

"You're the one with the head injury," I said.

"Bullet wounds trump head injuries."

"Since when?"

"Since forever," said Chuck. "Go to bed."

I sneered at him. I wasn't about to take orders from him or anybody. "Go jump off a bridge." It just slipped out. For a second, I thought he might laugh. I was ready to laugh, ready to leave it behind us and find a way into the future. Chuck didn't laugh. He had no expression at all. He turned on his heels and went to the spare bedroom. Marie said he'd been to the wars. If only I knew what war we were dealing with.

# CHAPTER THIRTY

Chuck didn't come out of the bedroom until Aaron came back from the cooking school. The little weirdo looked like he'd been in a flour fight and we dusted him off as best we could. He couldn't see the point in changing clothes before going out to enjoy the music festival. Aaron didn't think crusted on pastry cream was an issue. I hoped nobody would notice and question what exactly that substance was.

Since nobody cared but me, we headed out into the crowded streets. I'd been in Paris for the festival when I was six, but I didn't remember much about it. Aaron, of course, knew exactly what we were going to do, but he didn't share the plan. He just headed off, leading us to the Louvre for a drumline, then to the Orsay for a huge brass band. They looked like they were going to play heavy metal with all the black and tattoos, but they played Gershwin. It was kinda surreal.

We followed Aaron around the city without question and without speaking to each other. Something had to break the stalemate. I wanted to say that it would be okay, but how could I say something so lame, especially when I didn't know a thing about what Chuck was dealing with?

After taking umpteen trains and walking miles, we ended up close to the Rue Montorgueil apartment. With all the excitement, I'd forgotten our stuff was still there. With Angela revealed to the world and, according to Dad, Marius Bombelli on the run, we could go back and enjoy showers for the last few days in Paris. Dad thought Marius would be caught within days. The Gravano family had cut ties with him and had been uncharacteristically open about it, tweeting leads to the FBI and posting mugshots on their Facebook page. The media had reported the boat incident as a terrorist act and they named Marius as the instigator. The French and U.S. Government denied that it had anything to do with terrorism, but the media had their own ideas. Apparently, the Gravano family didn't want a thing to do with a suspected terrorist and Dad thought Marius's life expectancy was dropping by the minute. And without Marius paying Poinaré and his ilk, no hitmen would have any interest in Angela or me. I'd told Dad the cover story and he appeared to buy it. I left out the body in the sewer. It hadn't been on the news and I found myself wondering if a body could disintegrate in that muck. That would be nice and no more than what he deserved.

"You hungry?" yelled Aaron. We were in-between not only two DJs, but also a live band rocking out everything from Motörhead to Taylor Swift. It made for some weird transitions, but the guys had range.

"Starving!" I looked at Chuck, who was gazing into the distance at nothing in particular. "You?" I yelled.

"Sure!"

That was it. One word. This wasn't a good sign. I thought about calling Mom for advice. She'd been dealing with cop stuff for a quarter-century and would have more of a clue than me, but I was afraid she'd yell. She'd been yelling in the background when I was talking to Dad. For once, he was the calm one, probably because this whole boat thing was good for business, and hence, the family. Mom didn't care and let me know it.

Aaron pointed at a restaurant called Blend and I nodded. I would've agreed to anything, including crab, to get out of the music for a minute. The sliding glass door opened for us and I rushed inside into the cool modern interior. The door closed behind Chuck, cutting the sound to a dull roar.

"Aaron!" exclaimed a bearded man in a chef's coat.

"Is there anyone in food that you don't know?" I asked.

Aaron didn't have a chance to shrug before the chef rushed up to hug him and exchange cheek kisses. I gathered through the rapid-fire French that they knew each other from the old days. We sat down at a table and were enthusiastically told all about the bread they baked in house, the ketchup they blended, and meat they ground fresh daily. I struggled not to drool on the table and when Chef Andre was done describing the special meats he had in mind for us, I ordered an Agent Provocateur beer, even though it was an IPA. The name sold it and I needed some lubrication to deal with the booming music that flooded the restaurant every time the doors slid open, not to mention the glowering Chuck sitting across from me.

As if on cue, he said, "Let's see if we can sit outside. There are open tables."

"Are you kidding?" I asked. "We can't hear ourselves think out there."

Chuck took a drink of beer. I guess thinking or hearing wasn't high on his list.

"Fine. You want to go out? Let's go out." I took a big gulp of beer. It was hard to swallow, all of it.

"You're not going out there," said Chuck.

"I'll go out if that's what you want."

"No, you won't. It's too loud."

"I'll do it."

"You won't."

Aaron got up and trotted back into the kitchen.

"See that?" I asked. "You scared Aaron."

"Aaron's not scared. He knows you're not going out there."

I finished the beer and slammed it on the table. "You're getting us confused. I'll do what you want. You won't do what I want."

He drained his bottle and said, "I asked you to sing at the Cops for Kids benefit and you won't do that."

"That's different," I said.

"Oh yeah? How?"

"That's singing as opposed to sitting. It's different."

"Yeah, one's for the Children's Hospital and one's for me."

*What's happening?*

"You really want me to sing that bad?"

His icy blue eyes bored into me. "Yes."

*He's trying to get me to break up with him. Nope. Not gonna do it.*

"And if I sing, that'll change everything?" I asked.

"We'll never know," he said.

I stood up, snatched my second beer off the waiter's tray, and threw it back. "Yes, we will. We're gonna know right now! Aaron!"

Aaron peeked around the corner from the back. "Huh?"

"Where's that chef guy?"

The chef came out. "Oui?"

"What are you doing?" asked Chuck.

I stuck my finger in his face. "You want singing? You're gonna get singing."

"From the chef?"

"Quiet!"

I marched into the back, dragging Aaron and the chef with me. Like Aaron, Chef Andre knew everybody, including the band across the street. He introduced me and convinced them that I could sing. No, that's not the truth. They didn't buy it. They gave me a tambourine and said I could stand on the side. Then Aaron intervened and showed them a news report with the video of me jumping off the bridge. That video was magic. They would've let me sing if I sounded like Daffy Duck.

The lead guitarist asked what I wanted to sing as Chuck came out of the front door of Blend. The crowd was jeering and complaining about the lack of music as if the DJs on the other two corners weren't enough. My stomach twisted into knots, but I was committed. I would do it. I'd sing, even if my hero status got downgraded to idiot. I would do it and everything would change. I was just stupid enough to believe it.

I got up on stage and sang. I sang like I never sang before. I sang as myself, not as Marilyn Monroe. It was me, not a character. "When you can't find the light, that guides you on the cloudy days."

There were about 300 phones filming me, but I sang to Chuck. He gripped the back of a chair, expressionless.

I came to the end and gave it my all. "Till the break of day."

Chuck let go of the chair and pushed his way through the hysterical crowd. I was a hit.

He stood in front of me and said, "You sang Soulshine."

"I did. You want me to sing something by Van Halen?" That band was Dad's favorite, but definitely not mine.

"You'd do it, wouldn't you?" he asked.

"Damn straight. What'll it be? "Jump"? Or," *God help me.* "Hot for Teacher."

Chuck grabbed me, kissing me so hard and so well, I stopped breathing and I didn't mind. The crowd went batshit crazy and we took a bow.

"You made me forget," said Chuck in my ear.

"Good," I said. "So "Jump"?"

"Step back, woman," he shouted. "It's my turn!"

Chuck pulled the lead guitarist aside. In a second, there was smiling and nodding. They gave Chuck an acoustic guitarist and I got shooed off the small stage. Then Chuck took center stage, his natural spot, and played the score from *Chocolat*, my favorite movie. I knew Chuck played. I didn't know he was good, like really good.

But wait, there's more. He played with the band through songs by Prince, Green Day, and Metallica. I drank another beer, a record for me, and danced with strangers. My cheeks hurt from smiling and from the multitudes of kisses that were bestowed upon me. It was a perfect night, a perfect happiness. But the whole time, I kept thinking it would end and the happiness would vanish like Elias on the bridge, like it was never there at all.

But it didn't vanish. It changed. At one in the morning, we left Aaron sipping kirsch with Andre in Blend and went to the Rue Montorgueil apartment. Chuck unlocked the door and went silent as we checked to see if Poinaré had broken in, just in case. He hadn't.

*Please say something. Anything.*

"I guess that's it. Good night," he said.

*Not that.*

"Er...so everything isn't changed," I said.

"It is."

"If you're going in there"—I pointed at the tiny bedroom—"and I'm not, it's not fixed."

Chuck touched my cheek. His hand trembled slightly, but he didn't pull away, letting me feel the fear. "I don't want to taint what we have."

"I love you, but it's already tainted."

His hand dropped and I grabbed it, not letting go. "I thought you said you went to the therapist when you came back."

"I did." He wasn't lying. I could see that.

"Did you...tell the truth?" I asked.

He tried to get his hand back. Nope. Not letting go.

"Did you?" I asked.

"Mostly."

"But not totally?"

Chuck didn't answer.

"It helps to talk. It helped me. It's still helping me."

He leaned on the hall wall. "I'm not telling you. I wouldn't do that to you."

"Then don't tell me everything. Tell me something. Enough to help me understand. Why was it okay when we got together at Cairngorms Castle and not now?"

"I wasn't thinking then."

"And you started thinking?"

He nodded.

"About what? What is it?"

He shook his head. So I told him a story, the story Mom told me when I wanted to quit therapy for a second time after I killed Richard Costilla. After I was born, Mom had postpartum depression. It was pretty bad. She kept thinking she put me in the oven. She could see what it did to my little body. She could smell it. She got to the point where she locked me in my room and threw the key into the garden, so she couldn't get to me. Mom slept in the kitchen, on the floor next to the stove with the oven door open to make sure I wasn't in there. Dad found her there at three in the morning and persuaded her to tell him what was going on. As soon as she told him, it got better. Mom said it was like putting down a lead weight that had been nailed to her hands. She went to a therapist and it was over in a few months.

"That's different," said Chuck. "Hormonal. She only thought she put you in the oven."

"So you actually put someone in the oven?" I asked, getting more nervous by the second.

"Not me personally. I..."

I hugged him and wouldn't let go. "Put down the weight."

So he told me. Some of it. Not all of it. Thank goodness. I wouldn't have dealt with it as well as he had. Chuck's undercover assignment might be the worst in history. He knew what he was getting into. Or rather, he thought he did. Chuck went into the world of child porn. He saw things. He heard things. Things he couldn't forget. When he touched me, he saw them again.

"I let it happen." Chuck broke away from me and ran to the bathroom. The sound of his vomiting echoed through the hall. I stood there listening, nauseated myself. I never imagined that was where he was. I thought it was drugs and maybe he saw a dealer get murdered. This was so much worse.

When he finished, I got him out of the bathroom and into my bed. He didn't fight it, which surprised me. I tucked him in and pulled up a chair, sleeping there while holding his hand.

The smell of poitrine fumée woke me the next morning. It was bacon, one better. The smell called to me, but I couldn't get out of the chair. I had eight cricks in only one neck. I texted Serge while I was waiting to loosen up. He was at the Orsay, cataloging a new exhibit, but he was happy to give that up to come over and help me go through Elias's art. He'd come at noon, but I'd have to get moving first. Eight thousand and one texts were waiting for me from Mickey Stix. He'd seen a video of me singing and thought it was time for me to come back. DBD was willing to pay in a big way for me to sing. I'd rather stick a fork in my eye, but the bill from Madam Ziegler hadn't come in yet, so I told him I'd think about it.

"Need some help?" asked Chuck from the doorway.

"Only in a huge way. I think my joints are frozen."

He pried me out of the chair and straightened me up. It wasn't easy, but he waved some poitrine fumée under my nose to get me moving. We had breakfast on the balcony, surrounded by red geraniums and Blackie appeared, twisting around my feet.

"So..." I said with much hesitation, "how's that lead weight?"

"Your mother's a wise woman," he said.

"Don't tell her. I'll never hear the end of it."

He laughed a deep, resonating laugh and I realized I hadn't heard it in months. A real laugh. Real and deep. "Then I'm telling her."

"You just love to bother me."

"I do." His smile wavered. "Can I tell you something else?"

*Uh oh.*

"Of course," I said.

"First, I want to say that I'm going to go to therapy and tell her what happened."

"All that happened?"

"All of it."

I sipped my latte and regarded him with trepidation. "I'm waiting for the other shoe to drop."

He rolled his cup between his palms, leaving moisture on the glossy black surface. "I saw Elias."

"Before we saw him on the bridge?"

"In the apartment. Pretty much every day," he said. "I take it you didn't."

"I dreamt about him, remember?"

Chuck brightened up. "I wonder why. Was he doing something significant, something meaningful to you?"

"He was with members of my family and some Bleds in Nana's and he led me around an antique store here in Paris," I said.

"Maybe Elias was trying to tell you something."

I wrinkled my nose. "You don't really believe that, do you?"

"I've been watching a dead guy walk around, wringing his hands for a week. What do you think?"

"Well...if you think that means something..."

Chuck leaned forward. "What happened?"

"I saw Blackie."

"Blackie?"

I rolled my eyes. "Nana's so-called cat from New Orleans."

"Here? In Paris?" he asked.

"In Elias's apartment." I told him what Aunt Tenne said about the cat being a warning.

Chuck didn't say anything and went to make us some more lattes. When he sat back down, he said, "I'll buy that."

"You will?"

"After this week, sure. But I think there's more to it."

*Fabulous.*

"Like what?" I asked.

"Like I thought that cat only showed up on family property, your grandparents' house, for instance."

"I know. It's weird."

"I think Elias and Blackie are trying to tell you something," said Chuck, cocking an eyebrow at me.

"Of course."

He leaned back and laughed. His voice echoed off the buildings, bouncing back to us in joy. "I thought I was crazy."

"Oh, you're crazy. You're dating me," I said.

"I'll drink to that."

We clinked mugs and enjoyed the lovely Parisian morning with no place to be and no mysteries to solve. At least, not for a little while. A couple of hours. Maybe.

**THE END**

# PREVIEW

## My Bad Grandad (Mercy Watts Mysteries Book Seven)

The roar was everywhere. It pushed me, pulled me, and hurt my ears. I couldn't escape. I'd tried and failed, repeatedly. So, since I had no skills and even less sense, I found myself in a broom closet that smelled like an unflushed toilet and looked worse.

My plan was to hold my breath until it was all over, but like most of my plans, it didn't work. I went to slam the door shut just as my boyfriend stuck his big foot in to block my ostrich maneuver.

"What are you doing?" Chuck asked, tugging on the door that I was valiantly trying to close on his long fingers.

"Hiding. What does it look like?" The roar got louder. "Holy crap! Do you hear that?"

"That's a good thing. The place is packed, just like Mickey wanted."

"Mickey? I could kick him in the junk. He said small. Does that sound small to you?" I screeched.

"It sounds like 10,000 bucks." Chuck yanked the door open and his tall, lean form blocked most of the light coming into my barf closet.

I grabbed a sloppy wet mop, ready to thwack my way out. "He said small."

"This is small. Double Black Diamond usually plays stadiums. We're talking 50,000 people. The Pageant has a max of 2,300."

"I'm going to barf."

"I thought you already barfed."

"There's more in there."

Chuck darted in the closet and grabbed me. "No more barfing. You're on in ten minutes."

"I can't do it. I can't," I said, trying to wriggle out of his grasp. Hopeless. Chuck was a foot taller than me and infinitely stronger. Plus, I was wearing an unspeakable black leather getup designed to make me look even curvier than I actually was and I'd cornered the market on buckles and snaps. They were great handholds and all I had to defend myself were pointy fake nails in Harlot Scarlet and thigh-high stiletto boots. Chuck said I looked hot, but I really looked like walking porn. It was embarrassing. I'd spent my life avoiding looking like that nightmare. I was Mercy Watts and because of my uncanny resemblance to Marilyn Monroe, people expected the worst of me. I wasn't a drug-addled dingbat or a slut and I put a lot of effort into convincing the world of that fact. The opposite impression always seemed to happen, no matter what I did, and the outfit Mickey Stix picked out wasn't going to help.

"Okay. Fine. Give me your shirt," I said, hands on hips.

"My shirt?" asked Chuck, a frown puckering his high forehead. "What for?"

"So I can wear it. Duh."

"You can't cover that up. You agreed to it."

I poked him in the chest. "Mickey said a stage outfit."

"It is. Don't be a wuss."

I spun around and did an arm sweep. "I look like Cat Woman!"

Chuck grinned. "Yeah, you do. I have to thank Mickey. You can wear that home, right?"

Suddenly, looking like a slutty idiot didn't seem so bad. "Are you serious?"

The grin fell off his handsome face. "Not yet."

Chuck was a cop and he'd recently returned from an undercover assignment. It messed with his head in ways nobody expected.

I took his hand and squeezed it. He let me. Progress. I smiled and said, "I'll save it for later."

His grin came back. "I thought you'd burn it."

"Are you kidding? This thing cost like 5,000 dollars."

"Maybe we can sell it."

I did a fist pump. "Then I won't have to sing. Yes!"

He rolled his eyes. "It's one song. Two at most."

"No. I really can't. Stop distracting me."

"You signed the contract and we need the money." Chuck manhandled me into the hall. The roar got louder. I could barely make out Mickey Stix's voice over the din. "Hello, St. Louis! Let's rock The Pageant!" The place went batshit crazy.

"Oh, no," I said.

"You sang on the street in Paris. You sang at Cops for Kids."

"That was for you." I made a break for it, but Chuck captured me easily, hugging me tightly. It would've felt fantastic if he hadn't been preventing my escape.

"Who else is going to pay you 10,000 bucks for twenty minutes' work? We need the money."

We did need the money. That's what I was thinking when I signed Mickey's contract. DBD was launching an album and decided to try out their new material at a "small venue." I should've asked for specifics, but all I thought about were the bills I could pay. Chuck and I owed 6,000 dollars to a Parisian couture designer and that was with a seventy-five percent discount after we went toe-to-toe with a Corsican mobster wearing her designs. Our clothes went viral and suddenly, she was dressing movie stars. It was a hell of a discount, but I'd have gone naked before I'd put on a pair of boots that cost 2,000 dollars. I don't even want to talk about the suit.

The upside of our adventure in Paris was that we got new leads on The Klinefeld Group. My family's past was all mixed up with The Klinefeld Group, along with my godmothers' family, the Bleds. The German nonprofit's goals were as obscure as their location. The Klinefeld Group wanted some box they thought the Bleds had. That box had something to do with my parents, our house, and the disappearance of Josiah Bled. They'd sued, stolen, and murdered to get it, but hadn't been successful. Chuck and I had picked up great leads in Paris, but investigations are pricey. Our new info meant more trips to Europe to follow those leads and I didn't even have a regular job at the moment. I'd accepted a nursing position at the Columbia Clinic. They paid well and it meant no more bouncing around as a PRN nurse. Steady income sounded good at the time, but it didn't last. A mere week into my new job, there were torrential downpours. Rivers all over the tri-state area flooded and the Columbia Clinic was under five feet of water.

"Mercy, come on," Chuck said. "I'm getting sick of pushing you down this hall."

My heel let out a nail-on-a-chalkboard screech as he picked up speed and Freddie, DBD's road manager, came around the corner with a pained look on his face.

"Hey, Freddie," said Chuck with a load of false cheer.

Freddie looked even more pained, but he always looked like that. Maybe because we were the only ones who called him Freddie. Everyone else, including the band, called him Four Squared or Lucky. It was not a term of endearment. It was more like a fact. Freddie was DBD's sixteenth road manager. You'd think that was normal in the music business. People came and went, but DBD's people just went. Like in a bad way. They died in various heinous accidents: overdoses, drunk driving crashes, jumping out of hotel room windows on the fifteenth floor because they thought they could fly, that kind of thing. Freddie was Lucky because he'd lasted longer than any of his predecessors.

"What the hell was that noise?"

"Her heels," said Chuck.

Freddie tugged on his scraggly ponytail. He did that when he was nervous, which was most of the time. DBD was unpredictable on their own, succumbing to violent in-fighting and jealousies at the worst times. Freddie thought adding me was a disaster waiting to happen. Considering my track record, I couldn't blame him. "What's the problem?"

"Just some stage fright," said Chuck.

"Terror," I said with a juke to the left. Chuck snagged me by a buckle and I yelped. "It's stage terror. Terror, I tell you."

Freddie pulled out five strands of hair and twisted them around his pinkie. "Oh, is that all? You'll be fine. I thought you had a real problem."

"This is a real problem," I said.

"It's what you call common. All performers freak at one time or another."

"Mickey doesn't."

"He's been doing this since the seventies. He's so famous now he don't give a fuck. Back in the day, he had to be tanked and twisted to get on stage. Did you barf yet?"

"Three times so far," I said, thinking this was evidence that I couldn't go on. But Freddie slapped me on the back. "Then you're all set."

"Hardly. What if I barf on stage?"

"You won't. Nobody barfs more than three times. Believe me. I've been doing this for a long time. Three times, that's it. Done and dusted. Now, what's going to happen is—"

I grabbed his arm and squeezed until his skinny, tattooed bicep turned red. "I'm telling you I can't."

Freddie ignored the pain, fluffed my hair, and popped a mint in my mouth. "And I'm telling you that we have an iron-clad contract. You go on and sing your tuckus off or I'll sue you so hard that the only thing you'll have left is the paint on your toenails. I might even take that." He gently patted my cheek. "You'll be the highlight of the show."

"You're mean."

"It's my job, not me." He glanced behind him and yelled, "Dallas, get your ass out here!"

A second later, a hipster wearing a plaid shirt, blue stocking cap, and three chin hairs ambled around the corner. Freddie wore an increasingly pained expression as he saw Dallas. The guy reeked of affected boredom. "Mercy, this is Dallas, your bodyguard for the show."

"Are you serious?" asked Chuck. "This guy?"

"Dude, I got skills," said Dallas as he pushed his black-rimmed glasses into place on his small patrician nose.

"Dude, I will shoot you if you fail."

"Jesus, so uptight. Are you a cop?" Dallas showed no real concern.

By the state of his red-rimmed eyes and slight hand tremor, I thought he should've been taking a hike.

"Detective," said Chuck.

"You shoot people?"

"Not as a general rule." Chuck jerked a thumb at me. "She does."

"What?" I asked.

"You've shot at least two people that I know of."

My mind was a blank. I shot people? The only thing I wanted to kill was a large mug of hot chocolate. So good for my nerves, which *were* shot in a huge way.

"You shot Costilla, that terrorist in Paris, and what about Claire's bigamous husband?" Chuck grinned at me.

"I didn't hit Poinaré and I never even fired at Larry."

"You shot a bigot? Sweet," said Dallas, squinting with effort. "I thought you were just Marilyn."

"I'm Mercy," I said, rolling my eyes.

"Oh, yeah. Mercy. Is it time, Freddie?"

Freddie tore out two more hairs and checked his watch. "Thirty seconds. Off you go." He waved us down the hall. "Dallas will put you on."

"Are you serious?" I asked. "This guy is completely baked."

"Don't worry about Dallas. He knows his business."

"I'm not sure he can remember his business," whispered Chuck as we followed Dallas through a warren of hallways and up some stairs to the stage.

"I'm sure," I said. "He can't."

"I'll be right off stage. If anything happens, I'll take care of it. You just sing, get the money, and don't get sued."

I nodded because I couldn't speak. Terrified was not an exaggeration. I think I peed a little...or a lot. It was hard to tell. I was sweating like an obese bodybuilder. There was the stage. The crowd roared as the lead singer, Wade Cave, finished one of their songs from the new album. The crowd was certifiable with screaming, crying, and chanting, "Wade! Wade! Wade!" I would've done just about anything not to go out there amongst the screams and billowing smoke, but I couldn't form a plan fast enough. Dallas peeled me off Chuck. Tamberlin, the makeup artist, rushed over, touched up my lipstick and then maneuvered me behind the side curtains with hands that were like vise grips. Dallas blocked my last dash for safety and pushed me out. It took a village to get me onstage.

Wade finished his last soaring note and took me from Dallas. From there it was a smoky, laser-filled blur. I felt like I'd left my body, but my body kept doing stuff. Fortunately, it was the right stuff. Wade handled me perfectly, moving me around and feeding me questions. He was at his most charming, his most rock star.

I kept telling myself, "It's going to be fine. It's going to be fine."

"Here we go, St. Louis!" yelled Wade to the crowd. "Our very own Marilyn has a new one for you."

Freddie's voice said in the tiny earpiece that Dallas had put in my ear, "Dedicate it to Chuck."

So I did. "This one is for my man. A cop. A hero. And the owner of an awesome ass. Chuck Watts!"

*Where did that come from?*

"Hell yeah!" yelled Wade. "Give it to us, girl. Mercy Watts singing "F'ed Up Friend!""

The roar from the crowd was like a physical assault. It pushed me back. I grabbed the microphone and Wade steadied me with a hand on my back. I sang. I'm not sure how I did it. I was half-blind from the lights. That helped, but mostly, it was Chuck's reddened face in the wings. I wasn't the only one to be mortified. That's always a good thing. The song wasn't about drinking. It was about a guy that was an idiot in love. Mickey wrote it about himself and his wife, Nina Symoan.

The song went over well. Too well. Five guys and one girl rushed the stage. It happened so fast that I didn't have time to be startled. Dallas took them down hard. He grabbed one by his man bun and kicked the legs out from under another one. The video of my first song would later go viral. Not because of me, but because of Dallas's ass-kicking. I was a footnote, which was fine by me.

It went so well. Mickey announced from behind his drum set that I'd sing "Sexy Curve", my least favorite song in the world. My dad always sang it to my mom. Gross, but what could I do? I sang it. There might've been dancing. I'm trying to block that out. The next thing I knew, my time was up, but the crowd didn't want me to leave. I tried and Dallas pushed me back on. It became a crowd participation thing. They chanted, "Stay! Stay! Stay!" I chanted, "Go! Go! Go!"

Mickey came out and canoodled me, saying in my ear, "You need to stay. This is working."

"How much?" popped out of my mouth. I really didn't mean it to.

"An additional three thousand."

"Make it five."

Mickey raised his arms. "She's staying!"

Three more guys rushed the stage and one almost reached us before Dallas flipped him. I stayed on for the rest of the show and it was not glamorous. It was sweaty, hot, and surprisingly smelly. I was part of the smell. I'd never smelled before, but I did then. During the last set, all I could think was, *How'd I get so sticky? Did somebody pour something on me?*

After it was over, I don't even remember getting off stage. Dallas had me in a dressing room and Chuck peeled off my leather before I drank the much-needed bottle of water. Chuck pulled one of his tee shirts over my head and somebody pounded on the door. Before we answered, Mickey strode in with a huge amount of swagger. He and Chuck congratulated themselves on the greatness of the show while I struggled to pull on a pair of yoga pants without anyone seeing my thong.

"Mercy," said Mickey, wiping the sweat off his brow. "That worked better than expected. Our people love you."

This seemed like a good thing, but somehow it wasn't. "Er...yeah," I said.

"Let's do it again. I'm thinking Red Rocks." He came over, laid an extra-moist kiss on me, and was out the door in a flash. My mouth was hanging open. I was not doing that again. Yeah, it went well, but it was a fluke. Everything with me was. I couldn't count on it and even if I could, I think my leather shrank. Either that or I swelled. Neither was good.

*Maybe he'll forget.*

Mickey forgot things on a regular basis, like modeling dates for me and conference calls. He had a lot of kids and some were special needs. He was a busy guy. That's it. Mickey would forget and I'd be safe.

Freddie popped in. "So Mickey wants you back. The band voted. You're in. I'll call you."

*Fan-freaking-tastic.*

**Read the rest in**
**My Bad Grandad (Mercy Watts Mysteries Book Seven)**

# A.W. HARTOIN'S NEWSLETTER

To be the first to hear all about the A.W. Hartoin news and new releases click the link or scan the QR code to join the mailing list. Only sales, news, and new releases. No spam. Spam is evil.

Newsletter sign-up

## ABOUT THE AUTHOR

USA Today bestselling author A.W. Hartoin grew up in rural Missouri, but her grandmother lived in the Central West End area of St. Louis. The CWE fascinated her with its enormous houses, every one unique. She was sure there was a story behind each ornate door. Going to Grandma's house was a treat and an adventure. As the only grandchild around for many years, A.W. spent her visits exploring the many rooms with their many secrets. That's how Mercy Watts and the fairies of Whipplethorn came to be.

As an adult, A.W. Hartoin decided she needed a whole lot more life experience if she was going to write good characters so she joined the Air Force. It was the best education she could've hoped for. She met her husband and traveled the world, living in Alaska, Italy, and Germany before settling in Colorado for nearly eleven years. Now A.W. has returned to Germany and lives in picturesque Waldenbuch with her family and two spoiled cats, who absolutely believe they should be allowed to escape and roam the village freely.